PINNACLE BOOKS • LOS ANGELES

This is a work of fiction. All the characters and events portrayed in this book are fictional, and any resemblance to real people or incidents is purely coincidental.

CALIFORNIO!

A Pinnacle Books edition, published by special arrangement with The Bobbs-Merrill Company.
Originally titled: *Angelo's Wife.*

First printing, August 1979

ISBN: 0-523-40594-4

Cover illustration by Bruce Minney

Printed in the United States of America

PINNACLE BOOKS, INC.
2029 Century Park East
Los Angeles, California 90067

In memory of my mother,
HAZEL HOPE MYERS

Hope had a stunning amount of personal courage, and a terrific sense of fun, and she always believed I was a writer—even when I wasn't.

IN THE YEAR OF OUR LORD EIGHTEEN HUNDRED AND THIRTY

(IN THE SPRING . . .)

The last white bristles of frost are long gone. There is nothing but warm greenness over the land. The edge of the land is lavish with bays, inlets and coves. Down the tattered careless coast of California these wait to shelter ships that come and go away. Thin sunlight sparkles on the rippling surface of the great green water. The ships pause and wait like drowsing birds. There is no press or urgency.

(What man would be so discourteous as to hurry his fellow?)

Inward from the ragged shore the land spreads and myriad hills arise to the bases of ancient mountain ranges. Here and there are ranchos and haciendas of feudal immensity.

(What man could ride across his land in so small a time as one day?)

The surface of the land's wealth has been but lightly tapped. Time later to explore its possibilities and plumb its values. There is no need to do it now. Time, now, only to be pleased with living. There is much enjoyment here, much ease. The land is rich and endless.

(Who knows its size, for what man could compute so largely?)

Chapter 1

For the twentieth time, since the beginning of the hot tiresome journey from the harbor to the rancho, Petra raised the damp handkerchief to her lips. Mother of God, please don't let her be sick in front of all these people! She clung with one slim hand to the twisted bough which formed the side rail of the oxcart. If only there weren't so many rolling hills and valleys! If only the Indian who goaded the oxen wasn't so close! If only they had washed the oxen—or the Indian. *Oxcart!* Dull anger rose for a moment. Thousands of miles she had come—to be met by an *oxcart!* And the aunts in Sevilla had said the Estrada family was so rich! How rich were they if they didn't possess a carriage! After fumbling a little, she found her fan and stirred the tepid air before her face. How tired she was! And this noise! These people! This horde of pleasant, cordial, friendly people who had met the ship at the harbor.

She had leaned on the ship's rail and watched them on the shore—people from Los Angeles, and those in town from the ranchos. They were moving spots of brilliant color across the shimmering water of the harbor. She had breathed a great, almost tearful sigh that the long time of traveling was over. Now, if she could be taken to her destination quickly and allowed to sleep for a long, long time, perhaps she would begin to feel alive again. It seemed an interminable while that she had stood by the rail, waiting to disembark. The vessel dipped its flag again and again in greeting to the gathering crowd on the shore. And after a time the leisurely Mexican, corporal to the commandant, had rowed out to borrow enough powder from the captain to salute the vessel. He spoke like a grandee, had the manner of a duke and was barefoot. He presented the captain with a beautiful speech and a bottle of choice brandy from Mission San Fernando Rey. The commandant, he apologized, was out on his cattle ranch.

But at last she was in California! Now in the swaying, groaning *carreta,* she thought of the end of her journey with a derisive smile. The end! Really only another beginning! For before she reached the house of the Estradas, she must first cross the land of the Estradas. And over this land they had been jolting and lurching since she had landed in the thin sunlight of early morning. And the people! If only they would be silent for just a little while! Her fan moved languidly. It had been another little shock to meet all these people when what she wanted was quiet and a measure of peace.

She had been lifted from the ship to the small bobbing boat by the great sailor with the pitted nose. Over the shining waters of the bay they had gone, with another small boat following with her trunks and boxes. Then on the shore, she had been assisted by a dozen eager browned hands. She was surrounded and engulfed by the liquid sibilance of their Spanish greetings. There were a dozen hands to lift each of her boxes and trunks. She caught fragmentary allusions to her bonnet, the fairness of her hair, and all about her was the flash of white teeth in brown eager faces. She had felt for a moment a shade of thin exhilaration.

She might have been the queen! It was but a minute until her own party claimed her.

The crowd fell back to make way for the puffy man in blue broadcloth. He swept her a deep bow, flushing with pleasure at the sight of her. This, she thought hastily, was Don Xavier Miramontes y Santander. And where, then, was his mother? As she gave him her hand, her eyes swept the crowd for one who might be his mother, her godmother she had never seen. In bustling importance he cleared the way, profuse in greeting and apologies for anything and everything; he led her a little apart to the two *carretas* standing behind the sullen oxen. Members of the crowd detached themselves and followed. She got the impression that these who followed were friends, or part of Don Xavier's party. She endeavored to fit a few names she knew to some of the faces in a hasty glance before the complicated introductions began.

How impossible it was to try to sort them out! Even now, as they rode beside the slow *carreta* on their fine pacing horses, she did not feel she had it all clear in her mind. If only they wouldn't talk so much! The soft musical Spanish whirled and eddied about her and she, who sometimes thought in English, had some difficulty in keeping track of the conversation. There was the creak of leather, the snorting of oxen and horses, the jingle and clink of silver spurs, the dust-muffled clop of the many hoofs.

Her head was beginning to ache again. Her eyes felt hot and gritty from exposure to the brilliant ascending sun. And over and under and through everything was the incessant, hideous shriek, and whine of the solid wooden wheels as they turned on the solid wooden axle. Never, to her last day, would she forget her landing in California. Now they were beginning to sing again! Those two men—what were their names?—whose voices were so liquidly sweet. She eased her cramped back and tried to rest a little. They had been right, in their hastily covered astonishment, when she had chosen to ride in the *carreta* instead of on horseback. Anything would be better than this. Turning a little, she saw the other cart bobbing along behind, piled with her luggage, and straggling after it the motley procession of townspeople on foot and horseback, who for lack of something better to do had followed along for several miles as a sort of additional impromptu escort.

And why must it be so far! How generous the King of Spain had been to Francisco Estrada! She felt a sudden gust of fury at the openhandedness of the King of Spain.

"Oh, please sing something else!" she heard herself saying. Anything, to keep from having to think and talk to them when she was so tired. Delighted, their voices rose again in something unfamiliar, but exquisitely melancholy and Spanish. She was suddenly sick of Spaniards—everything Spanish. She longed with quick indescribable homesickness to see something English. The gray stone front, slick with fog, of the house in the shabby square rose in her mind. Everything was always so different from what she expected. First the great change from London to Sevilla, now from Sevilla to here. It was nothing at all as she had thought it would be. She had expected something like—well, like Sevilla—a city, paved streets, large houses and a carriage! And the godmother she had pictured as a vague replica of her Spanish aunts—the godmother she had never before seen, who was to conduct her to the house of Don Francisco Estrada.

Her mind skidded away from all thought of the Estradas. Think about Doña Ysidra Miramontes, whom she called aunt, who was her godmother, who sat before her in the rocking groaning *carreta*. That remarkable woman! Surely the largest woman she had ever seen. No wonder she did not rouse herself to walk from the *carreta* to meet her. And yet they said that once she had been beautiful! Even Mama had said so. Long ago, before she died, she had spoken of the beauty of Ysidra Santander—now Miramontes. To think, at one time she had been betrothed to a Quintana! She must have been lovely. How odd that she hadn't married him after all! It would have been a fine match for a Santander to marry a Quintana. But she had not. Mama had said—and Petra remembered with what bitterness her mouth had twisted—that Ysidra was of such a mind that had the Infante himself wanted to marry her, she would have refused if she set her heart on another. Which, it seems, she had.

And now, she was old and very fat, with a faint dusting of hair over her numerous chins. Difficult to imagine that once she had been slim and darkly beautiful. Only her hands remained small, and they were pale and strangely dainty. The end of the wild romantic union was the widow, Doña Ysidra Miramontes, who sat before her, old, penniless, making her home with her nephew Don Francisco. And the child of this wild romantic union was the Don Xavier who rode beside the *carretas* now.

He rode well, as did all Californians, despite his bulk, but he would soon be fat. He was fairer than his mother, with a fine network of red and violet veins crossing and recrossing on his puffy cheeks. She wondered how old he was, and did some slow mental arithmetic. Thirty-four! Then Ysidra herself must be terribly old. Again Petra calculated, surreptitiously counting the brins of her fan. *Fifty-three!* More than half a *century!* She gazed at her godmother with a shade of awe in her eyes.

She glanced again at Xavier—he did have a good voice—and unbidden, the thought rose that Francisco, Ysidra's nephew, was probably the same type of person. She could scarcely credit the fabulous tales she had heard about him. And Angelo, son of Francisco? No! Please, sweet, holy Mother of Jesus, don't let Angelo be like Xavier! *Not* soft pulpy hands. *Not* fat cheeks, flushed with tiny bursting veins. Her mind writhed away from all implication of marriage with any relative of Don Xavier's.

And marriage it was! For all the subterfuge and Spanish vagueness, she knew. All the long trip over the moving sea on the plunging vessel she had lain sick, disgusted and frightened in the dank little stateroom, fitting the pieces together—hating them, rebellious, angry, thrusting the thoughts from her—only to wake in the middle of the night, thinking them again. Not that anyone had told her anything! Trust the Spanish never to say what they meant! But she could add two and two.

Why the sudden interest of this godmother who, contrary to Spanish custom, had never expressed the slightest concern of her welfare before? Why the many whispered conferences between the uncles and aunts? She had hung perilously over the balcony to hear snatches of these conferences which took place in the house of one of the aunts in Sevilla. Why the sudden interest and inquiries of the Estrada family? Mention of their wealth, prominence and position in California? References to this son Angelo who had almost reached the age for marriage? Talk, talk, talk, drifting, incomplete phrases.

". . . but, José, dear brother, I have four daughters of my own. . . ."

". . . and the child is miserable here in Spain, otherwise I would not consider . . ."

". . . she could only forget her English ways . . ."

Then soberly: "Yes, of course, the foreign blood, that might. . . ."

". . . there are so few women of good family in California. . . ."

"Well, let us not speak of good family. . . ."

Then laughter. And Petra, listening to them shamelessly, felt the blood surge into her cheeks. They laughed at her father, her beloved, wonderful, gay, young father, who was dead, lost, gone. With stinging eyes she strained to hear the words which rose through the laughter.

"The Englishman went through Teresa's money so quickly, and Ysidra makes no mention of a dowry. . . ."

Then in quick relief: "Oh no, not in California, it is not considered important. . . ."

Petra tried to be subtly Spanish, and sometimes even bluntly English, in her wild endeavor to find out what they planned for her. Why must she leave the convent? Why must she go to her godmother? Well, of course, she hadn't *liked* the convent, but now she had changed her mind. She *wanted* to go back. She *wanted* to stay in Spain. Yes, yes, of course, she had *said* she didn't like Spain, but that was long ago—three or four *months* ago. Oh, but she *was* happy here—she *did* love them all. And always she became mired and enmeshed in the complicated patterns of Spanish etiquette. Always she was baffled by the well-meaning, kind but uneasy regard of her Spanish aunts and uncles. She admitted, grudgingly, privately, that they had tried their best for her. There was something to be said for them. They had daughters of their own to raise and present to the world. They had done, and would do, their best for the strange, fair, foreign child of their sister Teresa—who had married so badly. And

Petra would admit, in a burst of honesty, that she must have been a trial to them during the months since she had come from England with her mother.

For her mother, Teresa, upon the death of the husband she had so obstinately married had returned to her family penniless and bitter. There she had died, quite suddenly and grimly, as if she had only waited to get home and place her child—whom she cared little for, save that it was hers—in the hands of her sisters. To Petra, the death of her stern forbidding mother was only a minor shock in a series of shocks that had begun with the death of her father in England. She remembered with greater pain her last glimpse of the shabby square, which had once been rather fashionable, as the carriage had turned the corner. There had been a thin sunlight shining on the slick wet surface of the stone house in which they had lived. It had been a painful thing to see it for the last time, and know it was the last time.

Then, in the various homes of her three aunts, or in the convent for short stays under the supervision of these aunts. Petra had fitted badly and rebelliously into the gentle, mellow, complicated way of living. With all her careful spying, all her delicate, and not so delicate questions, what did she know, really know, of Angelo Estrada? Nothing! Except, of course, that he would one day be very rich, that he was—incredible in California—an only child, that his father was her godmother's nephew, and of course—oh, most important!—that there seemed to be no embarrassing mention of dowry.

But where were they, these Estradas, across whose land she rode, escorted by their friends? They had not been among the beautifully clad party at the harbor. In meeting these, trying to sort them out, facing the fact of another tiresome journey, she had not been able to think of the Estradas. She was too busy making the correct replies to her remarkable godmother, to Don Xavier, and all the people who seemed to be such great friends of the two, this delighted crowd of friendly people who had waved to the ship from the shore, who rode around the oxcart as if it were a royal carriage, whose extravagant compliments flowed in wordy Spanish, who sang songs, made poems and told jokes. Sometime, when she wasn't sick and tired and filled with dread, she might love all these laughing people.

But she couldn't come right out and ask. She couldn't say, "Dear Aunt Ysidra, I am delighted that you and your gallant son met me, but *where* is Don Francisco Estrada? And *where* is his son Angelo Estrada? I am sick and tired of waiting to see them." One couldn't. One accepted everything that came, with the beautiful, complicated, Spanish politeness—that the nuns, the aunts and the now dead mother had labored so diligently to instill in one. If the head throbbed, the bones ached and the eyes stung, one continued to smile and flutter one's fan.

Well, it couldn't be much farther—or they would have ridden across the continent. Soon she would at least see them. And she, who a moment before had wanted with violence to see them, now rejected with violence the thought. A start of terror skipped through her mind. Don Francisco! The Don Francisco across whose land they now rode. That fabulous person about whom she had heard snatches through the closed doors. He was the man, they said, who could remain in the saddle for three days without sign of fatigue, pausing only to exchange his dying mount for a fresh one. He was the man, they said, who could kill an Indian with a glance, who feared neither priest nor devil. Yet he could beguile the birds from the sky, so sweet was the honey on his tongue. Then, suddenly, the cart came to a stop and a ragged shout of greeting rose from the horsemen. The sudden cessation of the whining wheels left her ears ringing and straining for the sound. There were the snorting of the mounts, the confused speculation regarding the approaching horseman. Above the confusion of the voices, the sound of leather and spurs, the pawing of the horses, she could hear the sound—steady, rhythmic, fast—of another horse. She sensed the straightening of Ysidra's great bulk. Xavier rose in his stirrups and strained his eyes in the distance. There, topping the crest of a distant rise, she saw the horseman. There was a flash of red as he thundered toward the party on a golden horse. In the gleam of sunlight the horse appeared golden. Oh, fantastic! Nervously she bit her lips, twisting her fan in her suddenly damp hands.

"Who is it?" she asked Xavier without thinking.

It was another—Enrique? Teodoro?—she didn't know who that answered.

"Angelo, maybe," he said, regarding the horseman. "Angelo always rides palominos. They match his leggings."

Angelo! She would not faint. She would not be sick. Hail, Mary, full of Grace, the Lord is with Thee. Blessed—— But he was here! There was no time, no time for anything. As he hauled his shining horse to a plunging, hoof-flailing stop beside the cart, she saw him plainly, brightly, in the sun. No! Not him! Not that big dark man in crimson velvet! The gold-fringed poncho which swung from his shoulders to the back of his horse made him appear larger than life. He was too big. Too immense. Too bright. Oh, someone smaller, someone gentler, someone without blood on his spurs!

Grimly, after her first start of fear, she

gripped her hands together and found, to her dim surprise, that they were cold. Ysidra was now smiling so that her cheeks lifted like twin melons. There was pride in her voice as she began the introduction. "Allow me to present my nephew, the Don Francisco Ysidro Estrada y Santander."

Francisco! Relief made Petra go suddenly weak. So it wasn't Angelo. Her own name was being spoken now. Hastily she wiped the palm of her hand with her balled handkerchief and extended it, cool and dry, to the man who was to be her father-in-law. He swept her a low bow and kissed the hand. He raised his eyes and looked at her frankly, appraisingly, before he dropped them. Color stained her cheeks, and she was dimly surprised to find she was reciting the proper formula in Spanish.

Now, he was greeting the others—his aunt, whom he had seen so recently, with profound courtesy, as if she were a great and beautiful lady instead of a fat old woman; Xavier, his cousin, affectionately, and the others, his neighbors and friends.

Then—and she could have blessed him for it—Don Juan Acuña, one of the group, asked of Angelo. He seemed to have a special regard for the son of Francisco and his tone was sober. "They tell me the boy is sick again. Another attack?" It was part statement, part question.

Veiling a glint of something like anger in his eyes, Francisco Estrada turned his attention to the question. "He was taken ill during the night, Juan," he replied courteously. "That was why I could not ride to meet the ship of the Doña Petra." He bowed in Petra's direction. "I was greatly disappointed."

"How is he now?" persisted the other in a gentle voice.

Francisco shrugged. "He will recover," he said

dryly. "I've shut him up in his room, with specific instructions to rest and be presentable for the dance tonight." He turned again to Petra. "My aunt Ysidra, and my wife, have arranged to have a dance in your honor tonight, señorita. Does that please you?"

"It—it's very kind of them," Petra answered, appalled. Would she never be allowed to rest? God knew how much farther it was—and then to dress and dance all night. Impossible! She would die in her tracks.

She steadied herself as the *carreta* started its jolting way. The group took on new life. There seemed suddenly much to talk about. The dust rose in clouds from the restless pacing of the horses held in check to the speed of the *carreta.* Heat seemed to rise from the ground in bright shimmering waves of air. How much farther? How much longer? She turned her eyes frantically from the sweat-streaked Indian to the stinking oxen, and frantically from them to search the rolling vacant distance for a house—any kind of house. It was long past noon, and the sun began to descend, with no abatement in the heat. At last, when she felt she must stop her ears to shut out the noise and cover her eyes to hide the glare, they topped a slight rising of ground.

Don Francisco drew his horse closer for a moment to the *carretas.* "There, Doña Petra, my house," he said simply.

It was like no house Petra had ever seen—bigger, much bigger than a house, but not tall. It was squat, not more than two stories high in any place. It appeared to wind about in an indefinite pattern of long low buildings. The rippling roof showed not a turret or a gable, but was nearly flat and glowed dull red in the sunlight. The buildings themselves were of dull brown color.

They traveled for some minutes without seeming to get any closer, and Petra decided that the intervening distance was more than she had thought. It was hard to judge when no obstacle rose between to break the even monotonous flow of undulating land.

She felt dull and torpid. The ebb and flow of wordy Spanish swirled about her. It was of local topics. Father Patricio thought the vineyards would bottle nicely this year—it had been a good year for grapes. New groves of oranges from Spain had been set in at Las Palomas and Dos Ríos. Don Francisco's hand rested lightly on the pommel of his silver-mounted saddle. His fingers from time to time caressed the coils of rawhide *reata* which hung there. It was a large hand, but not fat. The thumb was quite long and the fingers well shaped. The nails were clean and short. He was a clean man, she decided. His skin shone, and his long black queue was neatly braided.

In the drone of the noise in the warm air she began to feel numb. Long ago she had become used to the shrill crying of the wooden wheels. She felt almost as if she could sleep. Then she became conscious of a nagging petulant worry in the back of her mind. Tired as she was, she was straining with dogged determination to listen to the flow of talk about her, trying to pick out something more of Angelo. There seemed, somehow, in the course of meeting these people and riding across the Dos Ríos Rancho something else to worry about, something new to dread. Grimly she searched for it.

When had the new apprehension plummeted into her mind and lain there until now, now that she must recognize it and drag it out? What had they said? They had said so much. At which utterance had the new fear been born? She realized that for some time there had seemed something solid and congealed in the pit of her stomach.

What was it, then? It was something she had just recently discovered. She should forget it. Banish it. Throw it off, as her father would have done. But the part of her that was Teresa made her search it out.

There! Now! She knew. It had begun when Juan Acuña inquired about Angelo. Yes. What had he said? *"They tell me the boy is sick again. Another attack?"* Sick *again.* Attack of *what?* And Don Francisco—what had he said? *"He will recover."* His tone had been anything but sympathetic. And later: *"I have shut him up in his room—to be presentable tonight. . . ."*

Think! That fitted with something she had heard in the house back in Sevilla, something about Angelo being *almost* the age for marriage. Hadn't there been some criticism because of the early arrangements? Yes, and he was an only child, the only heir to all this vast property and the holdings of Don Francisco. It had all seemed to hinge on the wishes of Don Francisco, not of Angelo. It was Francisco who had insisted on the early marriage of his son. Why? Because he had no other heir? Because he wanted a grandchild? Why—unless?

Even in the heat she became a little cold and leaned sickly against the hard side of the *carreta.* Was there something *wrong* with Angelo? And if this were so, what could she do? One lone girl thousands of miles from her home, among strangers and savages. What recourse, what redress, what law could protect her? Were not these Spanish dons their own law, so far from Mexico and Spain. And Ysidra, the godmother on whom she was dependent. Searchingly she looked at the godmother. Remote. Expressionless. Like a great stolid Buddha.

Petra opened her mouth to speak. She wasn't sure what she would have said, but before the words were formed she became conscious that they had come to the house. They had jolted into the courtyard and the *carreta* rolled to a stop. So they had arrived. The house looked larger now. Stiffly she allowed herself to be assisted to the ground. She cast a confused glance about, receiving the jumbled impression of a hard-packed earthen yard, a bubbling fountain, a wild fluttering of doves and chickens, dozens of dogs of obscure breed, and people—people everywhere. Strange creatures of another race, clad in skimpy garments, seemed to materialize from the very walls to surround the company and stare at the fair-haired visitor. There was a profusion of naked or half-clothed children, of varying degrees of darkness.

The great brass-studded door swung open and several women emerged from the dim hallway. Ysidra was now safely from the cart and was being led to the doorway. Already the Indians, in response to orders from Enrique Padilla—she remembered his name now—were untying and unloading the boxes and trunks from the other cart, that luggage which contained the wonderful amount of new and beautiful clothing on which the aunts had lavished so much money—out of regret perhaps, she thought wryly.

The hallway was massive and dim. The walls were of an incredible thickness, making the air cool and refreshing. So this was the end of the journey. This was the Estrada house. Even now her possessions were being carried in by straining, grunting savages. There was no escape. A little feverishly her eyes flicked over the people who congested the hallway.

A woman was coming slowly down the stairway to meet them. She was tall and very pale. Her almost colorless face assumed a smile with seeming effort, as she welcomed the group which came in the door. As if from a great distance Petra heard Don Francisco presenting her to his wife, the Doña Ana-Lucía. She was dressed in black, in cut and mode far out of fashion. The pattern asserted itself and Petra uttered the phrases expected of her. Even when she had been seated, still in her traveling gown, sipping a glass of cool wine, the talk remained impersonal—only of what a long journey she had had, and how tired she must be, and how she must have missed her siesta.

Rest, that was it. Petra felt she could lay her head down on one of the darkly polished tables and fall instantly asleep. At last she was allowed to go to the room prepared for her. There was a rustling of voluminous skirts as she and her godmother rose. The proud part of her mind that was Teresa Vega y de la Torre refused to let her show a tremor as she mounted the steps. Let them hide their Angelo if they did not wish to bring him out. But, drunkard, madman, idiot, or whatever he was, she wasn't going to let them *know* she cared.

Petra woke to the sound of a *carreta* and thought she was dreaming. Sleepily she sat up in the center of the massive bed. The sound of voices raised in greeting came through the open window. There was a tap on the door, which opened in response to her invitation. An Indian entered carrying a pitcher of water. Petra knew she was an Indian by the way she was dressed, for the room was too dim to distinguish her features. She moved swiftly to the washstand, set the pitcher down, and lighted the candles.

"I am Damacia," she offered, smiling at Petra. "I am Doña Ana's attendant." She seemed slightly proud of this, so Petra smiled. She was beginning to feel stiff and not a little sore from her long *carreta* ride.

"Tell me, Damacia," she said, "what time is it?"

"It is nearly time for the evening meal," Damacia answered. "Doña Ana sent me to help you dress. She will come in later to see you. She says dress for the ball, as there will be no time after the meal, for it is late."

The dance! Petra straightened and winced. Well, maybe she would feel better after she had washed and dressed—and eaten. She realized that she was ravenously hungry. There seemed to be an uncommon amount of noise from downstairs. More people had probably been coming while she slept. Petra sighed and slid to the edge of the bed experimentally. Well, she didn't feel too bad.

"Will there be many people at the dance tonight, Damacia?" she asked, commencing to unbutton her dusty bodice.

"Not so many, I think," Damacia said pouring water from the fluted pitcher into the bowl. "They could not know what day your ship would arrive and so those in Santa Barbara and Ventura and up in Yerba Buena do not know of it yet. Later the Don Francisco will give a great fiesta for you." She spoke complaisantly. "And they will come from all over the Californias. For days and nights there will be nothing but music and dancing."

Petra smiled at the girl. "That will be very kind of Don Francisco. You will find my combs and brush in that small dressing case. Did many people come while I was asleep?"

"Many ladies came," Damacia answered struggling to open the dressing case. Petra's heart sank. "Oh, the doña has brushes and combs of silver!" Damacia took them out and examined them appreciatively.

Petra watched the girl absently, wondering where her boxes were. Such a way to run a household! At home in England Sophie or Beth saw, at least, that the guest's clothing was brought up and unpacked. Indolent Spaniards! Well, when she was mistress here—she paused as the thought struck her, her fingers motionless at the bodice fastening. When she was mistress here! Well, someday she would be, if their plans matured. She looked about the room in interested wonder. This, not London, would be her home. This Indian girl, not Sophie, might be her maid. And she, not Doña Ana, would someday be the lady of this house. These very walls would be hung with what she chose to hang them, that bed covered with what she chose to cover it with. She found this idea fascinating and surveyed the room with slightly narrowed eyes.

There was a rap on the door. Doña Ana! And here she was still in her filthy traveling dress. Damacia rose quickly from her knees and opened the door to let in her mistress.

Color crept into Petra's cheeks as the other woman surveyed her with pale eyes. "I was so terribly tired," she began explaining lamely, "that I lay down in my dress—for only an instant I thought—and when I woke Damacia had come to help me dress. It was most kind of you to send her."

Doña Ana acknowledged this thanks with a nod and a faint smile. "Is there anything else you need?" she asked. "I have been very busy with the other guests and have not had time to dress myself yet."

"Oh no, nothing," Petra said hastily. "That is, if you could send up my trunks, there would be nothing else."

"They are in the hall. We did not wish to disturb your siesta. Damacia, get the gown the Doña Petra wants, and while we eat dinner see that the trunks are moved in here and unpacked."

Petra was relieved when she had gone, and she felt something very near anger at the other woman. Ridiculous! She hardly knew the woman. And yet her cordiality lacked the eager spontaneity of the others. In an instant she had decided on the gown she would wear. She decided in a sudden burst of gratitude to the crowd of people below who had ridden so many miles to welcome her to California, who had ridden at the side of the *carreta* and sung for her. Well, she would dress to please them—the most beautiful dress she had.

Damacia was in a state of ecstasy as she took out the white satin ball gown, trimmed in gold lace. She brushed Petra's hair until it shone like sunlight. It took less than three quarters of an hour to dress, and during that time Petra had gleaned a skeletal knowledge of the group downstairs. The names which sounded familiar could be matched to certain faces which had been beside the *carreta*. Acuña father, and son Teodoro. She placed them now. The mother and two daughters had come during her sleep. The Acuña rancho, Las Palomas, was to the north of this one. The two Acuña girls were Catalina and María-Fe. Catalina, Damacia explained, placing the combs in Petra's hair, was very pretty. María-Fe was very pretty and very kind. The one who had sung so beautifully had probably been Enrique Padilla, Don Francisco's *mayordomo* here at Dos Ríos. The one with the ruby in his hatband had been Don Candalario Sal. His parents and some brothers and sisters had just arrived from their rancho to the south. It was thought he would marry María-Fe Acuña—but not until Doña Catalina had married. Whom? One did not know yet. Was the name Quixano familiar? Don Jaime and Don Pedro Quixano had come with the *carreta*. Others of the family had arrived since. Don Cristóbal she could quickly place when she met him, for he weighed three hundred pounds and was now, Damacia said, dressed in plum-colored velvet. Don

Cristóbal had a great rancho farther south. He was about the best pistol shot in California and his uncle was a cardinal.

By the time Petra had finished dressing, her excitement had risen. Her fatigue had vanished. At last, after turning this way and that before the oval mirror, she was satisfied with her appearance. The mantilla of white lace interspersed with gold threads spread gracefully about her shoulders. The great bell of her satin skirt swayed with a satisfying swish. Washing and dressing in something beautiful certainly made one feel better. She looked quite regal, for she was taller than average. Peering contentedly into the glass, she grinned suddenly. Well, anyway, she looked regal when she was in white satin and gold lace. And she certainly looked older than fifteen.

She whirled, a little breathless, at a knock on the door. It proved to be her godmother, who came in majestically, carrying a small leather casket. She smiled when she saw Petra.

"You look very lovely, my child," she said in her husky voice.

"Thank you, Aunt Ysidra," Petra answered. She felt perfectly able to cope with half a dozen ailing and elusive Estrades tonight. On a sudden impulse she swept her godmother a deep curtsy. She was rewarded by the sound of Ysidra's sudden and delighted wheeze of a laugh.

"Beautiful! Get up, get up, my child. It's late. All the people are hungry. Here, take my pearls out of this. You may wear them tonight."

Petra rose in a quick motion. Pearls! She had no jewels, Teresa's long ago having been placed in pawn. She took the box, her hands shaking with eagerness. From it she took the long strand of milky pearls, and, after setting down the box, she clasped them about her neck. They hung in a delicate loop almost to her waist. They were not large, but luminous and perfectly matched.

"No," Ysidra said. "Here, child, let me show you." She plucked at the pearls with her small quick hand. Carefully she looped the strand together once and twice and twisted it loosely about. When she finished she had a short, thick, seemingly tangled mass of pearls which gleamed and glowed in the flickering light. These she wrapped about the base of Petra's throat, and there they lay in a flashing tangled collar, leaving a bare expanse of pale skin uncovered down to where the gold lace formed a stiff ruff above her small outthrust bosom.

"Lovely," she murmured thoughtfully. "Quite lovely. Well, come, we must go down to them. Here, don't forget your fan." She handed Petra the small fan of white starched lace. But even with the pearls to sustain her, Petra half wished that there weren't quite so many people to meet.

At the doorway Petra paused, thinking suddenly of Angelo. "Aunt Ysidra," she said carefully, fluttering her fan, "everyone is already down, I suppose. Was—was Don Angelo well enough——" She stopped at the sudden frank glance from the old woman's wise black eyes. Miserably she felt color rising over her throat and face.

"I couldn't say," Ysidra answered. "Come, let's go on down while you are still blushing. There is no point in wasting it on me."

The progress from the middle of the stairs to the main *sala* was nothing short of triumphal for Petra. Effortlessly she fell into the correct routine. "Doña Dolores Acuña," she was murmuring politely, fluttering her fan. "Doña Catalina, I am so happy to know you. . . . Doña María-Fe . . . Don Cristóbal Quixano, I am deeply honored, sir. . . ." Smiling, using her fan, she spoke out the patterns set for her, answering questions, making conversation: Yes, it had been a long way to come, but she was so glad now that she had. Yes, she was glad to be at last with her godmother whom she had not seen since babyhood. Yes, she had seen part of the rancho; they had ridden over half a continent crossing it this morning. Yes, she had lived in England for many years, only recently in Spain. Yes, she spoke English, most people in England did. She even spoke a few words for them, amid a great deal of laughter and wonder that people could listen all day to so harsh a tongue. And then, when she felt lightheaded and giddy, Doña Ana came in, and dinner was announced. Dinner! She had hardly time to notice that Ana was still attired in black. She had merely changed into one of stiff taffeta.

The food was plentiful and delicious. She concentrated for a time on eating well and abundantly. The others, however, did not let the food interfere with their conversation. All except Ana contributed to the talk. Petra was agreeably surprised to learn that Ysidra was not stupid or dull as she had thought her, but possessed a subtle and clever wit. Petra found herself laughing again and again in vast enjoyment. Repeatedly she had to remind herself that Doña Ana was the head of the table and she must direct some of her conversation there. But Ana seemed sunk in some pallid apathy of her own which all Petra's efforts could not stir. And she sensed before long that it was not Francisco's wife who was the lady of the house here, but his aunt Ysidra. She regarded the vast woman with increased interest. She wondered how this could be possible. Doña Ana was a much younger and better-appearing woman than Ysidra. Petra noted with some surprise that Doña Ana wasn't as old as she had first imagined. It was merely her bearing and lack of animation that made her appear mature.

As if to hurry the diners, fragments of music drifted in from the *sala,* and it was soon time for the dance to begin. Petra felt wonderful. She had never felt better. The dance began, and Petra held a delightful court in the corner of the room until the older people relinquished the floor to the younger ones. Oh, this was wonderful and beautiful and gay! She was glad she had lived in Spain for two years. She was glad she could dance with them and talk to them and listen to the compliments about her gown, her hair, her grace.

Then in sudden contrast to the velvet jackets and breeches, there appeared at the door of the *sala* a priest. He was clad in the rough habit of the Franciscans. The knotted cord at his waist swayed a little as he kept slight time with the music. It was a moment before the others became aware of him, and then a subdued cry of greeting went up. The name Patricio was on a dozen lips. Francisco went forward swiftly to meet him, and the two men embraced.

"Please," said the priest, "don't stop the music on my account. Dance, please, all of you. I must hurry up to see Angelo. I will be back shortly—— I couldn't resist looking in."

With a bow to the group and a signal to the musicians Francisco led the priest away.

"A priest," Petra said faintly. "A priest for Don Angelo." Was it possible he lay dying while the music soared and they all danced.

"Do not be alarmed." It was Doña Ana who spoke, her tone one almost of boredom. "It is nothing serious. Angelo often has these attacks. Angelo is a sickly person." She seemed to take pleasure in the words. "Angelo is a sickly person, and Father Patricio is often sent for. You see, we are rather isolated here, and the fathers at the mission act as physicians to our bodies as well as our souls in time of need."

But Ana's assurance did little to allay Petra's apprehension. A priest was a priest, and you sent for one when you were dying. Was it possible that Angelo would die before she ever saw him? A little vaguely she joined the dance again. She must be quite drunk to think what she was thinking, but nevertheless she tried to catch a glimpse of the stairs. Guests went up and down from time to time. She felt sure she had drunk too much wine at dinner. This was not England, she thought, as she saw the priest come down after a time. He disappeared with Francisco into the dining room. Spanish etiquette holds here, she thought, and feeling apprehensive and lighthearted she made an excuse to her partner and slipped into the hallway at the first opportunity.

Hurry, hurry, before anyone came! Lifting her skirts, she raced up the stairs, not pausing until she reached the comparative dimness of the upper hallway. Breathless, pressing her hand to her heart, she leaned against the wall. *What was she doing!* What a fool she was! What a brazen forward creature they would think her, if anyone found out! But maybe they wouldn't find out. And he was probably so sick—or something—he might not even know she was there.

She shrank against the wall, as a large Indian woman came out of a room at the end of the passage. She was carrying a tray. Angelo's room! Grimly she set her mouth. She would see him. And tonight! Chaperon or no chaperon. Swallowing with difficulty, she went to the end of the hall. The door was even slightly ajar. No sound came from the room, not even the sound of breathing. Boldly she stepped forward and pushed the door open. Boldly she walked in and closed it firmly behind her. Then all the strength seemed to leave her legs.

Now! Angelo! She would see Angelo. Every fear and dread she had nourished on the long trip from Sevilla sprang up at the moment. The dim room pressed down on her. Sweat of sheer terror broke out over her face and body and she tried to control the helpless trembling of her limbs. One hand clutched her heavy shining skirts, the other pressed against her shaking mouth. At the foot of the great bed was a chest of some strange carved wood. As she reached this, her strength failed her and she sank weakly on it.

Her eyes wide and dark with fear could make out nothing on the bed save an untidy heap of comforts and a trailing sheet edged with heavy lace. At last she summoned her voice and said in the faintest whisper, "Don Angelo?"

There was a light stirring among the covers and the dim shape of a head and shoulders appeared indistinctly in the gloom.

"It is I, Petra——" she managed to add.

There was a long, almost unbearable silence and then: "Petra?" It was scarcely more than a murmur. "Why, señorita, I believe you are as frightened as I am." The voice was faintly humorous, slightly mocking.

Relief so great that it was a physical sensation flooded Petra. This was Don Angelo. This was the man about whom she had built such tales of dread in her mind. His voice was a boy's voice. He was not a bearded madman. Or a mewling idiot. He was a boy. Frightened as she was, she knew his voice was gentle, hesitant—kind! She had been so terror-stricken, so afraid, so cowardly. And this was Don Angelo. She was surprised to find that tears fell on the hand still raised to her lips, tears of relief, almost of happiness.

"Angelo," she said at last, "I want to *look* at you."

There was a candle. She took it and went close to the side of the bed, to look for the first time on the boy she was to marry and love forever.

He was not unpleasing to look at, she decided, scrutinizing him much more closely than a Spanish lady should have done. He was thin, quite thin, and the thinness made planes and hollows in his high-cheekboned face. His skin was browned from many idle hours spent on the sun-dappled patios. His eyes, she noticed, were large, widely set and slightly uptilted at the corners. His face slowly darkened with embarrassment as she openly stared at him. He tried, with nervous fumbling gestures, to smooth his untidy hair into some semblance of neatness. It had not been braided into the long neat queue worn by the other men, and hung in tousled disorder.

"Señorita," he said with an attempt at sternness which didn't quite come off, "what are you doing here? I wanted to wait until tomorrow to meet you—not that I really wanted to even then," he added in a spurt of frankness. "And *what* are you doing in here without a duenna?" He clutched the disarranged bedclothes about his naked chest.

She began to laugh the way she and Papa had laughed at home in England. She hung onto the bedpost and the candle wobbled in her unsteady hand. She had been so afraid for so long and there was really nothing at all to fear. If they had only told her that he was just a boy as uncertain and frightened as she herself was! This Angelo whom she had feared all the way from Spain was here before her, a sick, nervous boy whose most positive emotion at the moment was his embarrassment that she should have come into his room without a duenna.

"I thought you were sick," she said when she could speak.

"I was sick—very sick," he said and added persistently, "Señorita, you must leave. I . . . haven't any clothes on."

"But you're covered," she pointed out logically, retreating a step in the interests of decorum.

"I don't seem to be sick any more," Angelo said in mild surprise.

Petra remembered her own fits of nausea in the *carreta*. "Something you ate when you were excited or upset," she counseled. "Papa always said that meals should be taken in calmness, and he would never quarrel with Mama when he was eating."

Angelo grinned, revealing strong white uneven teeth. "Your father must have been a wise man," he observed.

The door opened, and they both started violently. Color flooded Petra's face as she gazed in speechless consternation into the eyes of Don Francisco. He bowed slightly.

"You tired of dancing, señorita?" he asked with a faint lifting of his brows. "You mistook the room perhaps?"

There was something like a gasp from the bed. "Yes! She was looking for her room," Angelo said quickly. "Perhaps you could show her, Father. I'm not sure which one she has."

"I did no such thing!" Petra was astonished at her own utterance. She was suddenly quite angry. These Spaniards and their cumbersome patterns of etiquette! What difference did it make that she came to look at Angelo in his room without the benefit of a duenna. She had meant no harm. All she wanted to do was *look* at him. "I came," she said clearly, setting the candle down with a thump, "to see how Don Angelo was."

"And—you saw?" Francisco asked with a slight twitching at the corners of his mouth.

"Yes. He says he doesn't feel sick any more."

"I'm delighted to hear it," Francisco said soberly. "He felt miserable a while ago when Father Patricio was here. Of course Father Patricio doesn't wear a white satin dress trimmed in gold lace. Was there anything else you wished to discuss with my son now that the state of his health has been clarified? If there isn't, might I conduct you back downstairs. The guests have inquired for you. Or," he said, turning to the door, "if you like, I'll tell them you are engaged in conversation with Angelo and will come later."

Petra swallowed.

"I'm sorry . . . sorry, sir," she said in quick shame. "I didn't mean to . . . to be discourteous or——"

He smiled suddenly, the same wide smile that Angelo had. His eyes glinted with amusement. "That would be quite impossible," he said. "All the same I shall be glad to conduct you downstairs, if you care to go."

The boy on the bed watched them go. He grinned a little ruefully, wishing he were going with them. But he could hardly get up and dance after Father Patricio had come all the way from the mission to see him. All the worry, all the wild rebellious dread had been for nothing. So that was Petra!

How kind she had been after all! She had been frightened of him in the beginning. Of him! He laughed silently. Well, a person one had never seen, and knew nothing about, coming suddenly into one's life was a disturbing factor. And she probably knew as well as he did why she had been brought here. He had worried about her too. Suppose she had been—— Well, but she wasn't. She wasn't like anyone he had ever seen before. How her skin gleamed in the candlelight, and how fair was her hair, and how smoothly it lay!

Wouldn't it be odd if he fell in love with her? But of course that would never happen. He would not allow himself to fall in love with anyone at all. There was no point to it. One got badly hurt when one fell in love. Aunt Ysidra had fallen in love and what had she now? She was old and ugly and poor. She had to live here in his father's house. And what had she left of her marriage? Nothing except Xavier. That surely could not be very comforting.

Anyway, Petra certainly wouldn't fall in love with him. She was too healthy and lively and gay. He couldn't expect that. Still, it would be nice, it—no, he really didn't expect it.

But his father expected them to have a child, didn't he? His skin burned. How could he ever—with Petra? He recalled the shimmering stuff of her dress. She must be very proud and aloof. Even if he was a partial invalid, so to speak, his father's pride would not let a marriage be arranged with just anybody. Aunt Ysidra had said she came of a good family. True, on her father's side there wasn't much to be said, since he was English. But then Aunt Ysidra had said that he had some very noble Scottish blood—whatever that was. On her mother's side, of course, there were the Vegas and De la Torres. And on his side he had the Montoyas, and the Estradas were a very fine line. They were all right for each other when one considered backgrounds.

It was just the plain physical aspects of it that were so appalling. He would have to wear night clothes! How he hated binding twisting garments to sleep in. He sighed. Night clothes he must have. He must ask Guillermo tomorrow just what he had in the way of night clothes. He became mildly indignant. He should have night clothes. Even if he never wore them, they should be there, and ready, in case he had need of them—as now for instance.

Someone should run the house properly and see that everything was in order. Father couldn't be expected to see to things like that. And the women of the household—what good were they? Aunt Ysidra? She saw that her own wants were attended to, and beyond that she bent no effort at all. And Ana? Less than useless. She went about ill-humoredly and snapped orders at people. But the house would have run as well as it did now without her haphazard petulant direction. Each had his duties and they were, for the most part, discharged properly.

Maybe Guillermo had some night clothes he could borrow. Guillermo always had a lot of clothes. Francisco seldom refused him anything, so great was his attachment for the boy he had adopted from the mission. Guillermo even bore the name Estrada, although his veins contained more Indian blood than white. Francisco had adopted him for the sole purpose of looking after his own child. His place in the household was somewhere between a servant and a member of the family. The missions had very little trouble placing children of this sort for adoption, as they were usually superior and eagerly taken into families. He was, they said, the son of some white soldier and an Indian woman, long forgotten, who had deserted him almost at the instant of his birth.

"What white soldier?" Angelo had once boldly asked his father. Francisco, grinning, had answered, "Figure it out for yourself, Angelito. He is three years older than you are, and at your birth I was still in Spain." Angelo had been slightly disappointed at this indisputable fact. He would have enjoyed thinking of Guillermo as his brother, even if he was mostly Indian. And tomorrow he would ask him to do something about securing some night clothes. He had never yet had any problem so great that Guillermo couldn't handle it with ease and dispatch. Although—and Guillermo never failed to remind him of it—he would have made a much better *vaquero* than nursemaid.

He sighed gustily and turned. It was too bad his own mother had not lived. She would have attended to all those details. She would have taken care of everything properly. How beautiful she would have been gracing the head of his father's table! And if there were anything Petra needed to know——

He wondered if Petra's aunts had explained everything to her. Wouldn't it be funny if she decided she didn't like him? Or suppose she *did* consent to marry him, and *then* became difficult. That had happened to bridegrooms before. He blew out the candle and lay back, smiling a little into the darkness. It would be nice, of course, but if Petra chose to make even the faintest objection, he doubted if he would try to overcome it. The thin net which hung about his bed billowed slightly with a gusty night wind. He pushed back the covers with one hand and let the cool air play over his slim body. What kind of a girl was she, anyway? She hadn't said much, except that she had appeared glad he wasn't old. Then, too, she hadn't seemed the least embarrassed that he had had no clothes on beneath the covers. Say! Maybe she wouldn't mind—— No! He must wear night clothes. This was his house. It wasn't out under some tree.

The music swelled, and his slim fingers kept time on the bedpost. Oh, well, he couldn't dance tonight, but there was still tomorrow night. Californians didn't visit lightly. Now that they were here, they would stay two or three days. He might as well go to sleep. He closed his eyes and tried to shut his mind against the small worrisome problems. Tomorrow he would think of them. Tomorrow he would cope with them.

Chapter 2

Downstairs they had finished another cold lunch of chicken, ham, cakes, coffee and champagne and they had begun dancing again. It was two hours until daybreak when they would all retire to the rooms prepared for them and sleep for about three hours. Then possibly there would be a picnic in the woods. The weather was mild and warm. They would enjoy a *merienda.* Francisco opened the door of the small square room he used for an office and went in. He expected to find his aunt Ysidra there, for she often stayed up late, having never accustomed herself to the early retiring and rising in California. He went softly in case she were dozing, but though his tread was light as that of a fawn, her black eyes popped open the moment he entered the room. She was rocking gently back and forth in the large chair she was accustomed to using.

"Well, my dear?" she said as he closed the door, dimming the sound of the music and dancing.

Before answering her, he picked up one of her strangely dainty hands and kissed it. "My beloved aunt," he began, still holding her hand, "you have done me yet another great favor in bringing your goddaughter to Dos Ríos. I shall be grateful to the grave, and probably after."

She gave him a slight grimace and the slightest

possible bow. "Surely I have owed you that much—having made my home here for the last ten years."

"No," he said smiling, "let us say you have given us the pleasure of your association for the last ten years—another debt I owe you." He dropped her hand and all pretense of courtesy vanished. "Thank you, anyway," he added, easing his big body into a chair. He took a long slim cigar and lighted it. When its tip was firmly glowing, he tossed it in a gentle arc to Ysidra. She caught it deftly with one small hand which scarcely appeared to move. Relaxing with a sigh of contentment, she inhaled a breath of the pungent smoke. It came out her nostrils wispy and thin.

Smiling, Francisco lighted one for himself and lounged back in his chair. Presently he spoke. "Do you think she will make a good mother, *Mamacita?*"

A low wheezing chuckle rose from Ysidra. "You understand no such word as failure, do you, my dear?" she asked after a moment. "The fact that she is brought here and you plan she shall marry your son satisfies you, doesn't it? It doesn't occur to you that they might have other ideas?" He shook his head good-humoredly, and she continued: "As for her being a good mother, it is difficult to tell if she will be a good anything yet. She is still only fifteen, you know."

"And Angelo only eighteen," he mused.

"True, but eighteen is not too young—although it is considered so here—unless of course," she added dryly, "the Military comes through to draft young single men. Then no age is too young for marriage."

"It may be young for Angelo, though," Francisco said thoughtfully. "He seems no older to me now than he did five years ago. But, Ysidra, I can't afford to wait any longer. What am I building up this estate for if it isn't for my family and heirs? I've reached a point where I must see my own children—if not mine, then Angelo's—in my house. It seems useless, ridiculous, to go on building up wealth and an estate of this size with no family to pass it on to. When I think of Acuña and his eight sons——"

"Come, come, my dear," Ysidra murmured, her eyes filming for an instant.

"Angelo is young, but he will marry immediately if I insist on it. He's much too lazy to put up an argument about anything. And I will insist on it soon because I'm not so young as I once was. Smile if you like, Ysidra, but I'm feeling my age more and more."

"Where, my love? In bed?" she asked closing her eyes against the rivulets of smoke which crept from her nostrils.

Francisco laughed. "No," he admitted, "not exactly. I'll probably want a woman in my deathbed."

"And no doubt have one," Ysidra said; "which will be awkward, because of the priest."

Smiling, Francisco poured them each some brandy, and sipping this, they meditated. Many long evenings they had spent in each other's company in this manner. Sometimes it would be an evening of almost complete silence, if Francisco brooded sullenly. Other times the room rang with laughter from the ribald stories of which they were both fond. Then, again, there was quiet earnest talk far into the dawn. Long ago Francisco had learned that if one dug deeply enough into Ysidra one found a store of shrewd intelligence and business acumen. Many an idea presented by Ysidra had been used by Francisco to his great gain.

They had been friends a long time, the attachment antedating the residence in California. It had begun during the turbulent later years of his boyhood in Spain, shortly after the time he had been cast out by his family and the circle of which they were a prominent part. He had been eighteen, Angelo's age—he paused in wonderment at the difference between them at eighteen—eighteen, but far older in appearance, sophistication and intellect. He had towered above his elder brothers, of whom there were two, and his father, a stern cold Spaniard with whom he had little contact or understanding. He had been a wrathful, passionate, proud eighteen, filled with a complete and absorbing determination to get exactly what he wanted. The determination had changed none through the years, but he had acquired more subtle methods with the passing of time.

He could still remember, after all the years, the sharp sweet engulfing of his first passionate love. The fact that a marriage in any case was impossible for him for several years, and that the girl was already betrothed to Felipe Ortiz, seemed small obstacles to his youthful arrogance. It didn't occur to him that he had accomplished any strange thing when he had persuaded her—three years his senior, betrothed and member of a family more prominent than his—that she loved him better than her betrothed, her family and the complex and inflexible rules of a strict Spanish upbringing. She was his, and he wanted her. She had been his, in his mind, from the moment he had seen her. And so Guadalupe Montoya y Vasquez had flung aside, joyously and with complete abandon, everything in order to run away with him. They had shocked, stupefied and horrified all by eloping. They were quite heedless of everything in their wild and passionate attachment for each other.

Like a delicate cup shattered by lightning the sweet exuberant plan exploded in their faces. The whole of the Estrada, Santander, Ortiz, Montoya and Vasquez clans rose as a man to hunt them down. This proved a simple thing to do, and within a month Guadalupe, raging, was confined to a bed in an obscure convent. Francisco, with smoldering eyes, paced his locked room waiting for the time when he must kill Felipe Ortiz who had immediately challenged him, despite his youth.

The Estradas, grim and gray-faced, prepared for the death of their son and brother Francisco. He had disgraced them, flaunted his own will against the time-honored and valued customs of their kind. It came as a distinct shock to them all when he turned from the field with a smoking gun, his adversary lying quite dead a few paces beyond. "I'm really very sorry," he had said, bowing. And within an hour he had disappeared, swallowed up completely by the city, or the woods, or the sea—none of them knew which. His mother might have sighed a bleak sigh that he escaped punishment for the killing, but no sound of it passed her lips. They spoke of him not at all, after the first bitter frenzied discussion. He was gone. It was finished. They would live it down. And if Montoyas, Vasquezes and Ortizes passed them with closed and grim faces, they ignored it as did their circle of friends and relatives. They only hoped with bitterness that Francisco—outcast, outlaw, renegade—had gone so far that they would never be troubled or shamed by him again.

He was, in fact, remaining in the city. He was stowed quite comfortably in the cellar of Ysidra's small ugly house in one of the poorer sections of the city. He had gone there immediately, before the body of Felipe Ortiz had been covered with his cloak and carried from the field. Sickness and rage filling him, he had gone almost blindly and directionlessly through the early morning emptiness of the city streets . . . until quite suddenly he was at Ysidra's door.

She, who was already a widow, living on the grudging charity of her family, met him at the door as his hand was raised to knock. Her beauty had blown itself out and she was running to fat. Clothed in rusty black, she opened the door. He managed a stiff bow, as he saw she was dressed for going out, and automatic words of greeting and apology rose to his white lips.

"Come in, Pancho," she said quietly. "I was just going to find you."

He had no coat, having left his on the field, and the thin white stuff of his shirt clung damply to his magnificent chest and shoulders. He stepped inside the door, breathing heavily, dew resting on his crisply curling hair. He was suddenly struck dumb, nonplused, not knowing why he had come to her. He scarcely knew her; the family had not met with her socially since her disastrous marriage. He knew that his mother, whose sister she was, had given her sums of money from time to time. He had seen her on occasion in her shabby black, distastefully received by his mother and hurriedly ushered out. He had seen the grimy little house only once before, on his mother's single hasty visit in some time of sickness. Now it had suddenly become the only refuge his raging and confused mind could think of.

"You have no money, I suppose," she said matter-of-factly, removing her bonnet.

He shook his head. "I . . . not with me . . ." he stammered, thinking of the goodly sum in his bedroom at home.

"Well, no matter," she said easily. "We will get some when we have need of it. You are not leaving Spain immediately, are you?"

His muscles tightened in fury, his face congealed. "I have no intention of leaving Spain without my wife."

"I thought as much," she said dryly. "Well, come with me. I have made a little place for you that will not be too uncomfortable." He followed her into the depths of the dark cramped house. "Xavier has nailed a few kegs together and placed them before the door of a little cellar room so that they may be moved easily, but when they are in place, they completely cover the door. You may have a candle, as the light will not show. I tested it. There is very little water seepage in summer, so you will probably remain dry."

Xavier, even then plump and flushed, had met them in the cellar. "He did come!" he cried in surprise.

"Of course," Ysidra answered absently. "Where else could he go? Move the kegs and show him where he is to sleep."

Francisco, inspecting the hole that was to be his home for some time to come, could say nothing, so deep was his gratitude. He knew only that she spoke the truth, there was nowhere else he could go. And he had to have some place to go, some hole to crawl into, until he could make plans and carry them out.

He had spent little time in the cellar, using it only for sleeping and on the occasion when representatives of his family—or some other family—made a polite search. Ysidra had expressed cool surprise and allowed them to go through. Xavier, fifteen and thoroughly delighted, wiped the dust from the kegs off his hands and bowed them out the door when they finished. Francisco had wondered then, and a thousand times since, what he would have done had it not been for Ysidra. Her plump body seemed to stand between him and all the things that strove to beat him down and confound him. The glint of shrewdness in her black eyes found ways and means when ways and means seemed obscure to him who had never had to connive and plan deviously.

"Money," she had said, "is a troublesome thing, but it can be come by, you know."

"How?" Not wanting to seem discourteous, he kept his tone calm when anger and helplessness were beating at his temples.

She pointed to the polished handle of the beautiful pistol which lay on a shelf, to the glittering ring on his finger, to the jeweled hilt of the small dagger in his belt. "I have had experience at trading, my dear—when I have had anything to trade. I found the bread of charity slightly bitter to my palate and consequently long ago I made the acquaintance of certain gentlemen who buy and sell things."

So that's it, he thought in sudden sharp knowledge. That explained the ringless fingers, the plaster crucifix instead of one of ebony and bronze, the house so sparsely and comfortlessly furnished. He knew a moment's anger against the dead Miramontes for leaving his wife a pauper. Then in quick conviction he promised himself that he would alter all this—sometime, not now, in ways not yet clear—but he would.

It was Ysidra in the rusty black bonnet who took away a package from time to time and returned with certain funds. It was Ysidra who, cautiously disbursing portions of these funds, ascertained which convent Lupe was in. It was Ysidra who told him without emotion or expression that it was useless to think of running away at present, for Lupe was going to have a child. It was Ysidra who came to him one night in the cellar to tell him his wife was dead.

"Do you want the child?" she asked looking at his stony face.

With difficulty he made himself think. "It's mine," he said grimly. "Yes, I want it."

It was Ysidra who obtained it for him, visiting the convent with his and Lupe's marriage papers and his demand that the child be surrendered to her. There was little argument, for the Montayas would have none of it, and the Estradas did not recognize Francisco as having been a member of their family. Using her wits and subtle tongue she not only brought the baby to him, she brought him all the personal effects of the dead girl. And it was she who had found the Montoya diamonds, given to Lupe by her father, entangled carelessly in a mass of feminine trinkets.

"Will you sell these?" she asked.

"No," he said remembering them about his wife's throat. "They belong to the baby."

Silently, showing no regret, she replaced them in the box.

"Now what?" he had asked, standing before the small fireplace, holding the infant, red shadows leaping about them. "Now what?"

"Leave him with me for a while," she said after a moment's thought. "I've raised one; I can raise another. You can't spend the rest of your life in my cellar. You'd better go to one of the colonies and—" she paused, her lips curling a little—"get some money, Francisco. That is paramount. Of course," she added thoughtfully, "use your intelligence about getting it. You will be more use to your child alive than hung or shot. So be guided by your common sense. And send some money back here from time to time," she had finished dryly.

He sent it. At nineteen he was soldiering in Cuba, later Mexico, later California. Pay for the troops was slow in coming, delays amounting at times to months. Supplies were intermittent, but he obtained sums of money all the same. He grew up, hardened, became wise, wary-eyed and cautious beneath the Castilian veneer. In time, still young, he retired from the army and became a landowner along with other soldiers who wished to establish themselves. Eventually he was able to bring Ysidra and his little son from Spain. He was becoming wealthy in cattle. He needed no one. He was himself. He was the beginning of his own line.

He looked at Ysidra's hands, motionless in her lap. They were smooth now, not knowing the touch of work and covered with jewels. Each winking stone represented many hides from the bodies of cattle on his grazing lands, many vats of tallow rendered from those cattle. He felt a satisfaction in looking at her hands—covered with jewels as they were, and remembering they were the same hands, work-roughened and bare, that had carried his gun to be pawned.

"*Mamacita,*" he mused setting down his empty glass, "wouldn't it be like the hand of the devil if this girl Petra didn't have any children for Angelo—or died in childbirth like Lupe?"

"Petra would have an easy birth, I think. Did you notice her mouth? Quite large. A good sign."

Francisco grinned. "So that is a sign of easy birthing, is it? How do you women pick up these little signs? The mind of a woman must be a strange and wonderful thing. Is there something I can look for that will tell me whether or not she would have many children?"

"Well, my dear, something depends on the husband," Ysidra said.

He sobered. That was true. So much depended on Angelo. He moved uneasily in his chair. What strange perverted hand had arranged the matings of his house? He, strong, vigorous, passionate, saddled with the miserable weeping Ana, who had brought him nothing but seven stillborn girls.

And for Angelo, careless, lazy, childish, Angelo, who cared nothing for family, inheritance or responsibility, there was Petra, young, bold, new to marriage.

"Ana was sick this morning," Ysidra observed.

Francisco's mouth hardened. "You amuse me, *Mamacita*, as if I could have any hope of having a child from Ana. She has been pregnant before and each time the thing she brings forth isn't worth throwing to the dogs."

"Oh, Francisco, you worry too much. There is plenty of time. How old are you exactly?"

"Thirty-seven, and I should have half a dozen growing children."

"How old is Ana?"

"Thirty."

"Now, you see," Ysidra said complaisantly, "you don't look thirty-seven. On the other hand Ana looks much older. In fact, taken together, you appear the younger. Forgive me if I speak frankly, but Ana isn't well, and there is always the chance that Ana will die in the next confinement. Then you could marry again."

"You dream, Ysidra. Those sickly bowls of milk last forever. My only hope is Petra and Angelo. And if that doesn't work out——"

"You will do nothing foolish," she cut in smoothly. "You will always use your head. I personally will see to it." She opened her fan with a snap. "Besides," she added, "you're jealous—admit it, Francisco—you're already half in love with Petra yourself."

He laughed, his good humor restored. Ysidra was right. There was plenty of time for everything. They glanced up as there was a soft knock on the door.

"Come in, Delfina," he said, and as the door opened to admit her, his eyes swept her appreciatively. For an Indian she was quite pretty, due probably to a generous strain of white blood. Her last name was Ruiz.

"How did you know, Don Francisco?" she asked delightedly.

"I know your knock, little one. What is it you want?"

"Oh, yes," she said remembering her message. "Doña Ana is ill. She wishes to go to bed. Will Doña Ysidra come and relieve her as hostess?" And as Ysidra grimaced, she added, "She already knows Doña Ysidra is still up."

"Oh, well," Ysidra said rising with difficulty, "it is almost daylight. They will soon all go to bed."

Francisco rose courteously to bow her out of the door, but his eyes, suddenly smoldering, were on Delfina.

"Lock the door this time," Ysidra said dryly as she passed into the hallway.

At the foot of the stairs, she met Ana, who paused and turned to wait for her. "You do not mind?" Ana asked. "I'm very tired, and you know those Quixano boys—they dance until daylight."

"It's quite all right," Ysidra said. "Run along to bed."

Still Ana lingered. She cleared her throat. "Is Francisco busy? I'd like to tell him something."

"As a matter of fact, he is," Ysidra answered without expression; "talking business with some of the men. Can't it wait until morning?"

Thin color rose in Ana's face. She stared for a moment with unveiled animosity at her husband's aunt. "Yes, of course, I can always wait." She turned and went upstairs, her thin back stiff with anger. Talking business is he! And where was Delfina! She hadn't come back—that *Indian!*

Ana closed her bedroom door and leaned against it, her tall body sagging inward as if she could not stand without its support.

How tired she was! She should not have cried so long this afternoon. She should have lain down with a wet cloth over her eyes. She should not have sapped her small strength by weeping. At the memory of the hot bitter afternoon, revulsion rose in her. Oh, not again! Not to live through all those sickening months, and at the end twist and shriek like an animal to bear another dead infant—for which Francisco would despise her more! Why couldn't her babies be alive? Even Lupe had done better than she. Lupe's child had been weak and frail, but he was alive—such as he was.

Her sharp teeth worried at her lips. How smug she had been and how eager to become the wife of Francisco!

Hastily she swallowed her rising hysteria and glanced about the empty room. She must be calm at all costs and retain her dignity. Ana the desperate, Ana the frightened, Ana the infuriated, might tear at the bedclothes and sob her soul to ashes when no one was near. But when there was danger of Francisco approaching, she must try to hold herself together. The corners of her lips pulled downward and twitched slightly.

But after all, why try to keep the myth of her dignity before him? Hadn't he torn every shred of self-respect and decency from her? Hadn't he humiliated and shamed her beyond forgiveness? Well, was he asking forgiveness? Hardly! He, who left Guadalupe's picture hanging in their bedchamber. He, who came to her bed whenever he pleased and left it when he pleased. He, who planted in her unwilling body every year the seed of another dead infant.

Her eyes fell again on the portrait of Lupe. He had had it painted in Mexico from a miniature. Ana could remember Lupe. They had known each other slightly. And she had looked with small-girl wonder at the lovely, vivacious Lupe Montoya.

Well she remembered the scandal of the runaway marriage with Francisco Estrada.

Ana had snatched a glimpse of him, and to her naïve inquisitive gaze he had seemed to epitomize all that was romantic, wicked and fascinating. Ana had believed that if she ever saw the Devil face to face—and most holy Virgin Mother protect her from that!—he would look just like Francisco.

The younger girls had spoken in excited whispers of the lovers. Who would have thought young Francisco could be so bold! How lucky Lupe was! How exciting her life would be! What a future she had in store for her!

In a year she was dead.

And Francisco was gone—swallowed up in a vast nothingness.

Suddenly one day he arrived again in Spain. It was not for a reconciliation with his family, because he stayed with strangers. What reason, then, could he have but that he was looking for a wife? He who had become a man of property in the new world must have a wife to grace his household, a woman who could give him a fine family, finer children than the sickly boy Lupe had left him.

At the thought of Angelo a slow mottled red crept up under her pale skin. That sniveling weak helpless creature. If only he had grown strong and tough like Francisco! Then there would be no need for all the pain and agony of baby after baby after baby. Why didn't he get out of bed in the morning, brown and hungry and glowing with strength. Why didn't he mount the way Francisco did and ride out over the land, to inspect the cattle, the grain, the vineyards, and direct all the vast interests of the estate. Oh, no, he must lie abed like a woman and have milk and melon brought to him. Milk! Mother of God, no wonder he was weak! Even the Indians—savages that they were—would not touch cow's milk. Like a woman in childbed he was, so weak, so timid, so cowardly. He must not ride in the sun. He must not do that. He could not eat this. How stupid—no, he wasn't stupid. He was wise. He was clever, for all his youth. His room was directly next to hers, with a door between, and each time she cried out in the night, he knew why. He knew when his father came and went. He knew each time she went down into childbirth. Each time she broke down and wept and clawed like a madwoman, he knew it. Nothing could be hidden from the wise eyes of Angelo.

And he pitied her, that little beast, that pathetic litle excuse of a man! *He* pitied *her*, the Doña Ana-Lucía Soledad Estrada y Valdez, mistress of the rancho, wife of Don Francisco. How could she preserve her myth of self-possession before his candid eyes?

She pulled herself upright with an effort and walked slowly until she came to stand beneath the portrait of Lupe. To think how smug she had been about Lupe, leaving her spindly blue infant mewling like a half-dead kitten in the arms of a convent nun!

How she had hinted and gently suggested, then outright asked her family to make the arrangements! And what a triumph she had felt at the announcement of their betrothal! Never before or since had she felt such a thrill of victory and power. How lucky and envied she had been! Ah, she would show them! Where Lupe had failed and sickened and died, she would succeed.

She remembered, her long pale hands twisting and pulling at her linen handkerchief, she had wanted to be just like Mama, with tall handsome doting sons. How proud and humble and loving would Don Francisco be! Humble!

Probably the only reason he had chosen her was because she was the only daughter of a family of five children. He had forseen a family of tough vigorous men like himself for sons, men he could understand, men who could match him mile for mile on horseback, and glass for glass at the table, men with whom he could work and hunt—and, when he became old, men to whom he could leave with assurance his estates and holdings and duties. That was what he had wanted. She knew what he wanted And she had been the woman who was going to make all this possible.

She recalled the first time she had seen Angelo. He had just had fever again. How pale and wan he had looked! She had pitied him with a sort of humorous contempt. What chance did this colorless child of Lupe have against the sons she would bear? He would be the eldest, it was true, but Francisco didn't care for him or even try to understand him, so she had nothing to worry about. Francisco would do well by sons of whom he was proud.

Ana raised shaking hands to her face. She must not think about that. She must not think about anything at all. She must be very calm.

And Petra! In an instant her little shred of calm shattered. That Petra! That chit! That child! Coming to marry Angelo. Suppose . . . suppose it did happen the way Francisco and Ysidra planned it. Suppose the pitiful Angelo did father a child—a son—or sons. No!

"No." She said it aloud. It was a moan, torn from her to the empty room, to the portrait of Lupe.

Not her! Not Petra, with her fine gown and gold lace, her round white arms, her hair as bright as wheat. But she might. She would—with her boldness. How bold she had been with her English upbringing, how confident! Ha! Well, she would learn! Mother of God, how soon a woman learned!

She hated them all. Hate! Hate! Hate! Her face became loose-jawed and shaking. She was filled with it, saturated with it. Delfina, you savage, delighting him with your warm brown body. You horrible beautiful Lupe, safe and dead and smiling. You fat, fat Ysidra, ugly, smug and secure. You Petra, bold and young and triumphant. Angelo! You—Angelo—you'll die and be free of it all, live and die, scarcely troubling to leave your bed. Idiots! Fools! Devils! I hate you! I spit on you!

Suddenly she was choking. Her hands, frantic and filled with a gust of strength, tore at her bodice and collar. They came apart, scattering jet buttons that bounced across the floor like hard black bugs. Blood was rising in her throat to strangle her. In a frenzy she tore and ripped at her hair and clothing until the cloth hung in tatters and shreds, and her hair fell loose and hung in tangled disorder about her shoulders.

A long time later she lay on the floor staring vacantly at one small jet button. She knew distantly that time had passed and that soon Francisco would come up. Some small part of her mind bade her get up and set herself to rights. But the task loomed great and insurmountable before her. She would have to get to her feet, hide the torn dress, brush her hair and gather up all the tiny scattered buttons. She knew this, and yet she continued to lie limply on the floor, not moving, scarcely breathing. This was good—this unfeeling. Tomorrow she would feel again, hate, and ache, and envy. But tomorrow she could cope with them all. Now she must just lie here and rest. It didn't matter whether Francisco found her thus or not. She did not care. Even when she heard his boots on the stair, she did not move. She merely continued to look at the little dot of jet. So he found her.

His keen eyes picked her out immediately upon entering the room, even though it was lighted only by the unsteady flame of a single candle. In two steps he was beside her. He dropped to one knee and seeing that her eyes were open he said, "Ana, what is the matter?"

"I am sick," she said remotely.

Instantly he slid his arms beneath her limp body and without effort lifted her and carried her to the bed. "Sick? In what way?" he asked, his voice holding no shade of emotion.

"I am going to have a child," she said dully, turning her face away from him.

Without a word he laid her down on the great bed. She lay exactly where he had placed her, without moving while he summoned a servant. She made no effort to see his reaction to this announcement, which had been made seven times before. She could not have told anyway, for until the servant came, he stood staring out into the darkness, and all she could see was his broad velvet-covered back.

Francisco remained in the room while the Indian woman washed and undressed his wife. When at last she was clad in a plain white gown and the covers were pulled up about her thin body, and she fell into a deep unmoving sleep, he sank into a chair by the window.

As the sun rose she began to toss and move about uneasily. From time to time she moaned and whined like a fretful child.

Francisco remained silent and still in the chair. His brooding eyes never left the bed. As if sensing his gaze, she muttered and turned uneasily while her fingers plucked at the linen sheet.

Chapter 3

In difference to the many sleeping guests Francisco had ordered that there be no sunrise hymn. Some of the older Indians resented this and he had heard a defiant voice or two raised softly in the kitchen. He supposed that the custom would have to be resumed tomorrow, but many of the guests had been asleep only a short time and he knew they would want to be rested for the *merienda* in the afternoon.

He stood now staring down at his son. Angelo slept quietly, without stirring, though the bright sun lay across his face. There was something of Lupe in the wide-planed cheekbones and the wide-set eyes, but the mouth, large and expressive, was a reflection of his own. That never failed to give Francisco a feeling of pleasure.

"Angelo."

His son stirred, opened his eyes slowly, then closed them and stretched elaborately. Guillermo, who was laying out his clothing, shook his head at such discourtesy. Don Francisco was indeed a lenient father.

"Are you completely awake, Angelo?" Francisco asked. "I want to ask you two things, so please attend."

"I'm awake, sir," Angelo said faintly, turning

his face from the sun and half burying it in the pillow.

"First, I think it would be a nice idea if you weren't sick today and would get dressed and come downstairs. We're going to ride out after breakfast and show Doña Petra some of the rancho. Then we'll go into the woods for a picnic."

"All right, Father," Angelo said placidly. "Although I seem to get the impression that you think I wasn't sick yesterday."

"Never mind yesterday. This is today." Francisco grinned. "Now the second thing I want to talk to you about——Angelo, please open your eyes while I'm speaking. Thank you. I'm referring to the Montoya necklace. What do you think of giving it to Doña Petra?"

Angelo's eyes widened momentarily. "I beg your pardon, Father. *Give* it to her?"

"Yes, Angelo." Francisco's tone took on an edge of exaggerated patience. "Surely you understand that your Aunt Ysidra didn't have her come all the way from Spain merely for a chat about the latest fashions in Sevilla. It isn't possible that you are ignorant of the fact that I want you to marry her."

"No, Father, of course not." Angelo's face flushed on the pillow. "Only——"

"Only what?"

"Well—" he paused as if undecided whether to continue or drop the whole subject—"well, the necklace is the only thing I have of my mother. I place a rather high value on it."

"That is a weak argument, Angelo. You know you'd do as I ask you eventually, so in all probability Petra will be your wife. Won't you place a high value on her too?"

"Not necessarily," Angelo answered dryly, and Francisco's face darkened at the implication, which he understood perfectly.

"Well, in any case, I took it out of the strong box this morning. I'll leave it with you. If you decide within the next few days to give it to her, do so, by all means. If you decide not to, let me know so I can replace it. You know the value of these stones. They mustn't be left lying about for several weeks while you make up your mind."

"All right, Father."

"I may expect you down for prayers and breakfast?"

"Yes, sir, I'm getting up now," Angelo answered, not moving.

As the door shut after his father, Angelo breathed an uneven sigh of relief. "I would say, Guillermo, that the golden-haired Petra made a good impression on my father." He began to get slowly out of bed.

"I would say that you are very disrespectful," Guillermo answered.

"Yes, I guess I would say so too," Angelo returned absently. "I don't want to wear that hat anymore. There's a new one there some place, isn't there?"

Angelo mused, as he dressed, on what might have happened had he refused outright to give the necklace to Petra. It was his, wasn't it? He should have the right to say. He grinned a little wryly. He knew his father well. Behind the polite phrasing lay a definite order. He was to give her the diamonds, or—or what? What would his father do if he disobeyed? Francisco was possibly the most indulgent and careless father in California, but there was a definite limit to his leniency. Angelo could go just so far and no farther. They both understood that, and while he might venture a mild argument, he knew that in things of this magnitude he would do as he was told. It was possible, highly possible, that in the event of any great insubordination Francisco might take a whip to his back.

A shiver passed through him. He had seen Francisco wield a whip, and the sight had not been pleasing. Other people lived through it. He had seen Juan Acuña, their neighbor, lay a rawhide across the shoulders of Teodoro, and Teodoro was—Mother of God!—Teodoro was all of twenty-two. And there was that time Don Cristbal Quixano had struck his son Pedro, and Pedro was the father of four children himself.

One could carry the beautiful idea of parental respect and obedience too far, and yet it was an established custom. Why battle against an established custom? He was no crusader. He and Francisco had never come to an impasse yet in the matter of obedience. Angelo had seen to that. Besides, what good would it do? You either obeyed or you disobeyed. In the event you disobeyed, you were punished and obeyed in the end anyway. So it seemed rather unintelligent not to obey in the first place. Besides, having a length of rawhide cut into your back must be not only painful in the extreme, but an entirely personal and obscene thing. A person's body—sweet Jesus!—a person's *body* ought to be inviolate!

"Guillermo," he said, "I have a very peace-loving soul."

A white grin showed in the dark face of the other as he braided Angelo's hair. "Most assuredly. Would you like to have me polish up the diamonds a little before you give them to her?"

"Listen, wise one, keep a civil tongue in your head. That's fine, thanks. Where is my sash? It was right here a moment ago." He took the length of red satin from Guillermo and wound it about his waist.

He wondered what Petra would think if she

knew that at this moment she was the owner of some very valuable diamonds. He took them from their deerskin bag and held them up in the streaming sunlight. Brilliantly they splashed multiple patches of light and color over the room, as they twisted and twirled on their heavy chain. Well, where could he put them? They mustn't be left lying about. He shrugged. Poor little *Mamacita* didn't know that one day her necklace would adorn the throat of an English girl. The stones were so valuable that the point now was to give them to Petra as soon as possible, and then *she* could worry about them.

He pondered where on his slender person could he put them. They would make too big a lump in his pocket. His eyes passed briefly over his hat, rejecting it, and then in sudden inspiration he unclasped them and pushed the strand down under the top of his sash. Just the place. Strung out straight beneath the heavy satin folds, they were scarcely noticeable.

"The señorita's door just closed, Don Angelo," Guillermo said quickly. She'll be looking for Doña Ysidra or the chapel or something——Why don't you offer to show her?"

Angelo sighed deeply and went to open his door. "You have the ears of a lynx, and the soul of a clucking hen. Good morning, Doña Petra."

"Oh, good morning, Don Angelo. Are you well today?"

"Quite well, thank you," he said, bowing. "If you are looking for Aunt Ysidra, she's already gone down. Everyone will be in the chapel by now."

She said, "Oh," a little uncertainly.

"May I be allowed to show you the way? It's on the other side of the *sala*."

"Yes, if you please. I suppose it's late. I'm afraid I slept too long."

"We had no singing to awaken us this morning," Angelo said as they walked toward the head of the stairs. They weren't engaged yet, so he supposed they were still considered children and could be allowed together without a duenna. Anyway, Guillermo was here.

"Singing, Don Angelo?"

"Yes, the custom here. The first in the house to waken starts the morning hymn. Then it's taken up by everyone else as they wake—which they seldom fail to do. By everyone but my Aunt Ysidra. She thinks it's a barbaric custom and will have no part of it."

"I think it's a beautiful custom," Petra said delightedly.

Angelo smiled and bowed. There was no point in being impolite, but he could think of nothing that appeared beautiful at five o'clock in the morning. As he patted the necklace in his sash, a sudden thought came to him. Why not give it to her now? Then he wouldn't have to worry about it. Of course he would have to take it out of his sash, giving the impression of a swain pulling a chain of diamonds out of his stomach for a fair lady. Maybe she would think he was enchanted. The idea made him smile.

"Since we have this moment alone, doña, there is something I would like to say." As he saw a shadow of alarm cross her face he pulled the necklace from its hiding place. "These," he said thoughtfully, "are called the Montoya diamonds." He let them swing bright and heavy from his slim hand. "They have a fascinating and bloody history with which I will not take up your time this morning. I say merely that they last belonged to my mother who was of the Montoya family, and now you are to have them."

For a moment she appeared stunned. Her hand was shaking as she extended it. "Why, how kind of you!" she gasped. "How wonderful! I don't know what to say. To think you would want to give me your mother's necklace——"

Want to! He hardly knew the girl. For an instant his eyes hardened.

"You misunderstand, señorita," he said evenly. "I didn't say I wanted to. I just said you were to have them." He heard Guillermo's startled gasp behind him and saw the girl slowly redden. "I was going to hold them in my sash until a suitable time presented itself, but they kept slipping. Well, will you take them, please?" Already his momentary anger was diminishing. It wasn't her fault. Why was he acting this way? Even Guillermo had better manners, and Guillermo was only an Indian. Besides, if she became angry and didn't take them——Now there was a thought!

He took her hand gently and piled the necklace into it. "I am very sorry, doña. I have been unforgivably rude to you. You would be justified in never speaking to me again. Please take them. If I promise to mend my manners and behave with proper respect in the future, will you take them? Besides," he added in a sudden spurt of frankness, "if you don't take them now, it will prove very embarrassing to me."

She was silent long enough for him to become thoroughly uncomfortable. Humiliation began to stain his cheeks. What was the matter with him? Hadn't he any breeding or pride? Why didn't he act with instinctive good taste as everyone else did?

Petra silently wrapped the necklace in her handkerchief, and turning from him, she thrust it down the neck of her dress. Then, with her face still averted, she said coldly, "I will take them if you insist. I dislike causing anyone embarrassment. However, we will understand privately, between ourselves, that they do *not* belong to me.

And thank you very much, but I think I can find the chapel by myself."

Before he could speak, she was hurrying down the stairs. Silently he and Guillermo watched her wide skirt swish around the *sala* door.

"All right, scowl at me," he said wearily to Guillermo.

"I don't scowl," Guillermo said presenting a placid face, "I feel sorry for you. The doña is very angry. She will probably marry Don Teodoro Acuña. Or one of the Quixano men. Or maybe Don Candalario Sal. Who knows? In any case it will be very annoying to Don Francisco."

Old familiar apprehension stirred inside Angelo making him frown.

"Don't forget," the other went on, "that while you were sick in bed they were dancing all night with her. Of course if you make yourself pleasant at the *merienda* this afternoon, and—" his tone became cajoling— "no one can be more pleasant when he chooses——"

"Oh, be quiet," Angelo interrupted tiredly. Already there was a dull throbbing in the back of his head and uneasiness moved in the pit of his stomach. Ahead was the long ride, then the noise and hilarity of the picnic. Now he must go downstairs, say his prayers in the chapel and eat his breakfast with the others. Perhaps he would feel better after that. He had wanted to feel good today.

In the chapel, as he bent his head over his beads and murmured with the others, he thought about what Doctor Vaiz had said: "I find nothing wrong with you, my boy. Perhaps you suffer from acute attacks of laziness—for which there are several cures." But he had smiled as he said it, for Doctor Vaiz was a kind and pleasant man.

Angelo glanced up and caught his Aunt Ysidra's

eye and composed his face into smooth impassivity, trying dutifully to think of his prayers. But there was this business about the girl from Spain. He had known it would be troublesome the moment he had heard about it. It had affected him the way trouble always did. He had felt the old familiar churning of fear sweep over him, the cold had crept into the palms of his hands, and moisture had gathered in a faint film on his forehead. They were making marriage plans. *What if she wouldn't marry him!* He clutched for a convulsive instant at the rosary. Mother of God, wouldn't his father be furious! If the marriage came to pass it would be their doing and not his. What chance would he have against all the dashing splendid *caballeros* who would vie for her favor. None at all.

He glanced with faint disgust at the slender hands clasping his beads. How small they looked when one thought of the strong large hands of his father! Why must he be small and delicate-looking when almost everyone he knew was big and tough and extremely virile. Mother of God, he thought with sudden violence, how did Francisco Estrada father such a weakling as he? How could he compete with young men like Teodoro Acuña who rode so wildly, hunted bears with delight and took great pleasure in things which struck terror to his own faint heart. Didn't they ever enjoy anything quiet or painless or easy?

What other Spaniard in California had ever been thrown from a horse! There. The old nightmare rose up again. It always did at times when he was unguarded, defenseless, thinking of something else. The memory of it was so powerful that it could still make his mouth go dry and make him sway as he knelt praying. He, at twelve, had been unable to ride as well as children of three or four. How humiliating this had been in a land where riding was more commonplace than walking. Why, even the Indian servant rode out to gather firewood, lassoing the logs and dragging them to the kitchen door. The memory of being thrown, of crashing to the ground, was faint. But the memory of Francisco's white-lipped rage, the contempt in the faces of the other children was clear, quite clear still. The ache in his back had diminished. The scratches on his face had vanished. But his stubborn brain clung to the remembrance of it. During all the years since, it could cause him to wake, sweating with terror, in the night. It came upon him at any time at all—as now, when he was carefully thinking of something else.

How many times, he thought wearily, he must have embarrassed his father! But Francisco was kind and, to a degree, understanding. If he was sick, nothing was expected of him. Delicate things were sent up from the kitchen to tempt his unsettled stomach. Francisco came into his room and smoothed back his hair with a strong brown hand, talking and laughing with him to take his mind off his illness. Aunt Ysidra called on him during the day and delighted him with her clever delineations of Ana and others whom they did not like. They could talk together for hours in mutual pleasure at each other's sharp wit and subtly acid observations.

Yet when the sickness passed, the problems began to press inward on him again. Things were expected of him. He was supposed to take his place as the son of the family. Always there was the veiled annoyance of his father when he became tired easily, or refused to go hunting, or evaded entering into the sports. Sometimes, he thought, in loneliness and shame, almost the only times he and Francisco were perfectly friendly were when he was sick. In these last few years he got sick oftener. At times he thought that some saint was watching over him, and whenever anything threatened, the saint would extend a kind hand in strange blessing to make him sick until the danger had passed. It was an accepted pattern with him now.

He had vomited his dinner the day he learned why Aunt Ysidra's goddaughter was coming from Spain. When he found he would have to ride to the harbor to meet her, stay in the saddle all day, dance all night and compete—oh, worst of all, compete—for her favor, he had felt the faint stirring in his stomach which told him he was going to be sick again.

Which saint was it? Saint Joseph? Possibly. One of his names was José. Perhaps Mary herself, for one of his names was Mario. In any case, no matter who it was, he or she managed to save him from untold trouble and inconvenience. It was so much easier to be sick than to face all the things one had to face.

He did please his father in many ways. He was intelligent and clever. Francisco was always laughing at his jokes. He was a good musician and had a pleasant voice. Everyone liked to hear him sing. And he danced well. They all remarked how graceful he was. His manners weren't the best, of course. He would have to watch them more carefully now. He shouldn't have trouble with manners. After all he had been born in Spain. He wasn't any footless Creole with a shady background and vague antecedents.

As he rose from his knees, he thought, longingly as always, of Spain. From the dim pleasant memories he retained, he felt he would have been much more at home in Spain. Things there were mellower, slower, easier. He wished his father had stayed in Spain.

* * *

The sun was high in the sky by the time breakfast was finished and they were mounting for the ride. Petra had been given a magnificent black from Don Francisco's own *caponera,* that group of twenty-five picked horses which each gentleman kept for his own special use. She watched as the Indians brought out three golden palominos. These, she learned, were from Angelo's *caponera* of palominos. Francisco rejected two of them on sight. He had a way of knowing instantly if it were right for his son to ride. When Angelo arrived, she noted that Guillermo held the bridle until he was firmly in the saddle. Several other men mounted by the simple expedient of slapping their horses and springing up as the horse started off at full gallop.

There was a wild fluttering of chickens and doves as they swept out onto the road. Petra was delighted and exhilarated by the fast ride—they were all superb horsemen. What had seemed sameness and monotony the day before was now sweep and vastness. Their destination, Francisco had told her, was a particular hill from which there was a good view of a large part of the rancho. But on reaching the small mesa Petra was unprepared for the panorama of Estrada land that lay suddenly before her.

The group came to a laughing milling stop and waited while Francisco pointed out what he thought might interest her. "That way is the sea," he said. Petra strained her eyes, and could discern a thin blue rim which must indeed be the sea.

"And over there—no, back that way a little—is the house." Petra's eyes, wide with excitement, followed his hand. "And over that way," he continued, "are some citrus groves. More are being put in. There are oranges and lemons. We've been trying to get some limes. In that direction all that is just pasture. But over there you can see a small orchard, and that long line of bushy red and green is pomegranate. Angelo is very fond of pomegranates. Beyond that are some almonds."

"There are more almonds over to the left, señorita," Angelo said with the first sign of interest he had displayed. "They're hard to see from here because they aren't in bloom, but they're in a little valley shaped like a teardrop. When they are in bloom——" He broke off, conscious that he had interrupted his father. Teodoro would never do anything like that. Teodoro had impeccable manners.

But Francisco seemed not to notice. "Go on." He smiled. "You sound like a poet."

"He is a poet." It was Teodoro Acuña who spoke. He reached over and clasped Angelo's arm, his eyes glinting with affection. "Can the señorita see the *hera* from here, Don Francisco?"

"Perhaps." Francisco resumed: "See that round place in the earth, the one that is bare and level with the fences around? That is where the mares thresh out the grain. It is larger than it looks from here. It's able to hold a hundred mares without crowding. Then, of course, over there are the wheat and barley fields."

"Does this go clear to the sea?" Petra couldn't help asking.

"Almost." He smiled. "The land along the sea is used by the mission."

Petra recalled the little walled garden at home. How different this was! When they spoke of land, they didn't measure it as "this field of grain," "that meadow," and "this tract of timber." They said "those pastures," "these valleys," "those hills" and "these mesas." They did not compute in miles, but in leagues. Nor could they tally in acres.

On this land were innumerable people to attend to the interests of the Estradas and their household. There were men who slaughtered their cattle in bloody fields, cleaned the hides and rendered the tallow. Men who sheared their sheep and combed the wool. Men who planted the fields and reaped the grain. Men to gather the grapes and press the wine. Men who made the harnesses, tanned the leather, braided horsehair for the bridles, baked the bricks, churned the cheese. In the house there were women to clean the rooms, cook the food, pound the meal, make the beds. There were those who washed the clothes, and those who ironed and sewed, and some who sat at the loom.

Petra turned her eyes to the pleasant group on the mesa, the Estradas and their friends. And for whom was all this? There was Xavier to whom it did not belong, who lived on his cousin's bounty. There was Guillermo, adopted, but whose place was little above that of a servant. There was Francisco, a man grown, with one grown son. A tremor ran through her. This was for Angelo. He sat quietly on his shining horse which idly flicked its silver-white mane. All this was for Angelo. His flat black hat, secured with a cord beneath his chin, had fallen down his back. He glanced up and his large, widely set eyes met hers and dropped.

By the time they reached the woods, Petra was more than ready to eat. Ana, Ysidra and some of the older women were there superintending the servants in the broiling of countless tender steaks and the laying of the snowy cloths on the ground. The horses were tethered at a little distance from the party. They all found their places. Petra noticed as the meal progressed that the men began to acquire little bunches of flowers. These, she found, were gathered by the women who picked the small blooms that grew near where they were sitting. Pleased—everything seemed to please her now—she leaned over and gathered a knot of violets. Both Teodoro Acuña and Candalario Sal leaned forward, their eyes pleading, but she chose not to notice and laid the bouquet before Angelo, who glanced up in pleased surprise.

After the meal the young people, chaperoned by some of the married women, walked in the woods in search of flowers. Petra found herself walking with Angelo.

"Do you want any more flowers?" he asked suddenly.

She looked at him, startled. "No, not unless you do. Why, are you tired?"

"Yes, very. Let's sit down here. Don't forget I've recently been very sick."

Petra sat down on the exposed root of a pepper tree, a grin tugging at the corners of her mouth.

"Go on and smile, señorita, if it amuses you," he said. "When you have finished being amused, I have something to ask you." His blue-green eyes clouded and were rebellious for a moment.

Petra frowned slightly. "Well, we'll have to go," she said. "The others are getting ahead of us."

"Let them," Angelo murmured. "That was the point. I must speak to you, and it has to be soon."

Petra raised her brows, a look of alarm crossing her face.

Angelo leaned against the bulbous trunk of the pepper tree. "I think," he said dreamily, "I think I am going to propose to you."

Petra's fan snapped shut. "You *what!*" she gasped. She rose quickly to her feet. "We must go," she said swiftly. "They will look for us and wonder——"

"Wait, wait a minute. You don't understand." He rose quickly and caught her hand, surprising her with the intensity of his grip. "Listen, doña, didn't it occur to you that there might be a reason why you were brought clear to California from Spain?"

A flush began to rise in Petra's face.

"Didn't it?" he insisted.

"Yes," Petra snapped, her eyes suddenly stromy. "It occurred to me a good many times. And it also occurs to me that you are acting in a very improper manner!"

"Yes, but don't you ever get *tired* of it? Don't you wish that sometime—just once—you could think of something yourself?"

"Yes," she found herself admitting. She smiled a little unwillingly.

"And does it occur to you that Aunt Ysidra is your godmother and she'll be making all your plans for you? And I'm answerable to my father. Petra, do you know that if those two plan anything, inevitably it comes to pass on the proper date?" His eyes were glinting now with something like amusement.

"Well—" Petra opened her fan uncertainly—"I'm not sure what you're trying to say."

"Yes, you are," he said smiling. "I told you. I'm proposing to you—English-fashion. This is the way they do it in England, isn't it? They just ask?"

The fan snapped shut, and her eyes narrowed. "I will remind you," she said coldly, "that this is not England. This is practically Spain. And in view of that fact your conduct is extremely improper."

"It wasn't Spain last night when you came sailing into my bedroom. Let us make up our minds. Which code of etiquette are we going to follow?"

Petra turned to hide a sudden grin. "Oh, Angelo, you said yourself that it was virtually inevitable—— Why bother with all this? Unless it gives you pleasure to embarrass me."

He laughed. "You admit it's settled then?"

She pulled her hand away. "Of course. Now we must——"

"Wait," he interrupted quickly. "Will you

please me by wearing the necklace I so rudely gave you this morning?"

"You mean your mother's necklace?" she asked pointedly.

"Yes, if you please," he said humbly. "If you'll just put it on, we will go and find the others."

She took the necklace from its place of concealment and put it about her neck, fumbling with the clasp.

"Here, let me. I've clasped it before. I can't tell you what a great relief it is for me to know that you're willing to marry me. I hate to compete for things."

"Compete?"

"Yes, of course. Didn't you see the lovesickness in Teodoro and a dozen others? I had to ask you first or you would have passed me by. There, it's fastened now. I wouldn't have been very good at courting you."

"Courting!" Petra smothered a delighted laugh.

"Yes. You know—writing you poems, singing beneath your window. You wouldn't have liked the poems anyway. And dampness gives me pains in the chest."

He looked at her soberly for a moment, a shade of regret in his eyes. Then swiftly, gently, he leaned forward and kissed her. "Petra," he said, "I think you are a very nice girl."

It wasn't until after they had rejoined the main group that Petra thought suddenly of the necklace. She was wearing the Montoya diamonds! They hung heavy and sparkling about her throat. Merciful Mother of God, *please,* don't let anybody notice! But even as the prayer formed in her mind, she saw Doña Ana's small pale mouth drop open and then snap shut. She shot a panic-stricken glance at her godmother. Ysidra's eyes fell on the diamonds at that instant and glittered, shifting swiftly to Ana to see her reaction.

Seeming strangely pleased, she rose majestically and came toward Petra. "Lovely, my child!" she murmured under cover of the noisy preparations to leave.

Petra gulped, and glanced pleadingly at Angelo, who appeared not to notice. He had started toward Francisco.

"Where did you get them, my dear?" Ysidra fingered one of the bright hard stones.

There was no time to think up a lie—and who could fool the wise black eyes of Ysidra anyway? Petra's jaw stiffened. "Angelo gave them to me, but they really belong——"

"What did he say?" cut in Ysidra.

"Say? Why, nothing much. He . . . we just were talking."

"Very effective talk," Ysidra commented dryly.

Angelo's voice, low but clear, carried to them. "Your indulgence, Father, for one moment. Before we break up our party I would like to say something to all our friends." He stood, slim and graceful, waiting for their attention. Gradually the laughter and talk died and they waited for his announcement.

"Ladies and gentlemen," he said, smiling engagingly at the group, "something has happened that has filled me with such happiness I cannot remain silent about it. I want to tell you that the lovely Doña Petra Hutchins y Vega, who has graced our *merienda* today, has done me the great honor of promising to become my wife."

Mother of God, what had he done? Where was the pattern? He should have waited. Days—weeks—then a big dinner or ball and his father or Ana should announce it, not he. That scheming little devil! So he was tired of it, was he? He wanted to think of something himself, did he? Petra closed her eyes in momentary panic. Now she opened them. What must they think? *Two days*, and she wore the Montoya diamonds! Her betrothal was announced. She dared not look at Francisco—or Ana— or Ysidra. Oh, Mary, let the ground open up! If only she could faint! If only she wasn't so healthy!

At most no more than half a minute had passed, no matter how long it seemed. The silence was broken. It was Ysidra. "Come here, my dear, let me kiss you."

Quickly, too quickly, they all started to talk, embarrassed that they had been disconcerted and had allowed a pause to develop. From the babel of voices Francisco's carried: "You can imagine how overjoyed we are at this piece of news," he was saying. "We—his aunt and I—had hoped for something like this. But we hardly expected anything quite so soon." He laughed. "It would seem my son was a little precipitate, but I think in this case it can be overlooked."

And from Ysidra: ". . . De la Torres of Sevilla . . . we are so pleased . . . the joining of our two families. We hardly dared hope——"

"I can understand his hurry, señor. Surely the lovely señorita could have broken every heart in California——" This from Teodoro Acuña.

Petra found herself being kissed and made much of. Her cheeks were flaming with embarrassment. They were smoothing it over, these impeccable Spaniards. Beautifully, politely, kindly they were reassembling the pattern. One would think that every day in the week headlong engagements were announced. Assiduously they would follow the lead of their host. They would die rather than embarrass him. Ysidra, Francisco and even Ana registered nothing but pleasure at the unexpected turn events had taken.

After they had reached home, in the privacy of

her room Petra could still feel the heat rushing into her cheeks whenever she thought of it. She hoped, with violence and rage, that Francisco was angry. Furious! She hoped fervently that Angelo was regretting his heedless conduct. She wished with all her heart that Francisco would vent a ruthless and terrible rage upon him.

Francisco was, in fact, annoyed. However, it wasn't until late that night that he discussed the subject with Angelo. The dance hadn't lasted so long, for most of the guests were planning to leave in the early morning for their various ranchos.

"Well, Angelo," he said when they were alone in Francisco's office, "I suppose there is nothing I can say to you, since I myself set you a bad example by eloping with your mother."

Angelo leaned against the table, his face slightly averted. "I've angered you?"

"Yes, you have."

"I'm sure I don't know why," the boy murmured. "You asked me to give her the necklace. I did—almost immediately. You wanted me to marry her, so I proposed. Possibly I was a little abrupt. If so, I am sorry. But it was not shocking to the Doña Petra, because she was brought up in England, and——"

"That's enough, Angelo. We know where we stand. You were annoyed about the necklace and you chose this way of repaying me. I thoroughly understand that. The person most concerned—the innocent victim to whom you gave no thought at all—was Petra. It was exceedingly unkind. For a moment I thought she might faint."

"I did too. That would have been interesting. But she didn't——"

"I'm not making jokes." The difference in Francisco's tone made Angelo bow slightly.

"I'm sorry, Father." He began to turn in his

hand a silver candlestick that stood on the table.

Francisco came to stand before him. His tone was deceptively soft. "Since you have covered a vast amount of territory in a day, I can do no less. Arrangements will be made immediately for the marriage to take place. And while this is happening—with the incredible speed you deem necessary—I want you to think about one fact."

"What is that, Father?" Angelo asked carefully.

"That once you are married, you are no longer a child. There are certain responsibilities connected with marriage. If I should be killed tomorrow, everything would pass to you. You would be the master here, Angelo, and several hundred people would be dependent on you. Enrique Padilla is an excellent overseer. Guillermo is intelligent and reliable. The Acuñas and the Quixanos would assist you as much as they could, because they are kind people. But you will have to learn to depend on yourself. You have been spoiled—the blame is mine, I admit it. You've been allowed to play too long. You'll have to grow up now, accept responsibilities and duties. There is no alternative."

Angelo's face had lost color. He seemed unable to answer. The turning candlestick shook in his hand. The flame wavered and little torn shreds of smoke were sent crookedly upward.

"Don't misunderstand me, Angelito," Francisco added gently. "This is in no way a punishment. This would have come about in any case. I'm not a hard man—not with you anyway. I won't rush you or expect miracles of you. You'll be given time to learn and accustom yourself to something besides amusement. After all, Angelo, everyone grows up sooner or later."

He placed his hand beneath the boy's chin, lifted it slightly and looked intently into the face. The eyes veiled quickly, but not before he had seen the look of bleakness and defeat. Bending suddenly, he kissed the smooth face. "Run on to bed if you're tired—there'll be plenty of time to talk and make decisions."

"All right, Father." Angelo walked to the door and paused. "I don't know if you'll believe me or not, but I'm really sorry that I displeased you."

Francisco smiled. "I believe you, Angelo. Good night."

"Good night, Father," he answered tiredly, not returning the smile.

He went upstairs slowly, and when he reached his room, he lighted every candle and lamp there until it was brilliant. He didn't want to be in the dark for the moment. It might make him dream again, the same old hideous dream that had corroded his sleep for many years.

There were wisps and veils of yellow fog in the dream, enveloping and shielding the rocks, similar to those at Monterey but larger and somehow malignant. He had run away for a long time until his side ached and his breathing was labored and fragmentary. Finally—as he had known he would be—he was cornered and must face and do battle with the strange invisible adversary. They engaged in a long voiceless argument, and he knew that his only defense was to keep the Thing at bay. For during the interminable wordless combat what the Thing didn't know was that he could not turn and run away again. He was standing on the edge of a sheer drop hidden by the fog. The slightest touch of the Thing's outstretched hand could send him over, crashing down on the foam-covered rocks below. And once there on the stones, he must lie, quite dead and helpless, while the white salt foam moved and whispered about him.

The painful, horrid aspect of it, the aspect that always woke him, was that if he fell, everyone would come and peer over the edge to see him there, made helpless and vulnerable.

Slowly he began to undress. Why had he done it? Why had he asked her? Why hadn't he procrastinated and ignored the wishes of Father and Aunt Ysidra? If he had, surely Teodoro or somebody would have pressed a suit. After all no one could force the girl to marry someone she didn't want to marry. Nothing so terrible would have happened. Father might have been angry for a while, might even have punished him in some way. But it would have passed, blown over, and he would still have been more or less free. Yet it would have to come sometime. There was no escaping it completely. The only complete escape would be the priesthood—and probably that had its own set of complexities and problems. He was shaken by a small gust of mirthless laughter. He would make a terrible priest. He was completely unsuited to the priesthood. Besides, there was Father to consider again. He remembered quite vividly the moment of his father's white speechless rage when once he had suggested entering the Franciscan Order. He turned down his bed and slid between the sheets. To what *was* he suited?

Nothing. It always came back to that. He was nothing. He had never been anything. He would never be anything. Of course if he did fall down on the rocks, it wouldn't be like the dream. If people came and looked at him, they would do so in horror and pity, not ridicule because he had fallen. And anyway, he wouldn't know it because he would be dead. There was a lot to be said for being dead.

On coming up later, Francisco saw the light under his door. He opened it and went in. If Angelo were still awake and worried, he would say something to set his mind at rest. But the boy was sleeping. Francisco stood silently looking down at him. He put out his hand gently and touched a tousled lock of hair. Angelo stirred uneasily. Quietly Francisco went about extinguishing the lights. What a child, tumbling into bed too sleepy to put out the lights! He wondered, smiling a little, if Angelito would ever consent to grow up.

Chapter 4

In the room to which she had been assigned to sleep, Catalina Acuña began to pull off her ball gown. She didn't have a headache, as she had said in order to escape the rest of the dance. On the contrary her head was remarkably clear. With the gown half off she paused to look into the candlelit mirror, so used to her beauty that she did not notice it. Absently she began to take the necklace from about her throat and the rings from her hands.

So Angelo was going to marry the English girl—and suddenly too. But Angelo was only eighteen. It hadn't occurred to her that Francisco might think he had reached the age for marriage. With women it was different. She had been waiting. She paused in her occupation, dropping a ring on the polished surface with a little click. She had been waiting to marry Angelo. Always in the back of her mind had been the conviction that someday she would marry Angelo and live at Dos Ríos. It had been a shocking thing to hear his bland announcement of this afternoon.

Confusedly she picked up her rosary and went to the prayer bench, her gown trailing palely on the floor. She began to pray automatically. But what difference did it make? She didn't love Angelo. At times she almost disliked him. What was the matter with her, that she had held in her mind all these years the conviction that she would one day be his wife? Her fingers moved along the beads. She could not understand her own mind. It wouldn't be just that she wanted to marry and have children. God knew, she had had enough chances to marry before this!

Her smarting eyes closed for a moment, then the lids flew back as if scorched by the contact. It would be good to marry and have her first child, perhaps a great beautiful child such as Don Francisco must have been. It was time for her to think of marriage. If only she could have thought of it before Petra had come! Why couldn't Petra and Teodoro have married—he was already half in love with her. How could she have known that Francisco was planning to let Angelo marry so early? But she should have known that. He wanted, was obsessed by, the desire for children in his house. Why didn't his wife give him children? Why couldn't Ana . . . Ana . . . Ana . . .

She stopped, gripping the rosary, dimly surprised that she was cursing Ana. I *hate* you, Ana Estrada! God damn you, Ana Estrada! Hastily she put the rosary away. Wicked! Blasphemous! But from somewhere came the thought that she could still marry and live at Dos Ríos. There was always Xavier. Fat. Fool. Clown. Pompous buffoon. Xavier Miramontes—why, he was twice her age! Besides, she could have her choice of any *caballero* in California. Standing in the center of the room thinking this absurdity, this ridiculous thought, she began to laugh. And then she began to cry.

Ana Estrada, in her room, stood by the window and looked out. She was very tired. Guests, always guests. Francisco was never happy unless the house was overrun with people. And now that they had all gone to their rooms, now that the house was at last quiet, she could feel no relief from the strain. Tiresome, stupid, troublesome people! And Angelo—what was the matter with that boy, to embarrass them, humiliate them in such a manner? And what had Francisco done about it? Nothing, nothing at all. Her anger made her a little sick, and she pressed her thin blue-veined hand against her flat stomach. In doing so, she began to count up the weeks. So many weeks until she would feel the first revolting flutter and know that during this small convulsion the alien thing had shuddered into life. So many weeks after that and she would twist and writhe in the sea of scalding pain. Then amid slime and blood and human filth, the thing would be born, twitch pallidly and shiver into death. That was for animals! The skin stretched tight across her face. It was late and she was tired. She must undress now and go to bed. Good night, Lupe.

Ysidra, standing before her bedside table, removed the jewels from her fingers, examining the stones with a detached pleasure. That Angelo! That little pagan! He had set them all back on their heels. There was more to Angelo than one thought. He wasn't Francisco's child for nothing. Well, she must go to bed and get her rest. She must be ready for tomorrow. There were plans to be made, things to be done, people to see. The marriage of Francisco's child would be a splendid thing. There would be at least, at the very least, seven days of fiesta. How the house would swarm with people! She gazed at the jewels cupped in her small palms and smiled with deep enjoyment.

Chapter 5

Petra had stood numbly for what, she felt sure, had been hours. They had been up since four o'clock, busy with the preparations for her marriage. Ysidra had been tireless in her efforts to prepare her goddaughter for the ceremony. As for Petra, she felt too tired to do anything but obey blindly the directions anyone chose to give her.

Ysidra had decided that it would be better for Petra to be married completely in white. She felt it would be outstanding here in California where weddings brought out the gayest and brightest colors.

Petra's stiff gown of white and shadow-silver brocade stood out around her like a bell of parchment. A half-smile tugged momentarily at her drooping lips when it occurred to her that she might go to sleep standing, and the dress would hold her up.

When there seemed nothing to be added, Ysidra had had her idea which caused them much more painstaking labor. Gently she had taken the pearl necklace from its box and held it up.

"What are you going to do, Aunt Ysidra?" Petra asked wearily. "Angelo said I was to wear the Montoya necklace."

"Yes, I know," her godmother answered in a preoccupied manner, "but these will look well on your bodice. I'll unstring them and sew them on."

"Sew them on?" Petra echoed blankly, while the serving-women and the seamstresses looked on in wonder.

"Surely, child—sew them on singly, like this." Efficiently she began snipping the pearls apart. She threaded a needle with a strand of silver thread and sewed them on until it appeared as if Petra had stood under a shower of pearls and some of them had clung to her gown.

"You see?" Ysidra said with satisfaction. "They look fine. This is much better." She stitched away while Petra stood first on one foot then the other. "Hold still, child. I've got to get them on firmly. I can't have you losing any, but I will have you perfect. No one can ever say the child of my friend Teresa Vega y de la Torre wasn't the most splendid bride this country ever saw."

She left out Papa's name, thought Petra with an inward wail. Then in her fatigued mind she began to long for him. If only he could see how fine she was! If only she could twist and twirl before him to show him the flashing diamonds and the gleaming pearls! If only . . . if only—— Abruptly, desperately, she began to cry.

"Petra!" Ysidra's voice was tinged with dismay. "Petra, stop it! You silly child, compose yourself!" She shook her a little.

The Mexicans and Indians scurried about fetching cologne for her to smell, and wet cloths to press against her throbbing temples. This, they thought, was good. Brides were supposed to be overwrought and hysterical. The tall girl in her frosty white gown had been too calm.

Before Petra had regained her composure, Doctor Vaiz, who had ridden from Monterey for the wedding, had to be summoned to the room. He ordered the stiff gown removed and had her lie down on the bed with a wet cloth over her face. Catalina Acuña stood by and gently fanned her for some minutes. It wouldn't do for the bride to appear with a swollen countenance.

Petra wanted to go to sleep but her mind refused to close. There was too much noise. The sounds from the lower floor had risen in volume. Guests had continued to arrive by twos, by threes, by dozens, and finally by hundreds as the Indians came in from the distant rancherias. The *vaqueros*, rarely dismounted, swooped and wheeled about on their restless ponies. The Indians, decked in their best and gaudiest cotton clothing, clustered in large and small groups. There was laughter and singing and a great deal of raillery. The people of quality had been arriving since early morning. They came mostly on horseback, but several gaily decorated *carretas* had jolted in, carrying the old women and some young ones who were expecting babies.

Petra felt her excitement rise with the swelling sound. There were cries and called greetings. Horses—always the sound of horses. And from time to time a gust of music as the different bodies of musicians seemed to tear off a fragment of a melody in their eagerness for the wedding to begin.

Then the long waiting was over and things happened too quickly for her to take proper note of them. It was as if, during the morning, time had got stuck, and it would always be cold dawn, and she would always be standing woodenly in her wedding gown. Now, time having got unstuck, it whirred along and people seemed to flash past in quick clear-cut, brighter than life pictures.

Angelo had insisted that all the horses in the wedding procession be palominos. The Quixanos and Acuñas had willingly ridden far, and without stint they had put out their own *vaqueros* to round up all the available palominos in California. Now the nervous animals with their honey-colored bodies and silver manes and tails milled and pushed impatiently in their gay trappings.

Finally Ysidra stood back and stared at her goddaughter. Her round face held a look of complete satisfaction. "Good" she said shortly. "Now are you ready to go down? Wait a moment. You remember all the plans?"

"Yes, Aunt Ysidra."

"You've thought over the instructions that Father Patricio gave you this morning when you confessed?"

"Yes."

"You're sure you know what to do?"

"Yes."

"All right, we'll go down now. The hallway will be full of people, so pause at the head of the stairs." She opened the door and Petra stepped out. She was suddenly overtaken with a fit of trembling so great that the silver fringe on her crisply embroidered shawl quivered.

"Smile!" hissed Ysidra as they reached the head of the stairs, with Petra a little in advance. "Go down to them. I'll follow—and heaven help you, child, if you lose one of those pearls!"

This snapped Petra back to normal, and she stood in the sudden hush that her appearance caused, perfectly poised and only a little excited. The calm lasted only a moment, for the wedding had begun.

There were muted laughter, sighs and tears.

Through the doorway Petra noticed Angelo with a flash of pride. He was actually beautiful, astride the frisking palomino on the gold-mounted saddle Francisco had given him the day before.

He bent down to assist the Doña Antonia Peréa who, as padrina, would ride to church before him on his horse. Petra saw that his wedding clothes were as fine as hers. His light wool hat was lined beneath the brim with gold lace. His waistcoat was of cream-colored satin, with the pocket flaps secured by little topaz buttons. His close-fitting red-velvet breeches were buckled at the knee. Little puppets and animals worked of seed pearls dangled as minute ornaments from his buckskin leggings. His red-lined poncho was faced with velvet at the neck.

Petra was lifted to the saddle in front of Don Juan Acuña, who had been honored with the post of padrino. He bent down and saw that Petra's satin-shod foot was placed in the loop of ribbon which hung in place of a stirrup for her.

The long ride to the mission seemed only a matter of minutes. There was so much to see. The *vaqueros* and Spaniards seemed to vie with one another to show off their skill and horsemanship. The soldiers from the Presidio contributed their best. All manner of tricks and feats were performed. The beautifully trained ponies entered delightedly into the spirit of the occasion, careening wildly one moment and stopping instantly the next at some unheard signal from the rider, only to wheel and dash in the other direction.

There were laughter, shouted challenges. Short races were run, and swift wagers made. There were sudden bursts of singing and music. Never had Petra felt so exhilarated. This was her wedding day! There was nothing to mar or stain it. Everything was gay and loud and bright and beautiful.

The church, by comparison, was all the more quiet and dim. Her heart was thudding so that she could feel waves of blood surge through her veins. Everything now was a series of pictures. There was a picture of Angelo's profile as he knelt beside her before the priest. There was a picture of lace, and that was the altar cloth. There was a picture of flame, and that was the candles. There was a picture of sound, and that was the chanting, and Angelo's responses, slow and hesitant. A picture of silver was the cord, looped loosely about her and Angelo, which bound them together as man and wife. A picture of gold was her wedding band which reached almost to her knuckle.

Doña Petra Estrada.

There was color high on Angelo's cheekbones when they mounted to ride home. His eyes were brilliant. Petra was lifted to her place before her new husband.

The *caballeros* and *vaqueros* outdid themselves to provide diversion. There was almost an ecstasy in the looping and wheeling. Handkerchiefs and coins were thrown to the ground. Then in sudden hairpin turns and wild lurchings backward, never slackening the pace, they were retrieved. Halfway home the party was met by another band of musicians and verse after verse was improvised in honor of the bridal pair.

As they clattered into view of the house, Petra saw that a great canopy had been raised and tables set beneath it. Here the honored guests of the family were to sit. Scattered out over the grounds as far as she could see were groups of less important people, some at tables, some picnic-fashion on the ground. In an instant Teodoro Acuña and several other local *caballeros* were off their horses.

"His spurs!" The cry was taken up and Angelo was dragged from his horse. Petra watched in excitement and consternation as in the wild scramble that followed Angelo's spurs were taken.

He stood at bay, laughing with them, a little bent over as if from a stitch in his side.

"All right," they shouted. "*Aguardiente.* Are they worth it? One bottle. Two. Six. They have silver rowels. Brand-new—Don Francisco gave them to him yesterday. Pay. Redeem them. Don't you want them?"

"Yes, I do," protested Angelo. "I have it. That is, I had it. I arranged with Teodoro." He looked about in laughing dismay. "Where is it? Help me, my friend." He still clung with one hand to the pommel of his saddle. Teodoro came forward with the dusty bottles for the spurs and the barter was complete.

There was a sudden hush and Petra was helped from the saddle. The crowd fell back a little. It was time to go in to their own family now.

Francisco and Ysidra awaited them. The close friends of the family were grouped at a little distance in the flower-decked *sala*. The musicians stood ready. Angelo and his wife Petra approached the end of the room. When they came before Francisco and Ysidra they dropped to their knees. Petra caught Angelo's soft "Your blessing, Father?" Francisco's eyes were glistening with tears as he gave it.

On their feet again, Angelo smiled and raised his hand slightly to the musicians. White teeth gleamed in dark faces. There was an instant's pause and the swell of music burst forth. The feast had begun.

Petra felt she had no more strength, but was carried on from one thing to the next by little puffs of excitement. The dinner was a long one. The table was spread for the families of note. The Peréas, the Acuñas, the Quixanos, the Sals and the Vasquezes were all present. Snatches of talk passed in and out of Petra's mind. She heard, with no feeling of awe, the vast wagers laid on races to be run and games to be played. Don Cristóbal, whose three hundred pounds covered with green velvet overlapped his inadquate chair, took all comers in wagering on his two new race horses.

Sound rose and fell. ". . . and we got him, of course, but three of us had to use our *reatas*. He's the biggest grizzly . . ."

". . . Claudio says there is no other cock in California with spurs so long. He says . . ."

". . . So my mother said, 'Possibly in Mexico things like that are tolerated, but this . . .' "

". . . Francisco is matching him against a bull this afternoon, and I will lay you five to three . . ."

". . . ridiculous, my friend. The captain of the *Crescent* himself told me his hide capacity . . ."

". . . why, the smallest grizzly in the world would look like the biggest face to face, wouldn't it?"

A momentary diversion was caused when Petra was presented with a companion saddle to Angelo's. She made a dizzy half effort to total up the value of all she wore and used that day—the necklace, the pearls, the gown, the saddle and appurtenances. It was too much for her faulty mental arithmetic and she gave it up.

Then the cry to mount up carried. "They have begun to bury the cocks," cried Claudio Vaiz who was a champion at this sport, and there was a mad scramble to mount and join.

A place was made for Petra to watch. The live cocks were buried in the loose dirt with only their dodging heads protruding. One at a time the men rode at top speed, swung downward from the saddle, grasped the greased neck and, never slackening the pace, swung the bird high amid the cheers of the spectators and the fluttering feathers of the hapless cock. The man who failed—but they were few—was derided with hoots and jeers.

Later in the afternoon the grizzly bear, whose hind leg was attached by a length of rawhide to the foreleg of the bull, was soundly trounced, much to everyone's complete astonishment. He put up a good but losing fight and caused a minor panic when it looked for a few moments as if he might get over the wooden enclosure and onto the platform where the ladies were seated. In an instant the pistols were out and cocked, and the air buzzed with whirling *reatas* which would descend to entangle him in a moment. However, he changed his mind and re-entered the fray, only to lose it.

In the evening the dance was opened by the elders who soon relinquished the floor to the young people. Music now was continuous, for as soon as one musician showed signs of fatigue or thirst, he was relived by another, for everybody played—Spaniard, Mexican and Indian. Many new songs were composed and sung.

Everyone now danced, inside the house and out, and to almost everyone clung bits of colored, gold or silver paper from the *cascarónes*. For weeks the kitchen women had saved the eggshells whole, having carefully let the egg out a hole in the end. These had been allowed to dry and had been filled with bits of paper, with cologne or gold dust. Cracked over the heads of friends and favorites they let down a little rain of color. Angelo had decreed early in the evening that only *cascarónes* filled with gold dust could be broken over Petra. He was loudly proclaimed as an artist, for the effect was dazzling. The cause was taken up by the rest of the *caballeros*, and anyone approaching the bride with a *cascarón* was told of the decree and vigorously warned as to the dire things which would happen if he marred the lovely vision with bits of mere paper.

Petra danced until her leg muscles jumped with fatigue. She had danced several times with her husband. He was extremely graceful and the postures of the dances were becoming to his slender body.

Wedding day! Wedding day! Doña Petra Estrada, whose hair was shining with gold dust and whose bodice was hung with pearls. There was no such thing as fear. London was a mist. The realest thing in the world was lean fingers clicking castanets. And over and under and through everything was the music, swelling and ebbing, rising and falling.

The bedroom was almost entirely dark when Petra stepped in and closed the massive door gently behind her. Through the open windows she could still hear the sounds of revelry and music from the lower rooms, the garden and patio.

The remaining ones would celebrate her marriage until daylight and after. Then they would sleep long and deeply through the sunlight of the following morning because of all the fine wine they had drunk, and all the good food they had eaten. How many bottles and casks had she seen? How much food? Such a celebration! She felt tired and drained. She could not summon up any positive emotion about it all now. She realized almost dazedly that she would have to undress herself and go to bed. The task appeared hopeless.

"Petra." It was the merest murmur in the semi-darkness.

"Angelo!" A confused jumble of disjointed thoughts darted through her mind. He was here. In her room.

"I thought—— Don Francisco said he thought you were watching the cockfights."

"I imagine Father said that because he didn't want people to know how tired the wedding made me. I've been here a long time. I didn't realize how long it took to get married. I got tired."

"Tired. Yes, it was long. You probably need a good night's rest," Petra said with weary apprehension.

"You're not very tactful," he said in mild reproof. "Not that it matters. I am more interested in going to sleep at this moment than in anything else. I'm sorry to tell you that this is now my room also. My thoughtful stepmother saw to that. She says with the house full of people and overcrowded she can find no reason why a husband and his wife should not share the same room. Even while we were kneeling before the priest, my things were being moved in here."

Something inside Petra started to crack and tear. "But I don't want it that way," she wailed. "I want a room to myself. I've always had a room to myself. I can't sleep with anybody. I've never slept with anybody. I—I'm tired. I've got to have some rest." The last words wavered and took on a tinge of hysteria.

"Well, have it then," Angelo answered tiredly. "The bed is right before you—and I shan't bother you."

"I don't mean to be rude—or anything," Petra faltered as she walked with an effort to the dresser and fumbled with shaking hands for a candle.

"It's just that I'm so . . . tired. You are too. If you left the fiesta and came away, you must have been tired. And——"

Under her unsteady hand the candle wobbled into light. Its flame fluttered weakly—rose—grew—and was steady.

"And . . . and . . . what was I saying? Oh yes, how tired we were. And Angelo, there is so much time. I mean, we'll be married for years and years——"

"Petra," Angelo began with exasperation. "Please. Please don't upset yourself in any way on my account. Set your mind at rest completely. I only want what you want—like any dutiful husband," he ended dryly.

The candle cast a warm glow over the room and

she turned and really looked at Angelo for the first time since she had entered.

He was sitting, in the relaxation of utter fatigue, in a deep leather chair. His face was pale against its dark polished surface. There was no semblance of his queue and clusters of tousled untidy curls fell about his face. The long line of his throat shone smooth and golden. The white shirt was open at the neck and down the front where nervous fingers had torn it apart.

Petra could pity him. After all it had been as much of an ordeal for him as for her. She remembered how low his responses had been, and how, after they had been kneeling a long time, his breath had come shorter and shorter. How lucky she was, after all, to have her abundant good health!

"Well," she began hesitantly, "if we are both tired and want to go to sleep, I suppose there isn't any reason why we shouldn't . . . both use the same bed. It's a very big bed."

"No reason at all," he returned. "However, that is for you to decide, not I."

"That's very kind of you," she murmured formally. "We shall then. I think you will sleep much better in a bed."

"Undoubtedly," he agreed, "since I've never slept in anything else."

"Very well then. And since the washstand is behind you, you can just stay where you are comfortably while I . . . undress."

Petra set the candle on the mantel of the empty grate and passed him. Her fingers were stiff and clumsy as she took off her clothing. She had trouble with the buttons down the back of her bodice, but didn't want to call anyone to help her. Since her fatigued fingers refused to react properly, in a sudden gust of anger she tore roughly at the fabric. The gown came away. One of Ysidra's pearls came off and landed with a thump on the floor and rolled into a corner. She wondered foggily at her carelessness. These beautiful, beautiful clothes, of which she had been so proud this morning! Was it only this morning? So much time had passed. So much had happened. So many, many people . . .

After what seemed an age of fumbling, tugging and sloshing Petra was finally washed and clad in her nightgown. "I'm finished," she told Angelo and made her way to bed, stumbling a little over the hem of her long white gown. "There is another jug of water there for you."

She dragged at the covers and with a great deal of effort pulled them back and tumbled into bed. "Angelo," she called sharply, "your mother's necklace—I left it on the washstand. I forgot it. I—I'm sorry."

He was before the stand now himself. He picked up the diamonds, let them dangle, heavy and beautiful, swinging gently from his outstretched forefinger. They caught the candlelight and glittered with multiple colors.

"Where do you keep your things?" he asked. "Where shall I put them? I don't wear my sash to bed."

But Petra was breathing deeply and evenly, turned half on her side, one arm flung above her head in complete relaxation. Her pale wheat-colored hair clung in damp tendrils and spread about the pillow. Her lips were parted slightly. She was asleep.

Petra looked long at the square of paler darkness that was the window before she realized that she was half awake again. She moved her head slightly, with infinite gentleness, so that she might, if possible, look at Angelo.

His hand was clasped loosely and warmly about

her shoulder. He moved slightly and Petra was instantly still. She kept her breath light and shallow so that she would not fall asleep and miss this time of gazing on her husband's shadowed face.

Such a strange night of sleeping, and waking, and sleeping again. It was hard to tell which was part of a slow deep dream and which was real. She had not dreamed that first lonely waking in the blackness and stillness. No moon, no light or sound. There was only the darkness and the quiet slow rhythm of Angelo's even breathing as he slept beside her.

And then—had she slept and wakened again? Surely that strange new yearning which brought tears to her eyes was no part of a dream.

Angelo . . .

Waking and sleeping. Responding in slow languor to the warm insistence of Angelo's gentle mouth. Silence and darkness and his strange unfamiliar urgency. It was no dreaming which dissolved her resistance and left her helpless in wonder and longing.

And the new unheard-of strength of Angelo, willing her, forcing her, back into the down-filled pillows. There was nothing of dream in the pain of it, sudden, frantic . . . and her cry, sharp, ragged, "Angelo!"

Nothing of dream in the soaring, the rapture . . .

He moved slightly and sighed. Petra felt her eyes sting with a quick uprush of tears. Was there some little thing, some small humble thing, she could do for him? Would it wake him if she kissed his hand, very gently? Through half-closed eyes she could see the patch of sky becoming faintly colored with the first uneven smudges of gray and pink.

Angelo . . . Angelo . . . Angelo . . .

The first rays of the sun slid over the sill and into the room. After a time they crept across the wide planked floor and at length fell on the bed. Angelo stirred and turned. As he did so, something bright and flashing cast small lights and shadows across his sleeping face. Petra raised her dreamy eyes and there, clasped about the bedpost, the bright Montoya diamonds dangled just above her head.

Chapter 6

The old man sat in the sun. If need be, he might open his eyes after a while and look on the things around him. The sun was hot and the adobe against which he leaned warmed his brittle bones. This was good. The brilliance on his closed eyelids made them curtains of opaque color for him to look at. Purple tides rose and fell. Strange shapes moved, disappeared and reappeared before his sight. A ball of burned orange cavorted in stately motion from side to side.

No one could quite remember to which family or tribe the old man belonged. If anyone had ever known, he had forgotten. Anyone you asked said that the old one had been there before him. It is possible that all his people had been wiped out in one of the many epidemics which took great toll of Indian life from time to time. They said he had sat in that very spot for a hundred years, and who could say he hadn't, for who really knew? He was so old that sometimes he was unable to stand. It seemed a miracle that life remained in his shrunken body. His last tooth had gone decades ago—no one remembered his having had teeth. The sun gleamed on his scalp, which was almost bare save for half a dozen patches of stringy white hair that trailed down over his withered neck and large ears.

At one time when Father Gabriel Ortega of the mission had been a younger and more resolute priest, he had taken the old man there. At that time Francisco's house had been a rude affair built on a clearing in case of attack by renegade Indians. But the old man hadn't liked the mission and every few days he appeared again to lean against the adobe of Francisco's then much smaller house. No one knew how he got there, except that someone had taken him, as it was evident to all that the old man couldn't have made the journey by himself. But when questioned, no one knew. One day when Mass was over, and before the Indians scattered to the various tasks of the mission, Father Gabriel took them to task about the old man.

"Now listen to me, children," he had said. "The sun that shines on this house of God is the same one that shines on the hill whereon Don Francisco has his home. Let the old man be in peace. It is true that he didn't want to come here, but he is very old. If left to himself, he will become used to this place and forget the other."

The congregation remained respectfully silent before their priest. Nothing was said. No finger pointed.

"Here at the mission he could be protected in case of attack. There at Dos Ríos on that bare ground he sits all day without cover or shelter of any kind. Don Francisco and his men are busy. In case of emergency they have no time to bother with the old ones. You see what I mean? You understand the wisdom of letting him remain here?"

Heads were nodded, murmurs of "Yes, Father," rose and the next day the old man was squatting against the adobe of Francisco's house. If any Indian nodded over his task that day from lack of sleep, someone jogged his elbow. If one stumbled with fatigue under a load, another hand was outstretched to ease the weight.

Father Gabriel gave it up and concentrated on other more important things. He had wanted to ease the old man in his last months. Surely if he were as old as they said—and he certainly looked it—he couldn't last much longer. But Indians were children, and stubborn in the stubbornness of children. So let it be.

The old one seemed to have an affinity for that one spot of ground. Francisco had moved the boulder against which he leaned in order to build the house. Now he leaned in perfect content against the house itself. When Francisco brought his son, his aunt, and his new wife from Spain, the old man's place was briefly in danger. Ana had little liking for the house Francisco had built and planned extensive alterations.

"I know the old man sits there," she said sarcastically to the workmen, "but he will have to move a little. I plan to extend the living room out here."

She was met by the blank eyes and closed faces of the laborers. There was an uneasy shifting of feet.

"Make the house go the other way," Ysidra had said laughing. "Why disturb his nap?"

"That is the most ridiculous thing I ever heard," snapped Ana, "I don't mean to be disrespectful," she added hastily, as she saw Francisco's brows lift, "but surely some authority must be maintained. Can their every whim be gratified at our expense!" It had been her plan to extend the little *sala* into a space large enough to be a ballroom. The present room she intended to have built up to form a sort of dais for musicians in one end.

"Let it go," Francisco said easily. "That is practically my office, and all my papers and records are there. If they were moved I would never be able to find anything." That was his reason to his wife Ana, but there were those who said he didn't want to disturb the old one. So what had been intended for the big *sala* remained the small square office, and the newer larger part of the house jutted out in the opposite direction.

Now hunger stirred faintly in the old man. He pursed his withered lips and made the soft sucking sounds of a small baby. Someone would think to bring food soon. He eased his back against the warm adobe. They would come, they always came. They took good care of him. In the morning he was carried out by one of the Indians, and in the evening he was taken into one of the huts. There someone spread a coarse blanket over him and he slept. At times, even during the busiest day, a moment was found to set a bowl of food hastily before him. If he was very old that day and could not lift the food to his mouth, someone observed this and paused to feed him.

He raised his fingers with infinite slowness and lifted the lids of his eyes to look at the blurred patio. Someone clad in blue hurried by leaving a trail of fragrant scent in her wake. There were milling horses tethered close to the door. There had been much pleasure in the house of late, much sound. Now it was fairly still. His hands dropped to the dust at his sides, and his eyelids of a necessity closed. Tracing a slow illegible pattern in the dust with a gnarled finger, he thought of the little boy. When one was full of years one became confused. It had been some time since the curly-haired child had brought him sweet good things to eat from inside the house.

He pondered and gradually focused on the thought. The little boy was no longer a little boy. He was the young don. The old man wished the shadows would not drift in his head. In these later days—or was it years?—he could not rightly tell the passage of time. Whereas yesterday the child with the sea-colored eyes had been here, today he was the young don mounted on an animal of sunlight. Still again tomorrow it might seem as if he were the little boy again.

The sound of laughter came to him, the sound of the musical tongue spoken by the white people. He knew without raising his eyelids that some of them were mounting to ride off somehwere. There would be, by the sound of them, the white chief, the little—no, the young don and the fair-haired woman, so recently arrived. Yes, she was the one who had passed clad in blue and smelling of crushed flowers.

Petra was glad, delighted, to accompany Angelo and Francisco to the harbor to meet Xavier and Catalina. She frequently rode out with one or the other of them—not that she disliked the house, or her duties in it, but she was rapidly growing sick of Ana. Now, as she rode beside them, her color was high and her eyes held a dangerous glitter, for only just now she had come from her mother-in-law. *Step*mother-in-law, she reminded herself viciously. For she felt quite sure that had Angelo's own mother lived, they would have had no trouble at all. She couldn't help it because she had fallen in love with Angelo. She was, quite frankly and madly, in love with her husband. It showed in every look she gave him, and in every word she spoke to him. She couldn't bear to have another girl look at him, and she was worried and desolate if he left her side a moment. She was quite shamelessly jealous and possessive of him.

Ana apparently distrusted passion in women. She had taxed Petra with it that morning. "The afternoon siesta," she said cuttingly, "was designed primarily for rest or sleep."

Petra's color rose and she looked uncomfortable.

"It might be wise," said Ana coldly, "not to give too much, Petra. I am older and more experienced than you—I feel I have the right to offer you this advice. Men tire easily, you know. You'll be married a long time."

Petra bit back a sharp retort. What difference did it make to show openly that you loved your husband? If anyone was to give her advice it should be Ysidra, who was at least her godmother. And anyway, Ysidra was pleased that she loved Angelo.

"You might," Ana had persisted, "refuse him once in a while."

Petra turned quickly to stare at her dumbfounded. Refuse him! Refuse *Angelo!* Why, half the time it was she who began the love passages—wantonly she supposed—but she didn't care. There were times, moments of exquisite longing, when she felt she would go mad if she couldn't reach out and just touch his smooth warm skin.

"But Doña Ana-Lucía," she had protested in astonished frankness, "I couldn't refuse him——I've never wanted to!"

Spots of color showed suddenly on Ana's cheeks. "Ah! Such talk!" she snapped angrily. "But perhaps it's just as well. Maybe you'll have a baby every year and please everybody—excepting yourself."

"Myself too," Petra declared with some heat. "I happen to want a lot of children. I'll love having Angelo's children."

"Wait till you've had one," remarked Ana briefly. "We'll see how you love it." And turning, she went quickly down the hall. Petra, in a gust of fury, had hurried out the door to wait there for the others.

Now as the four of them rode along, she felt a glow of satisfaction. Angelo, Francisco and Guillermo, who led the two spare horses for Catalina and Xavier, were such perfect companions. After all there surely would be enough space here to hold the women. After Catalina came back she would make her home at Dos Ríos. She didn't know Catalina very well, but she seemed pleasant enough. Of course one never had to worry about getting along with Aunt Ysidra, because she was either too good-natured or too lazy to argue about anything. And later on, if she continued to have trouble with Ana, she could always request that another house be built. Sebastian Sal had built a separate house for his eldest son and his wife, for she had been a Quixano and they were notoriously hotheaded. Francisco was more than generous. She would think about it.

Petra had had little difficulty in fitting herself into the everyday routine of Dos Ríos. She found after the fiesta that she quickly became a member of the family and ceased being a visitor. There was a steady round of occupations which could be followed. The routine of rising early, prayers, meals, tasks and pleasures was very absorbing to her. She was clever and adaptable and never ceased to entertain a lively curiosity regarding the workings of the ranch and house. She knew that a great deal of work must, of a necessity, be accomplished each day. But it was spread thinly over so vast a number of people that it all seemed to get done with a minimum of effort. Indeed, the most active and hardest-working people on Dos Ríos seemed to be Francisco and Enrique Padilla, the *mayordomo*.

Many mornings she wakened earlier than anyone in the house and lay quietly enjoying the serenity of the silent dawn. She would go over in her mind all the things she planned to do during the day—knowing that some of the plans would be upset by one thing or another. Ana, of course, took a pettish delight in altering slightly any arrangements she made. Then Angelo was subject to moods and whims which must be catered to. The day which she had planned down to the last minute with housewifely care would be the day he decided they would go on a picnic. Without a moment's hesitation she consigned all her plans to the rubbish heap and joined him. She found a deep contentment lying in the shade listening to him sing. His voice was melodiously soft with a strange husky quality. There was an aching pleasure in watching his slim well-kept hands pluck at the guitar strings, and in hearing the notes drop singly in the warm air.

Sometimes it seemed that there were two Dos Ríos, one superimposed on the other, one visible to one person and one to another. Angelo's Dos Ríos consisted of quiet beautiful things, such as singing in the warm afternoon, or taking pleasure in looking at the patterns made against the sky by the flowering tree in the patio, or noting the wet gleam of the shale on the banks of a stream, or smelling the pungent odor of eucalyptus acorns—numberless things which were pleasing to his senses and which he shared with her.

Francisco's Dos Ríos was a gigantic place of sloping pastures, milling cattle and sandy vineyards. He took pleasure in his fences composed of adobe slabs along the top of which had been set at angles the long-horned skulls of cattle. This formed an impassable barricade for prize stock or cattle thieves and made a wierdly beautiful picture in the moonlight. He saw with satisfaction the sewed-up hides full of tallow which made them look like stumpy misshapen beasts of another world. Dos Ríos to him meant stacks of flattened hides as stiff as sheets of iron. It was a long stick in a brown hand on which each cut notch represented ten of his cattle.

Each Dos Ríos was separate and distinct from

the other. Petra could see and understand them both. She found moments to wonder and wish they might merge. Sometimes in an unoccupied moment on a hot afternoon or in the stillness of a morning there was time to think of this and wonder with a fleeting sadness why the differences had to be.

There was little time for sadness and much time for gaiety; much pleasure to be taken in looking after Angelo, and in learning and sewing, for she readily adopted the California custom of seldom being without some kind of needlework in her hands. She and the seamstress, Señora Llanes, were frequently together, and Petra learned from her a great deal about fabrics and stitches.

From the last trading vessel and from merchants in Los Angeles Petra had bought quantities of soft white cloth from which she hoped to fashion clothes for the baby that she must surely have soon. Señora Llanes observed this and in her spare time began to make lengths of fine narrow lace suitable to adorn the dress of a princess' child. She didn't mention it to Petra, nor did Petra mention her purchases, but they laid them away with a sense of contented anticipation.

Some fine morning Petra would enter the other's sewing room with a length of cloth over her arm and ask for a baby-dress pattern. Señora Llanes would sit back placidly, her dark fingers moving quickly in the fine white thread. This was good. This was the way it should be.

And Angelo. Always Angelo. He was never out of Petra's mind for more than a second at a time. She wondered how it was that one could think so constantly of another. No matter what she was doing, there lurked in the depths of her mind his image.

There was never any dullness in Angelo. He was a person of quicksilver moods and beguiling ways. It was impossible to stay angry with him. She got angry on occasion. He exasperated her sometimes beyond endurance, for he was an incurable tease. She found also that he possessed a stubborn streak that amazed her. He usually appeared so careless and indifferently good-natured about everything that at first she had been deceived into thinking he would be easy to manage. She had thought to wrap him about her finger and dictate to him, feeling sure that he would instantly agree with everything she said.

She found to her surprise and consternation that when he made up his mind to a thing, it stood. He didn't grow angry. Angelo never grew angry. He would merely shrug good-humoredly, spread his hands and say, "I'm sorry, my dear, if you don't like it, because that's the way it's going to be." He always won, because he was capable of ignoring her completely, something she was not able to do with him.

It annoyed her a little that Angelo could very nearly read her mind. There was nothing she could hide from him. Not that she wanted to hide much from him, but there were times when it proved exasperating.

The morning after breakfast as they all rose from the table preparatory to scattering to their own occupations was one such occasion. The sunlight from a window fell across Angelo's face throwing it into sharp light and shadow. His throat curved golden and smooth, and Petra had one of her inexplicable yearnings for him. Heat rose in her body. Santa María, just to touch him! Angelo caught the look, fleeting as it was, raised his brows slightly and murmured for her ears only, "And no siesta until this afternoon. . . ."

"What's the matter, Angelo, aren't you feeling well?" Francisco had asked once in the half-annoyed tone which he used when inquiring about his son's health.

"Fairly well, thank you, Father," Angelo answered.

"You look pallid," Francisco observed. "Are you sleeping well?"

Angelo's eyes flicked an instant to Petra and away again. He murmured with apparent innocence, "As a matter of fact I do have a little trouble getting my rest."

Petra felt the color rise in her face. Blast and damn that boy!

"Why did you say that?" she asked him hotly afterward. "I'm sure your father knew exactly what you meant."

"Oh, no, beloved, he couldn't have. It wouldn't enter Father's mind that a woman would wake her husband up in the middle of the night——"

"Angelo!" She rushed from the room with flaming cheeks.

They spent a great deal of time together, although Francisco had more than once suggested that Angelo start to take some interest in the workings of the rancho. Angelo's answer to this was usually a plaintive "But, Father, I'm still on my honeymoon," at which Francisco would laugh and drop the subject for another week or two.

Ysidra had said to Petra privately that they would all settle down after Xavier and Catalina returned to Dos Ríos. Petra wondered aloud what Xavier had to do with their settling down, and Ysidra explained that with all the activity of the past weeks in consummating both the marriage of Petra to Angelo and of Catalina to Xavier, there had been little time or inclination for thinking seriously of work. Now, she said, all that was over. They were well into summer, and by the first week of July the slaughter season would begin. According to Francisco's plans the slaughter this year would occupy the time until mid-October. There would be little community social life until this work season was finished. "After that of course——" She spread her hands and smiled. Petra knew that after that there would be another long idle period until marking and branding season was upon them.

Catalina's wedding and the week spent at Las Palomas had been as hectic and exciting as her own wedding and the fiesta following. For several weeks the seamstresses had been busy there on the wedding clothes and the supply of household linens. Catalina had cried in exasperation to her mother, "*Mamacita*, please, please, let them spend more time on the wardrobe and not so much on the linen——I haven't even got a house yet." But Doña Dolores was firm. Her child would not leave her house without suitable housewifely possessions. Doña Ana had sent the skilled Señora Llanes to Las Palomas to assist in the making of the wedding gown. She, in turn, took along some of Petra's gowns in order to adapt the latest designs and fashions for Catalina.

The week at Las Palomas had been especially enjoyable for Petra because she and Angelo were afforded more privacy. The center of attention was held by Catalina, the bride. Then Catalina and Xavier had embarked on a cruise up the coast, stopping at various places to see and stay with friends. Now they were coming back.

Petra sighed a little. It meant the end of an interlude, but she guessed it was as it should be. Angelo should take more interest and do his share, although it would not be so pleasant to have him ride off in the early hours of the morning and return to the house only for meals.

Halfway to the harbor they met Don Juan Acuña and Teodora also on their way to meet the ship. There were other girls in the Acuña family, but Catalina was the favorite with both of the Acuñas, and they had missed her more than they could say. Guillermo, leading the horses for the couple to ride home, sighted the water first.

The Acuñas and Estradas were invited by the captain to have dinner with him on the boat. They frequently did business with his firm. Contrary to Petra's supposition, Catalina seemed very happy. She was vivacious and talked and laughed. The meal the captain served them was lavish and consumed a good deal of time. Before it was half through, Petra was inwardly wondering if Xavier was regretting his bargain—he had been so wild to marry the black-haired Catalina. She realized, perhaps for the first time, how much she felt a part of the Estrada clan, for she resented Catalina's treatment of Xavier—she who had never given much thought to the chubby man before. It seemed to Petra that Catalina treated him abominably—nothing exactly that she could put her finger on, but in the soft insidious ways a woman can wound a man who is her husband. She had a way of making him appear incredibly stupid, for Catalina was clever. She used the same tone with him that she might have used to an overgrown but backward child. She had developed the trick of exploding into a gay derisive trill of laughter at everything he chose to say. Petra found herself observing the other girl closely, wondering why in the world she had married Xavier if she felt so about him.

The dinner was finished and they were in the hold of the vessel examining merchandise before the answer came to her. It came in an instant, and was gone in an instant. It was only a glance Catalina swept Francisco with when he reached to hand her a bolt of silk she asked for. Mother of God! Petra gave a little gasp of shock and swiftly sought Angelo's eyes to see if he too had seen. He had, because his face went immediately blank and expressionless.

"Captain," Petra said hurriedly focusing attention on herself, "I've been all over the hull of this ship and I fail to find any combs. I've been wanting one of tortoise shell. Have you any of tortoise shell?"

"I can find you one later," he said easily. "By the way I found some Spanish papers for Don Angelo. He expressed a wish for them when I was here last." He began to rummage around at the far end of the counter.

"There aren't any tortoise-shell combs," Petra said in mild exasperation. "I've looked."

"He will find it, little one," Francisco said with a sudden grin. "Merchandise finds a way of slipping behind the false side of the vessel. It helps in declaring cargo and paying duty. Say nothing to him of it, though. He would be embarrassed," he cautioned as the captain returned with the papers for Angelo.

Angelo took them delightedly, while a clerk made a brief note of it in his book, adding after it, "one tortoise-shell comb for three hundred hides." Petra felt a wave of apprehension. Holy Mother! It had better be a beautiful comb to cost that much. Even she knew that the hides were valued at two dollars each. Only the comfortable feeling that Francisco had unlimited resources made her refrain from deciding she didn't want the comb after all. She bit her lip a little nervously, wondering if she dared mention what else she wanted. Francisco had told her to make a list of everything. There was Xavier buying as he pleased and letting the clerk put the items down to Francisco's account. Francisco himself didn't bother to ask the price of an article. This was the attitude of all the family on the trading ships and at the stores in Los Angeles. The first time she had been shopping she had asked rather timidly for lengths of black ribbon for Angelo's hair, and Francisco had been surprised. You didn't *ask*, it seemed, you simply bought what you wanted, and the clerk marked it down.

As they disembarked from the Boston ship *Crescent*, Petra scanned the harbor in search of the Spanish ship *Santa Margarita*. When she spied it, she breathed a sigh of relief that it hadn't gone.

"Guillermo," she said, "hand me that list." Obediently, avoiding Francisco's eyes, the Indian took off his hat and from it took the list. It was a list of books. Angelo enjoyed reading, but there were few books at Dos Ríos—or anywhere but the mission. Father Patricio had tutored Angelo at times. During Angelo's childhood, whenever trouble with the Indians was threatened Francisco sent him to the mission to stay. These visits had been very pleasant for both Angelo and Father Patricio, and a great friendship had sprung up between the two.

As a rule the priests did not care to have the people too literate, and there had been some heated debates and troublesome times regarding how many books should come into California. But Patricio was fond of Angelo and respected him intellectually. He had stated on more than one occasion that a classical education would do him no harm, even suggesting that Francisco send the boy to Spain, France or America for study.

Francisco was inclined to doubt the wisdom of this. Had Angelo been of a different temperament, he would not have. But he disliked seeing Angelo curl up with a book when other boys his age were out hunting. Consequently, although he was more than generous in supplying anything

Angelo wanted, he was careful about how many books came to Dos Ríos.

Once, half jokingly, half to please Angelo, Father Patricio had made a long list of all the books he could remember having read and enjoyed. This list Petra now held in her hand. Guillermo looked blankly into the middle distance, as Petra cleared her throat and spoke to her father-in-law. "Don Francisco," she said, "have we time to board the *Santa Margarita* before we go to the alcalde's house?"

"What do you want on the *Santa Margarita?*" he asked. Then as he saw the list, his eyes suddenly became veiled. "Ah, those books again!" he said softly.

"Angelo didn't ask me to get them," Petra said quickly as she saw Angelo stiffen. "I—I thought of it myself. I'm sure that a library would be a pleasant thing to have at Dos Ríos. We had a large library at home in England and I miss it very much," she added, flushing a little at the bald lie. Reading bored her immeasurably, but if she could have a six-hundred-dollar comb she saw no reason why Angelo couldn't have a few dozen books.

"Let me see the list." Francisco held out his hand. His eyes passed expressionlessly over Guillermo who had darkened perceptibly. Petra hesitated an instant and then handed him the paper. As he looked at it, his eyes cold, Petra had a momentary fear that the next instant it would be dropped into the blue water of the bay. Her consternation must have shown in her face, for when he looked up his expression changed quickly.

"We haven't time to board the *Santa Margarita* today, Petra," he said. "In any event Captain Lopez wouldn't have any stock of books. The only way we can obtain them is to place a special order with him." He handed the list to Guillermo. "Go out to the *Santa Margarita* tonight, Guillermo," he said, "and give this list to Captain Lopez. Tell him to get these books when he arrives in Spain, and either bring them when he returns to California or send them by another vessel."

"Francisco," Xavier said in astonishment remembering the many refusals on books, "that will cost you a fortune."

"Be quiet, Xavier!" Angelo said, suddenly finding his voice. "Don't remind him of that. He doesn't care about that." He turned to his father, his eyes brilliant.

"I do deplore your lack of manners," Francisco said dryly. "Since when is it customary to tell your elders to be quiet?"

Hastily Angelo apologized.

"Never mind, Angelito. It's all right." Xavier laughed good-naturedly. "I guess we were both surprised out of our wits. Look, there's the alcalde waiting to meet us."

They turned to look and saw the alcalde with his staff of light-colored wood, topped with gold, its black tassels snapping briskly in the breeze. He and Francisco had been friends for some time, and when Francisco or members of his family were in town, they stayed at the alcalde's house as a matter of course. It was almost time for the evening meal now, after which there would be a little entertainment. However, they would probably not remain up too late because both Francisco and Don Juan Acuña wanted to leave early in the morning for their ranchos.

"You know, Petra," Angelo said to her before they retired to their rooms, "I can't remember how many times I've asked for some—just *some*, mind you—of those books."

Petra smiled in a superior manner. "You must not have done it the right way, Angelo," she said.

"Your father is most generous. He has never refused me anything yet."

Angelo laughed in quick delight. "Of course I'm only his son. I suppose father is as susceptible as any man to hair the color of yours. What is there about a blond woman that every man finds so appealing?" But he was deeply pleased and vowed to himself that his father would have less cause in the future to be disappointed in him. It would take two, three, perhaps even four years for the order of books to get back to California. But while he was—he grimaced slightly—while he was learning to be a ranchero, he would have them to look forward to.

The alcalde's house was crowded with six in their own party and two Acuñas, so accommodations were comfortable but haphazard. Catalina and Petra were bundled into the bedroom with the alcalde's daughters, the youngest of whom cheerfully slept on a chest covered with a blanket.

The bed was as lavish as all California beds. All the women made a fetish of the magnificence of their beds and bed linen, and the alcalde's wife was no exception. Petra settled herself between the silken sheets with a sigh of content and fell almost immediately asleep.

Catalina, beside her, stared into the darkness, nervously fingering the lace at the yoke of her gown. A little thrill of triumph ran through her. Xavier had bought it for her along with all the other clothing California men bought for their brides, but—here her cheeks burned a little in the darkness—Francisco's money had paid for every thread. The small exultation faded quickly. Mother of God, what had she got herself into! It was sheer madness to have even thought of marrying Xavier—much more actually doing it. It had started shortly after Petra's wedding, when the first fiesta was finished and they had begun the trip home to Las Palomas. She had realized that she was leaving Dos Ríos and Petra was staying there—Petra with her beautiful modish gowns, her yellow hair, the only pretty white woman on the whole rancho. If only Angelo had some brothers! But no, there was no one left but Xavier.

Ana of course would—such wickedness and sinning thought!—Ana would live forever. There was gossip that she felt extremely well in this latest pregnancy and expected to carry the child its full term and bear it. She probably would, Catalina had thought dolefully. She would probably give Francisco the child he wanted badly, and live to remain his wife forever. There was no place for another woman at Dos Ríos—except as the wife of Don Xavier.

Mother of God, he must be thirty or forty! Don *Xavier*—when Refugio Peréa and his friends had ridden all the way from Rancho Estrella Grande to serenade her? *Xavier*—when Candalario Sal had almost come to blows with Julio Quixano in order to dance with her?

Was she losing her mind? Was she planning to marry one man so she might live in the house of another? To lust after him who was husband to another woman? Who was she? Some Indian? Some half-breed with no morals, no upbringing, no background? Wouldn't they blanch and tremble if they knew the thoughts in the mind of María-Catalina Dolores Acuña y Ramiriz, whose blood was of the whitest and finest, whose father was one of the first gentlemen of California.

And yet, if she did—*if* she did—marry Xavier, she *would* go to Dos Ríos. And she would stay at Dos Ríos. That she was reasonably sure of. In her confusion she thanked God, Jesus, Mary, all of them, for the California custom of just *staying*. People stayed for life if they wanted to. Francisco's family was one of the smallest. In addition to immediate members, other families consisted of various aunts, cousins, poor in-laws and relatives far removed—anyone, in fact, who couldn't or didn't care to make his own way. Each family had an adopted orphan or two, besides its own many children. If the family grew too big for the house, one simply built more house. Adobe bricks were made from the earth on which one lived, and dried in the bright free sunlight. What difference did it make if one, two or seven steers were slaughtered for table meat? Cattle was plentiful. At Rancho Estrella Grande, the house of the Peréas, forty people sat down each day to eat together. At Las Palomas, her own home, twenty-nine people lived beneath the Acuña roof.

And as for Xavier establishing himself as a ranchero, that took time. It took years. The government was not noted for the speed and dispatch with which it handled legal matters. Francisco's land was extensive, but he could not alone supply Xavier with enough. Government land would have to be chosen, measured, mapped, applied for, before eventually the grant was made. It was not unusual for this business to consume two years or more. Then a suitable house must be built. She certainly wouldn't consent to living in a three or four-room affair with earthen floors and a rawhide door. No, she would have wooden floors, and they were difficult to get. There would be glass in her windows, and maybe even a wooden roof, before she moved an inch out of Dos Ríos.

Allowing credit where credit was due, she knew that Xavier would not expect her to take less than she had been accustomed to. He was very considerate in some things. In others—— She shuddered a little. Mother of God, if she had only known! In uneasy, painful remembrance she moved closer to Petra who slept beside her. What a fool she had been after all! What a price she was paying to live beneath Francisco's roof and torment herself daily with longing for him!

Well, by everything holy, that should settle it! If it cost this much in outrage, humiliation and revulsion, they would see many a year pass before she left Dos Ríos. That was final.

Chapter 7

The matanza season had begun. Francisco and Enrique came back to the house for their meal each evening tired and dirty, but satisfied with the way things were going. Grazing had been good and the cattle were fat. Consequently the tallow yield was going to be excellent. Guillermo asked and was given permission to accompany them. Angelo had had little need of him since Petra's coming, for it delighted her to tend his wants and keep his belongings in order. Guillermo was exceptionally intelligent and an instinctively good horseman. Francisco spoke to Ysidra about him one evening while they sat in his office.

"I'm thinking of training him as a *mayordomo,*" he said. "Enrique and I both believe his qualifications are good, and if I continue to increase my holdings, I'll need more than one."

"Yes, Enrique works too hard. So do you. Guillermo will be pleased. His talents are wasted in the house," Ysidra answered. "What about Angelo? Isn't the boy ever going to take a hand?"

"Ah, Angelito——" Francisco laughed. "I'm afraid we'll have to face the fact, *Mamacita,* that his main interest in life is pursuit of pleasure."

"Well, he's a good husband, anyway," she defended, smiling. "Petra is quite mad about him, thank God."

They were silent for a moment, then both spoke at once.

"I wonder——" Francisco bowed.

"You wonder what, my dear? Probably the same thing I do."

"Probably. I was wondering when she was going to have a baby. Apparently no sign of it yet."

"Sign?"

"Come, come, Francisco. One has no secrets from one's serving-woman. Bianca is well meaning, but, Indianlike, she will gossip. I imagine it's only a matter of time," she said letting smoke drift from her nostrils.

"I suppose so. How has Ana been? I've scarcely had a moment since the beginning of the week to speak with her."

"Ana? That is a difficult question, Francisco. She says she feels well, but judging from her disposition, I find it difficult to tell. It's all anyone can do to get a civil word from her these days."

Francisco frowned. Like all Spaniards he hated any open discord. Courtesy was as important as bread. "I wonder why," he said thoughtfully.

Ysidra tossed the burning stub into the fireplace and rose ponderously from her chair. "Do you, Francisco? Permit me to assist your faulty reasoning powers. I think that, quite simply, she is annoyed with the amount of attention you pay to Petra. Now you must look astonished and vow that you have paid her no special attention."

He had risen from his chair and failed to smile at her thrust. "It pleases me to pay attention to Petra. By the way," he added suddenly, "how do Ana and Petra get along? Petra has never mentioned the matter."

Ysidra gave the smallest possible shrug. "My dear Francisco, tell me of any girl who gets along well with her mother-in-law. Ana could be more pleasant, but it must be remembered that she is not well. I know one other thing that annoys her is Petra's interest in the household. Ana feels, I suppose, that Petra takes too much upon herself."

"In what way?"

"It's foolish of course. My goddaughter is an intelligent young woman, and Ana has never cared too much about running the house anyway. At this time she is frequently ill or resting in her room. I've made it a point to avoid as much responsibility in the house as possible simply because it bores me, so what is more natural than for the servants to turn to Petra for instructions? They come to her at all times of day with questions. Yesterday Delfina was sick and could not iron, and since it is she who does the fine things, someone had to tell Elena to iron the dresses. Last week four of the Peréa sons came to visit and Ana had not ordered any meat slaughtered. You know how the Peréas eat, Francisco. If Petra hadn't thought of supplies we might have been humiliated.

"I could run on in this manner for hours. These are small things, but they annoy Ana. On the other hand she would be annoyed if Petra or one of the servants came to her room at all hours with these little problems, so what can one do but ignore it?"

"Nothing. I suppose it would only make it worse if I spoke to her."

"Mother of God, yes, Francisco! I believe she already fancies you in love with the girl." There was the hint of a question in her tone, which he chose to ignore. She continued: "She can overlook the fact—of which she must be aware—that you take your pleasure now and then with Delfina. But Delfina is an Indian. Consequently there is no threat of——"

"There would be none anyway," he commented dryly. "Petra is married to my son—with whom she seems well satisfied, I may add. Don't worry. If things become unpleasant, let me know, and I shall take pains to correct the situation once and for all."

Ysidra's wheezing derisive laugh rose, and he grinned reluctantly as he opened the door for her. Ana stood on the threshold.

"Anita, my dear—" Ysidra smiled—"we were speaking of you only a moment ago. Are you feeling better now?"

"A little," she answered frigidly, lowering the hand she had raised to knock. "Are you busy, Francisco? I wanted to speak with you."

He bowed. "I'm at your service, as always, Ana. What is it?"

"I know you are inclined to be indulgent with young people. I find no fault with the way you have brought up Angelo considering he is your only son. However, I would like to insist on more courteous treatment from my daughter-in-law."

Francisco's face became blank. He turned slightly to Ysidra. "Perhaps you could attend to this, Ysidra. Petra is your goddaughter——"

Ana interrupted him. "I'm doubtful as to what kind of bringing up she has had," she said plaintively. "Perhaps it was a mistake to have her here at all."

"Set your mind at rest, Anita, my dear," Ysidra cut in smoothly. "I shall make a point of speaking to my goddaughter in the morning." There was an undertone of finality in her voice which seemed to terminate the interview, and with that Ana had to be content, for Ysidra stepped into the hallway and of a necessity Ana was forced to step back a pace.

Courteous good nights were said, and Francisco's door closed as Ysidra and Ana started down the hall. Thin color stained Ana's face. She was conscious that no point had been made at all. She felt she had been given no time even to state her grievance against Petra's behavior.

At the foot of the stairs she stopped. "You will speak to her," she insisted.

"Of course," Ysidra answered. "I'm sorry if she has annoyed you. I'm sure it must have been unintentional. But—" quickly she forestalled the other woman—"I shall speak to her."

Still Ana lingered, clasping at the newel post nervously. It was plain she had more to say. Ysidra smothered a sigh, as Ana seemed to make up her mind to speak.

"Ysidra," she began carefully, "you understand that there is nothing definite. It's merely her general conduct which I cannot condone. She is much too . . . forward. You must ask her to modify her actions. I don't mean to criticize, for I know she's young and inexperienced." She paused uncertainly.

With another small sigh Ysidra settled herself on the bench just inside the front door. "What are you trying to say, Ana?" Her voice held elaborate patience.

"I'm trying to say she should act with more decorum toward Angelo for one thing. You don't see Catalina clinging to Xavier's hand or rushing to light his cigarette. Catalina has been brought up to——"

"Catalina is perhaps not so deeply enamored of her husband," Ysidra commented. "Give Petra time; the wild infatuation will diminish. I shouldn't be too hard on her, if I were you."

"I'm not hard on her," Ana returned sharply. "It isn't only Angelo! Oh, Ysidra, how can you be so blind? The girl is bold. Careless." Ana sought painfully for expression. "She—she lacks respect. Surely, you *must* have noticed. I should think that Francisco, as head of the house, would merit more respect than she shows him."

"Ah," Ysidra said softly.

"She's much too familiar," Ana rushed on. "I'm sure if I had spoken so carelessly to my elders when I was a girl, I would have been shut up in a convent to learn better manners."

"I shall speak to her," Ysidra cut in, rising from the bench. "Think no more about it, Ana. Only remember that Petra lived most of her life in England, where I understand there is less formality. After she is more used to this life, has a child or two, she will settle down."

"Is she going to have a baby?" Ana's voice was suddenly guarded.

"I have no idea," Ysidra returned with some asperity. "If she is, she hasn't taken me into her confidence."

Ana laughed thinly. "One would think," she said, "that it might have happened before this. Wouldn't it be odd if—" she broke off to laugh again—"wouldn't it be odd if she never had any? Wouldn't it be odd if there were never any children here?"

"I believe," Ysidra returned coldly, "that is an unwise speech for one in your condition. Don't trouble you mind about it. I haven't the faintest doubt but that Petra will have several children in time. Now I am very tired. I think I shall go to bed."

In her room Ana began to undress herself, avoiding the mirror. Her misshapen body sickened her. She despised the thin shadows where the tissue had strained and parted beneath the skin over her distended stomach. This was the last time, so help her God! She would never again try to have another baby, whether this one lived or died. She buttoned the neck of her gown with yellow-tinged fingers. She must speak with Doctor Vaiz about her color. And lately her appetite had been poor. She disliked medicine, but she must do something to open her appetite. Water and *aguardiente* wasn't so bad if she put sugar in it, although she did not care for it. She knelt with an effort and took her rosary between her fingers.

"Hail, Mary, full of Grace. The Lord——" She paused and stared blankly at the dim face of Lupe in the portrait. A dark idea began to form in her mind. It grew like mold. What were they doing? What was happening here, in her own house, before her own face?

"The Lord is with Thee. Blessed art Thou amongst——" Did Angelo know anything? No. He was nothing but a child intent on his own pleasures and pastimes. But maybe he did know or suspect something. Perhaps she should speak with Angelo.

"Blessed art Thou amongst women. Blessed is the fruit of Thy womb, Jesus. Holy——" He should know about his own wife, his own wanton wife. Ysidra had said—what had Ysidra said? "I haven't the faintest doubt but that Petra will have several children."

"Holy Mary, Mother of God, pray for us sinners now and at the hour of our death." She held the beads limply in her fingers, searching for the idea that formed in her mind. Of what was Francisco capable? Was there anything he would not do in his hardness, his ambition to establish his own line? A man's blood was a man's blood. A child was a child. Who could tell by looking at the child from whose loins had sprung the seed? There it was. Unconsciously she rose to her feet and went to stand beneath the portrait of Lupe. That was it. She gazed childishly into the painted eyes of the portrait, running her finger along the edge of the heavy wooden frame.

"You see," she said gently, "I knew something was wrong. They are different. He is different now from the way he was. Ysidra is different. They all are—except me. I'm the same, and you, of course. I should have known before."

How long would it take him to bind his spell? And what would Angelo do when he found out? Ysidra—she must know, but she would not care. She could see no fault in him. He was her darling, her favorite. She was a sinful wicked witch. And Petra—bold, immodest. How long would it be before she was captivated, infatuated? Angelo should know this.

She was placing her rosary in the little casket which held it when she began to ponder on the door between her room and Angelo's. He had been wrong to insist on taking that room again with his wife when she had moved all his things out. She was mistress of this house and she should assign the rooms. But Francisco always tolerated more from him than any other father from a son. Angelo knew nothing of obedience. She nodded slightly. Ah, Francisco had good reason to tolerate his insolence now, clever, ruthless Francisco whose whim was law. It occurred to her with mild surprise that she had never passed through the door between the rooms. She herself had locked it a long time ago and the key still stood in the lock. It was possible to turn the key and go into Angelo's room to punish him. He needed punishing for he knew all of her sorrow and all of her humiliation.

She placed one long white hand on the key and turned it. It twisted easily in the lock. That was a sign, then, for it should have been difficult to turn. She opened the door with a feeling of pleasure akin to delight and entered. Petra had not come up yet. That was a sign also. Only Guillermo was with him, squatting Indian-fashion on the floor, speaking eagerly and expressively of his day at the matanza field. Angelo was undressing, laughing at something Guillermo had said, holding his unwound sash in his hand. Both started at her sudden appearance and were silent. Complaisantly she folded her pale hands over her stomach. Guillermo rose quickly and bowed to her.

"There is something I must speak to you about, Angelo," she said. "Guillermo will be good enough to excuse us."

Angelo made a small sign to his friend, who immediately left the room. "If you had knocked before you came in," Angelo said mildly, "I would have righted my clothes." He wound the sash about his waist again and was beginning to tie it when she continued. Then his hands became still. He stared at her blankly as she began to speak.

She tried not to grow excited, but the words came faster and faster. She must convince him. In eagerness she spat her facts at him. She was a sick woman and had not been able to give Francisco the children he wanted. Francisco had never loved her. Angelo was only a boy. If Francisco wasn't satisfied with her for a wife, how long could Angelo expect Petra to be content with him? Like wanted like. How long could Angelo expect to hold Petra? What could he offer in comparison with Francisco? Angelo knew how hard Francisco was. He would take anything he wanted. He was ruthless and without conscience. Why would he not want Petra? What made Angelo think, in his naïve and childish way, that Petra would resist Francisco's advances for long. Was Angelo an infant that he did not understand his father's attraction to certain kinds of women? Think! God alone knew how much she had had to overlook since her marriage to Francisco. Petra was a young, impressionable girl. She——

"Be quiet!"

She stopped, gulping back the words that would tumble eagerly from her lips. How pale he was!

But what was he thinking? She could tell nothing from the blank, carefully expressionless face. It was like looking at the pretty painted face of Lupe. The same wide-set tilted eyes regarded her with the same cool reserve.

"You are sick." Finally he spoke, coldly. "That is the kindest thing I can say to you."

"You don't believe me?" she asked a little wonderingly.

"I believe you are mistaken. Go to your room. You don't know what you are saying."

"Fool!" She spat. "Ask him. He would probably tell you himself. He's much too brazen to lie. Why don't you ask him?"

His slim smooth hands were occupied with his sash. The silence hung between them until the sash was tied to his satisfaction. "Argument about this is ridiculous, Ana. My father would be incapable of such baseness."

"Fool," she whispered again.

"Besides, if I put such a question to him, he would have me whipped—and with just cause. Not to mention the insult you have just paid my wife. Go to bed and get some rest. I'll be kind enough to forget this thing. I'll be kind enough to attribute these indecencies to the state of your health. Be good enough to leave, please."

She stared at him wordlessly. This was her stepson speaking to her thus. This was the son of her husband, the son of Lupe. In his veins mingled the old aristocratic blood of Estrada and Montoya. Once an Estrada had been examined by the Inquisition. They said on the morning he was taken he spoke of it with a shrug. Long ago a Montoya had met with assassination. They said he spoke regretfully, with a knife in his side, of interrupting the banquet. She could tell nothing from the calm pale face before her. She smiled, turning to go. Let him order her out. Let him reject it. He would think of it later. The thought would recur and recur, until he must live with it all the days of his life and look with doubt into the faces of his children.

When Petra came in, he was standing where he had stood to listen to Ana. He turned to look at his wife. A habit pattern older than his memory asserted itself and he bowed to her.

"I thought you would be in bed. You said you were tired," she said, smiling at him and kissing him lightly.

He regarded her carefully. "Guillermo was in. He was excited about the matanza. He always said he'd like to be a *vaquero*. He was full of it. He could talk of nothing else. You look lovely tonight," he added thoughtfully. She did. She was wearing a yellow gown, and her yellow hair was piled high before the tortoise-shell comb which was set with bright stones.

"You look as if you were spun of gold, and very precious." He watched her eyes darken and her mouth become unsteady as it always did when he spoke to her lovingly. How plainly he saw her! She, and everything in the room, seemed strangely clear-cut and brighter than life. Her hands, hesitantly eager, touched his shoulders and slid about his neck.

"What is it?" she whispered. "What are you thinking of, *querido?*"

"I am thinking of you," he said. "I love you. You are my wife."

Later, during the darkness, after the frenzy of their love was spent, he felt a remoteness, a withdrawing that was strange and alien. Even with Petra sleeping close beside him he could feel a sense of unutterable loneliness. He lay wide-eyed in the darkness thinking of his father who was proud and honorable, of his wife who was beautiful and good, of their estate and their place in the world. He thought with uneasiness and confusion of himself. He was Francisco's only son. Francisco must love him very much.

All men loved their sons. Sons are part of a man. They belonged to a man like arms and legs. There was no question of disliking your hand because it spilled a cup or was clumsy at turning a page. There was anger perhaps, exasperation at its inability, but deep in your mind was the fact that the hand belonged to you and was part of you. If the hand was wounded, you anointed it and bound it up. You mercilessly probed and exercised the stiff joints so that it would become firm and supple. If a child was sick you tended it and cared for it and tried in every way you knew to make it strong.

If he had had brothers and sisters, everyone's attitude would have been different. There would have been a feeling of good-natured competition as among the Peréa boys and girls. Or perhaps it wouldn't have mattered so much if he didn't care to compete and be outstanding.

There was Rafael Peréa. Surely he wasn't more useless or careless than Rafael. Rafael's brothers rallied about him quite naturally to shield and protect him. Nothing was said or thought about any lack in him. Things which he did well were accentuated and enlarged on.

"Let Rafael sing it" was a frequent cry, or: "Listen to that, no one makes verses like Rafael." Because he never felt inferior he was able to do more. He rode with his brothers and hunted with them. He raced with them though he seldom won. If it was the accepted thing that someone else take the initiative in all things where danger threatened, he was not offended and his brothers did not look down on him because of it. What point was there in Rafael losing his hand between the snapping jaws of a grizzly? Let Refugio handle the grizzly. Chances were he wouldn't lose a hand, and anyway his fingers didn't have nearly the touch that Rafael's did on guitar strings.

But Francisco had only one son who had to be everything, and when something lacked, it was noticed.

Not only that, but Francisco worried about Dos Ríos. What of the estate? He had Padilla, of course. Enrique was a good man and a smart one, but being such, he would not always be content working for another man. He was a Catholic, a citizen of Mexico. There was nothing to keep him from being a ranchero and landowner. He was ambitious, and proud as those were who claimed only Spanish blood, but whose skin was dark and whose eyes were liquidly brown.

If Francisco should die tomorrow, who would take charge? Who would be in reality, if not in name, the head of the house? Would Enrique feel bound to stay because of his love and respect for Francisco? Would it be Guillermo? Angelo's face burned in the darkness. Guillermo, an Indian, was better qualified to take the place as head of the house than he was. If only he could be like Teodoro Acuña! Don Juan Acuña had nothing to worry about. He knew that Teodoro could step into his place any day and discharge with efficiency and personal satisfaction the duties incumbent on him.

How to start? How to learn to be the kind of man Petra would appreciate? He would give his very soul to be like Teodoro. But there was so much to learn, so much to do, so much to accept, and with ease and poise. How could one accomplish feats of horsemanship and valor with that careless unconcern?

It was too late. The words formed in his mind and gave him an empty lost feeling. Even if he tried to apply himself now he would be a laughingstock. The Indians had a sharp sense of ridicule. He imagined their laughter in their huts at night about his pathetic attempts to be a *caballero*. It had been better when he hadn't wanted to be anything else. Everyone had liked him then. They respected him in an offhand way because he was clever, witty, sang and danced well and because he was Francisco's son. They might raise their eyes heavenward and say, "That Angelo! If he would only apply himself!" There had always been the possibility that he could do anything he wanted to if he just cared enough to try. But now, when he tried and failed, it would be different. He shivered slightly. How galling that would be to the pride of a Spaniard! He would be inferior to everybody. Even the Indians made fine *vaqueros*. They expertly used a knife, a gun and *reata*. They rode like the wind and knew their animals like brothers. Inferior even to the Indians. There would be the little embarrassments and humiliations to be borne when he didn't learn properly and did things badly, clumsily.

He felt his wrists in the darkness. How different from the strong muscular arms of Guillermo, Enrique and his father! Could those wrists ever move expertly enough to send a rawhide *reata* singing through the air with unfailing accuracy. Were they strong enough to tighten it on a bear and pull him down? In an emergency would he spur his horse and run away in terror? O Mother of God, protect him from that!

Why try? he wondered. Why make any effort? Why not shut his eyes and go along the way he had before? Petra loved him. She was devoted to him. She would always be. His father was a decent man. Fathers loved and respected their sons. They were good and just. Hard, perhaps, but just and decent and sometimes kind. Ana was an evil woman. Ana was vindictive and jealous and sick. Ana was wrong.

But Petra was so valuable. Petra was his wife whom he loved completely, and without whom he would be lost. He had to protect his marriage. He couldn't go on being a careless little boy who could be pushed about and told what to do or what not to do. He could not remain a helpless child about whose existence decisions were made regardless of his feelings and desires. He must, in some way, become a responsible adult, who was valued, respected and of some account.

One jumped into the water and learned to swim in order to keep from drowning. For some time the idea had dangled just beyond his understanding. Then he faced it. If he just *began!* Sharply, just like that! If he began! And took his place as the son of the family and *tried* to be like everyone else. And *made* himself into the kind of man everyone had expected him to be. Then he would be such a personage that it would not occur to anyone that he was to be trifled with. No one would think to disregard him, or question his rights, or covet his wife.

Here before him was a beginning. The matanza. His mind tried to twist away from the thought. That might be the start. He could let them think he was interested, and perhaps later he really would be. When he understood more and was more capable maybe he would grow into it all just as Teodoro had. But the beginnings, the painful, humiliating, galling little failures. Guillermo would help him. Almost as far back as he could remember Guillermo had been there to help him, loyally, devotedly and without question. He went to sleep thinking of Guillermo.

Francisco looked at his son silently for some seconds after the request. Angelo's actions and approach had been different and puzzling. In the first place he was on horseback. He had ridden out to meet them as they came in for their evening meal. He, Enrique and Guillermo halted their horses as he rode up to them. His manners might have been those of Teodoro Acuña, so perfect were they. He removed his hat and bowed, speaking with utmost courtesy.

"Father, would you mind if I went with you to the matanza field tomorrow?"

"The slaughter?" Francisco asked sparring for time. "I'm not sure you would care for that, Angelito." The diminutive form slipped out unnoticed, and he was sorry the moment he spoke, for Angelo stiffened slightly.

"I didn't say I intended to like it, sir," Angelo answered, smiling faintly. "But I'm nearly nineteen. I think it's time I began to learn a few useful things, don't you?"

"Of course," Francisco replied, still uncertain. The matanza was a difficult place to start. Angelo could have taken the matanza, bloody and rough as it was, in perfect stride if he had worked up to it gradually by becoming familiar with all the other crude, unlovely occupations which comprised the essential workings of the rancho. But if this were an overture, if he intended to make an effort, now was not the time to forestall him or place obstacles in his way. It had been on the tip of Francisco's tongue to persuade Angelo to pass up the matanza, to remind him that he was still on his honeymoon, and suggest that he wait until this slaughter season and the following idle season were finished. Then he could come out to the first rodeo. Francisco was field judge and there would be hundreds of things to do. It was an exciting time, half festival, half business. Instead he found himself saying formally, "If you care to come, I shall be delighted to have you, Angelo."

Petra spoke to Angelo that night in their room. "You won't like it, Angelo," she said flatly. "Why bother? Your father doesn't really need you there. Stay here with me."

He looked at her strangely. What did she know about the matanza? She had been in California only a few months. However, she was such a curious interested girl, it was possible, probable, that she already knew more about the business of the rancho than he did, who had been here most of his life. He sat down on the edge of the bed and leaned his head against the bedpost. Was it possible that a man's wife could be of harder and braver stuff than he? That would be a humiliating thing. Yet Petra occasionally watched with only a delicate wrinkling of her nose when they slaughtered a steer for table meat. Nothing could be bloodier than butchering an animal Spanish-fashion on its own hide.

"Angelo," she said, imitating his own plaintive tone, "this is still our honeymoon."

He smiled at her. "Kiss me and I'll tell you something."

Quickly she bent and kissed him. "What?"

"The honeymoon is finished. Now I turn my attention to becoming a serious and hardworking ranchero. Doesn't that please you?"

"No," she said bluntly. "It doesn't please me. You know how easily your stomach is upset. You'll be sickened."

He shrugged. "Oh, I don't think so. It's just part of the business. I'll think of it that way. Don't worry about me, my love. I'm not clever at outdoor things and Father won't let me get hurt. I won't do any of it myself. Neither do Father or Enrique, really. They just oversee. If any emergency arises they either do something to avert it or see that someone else does."

"But what happens? What do they actually *do?*"

"You understand that I speak only from hearing about it? I've never been on the matanza field during slaughter season."

"Yes, tell me what you know."

"Well, it seems the *vaqueros* work in pairs. The number of fat cattle to be slaughtered are driven into that corral by the field, and whenever two *vaqueros* are ready, one goes in, lassos a steer and brings it out. Then the other also lassos it, and they back up their horses until their *reatas* are taut and the steer is helpless between them. Then the one who is at the back end dismounts and ties its legs securely."

"He dismounts!"

"Yes, the horse keeps the *reata* taut. That's what they're trained for. They never allow an inch of slack. Sometimes I think the horses are as intelligent as the Indians."

"Then what?" she asked beginning to unfasten her gown.

"When it's tied up, he takes off the *reatas* and kills it."

"How? The way they butcher?"

"Yes, he just sticks a knife in its neck. By that time the other *vaquero* has dismounted and they take the skin off, a matter of a few minutes."

"Well, is that all there is to it?"

"Not exactly. I understand it's cut up. They save about two hundred pounds of the best meat for curing, the same old dried beef we have so often. They take off the fat to render it down in those big vats you saw, the same kind in which whalers used to render whale fat. I sound very efficient, don't I? I picked up all this information just listening to Father and Enrique talk business.

"Let me see if I know anything else. Oh yes,

there are two grades of tallow. The tallow inside the animal is inferior, and that's what we export. The tallow next to the hide is better. It's handled and rendered very carefully because it's for home use. I understand it burns easily. I've heard Enrique in a wild swearing rage whenever the Indians have let some scorch. Then they run it into bags made of hides. These hold—depending on the size of the hide, I guess—from twenty to forty-five arrobas, or between five hundred and eleven hundred pounds, approximately that is. The traders buy the inferior stuff, the *sebo*, for a dollar and half an arroba. If there is any of the good tallow, the *mancata,* that we don't need for home use, the Russians are delighted to buy it for two dollars an arroba. That's all, I think, except that the hides are staked out until they're dry. Then they're stacked up and eventually taken to the harbor and sold to the traders. The rest of the meat is left there for the dogs and bears. You see, there is nothing very difficult about all this. It's probably only tiresome."

"That is not all. I'm not a child. There is always a certain amount of danger where there are wild long-horned cattle."

"Petra, they are in the corral. I told you that," he said with elaborate patience. "That corral wasn't built to decorate the landscape. It was built to hold a hundred half-wild steers. Believe me, I'll be perfectly safe."

She sighed, and her worried gaze rested a moment on his face. "Angelo, I know you can ride," she began carefully. "Can you use a *reata?* I'm not doubting you, Angelo. I just want to know."

"Petra, I don't boast of being as proficient with one as my father, or Enrique, or Guillermo, or Teodoro, but I have managed to lasso moving objects from time to time. There isn't a man in California who can't use a *reata,* with varying degrees of accuracy, of course. Don't worry about it."

"But they bolt," she muttered sullenly. "Those steers get out and run away, and you know it, Angelo Estrada."

He shrugged and spread his hands. "All right, they run away. There's nothing dangerous about that. When one does, somebody lassos it. Maybe if he's in a playful mood he just grabs it by the tail and turns it over. Cattle aren't bold by nature, Petra. When a steer has been twisted over and flung on its back to the ground, it gets up and very submissively comes back to be killed."

"Angelo, you won't try to do that!"

In spite of himself he had to laugh. "Beloved," he said, "I can make you a solemn promise on that. All day tomorrow while I am at the slaughter field, you may be safe in saying to yourself that your husband is *not* hurling steers to the ground."

"Oh, Angelo, you make a joke of everything. Here, let me unbraid that for you."

But in the morning when Bianca brought their morning coffee and cereal, he had difficulty in laughing about it. He thought of it while he dressed and during prayers. Enrique rode out to the field to get the men started, and Francisco was busy in his office for a while. Between eight and nine the large breakfast was served, of which he could eat but little, so tense was he. The sight of the thick broiled and roasted pieces of beef and the fried beans of which he was usually fond failed to tempt him. Then the moment he had been awaiting and dreading arrived, and it was time to go.

"Change your mind?" Francisco grinned as they rose from the table.

Angelo shook his head. "No, Father, I haven't."

"Well, come on then." Francisco passed his arm

about Angelo's shoulders and they went out the door into the brilliant sunlight.

Guillermo was saddling a horse from Francisco's *caponera* of working horses. "I borrowed one of yours, Don Francisco, for Don Angelo. He hasn't any work horses." He turned to Angelo. "I used your old saddle. That's what you wanted, wasn't it?"

"Yes, that's fine, thank you." Angelo mounted silently, thinking what a commonplace occurrence this was to the others. Xavier was going. It didn't bother Xavier.

It was only riding a horse, he told himself. There was nothing so difficult about riding a horse. It might be a little different perhaps. There might be new momentary decisions to make in guiding him. Sudden turns. Necessary bursts of speed. Little things to cope with, but only little things. Surely he could do them. He would be tired of course. It would be hot. It would be dusty. There would be blood. But a day has just so many hours, and the time passes.

"If you get tired, Angelo, you can come back to the house," Francisco offered just before they started. "Continuous activity like this is very tiring. Sometimes I'm exhausted at the end of the day. You'd better not overdo on your first day."

Angelo looked at his father in polite disbelief. Was it possible that the strong muscular body of his father ever experienced fatigue. He smiled faintly. "I'll stay all day. I don't think it'll kill me." He would stay. Nothing could make him leave the field once he got there. It would be more stubbornness than any power of will, but what difference did it make just so he stayed?

The field, when they reached it, already held the carcasses of several steers. He felt a moment's thankfulness that he hadn't eaten much. It was going to be terribly hot. He was already sweating and he could see the faces of Francisco and Enrique glistening in the sun.

By midmorning he was tense in his saddle. Mother of God! It was just as he had described it to Petra the night before. But the difference, the stupendous overwhelming difference! He had told her how a horse could keep the *reata* tight while its rider dismounted to tie the steer's legs. He hadn't imagined the nervousness and intenseness of the horse as it stepped backward, forward, this way and that, with the movements of the struggling steer, its ears flattening and the whites of its eyes showing. Nor had he imagined the muscle-straining effort of the *vaquero* who secured the steer's thrashing legs.

He had said the killing and skinning was a matter of a few minutes. It was, but he hadn't imagined the blood, spurting, gushing, spreading, or the suet-muffled tearing of the hide as it left the body. How could he have foreseen, who had never seen it before, the aspect of sweat-drenched Indians, to the elbows in blood, cutting up the meat? Or known the croaking sound, which is half chuckle, half groan, that an Indian makes as he cuts up fat meat? Who could have known what they looked like, covered with grease and blood, appearing to absorb it, lave in it, eat of it? Who could have known how they smelled, men and women, as they squatted beside the masses which had once been steers, and wielded their knives in the eternal *scrape, scrape* as they gathered up the tallow? Presently there came the nostril-searing odor of boiling fat, and each hide bag was set up in the center of four stakes to receive the liquid.

The noise, the din, the never-ending sound which rose in confusing waves. The crash of a steer hitting the ground, the bellow of cattle, the rip of hides, knives striking bone, the Indians' croaking gobble, the pounding beat of horses, the shouted orders, the wild heart-stopping yells of *vaqueros,* the shriek of an Indian woman with a scalded arm, the scream of a horse impaled on a steer's horn. The strain, the intensity, in watching the *vaquero* leap from his saddle as the horse went down, and in a split second dodge the steer as it charged again.

He gazed, repelled, fascinated, as Francisco and his horse, seeming one being, leaped forward. In a moment the steer had crashed to the ground. There was the whir of a *reata,* a quick grin of thanks from the Indian, blood spurted from the dead steer's neck, and Francisco was somewhere else. And the dogs, the snapping, snarling, fighting dogs! Hundreds of them, scavengers of every breed and crossbreed who rooted and tore at the offal which lay scattered in red slimy heaps about the field.

He would not go home. He would not leave the field for one instant. He could—Mother of God!—he could do anything a half-breed Indian could do. He tried to stiffen his nerve by thinking of the Estradas and Montoyas who had gone into battle, made rough journeys and accomplished dangerous things. He thought of Francisco, no older than he was now, setting out to a new country, penniless and hunted. He thought of the small wiry Montoya men who had ridden a hazardous road on the king's business, when being a king's courier was a dangerous career. He thought of Santander men who had fought duels to the death with gleaming swords and gleaming smiles. They would have thought nothing of this. His father thought nothing of this. Would those men who were gone have quailed at the sight of some quivering dogs? The thought kept him straight in the saddle. It kept his face expressionless. It kept him from vomiting. It kept him from fainting.

The sun was a hot flaming ball almost directly

over the bloody, dust-choked field. In half an hour, fifteen minutes, ten minutes, they would stop for the midday meal. He could wait that long, surely. There would be a couple of hours in which to eat and rest.

The field looked like a battleground after a massacre. Activity had reached a fever pitch. For an instant he was alone in the midst of it. Everyone was gone from him on some quick errand or to meet some sudden emergency. At that moment a panic-stricken steer crashed out of the corral behind the *vaquero* who was busy at the gate. It charged, bellowing, in the direction of Enrique Padilla.

In a flash of revelation Angelo knew that Enrique would be unhorsed, perhaps gored. Instinctively he had his coiled *reata* in his hands and it was hissing like a snake in the air. He didn't even think while he was doing it—it was such a familiar act. He had seen it done hundreds, thousands of times. It took but a moment for a *reata* to snap through the air, drop its coil on the neck of a steer. In another instant his horse would back sharply, instinctively, and his end of the *reata* could be wrapped quickly about the pommel of his saddle, pitting the strength of the horse against that of the steer for a moment, while a *reata* would come singing from another direction to encircle the steer a second time. He didn't think consciously of this. He was thinking how humiliated Enrique would be if he were thrown from a horse.

It was over in a moment. His *reata* snapped about the charging steer like a trained serpent. He felt it rise and tighten instantly. He looped it about the pommel quickly as the horse began to back. There was a shout and he knew someone had joined him. The next instant before his fingers were free, he felt the rawhide encircle them like a steel band, bind them and crush them against the pommel of his saddle. There was one stunned second, during which he felt nothing, when he saw the fingers ripped from his hand. A gasp wrenched from the depths of him and his body arched convulsively in the saddle.

Francisco and Guillermo saw it at the same time. Guillermo's cry, harsh with anguish, cut through the din. "*Angelito!*" Francisco in lightning, savage rage, swung on the steer. Bending like a matador between its horns he drove his knife to the hilt in the back of its neck. It stood, as in a bull ring, dead on its feet.

Blood welled, then gushed from Angelo's mangled hand. He regained consciousness almost instantly, still in his saddle. His first thought, half prayer, was that he wouldn't fall or be thrown. Then Francisco was beside him, gripping him for an instant about the waist. Right after him were Enrique and Guillermo.

"I won't fall." Angelo's voice was clear but sounded dim to his own ears, and his father released him.

Francisco's hand hesitated a split second over his *reata*. Then he had his hat off and the cord ripped from it, binding it about Angelo's arm to stop the flow of blood which had already drenched the saddle and the neck of the horse. The Indians, mounted and on foot, pressed in a horrified group about them.

"Bind it up," Angelo said, not realizing he spoke. "It mustn't shock Petra."

Gray-faced, Xavier ripped off his jacket and shirt. They tore a sleeve out and bound it hurriedly about the hand. Francisco dropped quickly to the ground and mounted behind Angelo's saddle on the leather *coraza*. He dug his spurs into the animal's flanks. It leaped forward. The crowd melted before it.

"I can ride alone." Angelo's words were lost in

the wind that suddenly hit his face. He felt his body go lax and limp against Francisco and knew that his father was holding him up. It seemed only a minute until they thundered up to the door at Dos Ríos. He got a glimpse of Petra's white frantic face as she saw the blood-soaked bandage. He heard her scream harshly, "Get out of the way," to an Indian girl and send her spinning as Francisco helped him through the door and up the stairs.

"Angelo, *querido*, what is it?" she gasped, her voice thin and terrified.

"Get Ana's medicine chest," commanded Francisco, half carrying Angelo up the stairs, his face still colorless. "Heat some water and get some linen for bandages. Get some brandy——"

His voice diminished suddenly from Angelo's hearing as it smote his mind that his fingers were gone. Mother of God, part of his body! A hundred images imbedded themselves in his brain. Never again to play a guitar, or click castanets, or lift a glass, or caress his wife. He began to be sick, violently and convulsively, as he heard the other horses thunder into the patio. The confused babble of sound rose as those downstairs found that the right hand of Don Angelo was mangled and maimed and useless.

The raw nerve ends which had been numbed sprang to life and his arm was swept again and again with scalding pain. In his agony he was enraged with his father. In jumbled hysteria he thought that if Francisco hadn't coveted his wife he wouldn't have gone to the matanza and his hand would be whole and beautiful.

"Let me go," he gasped and wrenched savagely from Francisco's grasp, half falling on the bed, half fainting from the pain.

He was dimly conscious of activity around his bed. The hand was unwrapped. There was a hoarse unbelievingly cry from Ysidra as if to reject the sight her eyes beheld. Ana hurried from the room, sick and afraid. Catalina fainted without a sound. Petra gave one terrible cry and stared with glazed eyes.

Gently as a woman Francisco cleansed the wound, pausing only to force him firmly to take the brandy. He took it strangling, gasping, sobbing for breath, enough to make him drunk, enough to make him senseless. Only Francisco seemed to remain calm in the crowded noisy room. Grimly and tenderly he dressed the hand that had once been so beautiful, giving directions, issuing orders, telling them how brave Angelito had been, cleaning him, removing his jacket and shirt, putting him to bed.

Angelo got confused impressions of the noise receding, the room clearing of people, Petra clasping his other hand, kissing it and weeping softly, his Aunt Ysidra cursing quietly and luridly, Guillermo standing at the foot of the bed like a statue. Then he seemed to sleep, to diminish, to become nothing.

When he woke the day and night had almost passed and he lay in the thin predawn darkness. Petra sat beside the bed, tense and wide-eyed. His father stood where Guillermo had been, and Father Patricio was seated on the broad window ledge looking at him with loving compassionate eyes. He knew instantly that he was ill, and he closed his eyes for another instant as the memory returned to him. The thought sickened him, shamed him. It was an obscene and indelicate thing to be maimed and disfigured. He had never before known what quiet pride he had taken in his whole perfect body. Now it was no longer perfect. There was ugliness in him where there had been none before. He was more afraid than he had ever been. He wanted to hide. He tried to keep his mouth from shaking, and as if divining his desire, Petra rose from her chair and leaned down to kiss him gently, her streaming disordered hair hiding his face from the others in the room.

When he woke again he was cold with terror. He had been dreaming of the slaughter. The room was empty now except for Petra who stood wearily by the dresser removing her necklace, not knowing he was awake. Confusedly he tried to push the vestigial dreams from his mind. His part in the slaughter was finished and passed. Who would have thought it would come to him here in the dawn? Who could realize that sounds would echo and re-echo in a shocked mind? He moved, feeling he must get up and be free of sleep for a moment. The sound of the silken sheets was a steer losing its hide. The necklace dropped in its velvet box was a knife striking bone. And in the back of his mind, just beyond the edge of his hearing, was the turbulent sound of the dogs. Like shadow sounds they rose and fell, little brute noises, chopped off quickly as they glutted themselves with offal. Surely, here in his own room, he couldn't be hearing them. He was thinking it, or dreaming it, but he couldn't possibly be hearing it. The field was too far away. He struggled to a sitting position, feeling lightheaded and giddy.

Petra turned, startled, and came toward him. "Oh, don't get up, dearest."

"I want to go to the window," he said, and slid his legs over the side of the bed, pain suddenly rising from his arm and spreading up his shoulder. The air struck coldly on his damp body. Without help from Petra he got to the narrow window and leaned against the broad adobe sill. There was no sound of dogs in the air. They would be miles from here, out in the slaughter fields. There would be bears there too. And probably *vaqueros* taking great sport in fighting the bears. He closed his eyes. They were here. He could hear them. He opened his eyes again. It had been foolish to get out of bed, for his strength seemed to be melting. He turned from the window with a feeling of new alarm at the strange stiffening in his body. Then he began to shudder uncontrollably.

"It's just a chill," he managed to whisper to Petra. "Please, please, Petra, don't call anyone. It's . . . only a chill." And Petra, used to obeying him, covered him, heaped blankets and quilts over his shaking body, sobbing with terror as she did so. In a few minutes the shaking subsided.

"You see," he said, with an effort to keep his eyes open, "it was only a chill." He could feel heat flushing and throbbing in his face, and his eyes beneath the half-closed lids were brilliant with fever. As Petra, smudging the tears from her face, began to take off the extra covering, he became sick with a violent nausea and started to vomit. The pain in his arm mounted savagely and stabbed up his neck into his head.

This, he found, in the hours that followed, was the pattern which the pain followed: first the chill rigor, then the sudden flaming fever, then strength-sapping sweat and terrible painful sickness. This would surely pass. This would diminish and not grow worse. He had been sick before and got well again. But he must eat. Mother of God, he must eat or he would die! Each mouthful he swallowed was ejected, no matter how soft and palatable, no matter how daintily prepared.

Francisco seldom left the room. Petra, grim and white, was in and out continually, seeming never to rest or pause. Hot compresses were, agonizingly, wrapped about the stump of hand. Father Patricio ordered a calf and a pig killed to make a cataplasm of roast pork and veal for the pit of his stomach but nothing helped.

Everything at Dos Ríos had come to a standstill waiting for the sickness to pass. Petra's maid Bianca, who had been Angelo's nurse when he was a little boy, came in. Her face was swollen from weeping almost beyond recognition. Señora Llanes in the sewing room ripped out useless stitches. Delfina in the ironing room scorched a garment and then sobbed hopelessly as her iron cooled. There was a pervading air of sullen anger that the young don was crippled. It was a wrong and alien thing to them all. If *only* because of the music, it was wrong, they said. If *only* because of *that*. He who had made music would make no more. And that was wrong. They waited for him to get well, thinking of little things they could do for him when he came downstairs again, planning ways to make him smile and laugh—he had such a fine laugh.

The following day Francisco stood beside the bed and looked down at Angelo's face. It was bloodless and his sunken eyes appeared to be set in bruises. Was it possible that so short a time had carved such hollows in his cheeks? Angelo couldn't afford to lose any weight. For the first time Francisco admitted to himself that his son was desperately sick.

"Teodoro rode over to see you," he said.

"I'm not very presentable," Angelo whispered, not opening his eyes. "Thank him for me. Tell him I'll be better tomorrow. He'll stay, won't he?"

"He'll stay a week if you want him to. Is there anything you need?"

"No, Father, nothing."

Father Patricio, at the foot of the bed, beckoned to Francisco and together they went into a corner of the room, where the priest began to speak hesitantly and with humble uncertainty. "Francisco, forgive me, but I have done the best I know for him. There is only one thing else I know to do—and I don't want to unless Doctor Vaiz is here."

"What is that?" Francisco asked after a moment.

"It gets no better, only worse," the priest said, as if hating to speak. "You see that something must be done. There is only one thing to do. We can't let him die. You see that. Better no arm at all than to die." He placed his hand on Francisco's arm as he saw the man stiffen. "I am sorry, Francisco, but we can't let him die."

"Petra!" Everyone turned quickly toward the bed. Angelo was half sitting up, his face agonized. "Petra, don't let them take my arm!" Petra could stop them. His father would do anything Petra asked, because he was in love with Petra.

Two dogs in the patio began to fight. Angelo's body jerked convulsively, and he began to cry for the first time. This unleashing mounted instantly into hysteria, and he screamed with pain, not even knowing that he did so.

When at last he appeared to sink into sleep or unconsciousness, the priest rose from bending over him. The dogs had stopped fighting outside and the room was silent except for the labored breathing of the three people who had witnessed the convulsion.

"Francisco," the priest said wiping his face, "someone will have to ride for Doctor Vaiz. I . . . don't know what to do." There was fear in his voice.

Without a word Francisco went out the door and closed it behind him.

"Don Francisco, what's wrong?" It was Teodoro. He had been just outside the door with the other members of the family who had gathered on hearing the agonized cries.

Francisco's hand closed over the young man's arm and he gripped it. "Angelo is very sick," he said. "Father Patricio said to get Doctor Vaiz. He may be in Monterey."

"I'll go." The words came from Teodoro, Xavier, Enrique and Guillermo. The realization hit them all that if Father Patricio couldn't cope with the illness, it was serious indeed.

"He may not be in Monterey," Francisco said controlling his voice. "It is best that several go. Teodoro, you ride to Monterey. Padilla, you ride out toward Estrella Grande. Xavier, you ride south. Guillermo, cut over to the harbor and see if one of the ships carries a surgeon. If not, get the British captain or his mate."

"I'll stop at Las Palomas long enough to send my mother back," Teodoro called clattering down the stairs.

There was little need for words as the four mounted their horses. They said quick good-bys and each started off at full gallop. They were superb horsemen. They could ride for hours and never feel the ache of a muscle. When the horses became tired they could dismount and take others—it didn't matter whose. Horses were cheap and plentiful. Nobody cared. The harder and faster one rode the less time one had to think of the sick boy back at Dos Ríos. There was time only to catch and saddle a fresh mount, time to moan a curse at fingers finally made clumsy by fatigue, time to mutter a prayer. O merciful Mother of God, not Francisco's only son!

The pain rose in Angelo. It rose from the arm in red shadows on his flesh, up over his shoulder, onto his chest and back, up into his head. He lived in fragments and snatches. Petra and Father Patricio were there to cling to with the desperate twisting fingers of his good hand. At times he could feel, insanely, pain in the fingers of his good hand. At times he could feel, insanely, pain in the fingers of the hand where none existed. Brandy ceased to ease him. Drugs were brought from the small supply at the mission, fragments of rest.

Doctor Viaz came, stamped about the room, cursing savagely and beautifully. Angelo knew he must fight them all, continually and without end he must fight them. They must not take his arm. Frantically, distractedly he battled with them. But against Francisco he was helpless as always. With one hand his father could take his slender arms and bend them back over his head and replace the steaming compress. He could only sob and scream into his father's face, which was like the face of a graven image.

Sound came to him in waves, with blank intervals between. He did not know that Guillermo, weeping, whip in hand, kept the dogs from the patio. He did not hear Francisco's strained: "All right, Vaiz. Do it now!" He didn't hear Petra, suddenly savage: *"Give him something for the pain!"* Dimly, after a long while, he only knew that his arm was gone. And even now they did not know if the mounting poison had been stopped. It sickened him and shamed him to the depths of his soul. What was he now? He who had been inferior when his body was whole and beautiful—what was he now that it was no longer so?

Gradually the sickness and shame diminished and he was only tired, with fatigue so deep that he could scarcely open his eyes to look at them.

He must see them. He was so sorry for them all. They had all worked so hard and so long for him. He couldn't look at them enough. Petra, oh, lovely golden Petra. Father, godlike splendid Francisco. Guillermo, Teodoro, Father Patricio, Doctor Vaiz—he loved them all unbearably.

This is going to kill me, he thought, I'm going to die of this. He ached with a terrible longing to live, live a long time, live forever! His yearning swelled and rose and grew until it seemed to fill the room with the shimmering radiance of sunlight through tears. But he couldn't. His body was such a shoddy, poorly made thing. It couldn't be made to live forever. Or even a long time. *Or any time at all.*

"Petra, I'm falling!"

It cut through Petra's dream and she was instantly on her feet. "Help him!"

Vaiz lurched from the couch, crashing against the bedpost. *"Angelo!"*

Francisco stood as one turned to stone, gazing at his son, refusing the knowledge, disbelieving it, rejecting it. Dumbly he caught Petra as she sagged, fainting, against him. Dumbly he watched the doctor sink to his knees beside the bed in exhaustion and defeat. A wave of crashing shock smote him, and he who could throw a bullock or bring a grizzly to its knees found the weight of a fainting girl nearly insupportable as he bore it to the couch. He knew only this: Angelito was gone.

Chapter 8

There was no weeping left in her. She was hot, tired and miserable. The black stiffness of her dress had long since been reduced to rumpled untidiness. She had wakened in the sultry afternoon dimness of her room and gone through the same old dying that she always felt when she wakened. She wondered in slow torpid anger how long it would be before she could wake and know he was gone without feeling this dull desolation. Stiffly she sat up.

They were going now. All day the sound of horses and the endless cry of *carretas* had smitten her ears. All the people who had come to Dos Ríos in time of trouble were going home. Angelo was dead and buried, sleeping in the Estrada hillside with the little sisters who had never known waking. The weeping had almost stopped. The loud lamenting was ended. The mourning for Angelo was quiet now. It was only in the intolerable fullness of her throat and the softness of Guillermo's struggling sobs. She looked at him somberly. He was all Indian, squatting in the corner of the room, stricken and bereaved of his friend, his brother and his lord.

She thought, watching him, that the Indians had felt the loss more keenly than the Spaniards. After he died, they came from the farthest rancheria on Dos Ríos land to wail aloud and lament his going. They entered her room with exquisite hand-woven baskets and scattered it with piñon nuts as a token of loyalty to her who had been his wife. Their grief was savage and childish and to ease it they cried aloud and spoke to her in languages she could not understand. But she could understand that they mourned him and missed him. He had been such a beautiful white boy. He had had so much laughter. He had been good to them all. If a hand was slow in serving him, he did not care. If one was slow in coming at his call, he did not notice. His hand had never held a whip. They had heard him sing and watched him dance, and the sight of him had been a pleasant sight.

Her fair hair streamed carelessly about her drawn face. She had forgotten to wash, and her faltering hands were grimy. She looked at them with dim consternation. Angelo would have hated that. He was so neat. Francisco came to the door and was sent away. She faced him disheveled and unclean, not thinking about it. She was rude to him and it did not occur to her that she was.

Francisco closed himself in his office and stayed for hours. Only Ysidra ventured in. Sometimes he failed to notice her. Once he saw her and said, "I'm being weak."

"Grief is not weak," she told him and resumed her silence.

Ysidra, too, missed Angelo. The black eyes which had shed so few tears in her life filled and filled again whenever she thought of him. She felt defeated, confusedly enraged as if something valuable had been wasted. She had rocked her great body back and forth in unbelieving anguish the night he died. He had been important to her in ways she had not known. All the days of his life, from his birth to his death, she had seen him, lived with him, been annoyed by him, amused by him. She had pawned her wedding ring so that he might eat. She had nursed him through sickness. She had shaken him in exasperation. She had admonished him, given him advice and laughed at his jokes. She thought, sitting in her big chair and looking at his father, that someday the time would come when she would look up quickly to meet Angelo's eyes to share some secret amusement, and he would no longer be there. That would be a dreadful instant. There were so many things she had wanted to say to him which must now remain unsaid. She wished to cry again, but crying was difficult for her, and she remained motionless in her chair.

There was nothing to take up the time of bereaved people, because everything was done for them by their friends. Doña Dolores Acuña, the kind and competent mistress of Rancho Las Palomas, now took charge of Dos Ríos. Even as she wiped her eyes, she directed the servants and other women who had come, seeing that the house was kept in order, seeing that even in time of grief the hospitality of Dos Ríos might lack in nothing. People were coming from the farthest part of the land to be with Francisco and extend what help he might have need of. When the house was overflowing, still they continued to come. The candles of wax which burned high about Angelo's still form never ceased to flicker for the continued motion of silent people who came to kneel and pray for his soul as it struggled through purgatory.

It was Catalina who assisted Petra. Her own eyes were red from weeping. She could pity Petra when she was crushed and dazed and silently did as she was told like one in a dream. Very gently

Catalina took a wet cloth and bathed the other's shadowed face. Carefully she washed the hands which had always been so busy. She arranged the fair hair gently, pausing only to wipe her eyes from time to time. There was nothing bold or beautiful in Petra now. She was lifeless and desolate, and Catalina could pity her. If she had never liked her before and would never like her again, she could pity her at this moment. There was nothing to say and the only time they spoke was when Catalina told Guillermo to leave. The Indian was hunched in a corner weeping over some fragment of Angelo's.

"Go out, Guillermo," she ordered softly. "Your weeping must annoy Doña Petra."

"Let him stay, Catalina," Petra said listlessly. "It doesn't annoy me." And Guillermo was allowed to stay, moaning his soft lament and letting the tears roll unchecked down his dark face. After all whose loss was greater? Guillermo had known him better than anyone else perhaps. If anyone should weep for Angelito, it was he.

The people came, kind and subdued, eager to help a little. The activity was restrained, but things were accomplished, useful things and unnecessary things. They were there in case they were needed. In a burst of bewildered anger Teodoro broke up a dogfight in the patio and sent the animals scurrying for cover. Xavier worked with absorption, polishing Angelo's almost new saddle that didn't need polishing.

"The fault is mine, Ysidra," Francisco said somberly.

"Please, do not torment yourself, *querido.*" She stirred, moving her fan as if by a faint thrusting motion she could reject his voice.

He had always been going to know Angelo better. Sometime later when there was more opportunity, there was much he was going to say to Angelo, much he had to ask him. It had never occurred to him that someday the chance would slip away and Angelo would be gone. If only he hadn't always been so busy! No wonder the boy kept close to himself. No wonder they had failed to understand each other. Who had brought him up? Who had reared him? Not he. Not Ysidra. They had merely enjoyed him or were irritated with him. Guillermo had reared him, if in any sense he had been brought up at all. Perhaps Father Patricio had lent a constructive hand. What could he expect then? He had had little time to be with Angelo while he was young. He had been poor and he would never be poor again. It took time and effort to forestall poverty, to gather wealth. There had been too little time.

"Father, look, what do you think . . ."

"I'm busy now, Angelito, run along and play. . . ."

"Father, would it be all right if . . ."

"No. Well, all right if Guillermo goes with you. . . ."

And from this haphazard childhood he had expected—what? He had expected Angelo to emerge into a manhood similar to his own. How could he have expected it when he had given little time or thought to bringing him up? What was Guillermo? A savage. What was Father Patricio? A priest. Everything in the boy's mind had been put there by a savage or a priest.

The old man sat against the adobe and little by little it seeped into his consciousness that the young don was dead. He weaved his head from side to side on his withered neck, and a thin wail, ancient as time, rose and was lost in the shimmering air. *Ay-ee-e-ah.* The little boy . . . the little boy was gone.

Chapter 9

It was incredibly hot for October. Father Patricio's rough habit clung to his sweat-covered body like wet bark. The perspiration ran in little rivulets down his back and legs. He raised his arms and moved them, letting the loose sleeves fall back, hoping the motion would create a breeze about his arms. There was no breeze. His damp arms were bathed in air like warm milk. He went about his duties with conscious effort and even the simplest task took on the aspect of labor. Would the morning never pass? He was awkward and clumsy and the heavy cloth of his gown clung exasperatingly to his limbs and hampered his walking.

The molten minutes passed, and he gazed at the brassy sky for some time before he realized that it would be only another hour until high noon. It was time for the midday meal. He glanced from beneath the arch where he stood to the pot of bubbling *atole* in the center of the patio. He shook his head. How could anyone eat such hot food on a day like this? But the Indians would be hungry, for they had worked all morning. It was time to ring the bell which called them all from the fields and shops, but he paused another second, staring through the waves of shimmering heat. Was that speck a horseman coming from the direction of

Dos Ríos? He hesitated an instant longer and realized that it was nothing. Sighing a little, he went to ring the bells.

They came slowly because of the oppressive, heavy air. Listlessly they held out their plates for helpings of inevitable barley gruel, vegetables and meat which made up the noonday meal. They ate slowly and there was little laughter or joking among them, for their energy was sapped by the thick, hot air and the morning spent in labor. Some had been too disinterested to secure a proper plate or bowl and so used a curved piece of bark with the dust still clinging to it. They ate stolidly, without gusto, putting the food into their mouths from force of long habit and swallowing it without pleasure.

The thought of barley and fat meat was repellent to Father Patricio and he went slowly to the fig tree and took two black-purple pieces of fruit. They were warm and soft and split open with ripeness as he carried them back to the long building. Listlessly he entered the library, sliding his feet out of his sandals and walking barefoot on the hard earthen floor. He seated himself at the rude table, pushed aside a stack of sermons and began to eat. The centers of the fruit were sweet and sticky with richness, but it seemed joyless eating. When he had finished he would go into his cell and rest. The thought of his rawhide bed, stretched a few inches off the ground on pegs, was not particularly appealing, but he must rest. He must husband his strength in case the long-awaited, long-expected horseman from Dos Ríos came into view in his little cloud of dust.

Despite the competence of the midwife at Dos Ríos he had always managed to be there for the births of Doña Ana's babies. His friendship with Francisco was of long standing, and he had never failed to come when Francisco had need of him, although he had been told many times that his first duty was to the Indians and not to the wealthy rancheros.

Seven times in past years the horseman had come and seven times Father Patricio had taken his small store of instruments to the house of Francisco, either to assist Doctor Vaiz or see it through alone if Vaiz could not be found. And seven times there had been fiesta because the child of Francisco and Ana had gone to God its Father with no sin on its soul. Seven pallid infants he had christened Mary-of-Jesus, and seven times he had scarcely finished before another lay dead in his hands.

So now Doña Ana had carried her child its full term. It would have fingernails and perhaps hair as black as Francisco's. It must be whole, complete and living. His novena to Mary in its behalf was finished. It must be living and healthy, for it would be Francisco's last and only child.

And Angelito . . .

Father Patricio felt a deep yearning to hold out his hand and help Angelito wherever he was. But his sins were not many. He would not remain long in purgatory. Patricio sank quickly to his knees with a sudden feeling of urgency and began to pray. His prayers were not for the new baby. These were for Angelo, who might have need of them now, at this moment.

When the prayers were finished he rose and went toward the door, bracing himself for an imperceptible instant before stepping into the brazen glare. It smote him with a physical sensation. It stopped the breath in his lungs and stabbed at his eyes as he squinted into the distance toward the broad lands and rolling hills of Dos Ríos. Nothing. No speck. No form. The sky came down to meet the parched earth like a bright-blue bowl turned upside down.

By half past three his gown clung to him with not one dry thread. The buildings wavered. The trees drooped breathless and still. The Indians in the far field glistened in the sun. Patricio's head ached. He made his way into the long building again. He took the keys to the cellars and went down. Not thinking to ask assistance, he prepared several large earthen jars of sweetened vinegar and water. He carried them up, one by one, and strapped them to the sides of a donkey. His tongue in his mouth ached in thrist and longing for the tart, sweet refreshment. He slapped the dusty animal on its rump and it started obediently toward the fields. The liquid sloshed in the containers, dribbling over the side. The priest laid his hand on one and let a cold drop ease his skin. On raising it to his mouth he found it salt with sweat.

He argued with himself: Indulgence or not, the Indians could not work in such heat as this without some refreshment. They met him with tired cries of gratitude as they saw him approach with the laden burro. Gourds were found quickly, and those who had nothing from which to drink waited in childish impatience for others to finish, reaching out to feel the coolness of the jars, one or two bending to lay a scorched cheek against the dampness. This was good. Father Patricio thought of them in the heat and brought them this sweet cool drink. They outdid themselves promising payment for his kindness. One would give him a chicken from the flock raised about his hut. One would give him half the berries he got next time he went picking. One vowed he would no longer hang about the nunnery at night to annoy the women. Life was not nearly so hard as it had been a moment ago. They could lean against the burro, waste a few slow hot minutes talking to their priest, drink of the delicate, pungent liquid he brought them. And in a little more than one hour the day's work would be finished.

"Take a little, Father," said one offering the gourd to the priest. Patricio raised the last few drops to his lips. Before it touched his tongue he could feel it down to the base of his throat. He sipped it slowly, letting it run beneath his tongue and about his teeth, savoring it, making it last.

With one hand he raised his cowl and pulled it far down over his eyes. One by one the Indians dispersed and resumed work. He fell back into his habit of gazing into the distance for the long awaited messenger. The air moved before his smarting eyes. The smell of the wheat field was about him. The sounds of the Indian workers were in his cowl-shrouded ears. The roughness of the burro's coat was beneath his fingers. He stared at the horseman a long time before he actually saw him. Then the bells began to ring as they always did when someone approached the mission.

The house which had rung with the screams of Angelo's pain now rang with Ana's. Hers began as a whine of anticipated agony when the swing of pain started. It rose in intensity until it was a howl, then an inhuman animal shriek, maddening and shattering. The shriek lasted until after the pain had subsided, when it faltered, lessened and sank to a wail, a moan and a sob. Then there would be a small interim of peace before the upswing of the next pain.

Petra lay huddled in the next room on the bed which had been hers and Angelo's and tried to shut her ears against the sound. How long would it last? How much longer? How could bearing a child be such a foul unlovely thing? She braced herself for the next cry. *Couldn't they stop her mouth!* Hysterically Petra sprang up from the bed, catching the bedpost for support. So it was receding now. Was this the last one? Was the baby coming now? Was it over? One more and she would lose her mind. A feeling of insurmountable panic filled her. The room seemed to close about her. She must be free of it.

In frantic haste she stumbled toward the door, bumping into furniture, staggering like a drunk person. So she had run in her dreams, as one would run through heavy clinging water, never gaining proper balance. Outside! To get outside, away from the closeness, the blackness and the noise!

At last she reached the door and rushed out into the hallway, down the stairs, out the front door, her black skirts trailing behind her like a witch's garment. Recklessly she slammed the door behind her and tore across the patio, out through the garden, up the slope. She could see little in the darkness but continued to run. The ground became uneven. Great fingers reached out of the earth and lay coiled on the surface to snatch at her trailing skirts. She knew by this that she had reached the pepper trees. One of the heavy, upthrust roots caught at her skirt and she stopped, panting. Groping in the darkness, she found its shaggy surface. She sat on it, leaned against the bulbous trunk and rested.

There was no sound here. No woman lay screaming in childbed. No scuffling feet. No murmuring prayers. Nothing but darkness and a measure of peace. No one could see her, for she was clothed in black. There was only the pale blur of her hair and face to testify that she was any different from the darkness that surrounded her. In a moment, when she had rested a little, she would lift her skirt and cover her head, and so be invisibly folded into the darkness.

* * *

Ana's appearance had altered considerably since her labor had begun. Her flesh seemed to have fallen away, leaving her uncushioned stick-like body to writhe without protection on the hot sheets. She looked like some pallid tortured witch. Her eyes had red puffs of strain beneath them, and her face bore three long weals made by her own frantic fingers which had drawn her nails through her skin. Her hair hung sparsely, trailing in wet disordered wisps. Some lay across her lips which were flecked with blood where she had bitten them. By the time the baby was born Doctor Vaiz had not been found or, if he had, was still on the road to Dos Ríos.

Francisco turned from the scene and went to the window. He leaned out, but there was no coolness in the breathless night. He waited for the first disappointment, holding his jaws rigid. There was only the sound of Ana's hoarse breathing to show she still lived. Francisco pressed with all his weight on the wide sill and tried to shut his mind against that sound and the tense words which came to him from the others.

"Steady the head."

"The navel is bleeding."

"Hand me those. No, señora, the small ones."

He knew it was born now.

"Francisco, my son, it is a girl." The priest spoke tiredly.

Francisco turned his hard face from the window and caught a glimpse of his newly born child as the midwife handed it to the woman who prepared to wash it. Then she turned her attention to the woman on the bed and began to work over her. Great drops of rank yellow sweat rolled off her face and fell on Ana unnoticed.

At last the infant, pallid and shining with oil, was wrapped in a white cloth and placed in the eager hands of the priest.

"The name, Francisco?" he prompted gently.

"The same as before," Francisco replied without emotion.

Ysidra came forward quickly to stand as godmother, and Enrique Padilla was summoned from the hallway to be godfather. There was no time for a proper christening. Father Patricio spoke swiftly, slurring the words in despairing haste. His fingers fumbled in the vessel of holy water. Francisco realized the cause of his hurrying and his face was grim.

The words stopped. The child was christened. The harsh breathing of the mother on the bed became less spasmodic. The midwife dropped some blood-soaked rags on the floor and squatted beside the bed in weariness. She passed her hand over her face to wipe the sweat from her eyes and left a red smear across her dark brow. The silence became heavier and more oppressive. Reluctantly Father Patricio laid the still baby into the basket prepared for it and went with halting steps to Francisco.

He placed his hand in hesitant tenderness on Francisco's arm. "It is dead, my son," he said humbly.

Francisco turned blank and bitter eyes to the priest. "I know," he said. Then his eyes came alive and behind the bitterness there burned a deep and consuming rage. Turning, he went from the room in stonelike silence.

The priest sat down on the wide window ledge. Then, Mary, most gracious Mother of God, he is childless. From his deep fatigue Patricio knew he must pray for Francisco who must surely have need of it in his black and blasphemous rage. From pattern of long habit he knelt and closed his eyes.

* * *

Francisco rode through the darkness until his animal was spent. He did not leave his own land or go very far from his house, but circled about a few miles this way and that way across the broad fields and through the dark timber. When at last his horse could go no farther he dismounted and led the stumbling animal. Mechanically as they neared the house he unsaddled it and let it go. Carrying the heavy saddle and trappings, he turned instinctively toward the house. The darkness was almost a solid curtain before him except for the pinprick of light which was his window. Ysidra was waiting up for him. There was a fragment of satisfaction in this. There would be no dissembling before his aunt, no condolences to be got through. They knew each other too well.

Petra, shrouded in the dark drooping leaves of the pepper trees heard the approach of strange steps without terror. She was a little sorry she hadn't covered her head as she had planned. She knew disinterestedly that whoever was coming was a man and not an animal because she heard the faint clink of spurs. The man halted a short distance from her, and there was the muffled crash of a saddle hitting the ground. He had seen her in spite of the darkness, she thought in mild wonder.

"Are you ill, Petra?" So it was Francisco.

"No," she answered.

"What are you doing out here alone?" he asked after a moment.

"Nothing. It was hot and noisy in the house." She knew she should ask about the baby and Ana, but for a moment could not summon the necessary energy. The air was cooler now and she had been nearly peaceful for a while.

"You take little care of yourself, Petra," he said, not unkindly. "You should not be out alone.

It was only by chance that I saw you. Instead of my finding you, any number of things could have happened. For instance, think of the bears. Or my *vaqueros*, some of whom are only a step above savagery. This was a foolish thing for you to do."

"I'm sorry, sir." The apology came automatically and meant nothing. She sat up slowly. The peace was finished and the Estrada family were crowding in upon her again. She sorted about in her mind for the correct form. Oh, yes, Ana.

"How is Doña Ana?"

"Ana is all right."

"And the baby—has it come?"

"Yes. The baby is dead."

So it had died. All of that had been for nothing after all. Petra sighed, knowing she should say something else to him. How did one go about comforting Francisco?

"I'm very sorry," she said stiffly. Again the words came automatically and meant nothing.

"We will not speak of it," Francisco answered. "There is nothing to say."

Petra moved across the ground, her skirts rustling dryly, and leaned against the bark of a bulbous trunk. She raised her hand in the darkness and picked out the pepper berries which had embedded themselves into her palm.

"I am sorry," she said again suddenly, scarcely realizing she uttered the words.

He reached out and took her small hand. "I must suggest we return to the house now," he said courteously.

"Yes, of course." She thought dimly of the strength of him. He had said so calmly, "We will not speak of it."

"But everything is gone," she said dully, almost to herself. "Everything is lost." He released her hand and instantly it seemed the darkness closed about her and she stood completely alone in a black void. Where was her life? Where were her people, her friends, her family? Mother and father, both gone. Her aunts, remote in far away Spain. Angelo . . .

"Where are you!" she cried in swift anguish, groping for Francisco. *"Help me!"*

Instantly he reached out and caught her to him, filling the endless black void, diminishing the sudden panic. She clung to him, unable to cry for the force of her emotion. She gripped him as she might grip a rock on a cliffside if she had fallen, as she might grip the mast of a foundering vessel in high seas.

"I will die," she wailed from the depths of her desolation, "I will die."

"No, little one," he said gently, "people don't die of this." He held her tighter, as if to strengthen her with the very force of his embrace. She sagged limply in his arms, knowing he would hold her up, knowing she could depend on his strength when hers failed her. He was all she had left. She thought this dimly, a little eased. He was her family and her people because he was Angelo's father, and she had belonged to Angelo.

The darkness was thinning a little. Lights still wavered in the house which lay like a sprawling giant. Together they walked toward it after a time, and Petra, forgetful of the heavy saddle he carried, leaned on his arm for support. When they reached the house, he let the saddle fall to the ground again and opened the door for her. Wordlessly she went in and mounted the stairs. Beneath the surface of her grief was a new sense of hard bleak security.

Ysidra heard them come in and realized again that now he had nothing. It was like another blow on long bruised flesh and hurt the more. She winced a little and leaned back, closing her eyes.

Nothing now. The thought came again. She clasped her small hands over her ponderous belly and swayed like a worried peasant. Such a pity that Ana had not died instead of the child! Or even that she had not died with the child! Then at least he could have taken another wife. But no, Ana had lain like a bundle of sticks in her bed and made herself live through it. A tired sort of anger mounted in Ysidra. Why indulge in regret? There was no point in brooding about it.

There was, of course, the thin hope that Ana would yet die. She was still very sick. A prickle of excitement ran over Ysidra. Her eyes opened and she looked blankly at the candle. Did one pray for such a thing or did one only wish it? While she waited for Francisco, she stared at the candle, turning the idea over in her mind.

The door opened and he came silently in. "Ysidra, beloved," he said when he saw her awake, "you should have been in bed hours ago."

She shook her head slightly. "I was not tired."

He fell heavily into a chair and neither spoke for some time.

"Well?" he asked.

Ysidra shook her head. There was nothing she could say to him. Every way was so complicated and each path strewn with obstacles. The road to divorce was such a long and complex one. None of Ana's children would live, but Ana would. Ana would live on and on. But for Ana the house of Estrada would not end. But for Ana there would be children. But for Ana Francisco could take another wife. There was always too much to cope with, too much to solve. There was Petra, pale and thin from grieving. Angelito was gone. There was a small swift pain in thinking of him. Then she became cold and thought without emotion for a moment. He was gone. The dead had no hold on the living. But for Ana Francisco could have Petra.

She glanced up and Francisco's eyes were on her. They looked at each other, not needing to speak. The sun was rising and the room was filled with a dim glow that made the candle pale and sickly.

"We should get a little rest, should we not?" She rose ponderously. The light was spreading to the corners of the room and the candle flame was almost invisible. "Do not worry, my dear," she murmured. "This is not the end of everything." She reached over and with a quick, dark motion pinched out the flame.

It wasn't so hot the next day, but Ana was uncomfortable and had to be fanned constantly. She lay white and spent in her now immaculate bed. A servant, a member of the family or a friend sat beside her bed at all times waving the palm leaf which had been brought from the mission. It created a larger breeze than the small fan used by the ladies.

The baby lay covered with a blanket on a table in the main *sala*. Four candles flanked its head and feet. It looked, when one lifted the blanket, like an extremely small waxen doll. There gleamed below its lashless eyelids, which didn't quite close, a film of something which might have been tears. It was not an ugly baby as the others had been. On its head was a dim shadow which might have been hair as dark as Francisco's. As the people came one by one, two by two, and dozen by dozen, to look at the still infant, any tears shed were for Francisco and not for the baby, sinless and pure, whose place in heaven was assured. As they passed, they could smile and comment on the happy fate of Mary-of-Jesus who lay all unknowing before their gaze.

The news could not be kept from Ana for long. She had counted on this baby more than she realized. In her fragmentary wakings she wanted it brought to her.

"Rest now, my dear. Do not trouble yourself. You are tired."

These were excuses which she met with ill-humor and increasing alarm. "I want my baby," she said time after time.

Later, not knowing any time had passed, she would take up her insistent whine again. "Bring my daughter. I must see María-de-Jesús."

It seemed to her that there were different excuses each time. Different people from the mist around her. All in accord to keep her child from her. They would not bring the baby. They had hidden the little daughter. Finally she thought that if she could find Francisco he would tell her why the baby was kept from her. After a long time and many small sleepings and wakings he was there, vague and shadowy, at the foot of the bed.

He stood looking at her. She was thin and still. Her hair had been brushed back from her skull and she appeared as pale and fragile as ashes. Those who watched marveled that life remained at all.

After a time she thought out and formed the tormenting question: "Where is María-de-Jesús?"

Francisco answered unhesitatingly, "She is in the *sala*."

So her baby girl was in the *sala*. Truly that was a strange place for a newly born infant. It might be there being shown to friends, or it might be laid out with candles at its head and feet. Francisco would not lie to her. He did not care enough for her to shield her from pain. At least she could get the truth. From this she took some small dry comfort, but she felt regret that the baby should be in such a large and echoing room. Was there not some small room, a little and cozy place, that would be better for a tiny baby.

Carefully she formed her next query. "How is my baby?" In the dimness she saw that Francisco had stretched out both arms and clasped one hand on each of the bedposts. He looked not unlike a great veiled crucifix.

"Ana, the baby is dead," he said gently but without emotion.

"Ah-h." It was a long half-utterance, half-sigh. So the dear, longed-for, little daughter was not to be. And there would never be another. Never in all her life would she bear another. This was proof enough, even if the others had not been, that it was not God's will she should have a living child. There was a dry longing in her, which surely must be sacrilegious, to have a child of her own. So then there must be a reason for it.

Francisco.

She opened her eyes. He still stood in the wavering dimness at the foot of the bed. It was indeed God's will. He was childless. His line was ended. How bitter this must be in his mouth who thought so much of lines and children! Well, then, let him learn that God's will was the law!

And perhaps—such a sweet bitter thought—perhaps it was better for the baby that this was so. It was gone. Safe. There would be no pain for it, none of the small consecutive agonies which make up a human life, nothing for Mary-of-Jesus but eternal bliss.

When she woke again the two candles on the bureau had burned down a bit and her vision was much clearer. Francisco was gone and Ysidra sat at the bedside. She wondered if they would bring the baby now. No, the baby had died. She felt a small twinge of sorrow, but there was little feeling of any kind in her. She regarded Ysidra without emotion. Even the old hate lay dormant with her. Moving slightly, she could see the window. If they shot off the rockets tonight for Mary-of-Jesus she wanted to see them. It was comforting to think that another of her daughters should cause the sky to be lighted by many flashes of brilliance. Her eyes turned once more to Ysidra who sat stolid and immovable as a heathen statue. And suddenly, for no seeming volition, the term *instrument of God* popped into her mind. She pondered it for some time, wondering why she had thought of it. How could one serve God when one was surely going to die?

But then, suppose one did not die? She groped on, puzzling at this new train of thought. Well, then, one lived. How did one serve God, then? The term altered. *Instrument of God* became strangely *instrument of punishment*. Ah, punishment! She could understand the word *punishment*. She had punished Angelo as a little boy. She had punished him by telling him of Francisco's covetousness of Petra. She had punished Francisco too, in all the countless ways a woman can punish a man who is her husband. Yes, punishment she could understand. Was it possible that these people had not finished their just punishment? Angelo was gone, of course. But Francisco remained. And Ysidra, wicked, wicked woman! It was possible that she was meant to live and vex them further.

It was not Ana who inflicted the punishment really. It was merely that God used her as His holy instrument of chastisement. How fitting this was, how beautifully simple! She folded her pale hands in the old gesture across her middle. She would live or Francisco would take another wife. He could not. He must remain bound and helpless in the holy bonds of marriage, like a great moth tangled in the fragile film of a spider's web. He would continue childless, each sprout of his house cut off.

She, Ana the despised, Ana the ridiculous, Ana the ineffectual, Ana the unloved, would lie in her invalid's bed all the long years and watch them. Her face set in lines of purpose, and she closed her eyes contentedly. Now she would rest and save her meager strength for her new life of service.

I will wait, thought Ysidra for the dozenth time. She will surely die. She cannot last. There is nothing to her. Indeed it seemed as if there were nothing. Little more than skin and bones and perhaps the evil which kept the lot alive. There was only the intermittent breathing to show that life remained.

What was she thinking? What lay behind the forehead that protruded against the skin in bony prominence? What passed in the mind held in the skull that showed so plainly? And now the natural old gesture of folding the hands. The visible relaxation of sleep. Healthful, healing sleep? Oh no, surely not. Ysidra found herself counting the seconds between the breaths of the sick woman. Such a long time in between. She would wait and wait, thinking life had ceased, only to have Ana draw in another breath and release it with a sigh. Time after time she almost rose from her chair to peer into the other's face. Now! *Now* for sure. But no. Ysidra leaned back in her chair. It was possible, of course, that Ana would live on and on, outlive them all, live to laugh at their dust.

It was midnight before Ana woke again. She appeared much refreshed and seemed faintly surprised to see Ysidra still there.

"Still here, Ysidra? How kind!" There was the familiar sarcastic overtone in her voice.

"How do you feel?" Ysidra asked, falling into the old safe pattern.

"Much better, much refreshed," Ana replied.

"That is good," Ysidra said woodenly.

"It is a judgment." Ana pronounced with enjoyment. "It is a judgment of God."

"What is a judgment of God?" Ysidra asked dully.

"This," Ana said; "all this that has happened. Angelo dying." She smiled faintly as she saw Ysidra wince. "Then the baby dying. I shall never have another. Francisco will never have another child. That is finished."

"You won't always be sick," Ysidra said emptily, staring at the heavy coverlet heaped at the foot of the bed. Of what use was this pointless discussion? Why didn't she stop it? Why didn't she summon a servant to stay with Ana?

"I shall always be sick," Ana said complacently.

Ysidra looked at the other woman. Evil, pale skeleton of a woman, stopping everything, thwarting everything. What of the family? What of Dos Ríos? What of Francisco? She saw distractedly that Ana had tired herself with talking. Her breath came shorter and shorter. Ysidra moved to the foot of the bed and leaned her weight against the post, her hand hanging limply and brushing the heavy thick coverlet. Ana breathed on. There was no escape from the pale woman who held them all in the palm of her emaciated hand.

"No, Ana." Ysidra spoke more to herself than to Ana.

Ana's lids raised and she gazed wide-eyed at Ysidra. "I will," she said childishly. "I will."

A quiver passed through Ysidra's great body. Her fingers caressed the heavy coverlet. Such a fragile life. Such unsteady intermittent breathing.

A second and a second longer between one breath and the next would be a matter of life or death.

"I waited," Ysidra whispered, scarcely uttering the sound. Her small hand, without seeming effort, lifted the thick comforter and drew it up. She went softly, almost floated, to the head of the bed. There she appeared for an instant to hover over Ana like a great dark bird.

As she bent, Ana's vision cleared sharply. She could not see Ysidra's eyes, only the blind roundness of her cheeks. She knew a moment of utter and complete terror as the strange plumage of the bird descended.

Chapter 10

Ysidra came slowly and ponderously, as was her way, out into the hall. Peering down it in the dim light of her candle, she saw Ana's attendant, Damacia, dozing on a chest.

"Come here," Ysidra muttered, and with a slight but imperious gesture she beckoned the girl from her resting place. Damacia was young. She rose quickly and came.

"Sit here," commanded Ysidra, indicating the floor before Ana's doorway. "I will leave the door ajar and if the Doña Ana wants anything she will call you. I am going to bed."

"Doña Ana sleeps?" the Indian asked, obediently squatting down on the floor.

"She sleeps," Ysidra answered without emotion, and turned to go to her own room. She must be up early in the morning so she might be the one to tell Francisco. Softly she closed her own door and mechanically began to strip off her rings and pins, not pausing to take pleasure in the jewels. God, how she needed sleep! Her very bones were weak from fatigue. Weakness spread through her great flesh and she had barely the energy required to pull off her clothing and fall heavily onto the bed before sleep overtook her. As it closed on her, she chuckled a little grimly. Yet a little rest for the old woman whose soul was no longer her own.

She slept and dreamed she was a puppet attached to invisible strings. She admonished herself a thousand times over that she must weep for Ana at her funeral. Everyone was weeping for Ana but one balloon woman who was Ysidra. No matter how she tried, the strings jerked up the corners of her mouth and she smiled.

Ysidra woke from her sleep unrefreshed. Her room was pale with the first thin sunlight of the day. She wondered if others were awake yet, and the question was answered for her as she heard Enrique's voice raised in song, to be joined almost immediately by Xavier. She thought for several seconds before she could force herself to struggle laboriously out of bed. They were just now waking, cleansed and made whole by good deep sleep. A little groan escaped her as she slid her great knotted legs over the side of the bed and stood on them experimentally, holding to the post for balance. There was a prickling sensation in her thighs as the sluggish circulation was stimulated. With a strong effort she walked across the bare floor and stood before her mirror. Holy Mother, was it possible that she was so ugly? Her great rounded shoulders lifted in the old shrug which now sent an aching twinge through her body. She was getting old—very old, old and sick. Where was the buoyancy of her youth? Where was the vivid vibrant Ysidra of her young days? Here she was, right here before the mirror. She had only changed. She was covered now with great pads of flesh and all the quick rushing veins must be stopped with fat.

Then the little tasks began to loom. Hair must be brushed and coiled. Combs must be set in on an aching head. One must wash and put on clothes. She grimaced at the thought of the effort she must make to do these necessary things—and soon!—if she was to talk to Francisco first. Relentless of her weary flesh, she began to dress.

When at last she was dressed and presentable, she looked apprehensively at the clock and saw that it had taken her nearly twice the time it usually did. In troubled haste she went out into the hall. Petra was just coming out of her room and she composed her face instantly. "Good morning, Petra. Did you sleep well?"

"Yes, Aunt Ysidra, did you?" Petra answered listlessly.

"Very well," Ysidra returned, noting that Petra was wan and lifeless. It was probable she hadn't slept at all, or very little. Why did people utter such meaningless phrases. Why must they always speak out in set designs? "Do you know if any of the women have gone down yet?"

"None of the women have. Francisco went down early."

Ysidra fell into step beside Petra as they walked toward the head of the stairs.

"Did he wake before Enrique?" Ysidra asked in vague surprise.

"Yes, sometime before. I heard him go down."

"You go on down, Petra. I must stop off and see how Ana is," Ysidra said, pausing by the door. The Indian girl was still there, trying to look as if she were not just waking up.

"She did not call me. She wanted nothing," Damacia offered quickly.

"Not that you would have heard her in any case," Ysidra said testily. "I trust nothing disturbed your rest." She opened the door with a hand that was suddenly moist. Her knees quivered beneath her as she entered. The Indian followed her. A momentary panic shot through Ysidra's mind. What should be the first natural thing to do?

"Be quiet," she muttered to the girl. "Do you want to disturb her?" She went soundlessly to the window and drew back the curtains to let in the brilliant morning sunlight. It streamed in across Ana's bed, lighting the white translucent skin and shining on each fair hair of her sparsely covered head. Ysidra felt a second's horror. Holy Christ, did she live again? Ana's head was turned toward the window and she lay partly on one hollow cheek. The pale eyelashes glistened.

"Doña." The word came hesitantly from the Indian girl.

Ysidra started to caution her to be quiet, but was unable to.

"Doña Ysidra, she—" Damacia pointed to Ana—"she has died." And the girl fell on her knees, crossing herself, and uttered a sudden wail.

This attracted the attention of Doña Beatriz Quixano who was just passing on her way downstairs. She tapped softly on the door and then hurried in. She glanced with startled eyes to the cowering girl, to Ysidra, to Ana who lay dead on her bed. "Oh, Ysidra," she said, "we have lost her too." She knelt quickly on the floor in genuine sorrow, for she had liked Ana and pitied her childless state.

It was not a dream. It was true. It had happened. It was indeed a fact. Ysidra swayed a moment. This was going too fast. Two knew now. She must get to Francisco. She must be the one to tell him, for no one but she must see the unholy joy which would surely show for a moment in his eyes when he heard of his wife's death.

"What is it? Is Ana worse?" Doña Dolores Acuña bustled in without tapping, and upon perceiving the Indian babbling her prayers and Doña Beatriz kneeling, she flung up her hands with a wail. "Oh no! Not gone!" she cried.

Ysidra gripped her hands together. Move! Old

woman, move! Hurry, before the whole house knows of it! Things were happening so fast they were getting out of control. She must grasp the situation and mold it back into shape. She had a panicky feeling that if the news got beyond this room before she did, it would go leaping through the house ahead of her and everyone would know before she could tell Francisco.

With a mighty effort she composed herself. "Please," she said hoarsely. "Ladies, excuse me. I must tell my nephew. You will excuse me." Without waiting for their murmured agreement, she hurried from the room, mumbling, "He will be so shocked . . . so shocked——"

Once she was in the hall, she turned this way and that distractedly. Where was he? Where had he gone? Downstairs? Clinging for balance to the rail, she hurried down, her great bulk shaking. As if pursued by devils, she staggered down the hall to his office and flung open the door, ready to tell him in the privacy of the little room. Safe now.

It was empty. She paused for a moment, stunned. How could he not be here? In haste she withdrew and slammed the door again. Where? Where? She stopped. It was morning. There were guests. He would be—oh no!—not in the chapel. Reason returned to her. Of course he would be in the chapel. Stolidly now, without hurry, she went toward the front of the house and through the *sala,* which opened into the chapel. Francisco was alone in the room. He had lighted additional candles and had selected the passage in the Book and was marking the place. He glanced up somberly and saw his aunt.

"Come in, my dear," he said, placing the mark between the pages and laying the Book down on the altar. "Catalina has done well with the flowers, hasn't she?"

"Yes," Ysidra answered, her voice a little constricted. "Catalina arranges them very well. She has been extremely useful in our . . . trouble."

Francisco sat down on one of the benches and held out his hand to her. "Come, sit by me a while. I imagine the others will be along soon."

"Soon," she agreed, sitting down heavily beside him. "Francisco," she said tentatively after a moment. She must tell him and get it over with. Other people would be trailing into the chapel before many minutes had passed.

"Yes?" His tone was listless. One hand shaped like Angelo's, but larger, lay lax on the bench at his side.

Ysidra placed her hand over it. "Francisco," she said tonelessly, "I have just come from Ana. I thought to speak to you before the others came. Ana is dead."

There was a long moment of silence. A prolonged shiver passed through his big frame, the echo of which she felt in the hand she held. He turned to look at her.

"You are sure?" he said at last in a voice barely audibile.

"I am sure," she answered with a fleeting sense of pride for him. She might have known nothing could shake his poise. She had feared hysterically for nothing. His manner even before her was perfect.

"In her sleep?" he asked after a moment.

"No, she was not sleeping," Ysidra answered steadily and would not drop her glance before his penetrating gaze. Their eyes remained locked for the endless ticking of many seconds before, very gently, he lifted her hand and kissed it.

The little pool of calm was broken. The door opened and Xavier, closely followed by Sal, Acuña, Quixano and Padilla came in. Xavier hurried to his cousin and impulsively placed his hands on Francisco's shoulders. "Francisco, my mother has told you?"

"Yes, she has."

"I am sorry, my cousin," Xavier said, genuine emotion lighting his face. He kissed Francisco on the cheek and embraced him.

Ysidra leaned forward resting her weight on her hands. She wished, in a sudden streak of petulance, that the benches had backs. She was tired and needed something to lean against. Everything was all right now. Now everything would move along smoothly. The first foreordained acts were taking place and all was according to pattern. Xavier, well knowing that no love was lost between his cousin and his wife, was reacting according to the old safe pattern. If tears glinted in his eyes as he embraced Francisco, who could say he was a hypocrite, for they might be for Angelo? And the other people who crowded in behind him could find nothing amiss in their actions as a family. They were in complete accord. They were grieved, genuinely grieved. What difference if there were precious little of the grief for Ana. Who would know? Who would think to question?

One by one the other men embraced Francisco and offered their condolences. Francisco was a man doubly and triply bereaved and they extended their symapthy. Even now their wives were laying out the body of his wife and lighting the candles at her head and feet. They were being kind, and he and his family would have little to do, for they would take all the tasks and burdens on themselves for the next days.

The door that led from the chapel outdoors was suddenly opened and Catalina came in hurriedly, followed by Petra at a more sedate pace. Upon seeing the assembly, Catalina paused. Her arms were full of white roses and she knew she must make a lovely picture, so she stopped to let them enjoy it if they would. "Oh, I knew I would be late!" she said almost gaily, not noticing in the dimness of the chapel that some of the faces bore tears. "But I did hurry, didn't I, Petra? I made Petra go with me, for Don Francisco said she needed to get out more. I simply had to have white roses for the altar this morning. Oh, you have lighted the candles, Don Francisco. Why did you trouble? I was going to——"

She paused for a moment. Something was wrong. Her little tableau wasn't coming off properly. She heard Petra's apprehensive whisper behind her. "Catalina——"

She looked about the room at the men gathered. Her father had his arms about Francisco. Even now the women were coming in through the other door. Something like sickness stole over her.

"Catalina, my dear—" Don Juan Acuña stepped forward—"of course you do not yet know what has happened in the night or you would not indulge in such gaiety, but I am sure the company will excuse it." He turned, bowing to the people. His manner said, I know my child is in a house of mourning, but she is young and gay. She is a bride.

"You see, Catalina," he went on, "our friend Don Francisco has this morning undergone another loss to add to his great suffering of the last months. Doña Ana died last night in her sleep."

Catalina's hands, which had been holding the roses with careful grace, tightened and her flesh was pricked by the thorns. The realization washed over her violently: Francisco was free!

Her lips drew back from her teeth. God! Hot liquid rose in her throat and her frantic gaze swept over the chapel, flicking from face to face until it came to rest on the puffy florid face of Xavier . . . her husband.

She stared at him dumbly for several seconds

before the second realization crashed like a tidal wave through her mind. Suddenly she flung the roses from her. Furious, hysterical, she clutched with wild fingers at her shawl and began to shriek and fling herself about like a mad woman. She had no thought of the astonished assembly, no knowledge of her father and Xavier trying to subdue her. Only one thing was clear and coherent in her mind: Francisco was free, but she was bound.

Petra sat sedately with the other women in the *sala*. Apparently all the tasks they had set for themselves that day were finished. It was late, nearly time for the evening meal. The day had been all wrong. Beginning late, after late prayers, it had seemed that everything had been a little behind time. Catalina had had to be quieted and taken to her room, where she had remained all day, after sobbing and weeping herself into a dull sodden sleep.

Petra moved uncomfortably on the hard chair she occupied. The high neck of her black dress constricted her breathing as she bent her head over her sewing. Had they all deserted her? Where was Ysidra? She worked with awkward fingers on the length of embroidery. Why had she been left alone with all these people? Glancing about, she saw that she was the only Estrada in the room. Bits of conversation drifted to her.

"You know, I believe Doña Ysidra was afraid this would happen. The servants say she stayed with Ana until after midnight."

"Yes, I suppose she was afraid to leave her."

"She thinks the world of Francisco."

"She does. Even this morning she insisted on telling him the news. She has spared herself nothing in this."

"I wonder how Catalina is." Doña Beatriz Quixano was speaking to no one in particular.

"Still in her room, I suppose," Doña Camila Peréa answered. "I believe Dolores is with her."

Doña Beatrix shook her graying head. "I wouldn't have thought she would be stricken. Did she have a special attachment for Ana?"

No one answered this and there was a momentary pause. She had spoken unfortunately, for all knew that Ana was not a particularly easy person to get along with, and Catalina was a young woman who knew her own mind. Petra felt a warning click in the back of her mind.

She heard herself saying, "She is really a bride still. It has been very difficult for her with the house going into mourning almost on her honeymoon." She stopped, her throat filling. She had a hysterical urge to fling herself screaming onto the floor, to wail and beat her breast like a peasant to ease the ache and longing for her husband. But not she, not Doña Petra Estrada. Members of proud Spanish families did not do that. They sat sedately in their black dresses and spoke decorously, excusing with carefully chosen words the member who had for a time let hysteria grip her. The stitches she made were slow and faulty for she did not see the linen in her hand. She saw Angelo as she wakened in the morning, dreamy-eyed, soft-voiced, with his warm skin gleaming like honey.

The morning of Ana's funeral Petra woke in a cold sweat, reached blind groping hands for Angelo and then lay back with a muffled wail when she realized she was alone. The room was pitch-dark.

I could weep now, she thought, for there is no one to see me. But perversely no tears would come.

The room next door was empty save for the body of Ana on the table. In her mind's eye Petra saw the dead form beneath the blanket, clothed neatly and laid out gently, with its head on a stone. The stone had bothered Petra terribly when Angelo died. She closed her eyes and saw him again as he had been then, his slim lovely body clothed in a gray friar's robe, his one delicate hand on his breasts, and his fine head resting on the comfortless slab of stone. Her sleep had been disrupted night after night when she dreamed she stole alone into the room to remove the stone and replace it with a little pillow. Each time in her dream Angelo had smiled without opening his eyes and said, "Don't trouble yourself, beloved. There is no discomfort in this."

Petra raised her hands and tried to massage the ache out of her throat. She wondered for the thousandth time why she had let it be Francisco who removed the stone. She had hesitated to go against the custom, and now ached with a sort of jealous pain to think that he, instead of she, had been the one to perform that last useless little service for Angelo.

The dawn was thinning the darkness, and in a very few minutes the silence would be broken by the singing of Enrique or Xavier. The household would begin to wake and stir and prepare itself for the funeral of Ana, who would go to her grave clasping in her thin arms her daughter Mary-of-Jesus.

Enrique Padilla's fine voice was raised in a slow and melancholy hymn, singularly beautiful and sad. Petra got out of bed and began to dress herself. Much as she hated the thought, she must go with them.

It had been like hearing an old story again. The death of Ana had been like an indistinct, slightly distorted reflection of the death of Angelo. The

Indians had come, Dos Ríos Indians and those from the mission who had learned the chants for the dead. They had filed into Ana's room the day after she had died, before the break of dawn, while the world was still in the thick of darkness. The chanting had begun. Softly and gently they tried to sing the soul of Ana to its rest. The ceremony ended on exactly the instant the red ball of the sun rose between the peaks of the hills and filled the room with a radiance slightly cloudy. Then silently, as they had come, they left.

There had been the necessary and unlovely tasks of the midwife who laid out the body. Petra knew, although she did not see these things, what had occurred. She tried not to dwell morbidly on the physical facts of death, but she could not help but think of them in horror and grief. Why couldn't death be swift and beautiful? There were these ugly things that must be done to the vessel which had held the life. She had seen the lime being brought in and knew that a poultice of it was placed on the stomach to keep it from swelling. She knew that the jaws were tied up until they were rigid and sealed. She knew that coins must be placed on the eyelids. These things she knew and these offended her. She noticed more at the death of Ana than she had before, for she was not protected from these facts now. As pennies were placed on the eyelids of Ana, she knew that they had been placed on Angelo's. As Ana's jaw was bound up tightly, so had the cleanly cut jaw of Angelo been bound.

Many times during the day she had to stop and hold herself rigid to keep from screaming aloud at the sacrilegious acts. But they must be done, they must, she told herself again and again. These things had been done for years and would be done for years to come. If only—if only Angelo—— He had been human too, and his body no less likely to be limp and lax in death. But no matter how she reasoned with herself, the acts committed upon the dead in the sense of propriety were to her grotesque and hideous.

Then there had been the other things to do and be done. In the patio she had heard the Indians soaping the axles of the *carretas* to dim the squeak when they carried the funeral procession. She knew when the empty wooden coffin was loaded and strapped down with rawhide. She heard the muttering of the Indians who were to bear the dead body of Ana to church on a litter. She could see in her mind's eye even now the lace curtains which cascaded from the table to the floor and formed a white bier for Ana. She could hear through her mind the rustling, like the whispering dead, of the white paper cutouts which were pinned to the lace and which surrounded the candlesticks.

The mourners had come, family after family. It was like some perverted fiesta, a dream fiesta cut short in the middle and changed inexplicably into a funeral. They had come to the house to rejoice in a subdued manner for María-de-Jesús, and had remained to see her mother buried.

Petra put on her clothing with leaden fingers. The sky outside was graying. It would be a bleak day and perhaps rain would fall. The sky seemed low and weighted as if trying to press down on the people to muffle and smother them. Now it was nearly time to go. The people were climbing into *carretas* and mounting horses for the procession. There was the subdued sound of many voices, the hurried hushing of children who laughed or spoke too loudly, not knowing the cause of the solemnity. Now again would come the long trip to the mission. Now again the old patterns. You say this, and so I must, as a matter of course, answer thus-and-so. She was tired of it, filled with it, sick of it.

Her fingers buttoned the high neck of her black dress. The widow Doña Petra. She turned eyes, suddenly glittering and defiant, to the Madonna over the dresser. Well, was it so much to ask? Only Angelo. Only to be his wife and mother his children. Only to love him and care for him and take pleasure in the joy of his mind and the perfection of his body. Was that sinful? Was it so wanton that everything must be taken away? Was that too much to ask? Ah . . . blaspheming. Questioning the will of God. Wicked, wicked Petra! Sinful abandoned woman!

Petra's mouth flattened in impotent rage and pain. Had she been given her portion of happiness already? Was it so intense that it had to be cut off at the very beginning lest she get more than her just share? He was her husband and her lover and her little boy. Mary should understand that. She knew she should fall on her knees and pray for forgiveness for such black and blasphemous thoughts. Bitterness and despair were contrary to the will of God.

She set the last comb in her shining hair and draped it with the black lace mantilla. Now to the funeral of Ana, and in every clop of a hoof, every moaning cry of a wheel, every tone of a chant, relive the funeral of her husband, her beloved. Later she would be sorry for such thoughts. She would kneel humbly in the confessional and tell of them and be repentant, humiliated and ashamed. Patricio would intercede for her and Mary, in her all-consuming love and understanding, would forgive her. She knew this dimly in the back of her mind, but the hurt was too new and intense to allow reasoning.

She must do some small thing, commit some small error, to assuage and ease the raw pain of her bereavement. She turned from the Madonna, went out and slammed the door after her. Its crash echoed and re-echoed through the house of mourning, loud, brash and defiant.

Father Patricio read the service. His voice rose and fell, and the coming and going of his breath caused a flickering of the candle flames as he consigned the mortal remains of Ana-Lucía to the dust and the soul of Ana-Lucía to her God. He did this with a feeling of reluctance and a feeling of foreboding. It was as if the house of Francisco were falling apart and there were nothing he could do for his friend but assist ineffectually and offer up his endless prayers which seemed to avail nothing. He paused in his chanting and began again with more vigor. Was he doubting the wisdom of the Lord? Was he, human and faulty, presuming to question the will of God? His voice began to die away. He took a handful of earth and dropped it on the coffin of Ana. He nodded to Francisco, whose eyes were veiled and remote.

Gently Francisco took some earth and dropped it on the box which held all that remained of the woman who had been his wife for nine years, and the child who had been his daughter for a few minutes. It was a finishing and a commencing. He stood, clothed in black broadcloth, big against the gray sky, and let the last earth fall from his strong outstretched fingers.

So it came Ysidra's turn. The amount of earth in her hand was less, for her hand was small. She thought of it fleetingly, dryly. What difference whether her hand held a little or a lot of dust? It marked the ending of Ana and the beginning of a new era. She recalled Ana's pale glistening lashes and her rustling voice like the rustling of the paper still pinned to the stiff lace at home: *"It is a Judgment of God."* She had changed the Judgment of God to the judgment of Ysidra. Stubborn old woman. Softly she let the earth fall and passed the grave.

Petra felt again earth in her hand. This was not Angelo. This was Ana. It was of no consequence. She would pass on quietly and drop the soil gently. Today was cold and murky, and she would not remember the gleaming sun which had beaten on the raw new grave of her husband. But even as she assured herself of this, the feeling rushed over her again. It would never be any different. All the years of her life any funeral would be the funeral of Angelo. Any soil in her hand would be that of the grave of Angelo. And any death would be the death of Angelo. She dropped it and passed on groping, blinded by pain.

The long slim fingers of Catalina gripped the dirt with an intensity that caused her arm to shake. She would throw it—fling it—with such might that it would go through the lid of the coffin and spatter in the dead woman's face . . . the pale dead woman who had released Francisco and made him free. She should have lived to hold him ever bound. Now what need would he have of her, Catalina? What use could she be to him? Any children she had now would be unimportant to him, for he would take another wife and have children of his own. She would be nothing in his household except the wife of his cousin. She would hurl the earth. She would fling it at Ana. But the long years of gentle rearing, the veneer so painstakingly wrought by her parents and so seldom cracked, held good. She dropped the earth quietly and went on as the others had done. None knew to look at her that she blasphemed the dead and begrudged the dead its rest.

So the seemingly endless chain of people passed the new grave of Ana and dropped on it the soil. Each held his private thoughts of Ana. When the funeral was finished, the others departed a little from the family and left them alone for a time in the cemetery. Clouds rose and darkened. It promised early unseasonable rain which might wash the loose soil from the new grave of Ana and the nearly new grave of Angelo. Catalina clung to her father's arm and went with him, feeling unable to join the Estradas as she should have done.

The family stood, the four of them, Francisco, Ysidra, Petra and Xavier, alone in a silent group. Francisco looked at the plot which held the remains of his family. The graves of his eight little girls and his only boy. The mood of somber exultation which had gripped him was past. He looked at the silent mounds and had no emotion for the little girls whom he had not known, who had scarcely lived at all and who were Ana's children. But for Angelo, who had lived and who was the child of Lupe, there was a different feeling. He found himself wishing that it had been otherwise. He wished he could have kept Angelo—not as Petra's husband, for he already thought of Petra as his own—but as Angelito, who lived lightly and for his own pleasure as a careless little boy who would never grow up. He had only this one regret, one nagging plaguing sorrow; if only—somehow—he could have kept Angelo!

It began to rain, not thin and peppering but large, intermittent, splashing drops that fell like the errant tears dashed from the eyes of some passing saint.

The rain ceased almost as soon as it began, and a thin sunlight wavered over the lonely group. Francisco escorted his aunt to the *carreta* and helped her in. Petra clung like a bent reed to Xavier and they followed after. She appeared taller in her unrelieved black and wordlessly allowed herself to be assisted in beside Ysidra. She had elected to ride to and from the funeral in the *carreta* rather than on horseback as she usually did.

She leaned a little against Ysidra as they began the journey back to Dos Ríos.

Francisco, astride his black horse, rode beside them and from time to time glanced down at the cart. It held his two most valuable possessions: Ysidra, his friend and confidant, on whom he could always depend and without whom he would feel lost; and Petra, the widow of his son and the girl who would be his wife before many months had passed. A year is a long long time in the eyes of youth, and she was young. Now she was stricken and desolate, but soon, because of her very youth, life would spring up in her again and she would be radiant and dazzling and lovely. A vision of her descent down the stairs at Dos Ríos rose before him. All the years of her life, if she wanted to, she could wear white satin and pearls.

Petra was paler now. There came within her the same old sickness she had had during her first long *carreta* ride over the land of Francisco Estrada. She thought that all the fear and heart-ache had gone when she became the wife of Angelo, that nothing could ever break the enchantment in which she lived. Over this same sloping ground she had ridden to and from her wedding. Phantom shapes just beyond the line of her vision seemed to circle and wheel in some brilliant invisible sunlight. Just beyond the rim of her hearing there was the screaming, the laughter and the music—always the music. Forever and ever her dreams would be shot through and laced with fragments of music from her wedding day.

Not once during the journey did she glance up from the moving ground beneath the wheels. She seemed completely alone and in her unrelieved black presented a figure of utter dejection. The people who looked at her did not know that she wore the Montoya diamonds, wore them, not as a necklace, but as a badge of devotion to the boy who had given them to her. She wore them where she had first worn them—hidden. Beneath the black of her gown, against the warmth of her body, the jewels lay between her breasts.

Chapter 11

Catalina had been shocked at first by the impropriety of her brother's announcement. One didn't think of marriage with a widow so soon after her husband had died—at least one didn't speak of it. The shock had been succeeded by anger that she would be superseded in his affections—and by Petra of all people. She had given him a severe sisterly lecture, but after some thought the idea did not seem so terrible. Sad, of course, that it had to be Petra, but she had expected he would marry eventually. She had always thought of her brother's wife as some vague amiable little creature who would be a good wife and mother but who would take a definite second place in his regard.

Now, as she arranged the flowers on the altar for the next morning's prayers, she reflected that Las Palomas was a long way from Dos Ríos. If Petra were Teodoro's wife, she would live at Las Palomas. The idea was appealing. Perhaps that was the way she could achieve the long-dreamed-of post as lady of Dos Ríos. The idea of Petra so many miles from Dos Ríos was deliciously enticing. And Petra would *have* to marry. She couldn't mourn the rest of her life for Angelo. Why, if Xavier died——Catalina broke off the thought feeling a little guilty. After all, life did go on. She wondered what Francisco would think about it. He couldn't help but be pleased. Teodoro was a favorite with him. And Teodoro would certainly have the advantage over any other suitor because their two families were already united by one marriage, hers and Xavier's. The more she thought of it, the more she liked the idea.

"Still up, Catalina?" Francisco entered the chapel. "I thought everyone had gone to bed."

She gave him a brilliant smile and indicated the refurbished altar decorations, noting his expression with satisfaction. She spoke quickly as he turned to go. "Don Francisco." Anything to hold him.

He turned politely.

Should she mention the subject of Teodoro? It was too soon—indecently soon—but for a moment she felt she would die if he left her sight. He was less strict in matters of etiquette than her father. Nervously she twisted the stem of a flower, her eyes on the braid of his black broadcloth jacket.

"I . . . was worried about Petra," she said with slight difficulty, and was pleased to see his interest quicken. "She seems so . . . desolate."

"That is kind of you," he said soberly, "but grief must be lived out, you know."

"I was afraid," Catalina resumed hesitantly, "that she might let this . . . ruin her whole life. It seems a pity. I don't suppose she will . . . consider marrying again." There it was. What would he say? She didn't dare meet his eyes.

"It is much too soon to think of that, Catalina." His voice was quiet, but there was no anger in it. She breathed a little easier.

"Do you think it would be wicked for someone to be in love with her?"

"I don't think so," he answered.

She looked up quickly thinking he sounded amused. "Well, I'm glad," she said hurriedly, "because Teodoro is. Of course he has said nothing to anyone but me. And quite naturally he won't say anything to anyone else until the proper time has arrived. His feelings don't indicate any lack of respect for Petra or any less affection for Angelo——" She stopped at his sudden wince. "Oh, I'm sorry."

"Do you think," she asked after a pause, "that Teodoro would be considered?" This took an effort. Any girl would be glad to have Teodoro Acuña. The Acuñas had counted for something in Spain when God knew where Petra's antecedents had been.

"That would be for Petra to decide," he said remotely.

"Well, don't you think when the time came you could . . . well, influence Petra?"

"Oh, come, Catalina, you didn't want anyone's advice when you chose your husband. Marriage is a very personal thing."

"But I would respect my father's judgment. If he——"

"I am not Petra's father." His tone was cold. "I think Teodoro is capable of doing his own courting when the time comes."

She looked at him wordlessly, stunned at the rebuff. Then she rushed into angry speech: "You don't want Teodoro to marry her! I thought you and my father were the best of friends. I thought Teodoro was a favorite of yours. I thought——"

"You are being extremely discourteous."

". . . I thought I could count on you of all people. It seems to me, Francisco, that after our families have been friends for so many years you could have no reason——" She stopped. What was she saying? Quarreling with him as a wife might! Calling him Francisco! Even in her anger she felt a strange exultation. "Why do you refuse? Are you in love with Petra?" The blunt words hung between them. How had she dared say that? What would he say?

"If you have finished with the flowers you had better go up. Everyone else has."

"Well, you can't marry her," she said flatly, flinging aside the crushed flowers. "The Church would never allow it. She's your daughter-in-law. You can't get away from that."

"Catalina, my dear, do you propose to dictate to me in my own house?"

She stared at him. He didn't deny it. He all but admitted it. She was suddenly furious, revolted.

"Finish your flowers and come inside." His voice was only slightly annoyed as he turned to leave the chapel.

Catalina began to tremble and half turned, plucking with nervous fingers at the lace edge of the altar cloth. He hadn't even raised his voice or bothered to become angry. He thought her a troublesome child, when her body tingled at his nearness, when they had been so close she might have touched his hand, the shining black braid of his jacket.

"It won't do you any good," she said raising her voice. Her eyelids drooped and the corners of her mouth were turned down. "Petra won't have you." And this he didn't even answer. For a moment after he had gone, she struggled against hysteria. Then turning swiftly from the altar, she caught up her skirts and rushed from the chapel. She fairly flew past Francisco and up the stairs. Petra . . . Petra had everything. First Angelo, now Francisco. Was there nothing the yellow-haired *Inglesa* couldn't have! Even Teodoro!

She stopped in the upper hallway. Well. Think a minute. At least *one* of the Acuñas should have what he desired. He would if she could possibly manage it. Outside Petra's door she felt her lips flatten again in swift recurrent rage. And she'd fix it so that, for once, Francisco didn't have everything he wanted!

Francisco entered his office and closed the door behind him. So that was it. He might have known. But little Catalina, daughter of his best friend, wife of his cousin! He wasn't mistaken. He had seen that look on too many female faces, both light and dark, ever to mistake it. By God, right there in the chapel! He would have needed only to hold out his hand.

"Does something trouble you, my dear?" Ysidra asked.

"I'm not sure I should mention it," he answered. "It's likely to be a delicate subject."

"Francisco, I am extremely fond of delicate subjects, as you very well know. Please continue."

He grinned a little, then went restlessly to the window. "Very well, my dear. It is this: I have just come from your daughter-in-law Catalina. We engaged in a short discussion, during the course of which she apprised me, unwittingly, of a rather disconcerting fact. To be blunt, the girl seems infatuated with me."

"Ah-h." It was the merest whisper. "I was wondering when you would notice. You aren't usually so blind about those things."

"You knew, Ysidra?"

"Oh, come, Francisco, surely you don't think a child like that could fool me for long. Why else do you suppose she married my son but to come here——"

"You're joking!"

"On the contrary, my dear."

"Now there is a novel idea on which to base a marriage."

"Isn't it? I thought so at the time, but Xavier was so completely enamored of her that I said nothing, hoping for the best. It develops, as you said, into a delicate situation."

"I think," Francisco said after a moment's thoughtful silence, "that it is time Xavier had his own establishment. Don't you?"

"I do."

"Good! We'll go to work on it immediately. She should have had more sense. She must have a low opinion of my integrity. Not that I would balk at seducing her in any other circumstances, but after all she is my cousin's wife and the daughter of my best friend."

"I detect a slight tinge of regret, but I will pass over it. Do you think, my dear, that Xavier is capable of heading his own establishment."

"Certainly, *Mamacita.* Xavier has a very good brain. He's just never bothered to use it. Anyhow, I know all there is to know about ranching. I'll help him."

A wheeze of amusement escaped Ysidra at his conceit. "Let us look at the map," she said.

He got it and spread it out before them on the table. They bent their heads intently over it.

In her room Petra stared blankly at the door just closed behind Catalina. Was the girl completely mad! *Francisco!* Oh, surely *not!* But little facts began to troop through her mind. He had showed her, plainly, in a hundred different ways, but she had been too much in love with Angelo, too grieved at his death, to take any notice at all.

Color washed suddenly into her face. The *fool.* Didn't he understand that she would be Angelo's wife until the day she died? Well then, she would tell him. Her head lifted and her jaw set. That presumptuous, egotistical devil! She flung open her door until it slammed back against the wall, and hurried through the hall and down the stairs. Even at the door of his office she did not pause.

She wouldn't even accord him the courtesy of knocking. Angrily she turned the knob and walked in.

Surprised, Francisco and Ysidra glanced up from the paper which lay before them. Francisco rose instantly and bowed. "I thought you were asleep long ago. Are you ill, Petra?"

"I'm very well, thank you. I have just had a visit from Catalina."

"Catalina?" Francisco's face was a mask, his tone one of polite interest.

"Yes. She made a most outrageous statement which I would like either verified or denied by you."

"And that statement?" he inquired.

"She. . . . " Petra faltered for the first time. "Catalina said—this is ridiculous, of course—Catalina said you . . . wanted to marry me. Is that true?" Now it was out. Now let him look her in the face and admit such baseness.

"Catalina was most precipitate," he said dryly.

"Answer my question!"

Ysidra drew in her breath softly. People did not address Francisco in that tone. But he appeared not to notice.

"If I answer you truthfully, Petra," he said thoughtfully, "it will make you unhappy. However, I will not lie about it. Yes, I want to marry you."

Color sprang into her face and ebbed, leaving it pale. There was a dangerous glitter in her narrowed eyes.

"This has come too soon," he said. "I am sorry that you have been upset by it. Believe me, I would cause you no displeasure, but I offer you nothing dishonorable, Petra. You have lived in my house and I have come to love you very much. If knowing it offends you, I am sorry, but eventually I want to make you my wife."

"Well, let us understand this," she said harshly. "I will not marry you. At any time! I will not marry anyone. I consider myself Angelo's wife. That he has died doesn't alter the fact." She turned to the door, beginning to tremble, sick with fear that she would cry before them. At the door she stopped and turned. "I might as well tell you now," she said dully. "I should have told you before. I'm going to have Angelo's child in about six months, perhaps less. Now, let me alone." Without another word she left them.

They listened to her footsteps in a gathering silence. When these had diminished, Ysidra rose ponderously and went to shut the door.

"Well," she said tonelessly, "will you marry her anyway, Francisco?"

"Yes," he said distantly.

"The baby." She came to stand beside him.

"What about the baby?"

"It will be Angelo's baby."

He nodded and stared with veiled eyes across the room out the dark window. "One would think I would be overjoyed. This might be the heir I have so long berated heaven because I didn't have."

"Don't, *querido*, don't torment yourself needlessly."

He shrugged and began to walk restlessly about the room as if it had suddenly grown too small.

"Francisco," she said urgently, "put the idea out of your mind. Nothing but trouble will come of it. Choose someone else. Think of Acuña's lovely daughters. Juan would be delighted to join our families more firmly. Think of the Quixano women. Cristóbal has two daughters of marriageable age."

"Please, Ysidra. There is no point in discussing it."

"Francisco, I know Petra and I know you. Take an old woman's advice for what it's worth."

"Forgive me, my dear. There have been many times when I sought advice from you gladly and profited by it. This is not one of those times. My mind is set on this marriage. It happens that I love Petra.

"Don't be astonished. I know that when Lupe died, I thought I would never love another woman. No one will know what I felt when she died—except perhaps Petra, for she has lost Angelo. Ana—well, you know what that was. I never thought of Ana as my wife. I thought of her as the mother of the children I must have. Now Ana is gone. In Petra there seems to be everything I have wanted." His voice hardened. "And believe me, Ysidra, I will marry her."

Chapter 12

Catalina went with the men to the door and saw them mount. Petra had already gone about her tasks for the day, but Catalina watched the men ride into the distance, her eyes clinging to the diminishing figure of Francisco. When their forms were no longer visible and she knew that by now they had parted to go in different directions—Xavier to Los Angeles to see the alcalde, and Francisco to Rancho San Cristóbal—she turned back into the house.

Thank God, she wasn't as sick in her pregnancy as Petra had recently been. She felt extremely well, scarcely as if she were carrying a child in her body. Her appetite was the same, and she had had not a moment's discomfort.

The day's duties began to press on her. About the grinders, now, and the supply of meal. Two of the women had been sick yesterday. She pushed open the door of the kitchen and cast a practical eye about the adobe-floored room, noting with a small rush of relief that the two grinders were back in their places, and the stones moved rhythmically in the stone bowls. She crossed the wide room and asked how they felt, smiling kindly as her mother always smiled at servants. The brown hands of the women ceased to move as soon as she spoke. Trust an Indian to grasp any excuse to stop work, she thought, but the smile remained on her lips. She listened to their complaints, inquired into the medicines they had taken and the results obtained. She nodded from time to time during the recital and commented aptly where comment was indicated. Other servants, the cooks and a cleaning woman, joined the little group. Anyone's ills were the concern of all. Catalina was learning to be a good mistress. This house was very much like home, and she found that the more she patterned her conduct after her mother's the better she got along. Most of the servants liked her. She talked to them now, commiserating with them for their ills, asking after their children, telling them what to cook for the day.

While she pondered the meat supply, the corn supply and the medicine consumed by sick Indians, there beat in the back of her mind the knowledge that Francisco and Xavier had gone out to measure a portion of land on which she might have to go and live . . . away from Dos Ríos . . . away from Francisco . . . farther than ever from Las Palomas. Even while she had watched Francisco out of sight, unable to tear her eyes from his retreating figure, her soul had burned in anger that he would do this to her. He could have let them stay forever at Dos Ríos. If he had not talked to Xavier about being a landowner, Xavier would have been content at Dos Ríos. She had no illusions about Xavier's ambition. This was Francisco's doing. A slow deep flush rose up and stained the delicate skin of her face, and those who watched her thought she stood too near the fire.

Francisco halted his mount on the top of a hill within view of Don Cristóbal Quixano's house. He knew that the hoofbeats had heralded his approach and that Cristóbal, if he were home, would come riding out to greet him. It was a source of constant wonder to Quixano's friends that he managed to sit his horse at all, and much more that the heedless Cristóbal never bothered looking for an easy path but was inclined to urge his mount up or down hills which appeared to the eye as sheer drops. Francisco saw Cristóbal emerge from the house, mount and ride out. He was lost from time to time in the brush and foliage but in a few minutes he emerged and called out loudly and enthusiastically, "Well, Francisco, my friend, at last you have decided to pay my poor house a visit."

Francisco smiled. One was always sure of one's welcome at Rancho San Cristóbal. "I have been extremely busy, Cristóbal," he returned as the other man pulled his horse to a stop. The two men dismounted and embraced.

"Well, well, what is the news from up north?" Quixano asked. "I heard that your house is to be blessed with another child."

Francisco nodded. "Two," he said. "Petra believes hers will be born in April and Catalina is expecting in July."

"I'm glad. I'm very glad," Quixano said enthusiastically. "They will probably be boys," he added matter-of-factly. "Come, let us go down to the house. I was on the verge of tapping a new keg of wine I put down some years ago. I'm not certain of the quality, for that year was a bad one for grapes. Let's test it together. You are a good judge."

"You flatter me, my friend." Francisco mounted his horse again. A drink of cool wine in a vaulted cellar would be refreshing after his long ride, and the cellar was a good place to speak to Quixano. He hadn't wanted to leave Dos Ríos even for a little while with Petra's time so close, but he had chafed at a delay in seeing Quixano and settling this business with him. At the house both men dismounted again.

Cristóbal bowed Francisco in with the usual expression: "The house is yours, my friend."

In the cellar, when the wine was opened, it was, as Cristóbal had expected, inferior. He insisted on opening a dusty and cobwebbed bottle of excellent vintage from Spain to make up for it. "We must take the taste of that swill from our teeth," he grumbled, pouring Francisco's glass full. "I apologize for subjecting you to that vinegar, Pancho. I haven't done so well with wine these last years. I'm making the mission at San Fernando rich by my purchases."

Francisco nodded. "San Fernando puts out excellent wine and their brandy is superb," he agreed, tasting from the glass with pleasure. "Equal to this any day."

"Agreed!" Quixano said appreciatively, holding up his glass and looking through it. "Something is on your mind, Francisco?"

"Well, yes, but now that I'm here I hesitate to mention it. What I really came for was to ask a favor of you."

"A favor? My dear Francisco, you know very well I shall be delighted to assit you in any way I can. Ask it. Don't hesitate."

"Thank you. I knew I could count on you. There will be some little scandal about it, I believe, Cristóbal. You see, I wish to be married."

"Ah-h." Quixano pursed his lips.

"Obtaining permission is apt to present certain difficulties," Francisco added, apparently intent on his wine. The cellar was cool and dusty around them. Francisco's face was grimed from his ride and his eyes appeared strangely light and clear by comparison.

"Difficulties, my friend?" Quixano looked at

him in surprise. "What difficulty could you have in making a perfectly legal marriage?"

"With the Church. That's where you come in if you will be so kind. No, wait, do not commit yourself until I explain." Quixano closed his mouth obediently and waited for Francisco to continue.

"I believe it will be necessary to request permission of someone who holds a responsible position in the Church."

Quixano cocked one brow. "My uncle the cardinal looks on me most kindly. I am a favorite nephew," he offered, smiling a little.

Francisco's lips twitched at the other's eagerness. "Not so fast, Cristóbal. It is possible that you will not approve."

"Not approve? Don't be childish. We are both men of the world. The only possible objection is that your wife—God rest her lovely soul!—has died so recently. It is true that you have been married twice before but that is of no consequence. A man must have a wife, Francisco. Even the Church recognizes that."

"I propose," Francisco cut in quietly, "to marry my son's widow."

Quixano started visibly. The wine spilled over the edge of the glass as his hand jerked.

"That makes a difference, doesn't it?" Francisco observed.

"It does not," snapped Quixano, obviously cursing himself for the pause. "I said I would help you and I will gladly—yes, eagerly. You have been a good friend to me on occasions past." He ignored Francisco's depreciatory gesture. "Only the next time you fling a startling fact like that at me, tell me first to put down my glass. There is no use wasting good wine." He set the glass down now and wiped off his hand.

"Please don't hesitate to refuse if you want to. I shall not be in the least offended."

Quixano drew up his portly form. "*You* offend *me*, señor," he declared, "when you suggest that I would even want to hesitate."

Francisco laughed softly and relaxed. "I knew I could count on you. Be at ease, my friend. Don't stand there like a ruffled cock. What I am asking, you know, is no simple matter. It means a great deal to me, and it may prove difficult."

Quixano grinned at his friend. "Not so difficult," he bragged. "I have used my holy uncle's name many times in the past—in fact a good many more times than he actually knows about. You'd be surprised how simple it is. All I have to do is ask for something, laugh heartily—as if it were really nothing—and say, 'You know that reminds me of something my uncle Fernando, Cardinal Vallesca, used to tell me when I was a little boy.' While they are composing themsleves and trying to look as if they had not been on the point of refusing I regale them with this little story—which I usually fabricate on the spot."

Francisco laughed with him. "I'm afraid this won't be so simple. I am afraid you will have to write the cardinal."

"Hmm, yes, I suppose I had better. Let me see, what shall I tell him? Do you mind if I make you an extremely noble creature, Francisco?"

"Not at all," laughed Francisco. "Make me as noble as you like. It might be well to stick to the truth if you can, in case he seeks other avenues of information. Color it a little if you think it will help."

"Oh, I shall. I have quite a talent for literature. My spelling is weak, for I am better at bear fighting than scribbling, but I shall do the very best I can. Trust me."

"I do. And I will be extremely grateful——" Francisco began only to be waved to silence.

"Tut, tut, it is nothing. I am most happy to be of so small a service."

That night Quixano had occasion to regret the rashness of his eager promise, for he sat until early hours toiling over the letter. He had written very few letters in his life, and his schooling had been sketchy and obtained a long time ago. Jaime, his eldest, who acted as his father's secretary, did all the corresponding and there wasn't much. Very few occasions for letter writing had ever risen. It was much easier, when one wanted to do business, to ride over and see the fellow and stay a few days. There was usually a series of dances or parties in one's honor—— It made the whole thing much pleasanter. But this was one letter which had to be written, and he had to write it himself. Not that Jaime wasn't a fine lad, but he was inclined to confide too completely in his wife, and, Mother of God, when you told a woman anything!

Jaime remained up to assit his father. It wouldn't do to have mistakes in a letter to the cardinal. Long after his household and his guests were sleeping soundly, Cristóbal toiled over the paper. Jaime alternately dozed in a chair or read a book, helping when the need arose. Cristóbal's round red face contorted with effort. Sweat stood out on his forehead. From time to time his tongue crept out as he scribbled away intently on the important message.

"Jaime, how do you spell 'exemplary'?" he would ask, and his son would glance up and recite it for him letter by letter.

"That's the way I have it, but it looks odd," Cristóbal would lie, brazenly scratching it out and writing it over.

"Jaime, spell 'devout' for me, and 'wealthy' . . . Hmm, just as I thought." He scribbed away diligently, pausing to wipe his brow from time to time, realizing with dread that the whole thing must be copied over on clean sheets of paper to be presentable or even readable.

"Jaime, how do you spell 'upstanding'? And 'sincerity'? And 'honorable'? And 'generous'? and 'financially'? And 'pure'? And 'meritorious'?"

After a long time Jaime was allowed to go to bed. He went gratefully. He had offered courteously, "Just dictate it to me, Father. I'll write it down for you."

"Thank you, Jaime. I'll do it. I know how tired you must be. You just sit there comfortably and help me a little." And Jaime was too polite to say that had he been allowed to write the letter, it would have been done in one fourth the time and he could have been in bed hours ago.

Now the letter was written and all Cristóbal had to do was copy it neatly on clean paper, sign it and affix his rubrica. It was nearly two in the morning before he was finished. He had long since shed his coat to sit in his shirt sleeves. He got up at the end of each page and washed his hands carefully, for they perspired profusely from his intense effort. It would not do to have any smudges on the paper that the cardinal would read.

"Francisco, my friend," he muttered sleepily to the empty room, "greater love hath no man, believe me." He dried his cramped fingers and sat down again before the table on which lay his writing materials. He dug about the various papers in his desk, looking for some document he had signed, for he couldn't remember exactly how to form his rubrica. He found one and pulled it out with a groan of satisfaction and scanned its complicated lines, curls and scrolls with tired critical eyes. Why had he been so fancy when he made the thing? He had been young and inclined to flourish. Well, too bad, he would have to make the best of it.

He sat down and carefully began to write his name at the end of the letter, appending to it the complicated scrolling rubrica which set his signature apart from that of any other man. It covered nearly half a sheet of paper. When it was at last finished, he sat back with a great sigh. Good God, what a job!

He closed his eyes for a moment and then he was taken with curiosity to look on the lovely thing he had written. He opened his eyes. It looked very nice. To glance at it, one might think the writer a great scholar whose fingers were more used to the grasp of the pen than the whip. He lifted the pages carefully and began to read it over. He read it with deep interest and concentration. On one occasion tears rose to his eyes, so moved was he by his own composition. By God, he was a poet! He read on. And Francisco, his beloved and desperately noble and unhappy friend Francisco! Influenced by what he had written, he longed to rush into Francisco's chamber and fling his arms about his friend and kiss his cheek, assuring him that everything would be all right. It would move a heart of stone to tears, he vowed to himself, wiping his eyes and chuckling at the same time. Truth was indeed beautiful.

Well, it was very nearly the truth. There was nothing one could put one's finger on and say, "This is false." But reading it, a casual observer would never connect the man discussed in the letter with Don Francisco Estrada y Santander of Dos Ríos. It was, with slight embellishment in some places and slight understatement in others, a life story of Francisco. The main facts were in order, but they were set down in such a way as to make the most callous reader burst into tears at the unhappy fate of Francisco and his love for the widow Petra Estrada y Hutchins, who was an orphan, her father and mother being dead.

Nowhere in the letter was there mention of any child she was going to have. She didn't have it yet, so what point was there in mentioning it? Why confuse His Eminence with little details? If questioned about it later—the possibility of this was remote—Cristóbal could spread his hands and say with perfect innocence, "She did not have the child when I wrote the letter."

He sat back with a sigh of satisfaction. He was glad now that his signature was so complicated. Truly it was a chore to mark it down, but looking at its complex beauty was satisfying. He was a great scholar and a great man. He beamed on the letter. It was such a pity to send it away. The cardinal received a great many letters. After he had read it and been moved to action by its contents, it would be filed away, lost from sight forever. Such a pity! He mourned a moment for the fate of his beautiful letter. Maybe he could keep it, make a copy again to send to his uncle. Copy it! Oh no! God, no! What was he thinking of? It would take until after breakfast and he was exhausted. No, he would just keep the old one. It didn't look so pretty, true, but even if it was smudged and blotted and scratched over, it still contained the beautiful thoughts and flowing sentences. Yes, he would keep the old one as a memento and send the new one to his uncle.

Cristóbal, you are a good man, he said to himself as he rose from his chair. Lord, how his joints creaked! He was indeed getting old. He picked up his jacket and hung it over his arm. Taking the letters, original and copy, he held them carefully before him and went tiredly to his room for a bit of rest. He would lay them gently in the top bureau drawer in his own room. Nothing must happen to these letters. Sleep well, Francisco my lad, the world is yours if your old friend Cristóbal can get it for you.

Francisco easily avoided an extended visit at Rancho San Cristóbal. The next morning at breakfast he drew a deep frown. "Cristóbal, I need you again."

Don Cristóbal looked up, a little heavy-eyed from lack of sleep, and grinned. "I am your servant," he answered.

"I would like to have you come a little way to the north with me. Xavier has been insisting that we get out the map of the land he wants——"

"Grant? Land grant? Is Xavier going to set up as a ranchero?" Cristóbal broke in delightedly.

"Yes, and he has been champing like a maddened stallion for the last three weeks for us to be done with the measuring so that we may put the grant through. Once he made up his mind——"

Quixano rose excitedly from the table. "But, Francisco," he cried waving his arms, "this is wonderful news! I always said—didn't I always say, Jaime?—that when a man gets a wife he gets ambition. See how right I was. It's the doing of that little Doña Catalina! Xavier will make a fine ranchero! I always said Xavier would make a fine ranchero if he only chose to trouble himself. When will they measure?"

"I imagine they will begin this afternoon. Xavier was with the alcalde yesterday."

"Oh, we should be there, Francisco! We should go to the measuring." He turned to his elder sons. "Jaime, you and Julio and Pedro can make out here alone if I go, can't you?"

"Yes, Father," Jaime answered, glancing at his brothers, "There isn't really very much to be done," he added wistfully.

"Well, in that case, we could all go. What about that, Francisco? We could suspend our labors here, all of us, and join Xavier. Will that please him?"

His three sons breathed sighs of relief, and Francisco's laugh rang out. "Please him! He'll be delighted. You're all too kind."

Everyone began to talk at once but fell silent instantly when Don Cristóbal's voice rose above the din. "Come, boys, we must arrange to leave immediately. We mustn't delay now that we have decided."

His sons rose with alacrity. Riding, measuring land, racing, gambling, sleeping out on the ground! Maybe—oh, surely—they would find a bear to fight. The women rose like a bevy of bright birds in sudden flight. All at once there were a dozen things to do. Julio must wear his heaviest poncho because the nights were cool and he was subject to sickness in the chest. Had Pedro remembered to fix the faulty stirrup he had been reminded time and time again about?

"Listen," Cristóbal cried in rising eagerness: "We can have fiesta when we return." The cry was taken up. Of course they could have a fiesta. The women could make ready and when the men came back from the measuring they would begin. Think of the music, the dancing, the fun. Any excuse was excuse enough for fiesta. Besides, Don Xavier might have his feelings hurt if they didn't give at least a ball in honor of the land he was perhaps going to get in a year or two. Besides, they needed a fiesta. They were becoming dulled with too much labor. Look how the boys were drooping. Francisco listened with a faint grin at the wild clatter made by the boys as they made ready. Besides, they hadn't had a fiesta for a long time. There hadn't been a real fiesta since . . . well, come to think of it . . . since . . .

Voices trailed off in sudden embarrassment. Well, there had been but one fiesta since young

Angelo's marriage. A small spasm crossed Francisco's face. For a moment he was speechless.

"Of course," Quixano cut in quickly, "do not feel obligated, my friend. We only . . . we just . . ."

"Obligated! Oh, come, Cristóbal, obligated to accept your peerless hospitality!" Long years of habit and familiar usage asserted themselves. Instinctively Francisco rescued his host from embarrassment, though for one frantic instant he wanted nothing in the world so badly as to blot out everything of the past months, and be back at Dos Ríos, and have his boy back again. *Angelito.* "I'm not sure the ladies of Dos Ríos can ride so far at this time, especially Doña Petra," he was saying smoothly, knowing the thought of fiesta would revolt her, "but I think a fiesta for us and for anyone else able to come would be a splendid idea."

When the Quixano party arrived in very high spirits at the place where the measuring began, Zavier had already erected a pile of stone on which had been set a small cross. "What do you think of it?" he called as they rode up.

Greetings were exchanged and then Francisco advised him to plaster it up with adobe to make it more durable. The alcalde's assistant was drawing a sketch of the marker. Drawing on horseback was difficult and they courteously refrained from hurrying him.

When it finally began, there was no solemnity in the procedure. The *vaqueros* were chosen to measure, and each took one end of a chain of fifty-yard length. They secured the ends to long stakes. One Indian held his horse still by the pile of stones and thrust his stake into the earth. The second, holding his stake with the other end of the chain, kicked his pony and was off at full gallop.

A ragged cheer rose from the men. It had begun! Xavier's face shone with excitement. This was going to be his! When the *vaquero* had reached the length of the chain and it grew taut, he stopped his pony and in one swift motion bent and thrust the stake into the ground. This was a signal to the man sitting his quiet mount at the marker. Instantly his stake was withdrawn from the ground and he was off, riding at top speed, approaching and passing the second Indian, until the chain was again drawn tight. In this way a hundred yards of land were measured in a matter of moments.

The rancheros and the officials kept up intermittently with the surveyors. There was much time along the way for pleasure and activity. Races were won, bets were made. The sun rose hotter, and with it the dust. Excitement mounted, and the men became begrimed with sweat. By noon a good many miles had been measured off. Someone whose duty it had been had ridden ahead and killed a wandering steer. Pits had been dug and choice cuts of meat sputtered on stakes. The juice dripped down on the stones causing a tantalizing aroma to rise.

Squatting on the ground, the Indians ate some of the lesser cuts raw. Xavier, Francisco and the other Spaniards made for the shade of some large oak trees and flung themselves down on the ground to rest. At a safe distance because of flies an Indian was pegging out the hide of the steer so the owner would find it. It was worth two dollars. They were welcome to the meat, they knew, but they felt bound to leave the hide for the owner. Money was money.

"Here comes the meat," shouted Xavier as she saw the Indians approaching with the steaming food. They fell to ravenously, and when they had finished, they spread out their ponchos under the trees to sleep awhile. When the siesta was finished they set out for more measuring. There was some argument on whether or not the last fifty yards had been tallied, but finally an agreement was reached. Fifty yards more or less didn't matter, and they were all satisfied with the decision. A question of miles might have caused confusion, but why quibble about yards?

Time was taken to butcher and cook. Time was taken to sleep. Time was taken to stop and fight bears which came suddenly into camp as they went farther north. By the time the land was measured and mapped, all agreed that a substantial amount of work had been accomplished. It was definitely a time for fiesta.

It was not until the day following this entertainment that the Dos Ríos party started home. Due to a late start they were still on the road at nightfall.

"What do you say, Xavier, shall we sleep on the road or shall we go on?"

"Whatever you think, my cousin, although it would be nice to get home tonight."

"So I thought. A little night riding won't hurt us—if my *vaqueros* can stand it," he ended, raising his voice. There was a murmurous scoffing from the Indians who rode behind them, and the ride continued.

"We're on Dos Ríos land," Francisco observed once, an undertone of satisfaction in his voice.

"How can you tell, Francisco?"

"I don't know. I suppose I recognize it. I know this land as well as I know the palm of my hand."

"Do you suppose I shall know mine so well?"

"In time, I'm sure. You have to become used to it—as you do a woman. It takes time."

Xavier was silent. Perhaps in time he would know his land and his woman. He grimaced in the darkness. Let us pray that his land would not be so hard to know as his woman was. He wondered if he would ever be completely at ease with her, if she would ever be completely his. Perhaps after they had their own home, things would be easier. Perhaps when he was master in his own house and not taking second place to his cousin, things would be different. He had Francisco to thank for it. This was all Francisco's doing. It was at Francisco's instigation that he would one day be a landowner. When the time came, in the presence of witnesses and officials he would know the joy of entering onto his own land, and walking on it, breaking branches from trees, scattering handfuls of earth and performing other acts which showed to all that the land was his. He would hear the magistrate order that from that time on he would be held true owner and possessor of that land.

"I love you for this, Francisco," Xavier said suddenly.

"No thanks, please, my cousin." Francisco laughed. "It would have happened sooner or later anyhow. Little Catalina is not one to share another woman's house for long." They both knew he lied, but neither spoke of it. "There is the house, Xavier, home at last."

"Where, Francisco?" Xavier strained his eyes in the darkness.

"Don't you see it?"

"No, and I don't think you do."

"I see it. I swear." Francisco declared. "I'll race you!" He spurred his horse suddenly in the direction where he knew his house stood, silent and solid in the darkness.

Chapter 13

By the tenth of April the marking season at Dos Ríos was entering its last stages. Francisco and Enrique foresaw its close sometime before the middle of May. It had begun the first of February at Dos Ríos after a series of rodeos up the coast, starting far south at Rancho San Cristóbal. The labor had been heavy, for the animals seemed to have multiplied since the last rodeo and there was a vast amount of cattle to brand, earmark and castrate. Francisco, Enrique and the Dos Ríos *vaqueros* had gone with their tame cattle first to the south and then to the north to attend the rodeos and sort out the Dos Ríos wild cattle which had become mixed with that of other ranchos. Enrique never seemed to leave his saddle, and Francisco spent little time in the house. Xavier, contrary to his past habits, joined with vigor in the work, trying to learn everything he could.

Guillermo had reached his element. He rode constantly at Francisco's side and seemed to delight in the difficult feats and tasks required of him. He learned with remarkable speed, and more than once Enrique wondered hopefully if perhaps in a year or two Guillermo might be qualified to take his place at Dos Ríos. Enrique's regard for Francisco was great and he would never leave until his place could be adequately filled, but he longed for land of his own. He spoke of this to Francisco, knowing that their understanding was so great no offense would be taken. Francisco looked thoughtful. Guillermo for *mayordomo?* Then he laughed. "Well, we'll have to get some of the Indian out of him first." Enrique grinned. That was true. A little authority went a long way with Guillermo and the savage, despite the white blood, seemed just below the surface. Indians were notoriously hard taskmasters and Francisco was firm in his belief that excess brutality gained one nothing.

On the morning of April tenth Doctor Vaiz arrived at Dos Ríos. He had ridden at almost breakneck speed for the last ten miles, in sudden panic that he would be too late for Petra's confinement. He was reassured as he clattered up to the door by seeing Petra herself watering the potted plants which hung from the roof of the loggia.

"It is Don Claudio!" The shout went up from the Indians in the yard. One rushed forward to take his horse's bridle. Claudio Vaiz was well liked. He had relieved a good deal of pain, and the more civilized Indians thought much more of him than of any tribal doctor. The tribal doctor cared more for ridding the body of the evil spirit than of quelling the pain the spirit caused. Not so Claudio. They thought of him with affection because of this.

"Put down that watering pot, young woman," Vaiz commanded cheerfully as he dismounted. "Though I will say you are looking very well."

"Thank you, Don Claudio. It's a relief to know you're here." She smiled, obediently setting down the pot and offering him her hand.

The cry, "It is Don Claudio!" had echoed throughout the house, and people began to pour out the door to welcome him.

"Claudio!" Francisco cried, and the two men

embraced. "I'm so glad you got here. It is only my good fortune that I was here to meet you. I spend little time in the house these days."

"I can well imagine." The doctor laughed, leaning over to grip Guillermo's hand. "How are you, boy? How does the marking go, Francisco?"

"Extremely well. We should be finished by next month. You will stay awhile, won't you, Claudio?"

"Ah, Doña Catalina," the doctor said tilting up the girl's chin. "Shall I stay on until July for the new Miramontes?" She fled, laughing, back into the house.

After the doctor had finished his examination of Petra, he told her he believed that the baby would be born on the twelfth or thirteenth. He cautioned her to let him know the moment she felt anything faintly resembling a pain. She assured him she would, for she wanted to take no chances with this baby—all she would ever have of Angelo.

Petra woke the next morning with the sensation that something had just happened. She glanced down with sleep-hazy eyes, saw her distended body under the cover and thought with mingled fear and eagerness that perhaps her baby would come today. She was almost ready to go down to the chapel when the sensation came again. Even though the other feeling had occurred during her sleep, she recognized it as the same. It was so slight as to be almost nothing. Something between a tremor and a flutter seemed to pass through her. She waited, with her hand on the doorknob, but there was nothing else. Smiling to herself, feeling uncertain and hesitant, she opened the door and started to the chapel. It would be today then.

Despite Doctor Vaiz's injunction she found she could not tell anyone about it yet. The morning prayers were a faint and meaningless murmur in her ears. The breakfast might have been so much bark for all she tasted it. She was held in a dreamy lassitude and could do little more than wander from room to room accomplishing nothing. It was midmorning before anything else occurred. This time it was stronger, less a tremor and more like a mild cramp. She realized with sudden fright that she must hurry and tell Don Claudio.

But when she reached the door and saw him talking with Francisco in the yard, she was seized with a fit of embarrassment. Why, she felt fine now. It would be a pity to call the doctor from his conversation, especially when Francisco was taking valuable time from his work to visit with him. Suppose it was only a cramp and nothing concerning the baby.

She went back into the *sala*, her cheeks flushing. Aimlessly, she went from mantel to table, to window, pushing a lamp here, moving a dish there, tugging a bit at the drapery. She knew what would happen as soon as she told them, and she was reluctant. There would be a great turmoil. People would rush about, getting things for her that she didn't want, asking how she felt, talking, talking, talking.

Having a baby should be a private thing. There would be plenty of time to tell them—having a baby took a long time. God knew it had taken Ana long enough in the darkness of that stifling midnight. There was plenty of time, and now she felt only a vague desire to stand perfectly still and look out into the pleasant sunlight.

It took her until midafternoon to summon the doctor. During the interval she experienced several pains. She would think, catching her breath and clinging to doorway or mantel, that she would call him now. Yes, this was pain. When it had passed there seemed no point in disturbing him until next time. Then it happened just as she had known it would. The knowledge seemed to leap, permeate and spread over the entire household in an instant. Laggard steps were quickened for no reason. Inconsequential tasks were rushed to with senseless speed. The house was filled with a wild excited urgency.

It is time. It is time. Word went about. Would it be a boy? Many thought a girl. Others said with sudden twisting of the lips, Never mind boy or girl, just so it *is*. Just so it *lives*. What a pity if the fair-haired doña lost the last of her lost husband. And those who had wailed and mourned for the young don sucked in their breath a little and some of them clasped their beads in prayer. Lugarda, who dampened the clothes, pursed her lips and argued, "Have no fear for Doña Petra, a girl of great determination. She will have this child." Delfina nodded as she pressed with care the ruffled edge of one of the doña's petticoats. Those in the kitchen who ground the meal sat against the walls and made less noise in order to be sure they heard when first she cried out in the pain of bearing the child.

In all the house they were a little admiring because it was almost dusk before Petra surrendered enough to cry out. She, clutching at the rank and rumpled sheet, heard her own wail of anguish with a feeling of dismal disappointment. She was just like the rest of them: weak as water when it came to birthing a child. But men too cried. Angelo had cried. She squeezed her eyes shut and tears seeped from beneath the lids. She hated looking at the disordered room. The candles had not been lighted and dusk crept in, gathering in gray shadows in the corners. She longed for the sunlight, for some brightness.

"My necklace," she sobbed, "my necklace that

Angelo gave me!" They thought she was delirious and sought to calm her. She found this infuriating, but speech was difficult with her swollen and laggard tongue. "My necklace, my diamonds!" she wailed in wild despair.

She got the necklace, and had the impression that it was Ysidra's small hand which had pressed it into hers. *Now!* She had the bright necklace! With every wave of pain she clutched it tighter. The stones bit savagely into her palms. She could rest a little from the great pain in feeling the small pain. Just so had Angelo bitten his arms and scratched his chest.

Her cries came to the ears of the old man against the adobe wall, and he knew the sound of raw agony which meant a child was being born. He sat still in dozing wonder and hoped the child would live to play in the patio. The cry came again and he moved uneasily and settled himself more firmly against the house. It was well that it was warmer this day. He would sleep and sleep again. After many sleepings and wakings another child would either play in the sun or be dead; another little boy, perhaps, with curly hair. Dimly, with vague motions, half-formed and forgotten and taken up again, he lifted his eyelids and looked about the hazy patio. He hadn't seen the little boy in a long time. He pursed his withered lips and made a sad clucking sound. Ah yes . . . the young don. And the younger don was gone. He sighed a little as the cry of the girl came again.

At the mission the two suspects stood side by side, sullen and silent, facing the priest. Father Gabriel looked at them with something like regret in his face. He hated thieving Indians and nearly all Indians were thieves. The cloak of Christianity and civilization was yet a thin finish.

"Well," he said with flat finality, "one of you did it. We know that. It will go easier with you if the guilty confesses—for I will find out so as not to punish unduly the innocent." He closed his lips thinly and waited. Neither Indian moved. Each maintained his own innocence and accused the other.

Father Patricio stood a little back of his superior, his stomach writhing in the thought that one or both of those men was going to be whipped. He hated whipping with all the energy in his hard body. Man was not made to be whipped. But Gabriel was right. If they escaped once, the offense multiplied; countless others who held back for fear of punishment followed in their tracks.

The elder priest shrugged. "You are both foolish children in the eyes of God," he said, "for the evidence has been before me. Consider that I have been shown the half-butchered carcass of the mule. Consider that one of the mission mules is missing. Consider that I myself saw the brand on its hide. Consider that both of you have mule meat in your cabins. Now which one killed it?"

He paused. Neither answered. He went on: "It is as if you didn't get enough beef to satisfy your stomachs. I realize that you vastly prefer the meat of the mule, but beef is of the same value to your body and you weren't put on earth to satisfy its desires. Now answer me. Which of you conceived and executed this idea?"

He spoke sharply now, weary of haggling, and both Indians shifted uneasily and glanced about. They had heard the difference in his tone. Patricio heard it too and his eyes pleaded with them to speak up and so lighten the punishment that was sure to follow. But some stubborn instinct kept the guilty one still.

Gabriel turned to Patricio. "Get me a flat bowl of water," he said.

Patricio sighed and turned from the room out into the sunlight of the patio. Those foolish children, did they think they could hide anything from Gabriel? As he secured the bowl he turned his gaze out over the plain toward where Dos Ríos lay, wondering if Vaiz had reached there yet, wondering if Petra's time had come. She had got so thin since her bereavement. He worried lest she were too frail to bear the baby healthily, though he had cautioned her to eat for its sake if not her own. He balanced the bowl of water carefully and took a long time walking back. He must not spill any, for the bowl had to be as nearly full as possible. This also gave him a chance to look just so much longer in the direction of Dos Ríos; in case someone was coming with news he would know immediately instead of having to wait for the hoofbeats. At last he gained the dim doorway of the room, stepped carefully inside and gently set the brimming bowl on a table. The surface of the water moved from the motion of carrying it. Father Gabriel waited with nerve-wracking patience for the last flicker of a ripple to fade. When the surface was as smooth as glass he raised his eyes to the two suspects.

"Come now," he said in a tone almost friendly. "Which of you actually stole the mule from the mission?"

Both savages glistened with sweat and remained immobile.

"But I will find out anyway," he pressed almost disgustedly, "for some years ago a friend of mine explained to me this method of telling whether or not a man is lying when he speaks." He waited again. Then as he saw that there was nothing to be gained by waiting, he signed the nearest Indian to approach.

"Ramón," he said, "step over here and place—carefully!—the first finger of your hand into the water. Do not touch the bottom of the bowl. And try not to disturb the quiet of the water." His tone was brisk and businesslike and held authority.

Ramón's eyes shifted uneasily to his companion and he did as he was told. Fresh drops of sweat broke out on his face and shoulders as he gently placed his forefinger in the exact center of the bowl. What business was this? How could a bowl of water speak out who lied and who didn't? He knew he was innocent of the actual planning and execution of the butchering. He had eaten of the succulent meat when it was offered him, but he hadn't stolen or killed the animal. He glanced up and saw the priest was watching the slight ripple disappear from the surface of the water.

"Be very still, Ramón," the priest cautioned, bending low as if to listen to the bowl. Ramón was completely still. "Now, tell me, please, if you stole our mule."

"No, Father, I did not steal it," he said waiting for whatever the bowl was supposed to do. Long unbearable seconds ticked away while he kept wondering sickly if the bowl was supposed to speak.

After what seemed an interminable length of time the priest straightened. "Now, Teobaldo," he said to the other Indian, "do the same as Ramón has done."

The other Indian stepped forward. Sweat trickled in little rivulets from his armpits as he thought of the whipping he would receive if the bowl proclaimed his guilt. But how could an earthen bowl talk? He placed his finger in the water and again they all waited for the slight ripple to disappear.

"Now, tell me if you stole our mule," Gabriel said bending low to gaze on the surface of the water.

"No," Teobaldo answered noting the little ripple that widened about his finger as he spoke the word.

The priest straightened. "You lie to me, Teobaldo," he said regretfully. "Your tongue lies but the muscles of your finger cannot, and they speak out that you have lied. So you must be whipped not only for stealing but for lying. And you, Ramón," he said turning to the other Indian, "you undoubtedly ate of the meat."

Ramón nodded dumbly, as there was no point in lying to the padre if he could ferret out which was a truth and which was a lie.

"Then you too shall be whipped—but only a little."

The muscles in Patricio's back arched and strained. He turned a little sick and let his gaze bore for a moment into the adobe wall of the room. In a few minutes both Indians would be lashed to stakes with rawhide and across their naked backs the singing whip would cut again and again and again. His hands were damp with dread. There was something that sickened him about a human being tied like an animal to a stake. Rebellion rose. If they were all children of God and created in His image, they should not be treated like animals. Immediately his mind could hear the often repeated logic of Gabriel. Even children need chastisement for wrongdoing, else how can they learn to do right? Even Christ himself suffered chastisement. There was no arguing the placid logic of Gabriel.

The whip was already restless in the hand of Joaquin, the Indian *mayordomo* of the mission. From the movement of his eager muscles the whip danced and twisted on the earth floor, waiting to begin with, it seemed, an evil impatience of its own. Patricio looked at the immobile face of Joaquin. He was a strong hard Indian. Put into a position of authority, he was merciless to his less fortunate fellows, as was characteristic of such cases. He appeared to take a primitive delight in cutting the whip into their backs. Patricio had seen it before. It was as if Joaquin were punishing the whole Indian race for their subjection. In punishing them he made them even more humble. He waited for the two culprits to be bound and led out into the open. The restless twisting of the whip handle made it continue its writhing dance on the floor.

Patricio would have to watch the whipping. There was no avoiding that. He could ill afford to gain a reputation for being fainthearted. If he did then the Indians would begin to take advantage of him and so many more punishments would occur. He must go out and watch it. The muscles in his shoulders jerked convulsively in an echo of sympathy for those in the backs of the Indians. He thanked God weakly that Gabriel was in charge. Patricio, certainly, was much too weak-willed to discharge the duties incumbent on the head of a mission. He stepped into the yard and though he appeared to watch the activity preparatory to the whipping, he gazed with wide eyes at the confused melee of movement. He had a trick of not actually watching, but of staring at some insignificant thing until the rest of his vision became hazy and out of focus, and so he never actually saw distinctly any whipping that occurred. Naked children ran about eagerly getting their laggard parents lest they miss the show. Indians hurried from all their duties and milled in an anxious excited crowd, craning for a better view.

Then almost like a deliverance to Patricio he realized that above the mutter of the crowd there rose the sound of approaching hoofs.

Finally the baby was born and a deathly silence settled in Petra's room. She had sunk into unconsciousness from the last unbearable pain of its birth. The baby was passed quickly to the midwife and Doctor Vaiz turned his attention to Petra, begrudging what little blood of her could not be saved and fell down to stain the sheets.

Word came to those who waited . . . little snatches, eagerly heard and passed along. It is alive! It is a boy! The doña is well.

Father Patricio, grimed from a long ride, laid a hand on Francisco's arm when he saw the baby. "We can wait for a proper christening for this one," he said smiling. "This is such a healthy, sturdy little baby!" He held the child after the midwife had cleaned it, and was reluctant to put it down, gloating over it a little.

Petra slept deeply and restfully, oblivious of the news which spread over the rancho that a living boy had been born. Riders set out to the neighboring ranches to tell of it and invite all who wished to come to the christening. Xavier, choking with emotion tiptoed in to pat her sleeping hand. Catalina, sobered by Petra's torment, was only slightly annoyed that it had not been a girl. Guillermo, his face stiff and blank, had a sudden urge to seek out a private place to pray. Francisco drew up a chair and sat down by the bedside. He looked for long quiet minutes at the baby in its cradle.

"It is not an ugly baby," Ysidra offered thoughtfully.

"Nor was Angelo," he replied remotely.

The baby slept quietly and peacefully, its waxen eyelids exuding a faint shining moisture along the edges. Its tiny fist curled warmly against the exquisite, hand-worked coverlet.

The sounds of the house were subdued because the mother slept, but no one could see or hear the muffled activity without knowing that something of great portent had occurred. People went about swiftly on pointless errands, stopping to greet one another with broad smiles and sometimes moist eyes. A boy—have you heard! A little boy at Dos Ríos! A little child in Don Francisco's house! The spirit of fiesta drifted and rose. Oh, surely the don would have a great fiesta now. What if the house was in mourning! Don Angelo would be the last to care. Hadn't he always loved fiesta? Remember how he could dance. Remember how the white satin of his jacket flashed in the candlelight. Remember how the ends of his red sash gleamed. Surely no one could think of Doña Ana who might rest uneasily in her grave at the thought of fiesta. What place had that pale shade in this house of living mothers and babies? Oh yes, the don would arrange for a great fiesta.

Well, then, it was time to look to clothing. Many hands shook out the brightest cottons. This yellow skirt was fullest. This green sash could be washed and pressed. This necklace was gaudy enough. Excitement mounted and voices were lowered with an effort and many times laughter bubbled up and was suddenly muffled. Guitars pinged in secret tuning and some smiled vacantly into space trying to compose a new song.

Dust rose in the hard-beaten patio from the many hurrying feet. The old man sat against the wall and waited for his dinner. His withered lips moved a bit in anticipation of the food. He kept thinking that there was something he should remember. It was almost dark when someone thought to feed him. When his hunger was appeased he remembered. It was the child. It had been born, then. He negotiated the raising of his eyelids and looked about the darkening patio, smiling to himself. Such activity could mean only that the child lived. He hoped it was a little boy, and wondered if he would live to see it running about the patio with the sunlight making a brightness in its curly hair.

* * *

Petra wakened late in the evening. Her sleep had been deep and refreshing. She opened her eyes to see the great bulk of her godmother beside the bed, conscious that the woman had just finished speaking. She turned her head on the pillow and observed Francisco.

"Where is Don Claudio?" she asked, faintly alarmed that her voice sounded so dim.

"Having a well-earned dinner, my dear," Ysidra replied.

"My baby!" Petra gasped, suddenly remembering the dark nightmare which surely must have brought it forth.

"Right here." With strange swiftness Ysidra lifted the sleeping infant from its cradle.

Petra took it with hands maddenly weak and tugged in panic at its wrappings. Nervous tears welled in her eyes. "It is all right?" she managed to ask. "I must see if it's all right!"

Ysidra laughed. "Of course he's all right. He's a perfectly beautiful little creature."

Petra left off her agitated fumbling. The baby had stirred at her movement and now lay still and sleeping again. She gazed at the small feet she had uncovered. Tenderly she covered them up and eased her sore body so as to create a little well between herself and her arm for the baby to lie in. How many times had she so eased her body in slight movement for the comfort of Angelo? She closed her eyes. She must pray. She really must. She must thank Mary for the baby's safe arrival. But she was so full of this strange new ecstacy that she could think of no coherent prayer. But Mary would know. Mary herself must have felt this same way.

Chapter 14

Delfina Ruiz laid a stack of freshly ironed clothing on a table and allowed her iron to cool, for her day's work was finished. Precious little work had really got done that day. Her face, delightfully fair for an Indian's, was wreathed in smiles. Her mother was from the north, or the Karok tribe. Her father, Ruiz, called himself a Spaniard, but the darkness of his face bespoke much Indian blood, even if the mixture had occurred some generations back. Delfina's eyes, though large and brilliant as Karok women's usually were, had a lighter shade, amber flecked with green. Their clearness in her smooth dark face was pleasantly exotic. Because of her unmarried state, her hair hung in two thick braids down her back. She had reached her fifteenth year and there was a subtle ripeness and womanliness about her warm red lips and rounded body. She was, Lugarda in the ironing room often said, the best dress ironer in California.

Now as Delfina laughed and talked with Lugarda and took the older woman's direction in matters concerning the clothing, she felt a swelling of secret amusement. What, indeed, would the other woman say if she knew that little Delfina was beloved of Don Francisco? As yet, who knew? None, save she and her lord Francisco. That was another proof of her superiority. Had she bragged and boasted to the other women over this? No, not she. She had conducted her affair with utmost decorum. She was a lady. Yet the knowledge burned within her and she longed to drop just a hint, just a word. How respect for her would soar! For a moment she ceased to be Delfina Ruiz and became Doña Delfina, Spaniard, lady of this house. Her pert face assumed a look of housewifely care as she studiously observed the pile of clean clothing. This room was hers and everything in it belonged to her, including Lugarda who dampened the clothes. Beyond this room lay the rest of the house impatiently waiting the guidance of her hand.

The bubble burst and she smiled at her fancy. Oh, what a wicked creature she was! (She told herself this often.) At times she considered with alarm her last resting place in hell. She knew her catechism forward and backward and had heard many a Mass with feeling and fervor, but first she was an Indian. Some of her dim ancestors might have been reared in gentle Spanish homes, but others had lived in caves across whose walls were scratched red pictures of now forgotten things. The smile on her face remained fixed, but the sick finger of dread traced an image in her mind. Now she was afraid again. What had she done! What a fool she had been! She was no different from any of a hundred Indian women who looked at the big form of Francisco Estrada with longing in their bodies. What demon had possessed her and made her weak! But it wasn't all her fault, she thought savagely. How could she have resisted him anyhow if he wanted her? He was Don Francisco.

She remembered with a quick singing in her veins the first time he had ever kissed her. The gentleness had given way to insistence, rough and needful. There had been a melting in her bones.

When the kiss was finished, she looked frankly into his eyes. Innocent as she was, a message, old as time, passed between them. He had let her go—and this surprised her, for she had thought he would thrust her down roughly for his pleasure. She was an Indian and had seen, as all Indian children saw, sights not meant for their eyes. He had let her go easily and she had stood back from him, shaking in confusion. What was she doing? She, a good girl, a Christian! What was she thinking of!

The same fear rose up in her that every Indian felt for every white man, however deep he might keep it hidden. There was the knowledge embedded in the fibers of every Indian child's brain that no matter how long or how desperate the struggle, the subtle ways of the law, the custom and the Church foreordained the white man supreme and unbeatable. One knew from birth the frailty of the Indian before the white man's wrath. Only one body you had, and even that body was subject to the white man's wish. The flesh could be laid open by the whip of him who always held it, and the very blood that ran in the veins let out.

Delfina knew the ways of the Spaniard, for she had lived many years with them and didn't some of their blood sing in her body? She knew that many and uncountable were the cases of Spaniards and Indians being together. But this was not for her. She wanted safety and a good marriage, and they did not lie this way. Frightened, she had turned and would have run like a rabbit from Francisco's sight, denying the delight of his embrace, washing the joy of it from her mind. But he had stopped her.

"Stay, Delfina." His voice had been pleasant. There was no need for him to speak loudly. He would be obeyed, and he knew it. "Go on about your work. I am leaving." Then he was gone.

During the uneasy nights that followed she totaled in her mind the number of Indian women she knew who consorted with white men. Look at Concha! Concha had even had a child which was certainly not her husband's. Concha went free. She did not have to kneel with Don Xavier, tied to him, before a manger of grass, to show the world they had lived like animals. She didn't have to stand by the church door with a wooden puppet held to her breast to show she had tasted the joy of sinful love. Law was the law, and right was right, but to her knolwedge no one of Don Xavier's or Don Francisco's standing and wealth had ever had to undergo these humiliating punishments. There would be no danger for her, no risk at all. But one.

Now the smile on her face became a little thin. Even the old game of what-would-they-say-if-they-knew lost its appeal. Surely she must have realized that this must come to pass. And she would have had it no different. She was his beloved. She had lain against his great body in exhaustion. She loved him with a passion inconceivable a few months ago. That should be reward enough for anything to come. True, he was a Spaniard, but there was no sneaking in him. She knew what paltry passions and shamefaced regard certain white men held for certain Indians. There was no skulking in Don Francisco. Their love was not to be snatched in dark corners, at odd moments, got through quickly in an embarrassed and unclean manner. Francisco was a kind and careful man. If Delfina did not love him madly for any other reason, she would love him deeply and gratefully because he treated her as he might treat a Spanish woman. She held this thought triumphantly. And always she had closed her mind to the thought that, one day, she might have a child by him. Ah, and she had no husband as Concha had to father it. She would have to marry—quickly—just anybody! So the child would be fathered in the eyes of the Church, and she would still be a good woman. She had been lucky for a long time. But she had really known the luck couldn't last forever—not with Francisco for a lover.

There was her mother to be considered, a strong-minded woman, always conscious that she had married above herself in marrying the excellent shoemaker, Pablo Ruiz. She herself presided over the great kitchen of Dos Ríos. Well, Delfina could put it off no longer. She took up her shawl and flung it over her head and left the house. As she walked toward the *indiada* where she lived with her parents her steps lagged. When she got there she was relieved to see that the children had been put down to sleep. Ruiz and her mother sat before the door talking of the birth of the new baby.

"Ah, Delfina," Ruiz said smiling, "you took some things upstairs. Did you see the baby?"

She fixed the smile back on her face and regaled him with the bits of gossip she had accumulated against this time.

Her mother nodded, her eyes gleaming darkly in the night. "Yes," she would say from time to time, "yes, that is so."

Ruiz smoked in contentment, nodding and chuckling. "Fiesta now," he said finally. "The don has what he wants—a child."

"Let us have a private celebration of our own." His wife laughed. "I brought a thing or two from the kitchen today."

Ruiz laughed and slapped his thigh softly. That was one of the beauties of marrying an Indian.

Their fingers had a magic in picking up useful things. "What did you bring, my angel?"

"We shall have a cup of the don's fine coffee to celebrate for the new baby. And some sweet dried figs," she said going into the cabin.

Delfina sighed a little as she followed her parents inside. Her mother was so occupied with laughter and gossip as she prepared the treat that she failed to note her daughter's unaccustomed silence. Delfina accepted a cup of steaming coffee with thanks and commenced to drink it.

"Did you hear me?" Ruiz asked her.

"What, Father? I beg your forgiveness. I was thinking of something else."

"I said, my girl, I have made a pair of red satin slippers for just such an occasion as this coming fiesta but I don't know who will get them. I didn't use much satin, for satin is dear, and I doubt that there are feet small enough to fit them." He grinned at her with crooked yellow teeth.

Delfina swallowed. He favored her above all the others. Then her eagerness rose. Red satin! "Father, where are they? Let me see them!"

He threw back his head and laughed delightedly. "Oh no, they are not for such as you. I was thinking of offering them to Doña Catalina, though I bought the satin from a boat and it is mine."

"Oh, please don't tease me. Let me see them!"

Pretending to grumble, he rose from the table and secured a bundle from a dark corner. "Man can't even have a cup of coffee in peace," he growled. "Here, look at them and leave me in peace."

Delfina undid the package with shaking hands. Oh, they were lovely! Quick tears rose to fill her eyes.

"They are so ugly that you weep?" he teased softly, so as not to wake the children.

"Now don't plague the girl," her mother scolded

him, cuffing his shoulder. "Women always weep when they are happy. You are happy, my angel?"

Delfina nodded, looking at the strangely hazy forms of her parents. "I'm very happy," she said, "because of these and because I am going to have a baby."

Her mother was pouring the last of the coffee for Ruiz. The pot jerked convulsively in her hand. She set it with a thud on the table, her face changing. Swiftly she raised her hand and struck at Delfina.

Ruiz caught at her arm. "No, old woman. Wait. No!"

"He's a Spaniard, Mama!" Delfina's words weren't uttered quickly enough to forestall the first blow, and her cheek went numb. But there was no second.

A Spaniard.

"Who?" Señora Ruiz asked, something like pride on her face. A Spaniard. That was something else entirely.

Delfina rubbed her cheek with one hand and clutched the red slippers in the other. "It is Don Francisco," she said.

Both her mother and her father remained silent for a long time, their dark faces intent. "Don Francisco!" They breathed the name softly. Ah! Why hadn't she spoken of it before? thought her mother. Any other woman he lay with spoke of it, bragged about it, became insufferable to live with! Many who had only had a kind word from him exaggerated it into a love passage. She sat down at the table slowly. No, Delfina wouldn't boast of it. Delfina was a lady. She regarded the amber tint of her daughter's flesh, so much lighter than her own. Ah, blood would tell!

"When?" she asked, breaking the silence.

"I . . . think in November," Delfina answered uncertainly.

Ruiz drummed his fingers on the table. "Have you thought of anyone you would like to marry?" he asked after a time.

She tossed her head with a little of the old pertness. "Yes," she said. "Don Francisco."

Something between a rasp and a chuckle escaped her mother. "Talk sense!" she snapped, and added in the same breath, "Not an Indian."

"Oh no," just as quickly Delfina agreed. She might have to hurry a marriage, but she would marry her equal or better. Her eyes were veiled for a long moment as she thought about it, seeing in her mind all the faces with which she was familiar.

Guillermo?

Guillermo, whose father was an unknown white soldier and whose mother had been an Indian as hers was. She thought of Guillermo as the adopted son of Don Francisco, living in the great house, riding at Don Francisco's side these past months. Guillermo had his own *caponera* of pleasure and work horses, splendid clothing, beautiful saddles and spurs. And his name—a wave of pure exultation flooded her—his name was Estrada!

Her eyes had become dark and brilliant when she raised them. "I will marry Guillermo, Father."

Ruiz threw back his head to laugh, choking, strangling with sudden unbearable mirth. "Delfina! Little pet! Little owl!" he gasped, wiping his eyes. "Oh, little wise one!" He turned to his wife. "You know the talk, old woman. You have heard them say that Don Francisco so loves that boy he will make him *mayordomo* of Dos Ríos. Well, then—" he struggled against his laughter—"well, then, who will be the *mayordomo's wife!*" He ended with a howl of pure delight, waking the children.

"Little wise one is very sure of herself," commented his wife as she hushed the younger ones and made them shut their eyes again. "You know what airs that young cock takes upon himself. With his grand notions, and his name being Estrada, he is planning a better marriage than to such as Delfina."

Her daughter laughed, although a little weakly. She knew the thought was a daring one. What would Don Francisco say? They would have to secure his permission because he was, by law, Guillermo's father. She turned suddenly to her mother. "Oh, you mean he might not want to marry me! Oh, Mother, I'm not such a child as you think. I could have had Guillermo long ago. I have only to lift my hand. I do!" she insisted as her mother began to laugh again. "He's only a boy, lovesick for any pretty girl who gives him a smile!"

"Well, if you could," Ruiz cut in, "and mind I say *if* you could, it would be an excellent marriage. Of course there is Don Francisco to consider. We don't know what he would think of marrying his adopted son to you—in the circumstances." A new thought occurred to him. "He couldn't very well refuse you some money. Look at what he spends on Guillermo! When I think of that Indian dressing like a don! And you know how lenient Don Francisco is. If Guillermo *wanted* you, Don Francisco could never find it in his heart to deny the boy."

"He will want me," Delfina said flatly, and both her parents looked at her with new respect in their faces.

Don Francisco would be generous to her, thought Delfina, and with Guillermo. Guillermo would want her. That would be a simple matter to arrange. Yet with all this assurance she went to her bed carrying a heavy grief in her heart. She stared at the reed-thatched roof above her head and thought of those in the great house: how they had hung over the cradle of the new little baby; how the doctor had hurried from Monterey for its birth; how the priest had rushed from the mission to christen it; how they all rejoiced because Don Angelo's child had been born alive and well. They planned a great fiesta in its honor. And Don Francisco's own—*his own*—child would be born in the *indiada,* without even a midwife, with only some fine Spanish blood it couldn't lay claim to. She buried her face in the covers and began to sob dismally, because she had not thought of these things before, and because thinking of them now was a painful thing. It must be a girl! How could she face a man-child and let him know that, except for his mother, he might be the lord of Dos Ríos.

During the next few days no one could tell by looking at her that her life had been ripped apart and that she had set about with stolid grimness to repair it. She joined with the others of the house in the excited gossip. With outward absorption she discussed the new baby's name: Angelo José Mario Teodoro Graciano Estrada y Hutchins. She listened with interest to the news that the godparents had been chosen: Doña María Luisa Quixano and Don Teodoro Acuña. She knew with what pleasure they accepted the honor and already felt their families drawn closer together because of it. But even as she learned these details and smiled and talked, they were bitter in her mouth. However, the bitterness did not reach her pretty smiling face, and her gaiety became less forced when she saw the unbelieving delight with which Guillermo responded to her sudden interest. Oh, this is easy! she thought. He is only a boy. He knows nothing at all. He will soon be my husband.

* * *

Teodoro Acuña stood in the doorway of the loggia, flushed and pleased, having spent the morning accepting congratulations on his godson. This must be almost how it felt, he thought, to have a son of one's own. *Graciano.* He even thought the name with pleasure. But beneath the pleasure in his mind stirred uneasiness. His father had finally agreed to speak to Francisco about Petra. They had been closed in Francisco's office for, it seemed, hours. Perhaps it was already settled! Well, if it was, they should have the kindness to tell him about it. For a moment he was alone and was seized with an uncontrollable desire to go boldly in and find out. Quickly he snuffed out his cigarette in a flowerpot and rapped on the door. It wouldn't do to smoke in front of his elders.

Francisco himself opened the office door. "Come in," he said extending his hand.

"I don't mean to bother you, sir, if you are busy," Teodoro said taking the hand. "If you are, please tell me and I shall come back another time."

"No, please come in. I can't think of anyone I'd rather see."

"You're too kind," Teodoro murmured bowing. He noted with relief that his father was seated easily in one of the chairs.

"Sit down, Teodoro." Francisco pushed forward a chair, then seated himself on the wide window ledge. With his back to the light it was difficult to see his features. There was a small silence, unnatural and strange before he spoke. "Teodoro, your father has been speaking to me with regard to making provision for Doña Petra and little Graciano."

Teodoro felt his pulse quicken.

"Provision has been made, Teodoro," Francisco continued quietly. "If this knowledge causes you pain, I am deeply sorry. My affection for you is not slight, as you know. That is why I choose to tell you this myself rather than have it come through another person."

Teodoro's head had jerked up and he rose to his feet. He tried to speak twice before he succeeded. "What provision, sir?"

"I tell you this in confidence, Teodoro, because of our close relationship. As Graciano's godfather you will naturally have a certain amount of control over him. But I want him—and I think Angelo would have wanted him—to be reared here at Dos Ríos."

Color began to ebb from Teodoro's face. "I . . . don't understand you, sir."

"It is settled that a marriage between Doña Petra and me is the most sensible solution of our problem."

Teodoro concentrated a moment to hold onto the remains of his suddenly shattered poise. Petra's figure was once again dissolving in the mist. First to Angelo, now to Francisco. For an instant of raw male fury he wanted to strike out at Francisco, strike him dead.

"You cannot!" he cried harshly. "The Church won't allow it! *I* won't allow it!" He was oblivious of the fact that this was the first time he had ever spoken discourteously to a living soul.

"*You* will not!" Francisco was standing before him, Juan Acuña had risen quickly from his chair, astonishment on his face.

"I'd kill you first."

In quick rage Francisco's hand lifted and he struck Teodoro across the face. "You keep a civil tongue in your head, boy."

Juan Acuña flushed deeply, then paled. The cords in Teodoro's neck stood out in fury. He was unable to speak. His father bowed stiffly. He spoke coldly. "My son will apologize immediately for his unspeakable rudeness. I regret, Don Francisco, that I have reared so ill-bred a child."

The silence hung heavily in the room. Teodoro was visibly shaking. Years of breeding battled with his sense of outrage and loss. Finally he bowed. "I am sorry, sir," he said thickly. "I do humbly beg your pardon and forgiveness. Such a thing will never occur again."

Silently Francisco stretched out his hand. Teodoro took it and, bending lower still, kissed it as an added mark of respect. His face was ashen.

The chill voice of Don Juan Acuña fell again between them, changing the subject, speaking of the christening to come. Francisco's face was expressionless as he replied in a similar manner, adhering carefully to the pattern of courtesy set by Acuña. He knew that Acuña, his best friend, would have died rather than allow his son to show any discourtesy to an older person. But the mark of his hand was still on the boy's face, and Francisco knew with a feeling of regret that the perfection and wholeheartedness of his friendship with Juan Acuña had come to an end before the sound of the blow died. Acuña would not leave. Nothing could have forced him to treat Francisco with anything but his impeccable politeness in the future. He would remain to attend the fiesta. No breath of this occurrence would ever leave this room. Teodoro, because he was like his father, would be Graciano's godfather and discharge his duties to the little boy with kindness and affection. Yet the essence of their friendship had altered. Never again would they love him as deeply or respect him as much. The loss, veiled by Francisco's blandly gracious conversation with them now, was a bitter one.

By dusk of the baby's third day of life the fiesta at Dos Ríos was well launched. It was not yet time for the evening meal. At the sound of *carreta* wheels in the distance, Francisco mounted to ride out to meet additional guests. These would be from Rancho Estrella Grande which was situated the farthest of any from Dos Ríos. He had gone some distance before he realized that someone was following. Courteously he drew rein and waited for the lone horseman.

The horseman was Pablo Ruiz. Francisco smiled automatically as the man pulled up and swept off his hat in a low bow. "Good afternoon, Señor Ruiz, were you trying to catch up with me?"

"I was, Don Francisco," Ruiz answered. "I have a little present for your grandson, if you will please me by accepting it." He extended a small package to Francisco.

"Thank you very much." Francisco smiled, beginning to open the package.

"I would have gone up to the house to give it to the Doña Petra but with so many guests I felt everyone would be too busy. It is only by accident that I saw you ride out. How are the Doña Petra and the fine new boy?"

"Both are well. You should have come, though. My house is always open to you, as you know." Francisco finished unwrapping the gift and perceived that it was a pair of exquisitely fashioned deerskin shoes, scarcely the width of two of his fingers.

"This is a fine gift," he said, "and in the name of my grandson, I thank you."

Ruiz bowed, scoffing. "It is nothing, sir. I shall make him something really fine when he begins to walk." He paused and continued quickly, "Who knows but I may have a grandson of my own one of these days since Delfina is planning her marriage."

Francisco felt a stiffening in his backbone. He

began carefully to rewrap the shoes. "Who is the lucky one?" he asked.

Ruiz's face took on a look of acute surprise. "I beg the don's pardon," he began confusedly. "I thought the don knew of this. I am very sorry. It seems I am premature, but the young Guillermo said——"

"Guillermo!" Francisco's voice had the toneless quality which made the Mexican stay a quick impulse to wheel his horse and flee. He held his ground with an effort. Francisco said thoughtfully, "Guillermo has not spoken of this to me, as is the proper procedure. It seems a very sudden development."

"Perhaps you have been so busy with your guests that the young Guillermo hesitates——"

"Possibly." So that was it. Francisco felt a miserable rage. Nothing on earth could have led Delfina into a sudden marriage except sudden necessity. It would be his child as much as Angelo had been. Yet he could not claim it and it would have no heritage.

Guillermo was his adopted son. Guillermo had a heritage, a positive future in his employ at Dos Ríos; proud, intelligent, ambitious Guillermo, almost as dear to his heart as Angelo had been. If Guillermo wanted Delfina enough to marry her, perhaps that was the answer. Through Guillermo he could at least provide for this unborn child. But what about Guillermo himself? Did he know? Had he any illusions to be shattered? If the marriage was permitted, could Francisco make it up to Guillermo later? Even as he thought of all this he felt an underlying sense of jealousy that Delfina would be no longer for his own delight but for another man's. And here was Ruiz, silently and obviously waiting; Ruiz, looking after the future of Delfina.

"No harm is done, Pablo," he heard himself saying. "Guillermo will mention it to me in good time. Then proper arrangements can be made. Marriage is an expensive affair," he added.

Ruiz shook his head ruefully. "It is indeed, sir."

"Give me the pleasure, then, of handling the expense for you."

"Oh no, Don Francisco, we could not do that——" began Ruiz.

Francisco had a sudden impulse to lash out at him. Why must they always play games and speak in riddles. Ruiz knew he would accept the money. That was what he had come for—to insure the legally wedded future of Delfina. But he must make gestures of surprise and refusal.

"You must, Pablo." No anger marred Francisco's poise. "Indeed, I demand the privilege. Hasn't Delfina's mother been in my employ for the last fifteen years? Not to mention your own services to me and my family. It would give me great pleasure. Let us handle it this way: Allow me to make Delfina's mother a gift for the wedding expenses and new clothing for Delfina. All other assistance can come through Guillermo to whom, naturally, I will be very generous; since he is my adopted son."

Pablo Ruiz drew a sighing breath. That would do it. Francisco Estrada was a just man. "You are most kind, Don Francisco."

Francisco brushed this aside. "Do not thank me, my friend. Pablo——" He stopped and stared at the *carretas* which had appeared on the horizon. "My guests," he said absently, not even knowing he said it. "Pablo," he continued suddenly, "if you do have a grandchild soon——" He looked at the *carretas* for a long moment. His eyes were strangely light and clear. "I will be its godfather when it comes."

He turned again to face Ruiz. The eyes which had appeared so distant and veiled dropped their haze and fixed themselves on Ruiz's. The two men looked at each other for an instant of perfect understanding.

"I shall see to it, Don Francisco," Ruiz said. He turned his horse, spurred deeply and galloped off.

Chapter 15

Petra walked into her room, set the candle on the dresser and stood in the small pool of light that it created. Dimly she could hear music and the sound of revelry. Out in the patio and about the house they were still dancing in honor of Guillermo's marriage to Delfina. She stood for endless moments staring blankly at the wall, the crucifix, the bedpost, not seeing anything at all, thinking of the shocking, astonishing things which had happened to her that evening. How much shock could a person stand? How long did astonishment last? Would she be forever numbed by it, feeling nothing, seeing nothing. And where was Angelo? She thought of him at this moment quite without pain for the first time since his death, in a puzzled and bewildered manner. Where was Angelo that his spirit did not return and manifest itself in wild turbulent rage? Why didn't his soul shake the very foundations of the house and tumble the roof about them, crushing their heads like so many eggshells?

With the thought of eggshells came again the thought of Delfina's wedding, remembrance of the *cascarónes* which had been broken, scattering bits of tinsel and bright paper to cling to the violet silk of her dress. She was thinking with absorption of Delfina's pretty costume when a soft knock at the door reached her ears. She went to open it almost knowing it would be Francisco. He bowed.

"I knocked softly so as not to disturb you if you were sleeping," he said quietly.

"I don't seem to be tired now," she said after a moment. She felt obscurely puzzled at her poise and cordiality.

"I brought you a gift." He extended a velvet box obviously containing jewels of some sort.

Petra put out her hand and took it. "You shouldn't have," she murmured automatically, making no attempt to open it.

"They are pearls," Francisco said, "not a very original gift, I fear, but it is often said that a woman can't have too many pearls, so you may put them with your collection."

"I have no collection," Petra answered politely. "The ones I wore before were my godmother's."

"Then I'm glad I got you these. I hope you enjoy them." He left, bowing again. "Good night, Petra."

"Good night," she said and closed the door, holding the velvet box in the other hand. She really didn't need any pearls, she was thinking. She had the Montoya diamonds which were far finer. But she put the box on the dresser and pressed the catch that secured the lid. It flew back with a muffled click. There seemed, she thought, to be a great many pearls. She took them out, a long rope of them, and let them pour into her palm, unconsciously imitating an old gesture of Ysidra's. They were too many for her hand and spilled over. As she spread her fingers to catch them, they spilled in heavy drooping lengths between her fingers and hung and swung there. They were finer than Ysidra's, she thought, with only slight interest; much finer. Ysidra's were milk white. These were great lustrous pearls,

pearls with gray in them, gleaming darkly as they sagged in melancholy loops between her fingers.

I'm going to remember, she thought with dull panic. She could see him quite plainly in her mind now as she had seen him when she had gone downstairs shortly after dawn. He had discarded the black broadcloth of his mourning. She had thought, It's too soon for that! Worry filled her eyes as she looked at him in his white velvet jacket and red satin sash. There was a sparkling emerald set in the silver cord that bound his soft wool hat. The activity of Delfina's marriage pushed it far down in her mind, so that every time she looked at him she was startled afresh. The wedding was splendid—too splendid for a servant, she thought more than once, only to quell the thought because it was Guillermo's marriage too. That made it different.

At the end of the long day Francisco stopped her from going to bed. She had paused with one foot on the bottom step, feeling rusty and old before his splendid attire.

"I wanted to talk with you, Petra. Would you mind coming into my office?"

"Not at all," she replied courteously and preceded him into the small square room. She noted with satisfaction that it was empty. At least whatever he had to say was not to be shared by Ysidra this time. She turned to him, smiling, and waited.

"I shall come directly to the point, as I believe it is in your nature to appreciate statements shorn of all unnecessary words. It is this: Have you given any more thought, Petra, to my proposal of marriage?"

Petra's eyes flew wide, her body tingled with shock. "Marriage! I had thought that was settled. I told you quite plainly how I felt."

"I know you told me how you felt about it,"

Francisco said gently. "I understand that. Have you considered it from any viewpoint save how you *felt* about it?"

"I have considered it from every viewpoint I think necessary. That should be sufficient. The answer is no. It will continue to be no. That is final, sir." She held herself stiffly, making every effort to keep her face as immobile as his.

"Oh, come, Petra, forget just for a moment that you are a widow. For one moment forget that you were married to Angelo."

Petra gasped a little and saw a look of acute sympathy flash for a moment in his eyes. For some unaccountable reason this angered her.

"I am sorry," he was saying kindly, "but I ask you to consider the bare facts of the situation." He came to her side, took her arms and pulled her gently about to face him. Her head tilted back, but she kept her eyelids lowered, leaving her face pale and expressionless beneath his.

"Think back to the beginning, Petra," he said with quiet insistence. "Think back to the first day you came to Dos Ríos. You didn't even know Angelo. He was just a name to you—a fearful one, I believe. Suppose it hadn't been Angelo whom you had come to marry. Suppose it had been Francisco. From the very beginning—be honest, Petra—if it had been me you had been living with all this time, don't you think you could have loved me as you love Angelo now?"

She hated him standing so close to her. She hated the touch of his hands.

When she did not answer him, he continued: "Consider it further: if there had been no thought of Angelo in the very beginning save as my son, would you have had this love for him? Affection, yes, because he was lovable, but not this great feeling that blinds you to everyone else. Suppose he had never existed, Petra. Don't look so stricken. I can say that who was his father. But suppose I had never had a son, and you came to California and we had been married. Petra, have I not the makings of a satisfactory husband? Am I dull? Am I unkind? Am I poor? Tell me if you think you would have had this aversion for me if you had not been married to Angelo."

"Must you keep harping on Angelo?" She hated herself for saying it, wanting to ignore him.

"Yes, I must, because everything you say to me or think of me is colored by your thought of Angelo. You never think of *me*. You think of me *in relation to Angelo*. That attitude lacks fairness, Petra. I know you loved him. But I maintain that even if you loved him endlessly, you could still love someone else. You could love Candalario Sal or Teodoro Acuña because they are people easy to love. You could love me also—if you thought of me alone, apart from Angelo."

"I don't care," she said distractedly, "I can't. You can make it sound as sensible as you want to. But what you forget is that I *did* know Angelo. I *was* married to him. I did—do—love him, and no matter how you reason it out, that is the way I think and I can't think differently." She stopped because she was afraid she would cry.

"Very well then," he said smiling wryly, "at the cost of considerable masculine pride I must ask that you consider my offer from the cold standpoint of security alone."

"Oh, Francisco," she cried, "I can't! A person can't be cold about such a thing as marriage."

"People have been, my dear," he said dryly.

This steadied her a little, and she strove desperately for poise. "Undoubtedly," she said finally, "but I can't. I don't care how sensible a thing it seems to be, I don't want it." Suddenly she pulled away from him sharply. "I don't want to marry anybody. I don't want to marry you—especially."

She saw his face darken but remain devoid of expression.

"You will marry somebody," he said after a time.

"Why?" she asked passionately. "Why must I ever marry anyone at all?" Her head was throbbing and her eyes stung.

"Because—" his tone was hard, and she felt apprehension growing within her—"because I know you will. I have lived a good deal longer than you have. There are certain things I have learned to be facts. One of them is this: Grief dies, Petra. Someday, in a year or two or even ten, you will want to marry. I say you will *want* to. And when that time comes I do not want to have married someone else. I want you. Now you think I am cruel and unfeeling, but, believe me, I know what I am talking about."

"Well," she said flatly, "you waste your time in even talking about it. Now I am tired and I am going to bed, so I will ask you to excuse me."

"No, I will not excuse you. This interview has not terminated. Make up your mind, Petra, that when you leave this room tonight, it will be with the understanding that we are betrothed."

She wheeled to face him, her eyes glinting dangerously. "Please don't be too astonished when I leave betrothed to no one."

There was a moment of stark silence during which she felt an angry triumph. He wasn't used to being talked to like that. Well, let him see how it felt. Let him see that she wasn't a child, a chattel, who did his bidding without murmur. She would stand her ground and tell him what she pleased. There was nothing he could do about it but take his whip to her—but he wouldn't do that. The thought was startling enough to stop her headlong flight and make her pause to listen to what he was saying.

"I didn't want to quarrel with you, my dear," he said patiently. "I am hurt and not a little humiliated that you refuse my offer of marriage so lightly. However, you must know that even if you refuse, it will not end the matter. If I cannot appeal to you emotionally—as it appears I have not done—and if I cannot appeal to your common sense—as it appears I have not done—then I have yet one other alternative."

"Please, tell me what it is."

He bowed and smiled slightly at her sarcasm. "The one unalterable hold I have over you, Petra, is my small grandson Graciano."

"How could he affect whether or not I choose to marry you?" She tried to keep the alarm out of her voice but did not succeed.

Francisco shrugged. "I'm sorry you force me to use the baby as a weapon," he said, "for it will probably incur your lasting enmity. You will marry me for one reason: to protect your son's inheritance."

Her hands flew together in a sudden betraying gesture of nervousness. "Surely Graciano's heritage is secure. You didn't mean that. The mere fact that he is Angelo's child should——"

"Yes, it should, but it doesn't."

"I'm not sure I understand you."

"I grow tired of this discussion, Petra, so I shall be blunt. If Graciano is to inherit, he must stay here with me and be brought up at Dos Ríos. Now you cannot remain here in *any* capacity except as my wife. If you still refuse, I shall send you to Spain. I shall undoubtedly take another wife. There will undoubtedly be other children. If I allowed you to take the baby with you, his inheritance would be gone. Do you think I would want Dos Ríos to go to some strange European youth whom I did not know? And what of the other wife and her children? Graciano would have little chance of any estate at all. Not only that," he continued, his tone casual as if he were a little bored: "I might even be so despicable as to send you away and keep him here."

"Nobody," she said with finality, "can take my child away from me."

"Petra," he said levelly, "believe me, if I forbade you to take Graciano out of California, you would not take him."

She turned her back so he might not see her face. Thoughts, ineffectual as gnats in a strong wind, darted meaninglessly in her mind. "About the marriage," she said with difficulty: "you couldn't. The Church would not permit it."

"Oh, Petra," he said gently, "you little fool."

She turned to him quickly. "But they wouldn't. What about that other man—that Vasques? What was his name? Remember? The Church forbade it because the woman was his wife's cousin. Just her cousin, Francisco, and his wife had been dead for years. You see——" She stopped in wide-eyed consternation as Francisco turned to the desk and lifted from its top a rich-looking paper, resplendent with crests and seals.

"I have the Church's permission." There was something like apology in his tone. "This is a letter from Fernando Cardinal Valesca, wishing me long life and a happy marriage."

Petra stared, fascinated, at the paper, then lifted her suddenly dark eyes to his face. There was nothing but empty politeness in it. "My aunts," she said carefully. "I have written to them. They—I expect they will ask that I come back to Spain with my baby."

"I beg your pardon, I'm sorry I didn't think to give you your mail sooner, but the day has been so full it slipped my mind. We both got mail from Spain today. This is possibly from your aunt." He handed her another letter.

She took it, trying to hide her reluctance. She slid her fingernail beneath the seal and cracked it away from the thick paper. They must call her home! He could give orders to a defenseless girl, but would he speak so firmly to De la Torres of Sevilla? She had a swift vision of her uncles arriving on the next ship to take her back to Spain. How haughty and grand they could be when they chose! How disdainful and condescending they could be of the rancheros, who were, after all, only colonists.

She began to skim automatically through the formal beginning of the letter; going over the condolences for Angelo and good wishes for the new baby, for whom gifts had been sent; on down the beautifully written page. Phrases appeared to spring into blacker script for her attention: *Don Francisco shows amazing practical and common sense in asking you in marriage.* And: *All here are in complete accord.* And: *We sincerely advise you to consider his proposal.*

Suddenly dull with despair, Petra let her hand fall to her side, the crisp paper rustling against the black of her gown. All strength seemed to drain from her body. Francisco had returned the cardinal's letter to the desk, appearing remote and preoccupied. She had the idea that she had exhausted all her reserves, and he had not. She felt he had loosed only a small portion of his energy to batter down all her defenses, and that easily, without effort, he might shatter her completely. He had only to lift up his hand to strike and she would crash helplessly against the wall. He had only to speak a few words and her child might be taken from her.

"I'm afraid you are overtired," he said. "Let me suggest that you go to bed and rest. It is quite late. You have had a trying day."

She looked at him wonderingly. She had expected him to drive home his triumph and make her say the very words which would seal a betrothal between them.

"I am tired," she found herself saying painfully. Stiffly, with an effort, she turned to the door. Once there she paused and turned back to face him again. He observed this and bowed politely. His face was composed and quiet, but Petra got the impression that he was no longer sad. His mourning was over, and in his mind it put a finishing to Angelo.

"Good night, Petra."

"Good night, Francisco," she answered looking with detachment at the splendor of his garments. Everything about him gleamed, the gold braid, the red sash, the highly polished boots, as if the very clothing that covered his body were alive.

He was going to be kind and ignore her defeat, but for some perverse reason she could not let it stand that way. Because she could not cope with him, because she had lost, it behooved her in the spirit of sportsmanship, or feminine pique, or plain reasonless despair, to utter some word which would settle the matter between them. Angelo was gone and Dos Ríos and Francisco went on. Things kept happening—living, active things—in which Angelo had no part. These things that happened this week, today, would be memories in a year, memories which held nothing of Angelo. She leaned against the door, an intolerable ache in her throat. Was it possible that Francisco would eventually blot out the image of Angelo, that one day she would think of Angelo and be unable to remember the color of his eyes or the shape of his head?

Francisco was waiting for her to leave. She looked at his calm, closed face and wondered what it was she had been going to say to him. Then it came to her that she was going to marry him, and she must tell him so and settle it between them.

Vestiges of some deeply embedded form asserted themselves in her mind and she spoke with courtesy and decorum. "Very well then, I will marry you, Francisco."

"I thank you, Petra. I shall try to make you happy," he answered quietly.

Now, alone in her room, she remembered it all over again and clasped her hands to her throat. In so doing she realized that she no longer held the pearls which Francisco had given her. She glanced down distractedly and saw that they were back in the velvet box. She couldn't remember having put them there, but she must have—carelessly, untidily, as if they were a handful of pebbles. They hung half in, half out of the box, spilling over the edge and spread out on the dresser like dark gleaming teardrops.

Angelo was dying. In the dim confusion of her mind she could hear him, distinctly, insistently: *Petra, I'm falling!*

Chapter 16

Almost before Petra had fully awakened, she sprang from the bed, clumsy with sleep. It wasn't true! She had dreamed it. As this protective thought formed, she reached the dresser and fumbled at the clasp of the velvet box. One second, two, three, and she would know. The lid snapped up and she stifled a small sound. The pearls were there. It was true. She had promised to marry Francisco. She shut the box and turned to the baby who was beginning to fret and stir at the sudden sound she had made.

"Well, it's all right," she said to herself or the baby. "I would have to marry someone someday, anyhow." She began to take fresh clothes for Graciano from the drawer. She laid them in a neat, precise stack on top of the dresser and closed the drawer with care because she had formed a habit of closing drawers evenly. Angelo had always been annoyed if they were pushed in crookedly. She lifted the baby's clothes and, unfolding them, spilled rose petals unnoticed on the floor.

When the baby was clean and dressed and fed, and she herself was ready to go downstairs, she stared wonderingly at the grumbling Bianca as the woman swept up the petals. Petra left her and went down, knowing the people would be gathering in the chapel. As her foot touched each step she thought of Angelo.

Angelo . . . Angelo . . . Angelo . . .

How odd! How ridiculous that she, who was Angelo's wife, would marry someone else! That was impossible of course. She might marry Francisco but she would always be Angelo's wife. She had vowed to be Angelo's wife before the altar lace and the flickering candles, with a round golden ring, to be Angelo's wife until she died. Now there would be other lace and other candles. In place of the round golden ring—*oh no,* not her wedding ring! She couldn't give up her wedding ring that Angelo had placed on her finger. That was the ring she must live with and die with.

What did you do with your first wedding ring when you married again?

She leaned against the newel post at the foot of the stairway and turned the ring experimentally on her finger. It had never occurred to her that she would ever have to take it off. How often she had looked at it, dreamily, warmly content, because it signified that she was a wife! It showed she belonged to her husband, was his wife, his chattel, to do with as he pleased. It had given her a womanly, a wifely feeling to look at it any time of day, to watch its gleam as her hand darted this way and that, in household tasks, in sewing, in brushing her hair. It was always the round golden symbol without end or beginning to show that she was Angelo's. There was something mystical, final and satisfying about being a wife. It was a state differing from all other states—belonging definitely and specifically to one man and being as necessary to him as his hands, the sight in his eyes, his wide-set sea-colored eyes.

Made a little sick with dreaming she turned her eyes again to the ring. Something would have to be done about the ring. Francisco didn't speak of things like that. He spoke sensibly of practical things. Graciano's heritage was important of course. Angelo would not want his child to be a pauper. It was sensible. Nobody could say she wasn't practical. But in the end it was she, Margarita Petra Estrada, who would, at last, have to take the round gold ring from her finger and lay it down.

She went to the chapel nodding and speaking courteously to those who greeted her. From long habit she said the proper things and joined with the others in the ancient and beautiful prayers.

Now, she thought. It is now.

When prayers were finished and the hungry supplicants rose with rustlings and subdued clatter to be about their breakfasts, Francisco rose and stepped to the altar. "Just a moment," he said, and all eyes in the room turned their gaze to him.

Now, thought Petra, with a sudden shocking panic. Why couldn't he have waited until she was gone?

"I will keep you only a moment," Francisco was saying to the assemblage. "It is only that before you go I would like to have you share in the news of my good fortune."

Petra's lips tightened. Why did he have to tell them all, housewomen, grinders, washwomen, foremen, all of them? Why couldn't he have waited and told just the family? Her head rose a trifle, and she tried to copy the Estrada knack of keeping her face absolutely blank under emotional stress.

"You all know the losses the Doña Petra and I have experienced during the past year—I, my wife and son; the Doña Petra, her husband. These losses are bitter to us and difficult to bear. We all know that none can fill the places of those lost in death." He turned his eyes toward Petra for a moment. "We do not try to fill those dead ones' places," he said gently. "We try to make out with those who are left.

"Since the birth of little Graciano, Doña Petra and I have discussed the situation at length and have come to the conclusion that we want to do what is best for him as well as try to get over our own losses. I have asked that the Doña Petra become my wife. She has very kindly and graciously accepted. The first banns will be read at the mission Sunday and in about three weeks from then the marriage will take place. Naturally there will be a fiesta to which you are all invited. This will come as a surprise to many of you, but I wanted all my family and household to know of it and share with me in my new happiness."

He stopped speaking and looked directly at the group. There was complete silence for some moments during which expressions shifted and changed. There was an uneasy rustling and scraping of feet, bare, moccasined and shoe-covered. What was this strange thing the Don Francisco was saying? The new and unfamiliar idea rested uneasily in the minds it entered. The servants stared blankly, for theirs were deeply religious minds, peasant minds, slow minds, which shrank from any new thought. They endeavored to adjust themselves to the idea that the don's daughter-in-law was going to be the don's wife. This was a strange and not altogether acceptable thing. But he was the master after all. He was Don Francisco, the Spaniard, the lord of Dos Ríos.

With the exception of Ysidra who fanned herself placidly, the Spaniards and Mexicans in the room were dumbfounded. They showed it, hating themselves for showing their discomfiture. For several long moments they struggled for something old to cling to, trying to fit the situation into a well-known groove or design. Padilla's gasp was audible. The seamstress, Señora Llanes, allowed her mouth to drop open in amazement. Xavier's body jerked like a puppet on a string. Catalina turned the color of ashes, but it was she who broke the silence, striving to make her voice normal and gay.

"Petra, my dear, I am so glad." She hurried to Petra and flung her arms about her neck, kissing her pale cheek. "I'm very happy for you. We all are." Her tone held something of challenge to the rest of the group. It told them plainly that irregularity or not, Don Francisco was not to be embarrassed by any sullenness or reluctance. This broke the spell of suspended animation which held them. They all surged forward now, all of them kind, eager to blot out the fact that they had been silent and astonished. Petra caught snatches of eager words:

"Happiness, doña!" Señora Llanes was saying. "We must make you a gown, a splendid gown——"

Enrique Padilla bent low over her head. "How lucky a man is Don Francisco!"

Guillermo, his eyes shining, forgot his bride to come and kiss her hands.

Xavier hurried to her. "Petra, my dear, this is really the best possible thing. You will be happy——"

In the confusion the Indians began to come up, a little slower, less willing to accept the newness and the change, considering it ponderously in their minds, adjusting themselves to think of it as right and old. "Happiness, doña . . . Happiness, doña . . . A good thing for the little one, doña . . . Santa María bless you, doña . . . Long life and happiness, doña."

She stood smiling at them as they passed one at a time, giving them her hand, answering them. "Thank you, Concha . . . Thank you, Pablo . . .

Yes, of course, thank you . . . That is kind of you, Damacia. . . ."

It was the beginning. The wheels were beginning to turn. They would go outside and talk and wonder and hail their fellows to spread the news, eagerly now because they were becoming excited over it. *It is true! The Doña Petra and Don Francisco . . . Have you heard the news? . . . We will have a big fiesta. . . . The banns are to be read next Sunday for the first time. . . . Let us go to the mission to hear them read. . . . If the priest says so by the altar then it is true. . . . But it is true! Damacia heard it from the don's own lips. . . . There is Mateo! Ay, Mateo have you heard the news? . . .*

And finally all of California would know that Francisco Estrada was going to marry his daughter-in-law. Even down in Mexico they would speak of it at night by campfires on the range. Even in Mexico City they would nod over the cups of chocolate and murmur to each other, *How shocking! . . . How scandalous! . . . It is that Ingelsa of course. . . . They say that when she came, she spoke the Spanish with many a pause and falter, so foreign is she. . . . They do say she was betrothed to his son on her first day in California. . . . No! . . . Yes! . . . How on earth was she brought up? . . . Ah, well, what could you expect in England? . . . Where is England? . . . Ah yes, of course. . . .*

As she stood in the chapel and received the good wishes of the household, Petra could see the news leaping and spreading. But they would come to the wedding! They might cast their eyes heavenward and shriek in scandalized amazement, but they would all come to the fiesta, everyone who received an invitation and many who did not, for one's house was open to all. From all over California they would come—disapproving, perhaps shocked, perhaps whispering behind their fans and hat brims, but they would come. Up from Mexico the elite and dignitaries would come. Down from the north the Russian officials would come. Dos Ríos would be a madhouse for days.

Then back home in Spain . . . all the relatives . . . when the boats put into port. Letters from California and Mexico. Behind the grillwork and pink stucco walls the ladies would rustle and squeal at this tidbit. The men would stride across bare polished floors and laugh in faint envy and admiration because Francisco Estrada was three times married. And now to his *daughter-in-law!*

But they were really kind, Petra thought. Californians and Mexicans were fundamentally kind. In a little while, a month, a year, it would be forgotten, all over. She would be Francisco's wife, even as she had been Angelo's wife. Things would slip back into their familiar rut. People would visit at Dos Ríos, and they would visit back. Other people would marry. Other fiestas would occur and by and by it would cease to be shocking. It would be an old and accepted thing.

But now it was new. It must be lived through. She was that Englishwoman. She would walk into rooms amid sudden silence. She would offer embarrassed explanations of Graciano's relationship to Francisco. *Well, no, not exactly his father. You see, the baby's father was . . .*

And Graciano? He would grow up remembering no one but Francisco. Petra closed her eyes and felt another little bit of Angelo diminish and disappear. His wedding ring would be lost in the depths of some jumbled jewel box, and his son would never have seen his face. The chapel was clearing and breakfast must be eaten. Tasks must be looked to while the news went its wild excited way over California and farther. Outwardly calm, Petra thanked the last of the well-wishers. Keeping her face composed, she left the chapel, not saying a word to Francisco, not even looking at him.

Catalina watched her go and sat down suddenly on one of the benches. Her vision seemed oddly diffused. The chapel blotted itself out before she realized she had buried her face in her hands and was rocking back and forth like an Indian in torment. What was she? A savage? A peasant? She was nothing. Less than nothing.

"Catalina, are you ill?" It was Xavier, who had missed her and come back. "It isn't the baby, is it? Are you all right?" He came into the room, kindly and puffy and stupid. This was her husband, when she might have had Francisco. Rising to her feet she placed her hand on his arm. She might loathe and despise him and shrink from the touch of his hand, but she had married him. The baby within her moved in a sudden thrust, as if the blood in her body had stopped and stood still from shock, a shock that reached and disturbed it. She took a step forward.

"It was the baby," she said listening with detached interest to the smooth sound of her well-bred voice. "It moved a little." She waited a moment, then added, "But it is nothing. Let us go in to breakfast. We must not keep the others waiting."

She slid her arm through Xavier's and walked beside him to the dining room, hating him, hating herself. How horrible she must look with her lurching walk and her distended belly, how vile and ugly! And Petra was going to marry Francisco.

She doesn't want to. This thought slapped at her brain and she faltered so that Xavier looked down in worry. She smiled up at him reassuringly as they entered the dining room, but she wasn't smiling at Xavier, she was smiling at the joke of it, laughing at it in her own mind. Petra didn't even *want* him!

When the meal was finished, both Petra and Catalina waited before they set about their daily tasks. Francisco was leaving for the day, and courtesy demanded that they bid him good-by.

Petra stood resenting him, hating him, wanting to fly at him and dig her nails into his tough swarthy skin, wanting to cause him pain, *hurt him!*

Catalina wanted to fly at him, cling to him in passion, make him notice her and respond to her, force him to stop and think a minute and want her—above all want her!

They waited quietly. Because of their strict upbringing and careful veneer, their faces were smooth and pleasant.

"Well, my ladies, I am going to leave you." Francisco smiled. "I must ride over to the mission to transact certain business and make the arrangements." He seemed sorry he had uttered the last words, for Petra's face appeared to chill and harden. Catalina's was no less rigid.

"What arrangements?" Petra asked coldly.

(Catalina put out her hand and rested it on the banister almost touching him, with only the space of a thread between her hand and the cloth of his sleeve.)

"The arrangements for the banns, Petra," he said gently, almost apologetically.

(Catalina thought, I can take his arm and dig my fingers into it, and grip it, and he must turn and look at *me!*)

"Is there need for such haste?" Petra asked, matching his calm.

"Is there need for delay?" he countered, still gently.

"You act like a lovesick fool," she said cuttingly. Belittle him, shame him, hurt him a little because Angelo's wedding ring was going to become nicked and dulled in the bottom of her jewel box.

He smiled. "Better men than I have been lovesick fools." But his face darkened because she had said it.

Petra's eyes were brilliant and she widened them for fear the tears would spill over. She couldn't, would not, cry before him.

(Catalina's hand slid an inch down the banister and passed the edge of his sleeve. If I were slim, she thought, if I were slim and free, I would leap up and cling to him and never let him go. All the days of my life I would hold him, touch him, with my hands on his body.)

"There is a new ship in the harbor. Do you want to buy anything? Gowns? Clothing? Anything?" Francisco asked. "If you do, let me know when I return, and I will go up and get you some money from the box." He swung the deerskin bag he held and there was the soft muffled jingle of gold.

"I need nothing, I want nothing at all," Petra said.

His dark brows rose. "Nothing? Surely you want a new gown. A woman who wants nothing new is a strange thing to me, Petra."

"I have a gown," she said disdainfully. "I have dozens of gowns."

"But surely you want a new one for your wedding."

"The ones I have are good enough," she said keeping the pure savagery from her tone with an effort. Resist him, thwart him, in everything disagree with him!

"Well, unfortunately you will have to have at least six of every kind of garment," Francisco said with mock apology. "I am sorry to burden you with them, but you know it is the custom here for each man to outfit his bride so."

"We will make them black then," she said, "because I am in mourning for my husband."

His head came up. All expression washed from his face, leaving it blank and closed. Angelo, she thought in sudden panic; that's the way Angelo did, never letting anybody know when he was hurt—hiding it, covering it up.

(Catalina's hand tightened on the banister. She could break it, break the wood, break her fingers—break something.)

Francisco said quietly, "You may wear black for your confession, Petra, but for your wedding fiesta you cannot."

"Cannot! Why not, if I choose to?"

"Because I forbid it," he said spacing his words carefully. "If you continue to insist you want no new wedding gown, I will bow to that. It doesn't matter a great deal if you prefer not to wear the gowns I buy for you. You may wear the dress you wore your first night here, the white one with gold lace."

"I will not," she said flatly.

He looked at her a long moment. His eyes, despite his control, were menacing, as light and clear as the emerald in his hatband. "Yes, you will," he said with deliberation. "In all kindness to you, Petra, I tell you not to pit yourself against me. You may have as many new gowns as you wish, or none if you wish. But you cannot come to our wedding in the clothing of a crow. I will not permit it. That is final."

She was speechless, filled with rage. She watched him stonily as he bowed to both of them and went out the front door, striking a pale spark as his spur hit the step. It was lost at once in the brilliant sunlight. Grimly Petra turned and would have gone upstairs but the pallor of Catalina's face stopped her.

"Are you ill, Catalina?" she asked, her voice only slightly constricted now.

"Yes, I'm ill," Catalina answered remotely.

"Perhaps you had better go to bed for the day. I'll see to instructing the kitchen-women and whatever else you planned to do."

"Yes, perhaps I'd better. I'll lie down. I'll keep the room dark. Will you ask Xavier not to come up because I'll be sleeping?"

"Yes, of course, Catalina," Petra answered, knowing that Catalina would not sleep.

They went upstairs together, each thinking the other a fool.

After Petra had left Catalina at her doorway, she went into her own room and closed the door. She opened the wardrobe and looked at the array of gowns there. White satin. She picked out the shimmering heavy folds, edged with lace like wrought gold. She pulled the dress roughly, half hoping it would somehow tear and fall to pieces in her hands. It was more than a year old, but the heavy satin crackled like paper. Nothing could harm this dress because Francisco wanted her to wear it for the wedding. Disdainfully she let it fall to the floor. It made a shimmering pile of white and gold, heavy, stiff and beautiful. She kicked it, making it sail and slither across the floor. Why had she let Francisco bully her? She should be allowed to wear what she chose. Her eyes narrowed, obscuring her vision, distorting the image of the dress. If only—if only the hateful thing could be transmuted into ugliness, into mourning black!

Chapter 17

Petra woke to the sound of whining, petulant and insistent. At first she thought that Graciano was crying, and she started to get out of bed. Then almost before she was in motion, she realized that he wasn't crying, and it came to her with a fleeting sense of nausea that this was her wedding day. The whining was the sound of *carretas* approaching.

Wedding day! Light was just beginning to diminish the blackness of the sky. In a few minutes the sun would come up and it would begin. She counted over in her mind the things that would occur, almost as she would say her beads. First they would dress and go to prayers, to a congregation swelled to overflow the chapel because of the guests who had been arriving. Then they would break their fast with chocolate or coffee and bread. Then in a little while, about midmorning, they would all sit down to the large breakfast. Then she would go to confessional and when that was finished and the altar was freshly decorated in the *sala,* she would come down the stairs and the wedding would begin. After the ceremony she would be Francisco's wife. There would be a big dinner, and the rounds of entertainment would start. Such magnificent bulls they had brought in, such huge bears, such bright cocks! The music and the dancing.

All over again.

She buried her face in her hands. After the dancing was finished—before it was finished, while people still danced and sang and played and ate and drank—the time would come when she would inevitably have to face Francisco as his wife.

There was one small satisfaction: Francisco had without demur granted her request that the wedding be held here at Dos Ríos instead of at the mission.

Against her will, hating everything she did, she began to dress. It was hot. The dawn was breaking, and she lifted her eyes and looked out the window. It struck her that the air did not glitter as it had on her other wedding day. The very air was dull, sodden and weighted, lacking any life or brilliance. Yet it seemed so warm and stifling.

During the morning the noise rose in volume. The guests no longer frowned on Francisco's choice. The spirit of fiesta was intoxicating them. It didn't seem so odd now that Francisco Estrada was going to marry his daughter-in-law. It was all right. Everything was all right. They had eaten splendidly at his table and would soon be listening to the strains of his music. Their feet would be tapping out the complicated rhythms on his polished floors. The wait was long.

By midmorning the continually increasing noise had risen in crescendo. There were errant fragments of music, much talk and laughter, the sound of boot heels, the occasional twang of spurs. The ladies' fans moved constantly, for the air was oppressive.

Petra could hear the noise as she at last finished dressing. She would silence them all in a moment. She would start down and every face in the packed hallway would look up and they would be still, for she, the bride, was coming.

At the head of the stairs she paused. All over again. Her hand tightened on the banister for an instant. Her chin rose and her lips smiled. Regally, gracefully, she began her descent. A small feeling of exultation quivered in her. It wasn't quite the same because of the gown, the one he had insisted she wear. The satin of it shone and glimmered richly. It had taken the black dye very well. It was almost mirrorlike in its very *black* blackness. The gold lace was gone and in its place was black lace. A high black comb was fixed in her hair, from which trailed a filmy lace mantilla so long that it swung almost to the hem of her gown. Twined, half-hidden, in the pale coils of her hair were the dark pearls that Francisco had given her, but at her throat blazed the dazzling Montoya diamonds.

Francisco appeared not to notice and the hand he extended to her was calm and unshaken. It felt warm to her cold fingers. She was in mourning, she told herself repeatedly, allowing it to echo through her mind as they went to the altar. She had thwarted him, disobeyed him, and there was nothing he could do about it. Yet it seemed small comfort with his hand calm and unperturbed beneath hers, and the altar solid and immovable before her. She had to swallow several times and she wondered if her voice would fail her in the responses. The candle wavered in her unsteady hand.

Then the patterns began to emerge. Lace of the altar cloth . . . flame of the candles . . . chanting of the priest. She was being married to Francisco Estrada and nothing could stop it.

There was a pause. She had faltered, forgotten her response. Father Patricio repeated, and she took up her words hesitantly, awkwardly, ashamed to stumble and stammer like a child reciting a half-learned catechism, waiting to be prompted.

The silver cord emerged, was twined about her and Francisco, and she felt an incredible sense of finality, for she was Francisco's wife. She hated him. She hated the priest. She hated the hands that had draped the cord. She rose to her feet without the aid of Francisco's outstretched hand and turned to face him, furious, loathing everybody. Spaniards! She was sick to death of all things Spanish. If she could smite them, strike them all dead, send the altar crashing to the floor in fury! She stood poised for an instant, white, her eyes glittering. Then Francisco's hand closed sternly about her arm and the whole room seemed to hold its breath. She felt a fleeting moment of amazement that Francisco should grasp her so roughly before the assemblage.

A flutter and a shiver went through the very walls of the house, causing the pictures and crucifixes to move convulsively and hang askew, causing the draperies to quiver. The silence was of an appalling quality, as dense and lifeless as the sullen air outside.

Sickness churned in her stomach. Was she going mad? She turned amazed eyes to Francisco and saw that his face was like granite, as the house shuddered in shock, rocking on its foundations. There was a tearing and a thumping. Things were falling down and breaking. Dishes on tables chattered like chilled teeth. On the end of that shock came another. The house rocked in fury. The altar came forward and slammed against her back.

In blind terror she thrust out her hands toward the suddenly malignant wood. Francisco's arm circled her waist and snatched her forward. The altar crashed deafeningly to the floor and lay split in two. It broke the spell which held them all.

Minds which had refused to accept, accepted this. A dozen voices rose in fear, excitement, terror:

"Earthquake!"

Screams rent the air. There was a concerted rush to doors and windows. The priest's voice rose and was lost in the din. Another shock struck.

Ladies were thrust unceremoniously from windows onto the loggia. People clogged the exits, pushing, stumbling. Fans were dropped, necklaces broken, earrings trodden on.

Francisco had gone. Petra was alone in a maelstrom. *"My baby!"* she suddenly screamed and rushed into the melee like a mad woman. Her mantilla snagged on a piece of furniture and was snatched from her head, the fragile lace ripping and tangling in the push of bodies. She flew up the shaking stairs, crashing into someone midway.

"My baby!" she screamed trying to claw her way past.

"Stop that! Here he is." Francisco thrust the startled, wailing infant into her arms. The stair rail moved against her side as she gripped Graciano. Dust clogged their nostrils in a sudden noxious cloud and everything was unearthly still. The house had emptied. Silence hung deathlike and tangible in the torpid air.

From outside wailing and praying arose. Turning dark amazed eyes there, Petra saw them all on their knees or flat on the ground. She had a sudden panoramic view of upflung hands, tightly held children, torn garments, straggling hair. A babble of sound rose from the scene. Everyone was praying wildly, in a dozen languages and dialects. She sagged against the banister, shaking so that it was almost impossible to hold the angrily squirming baby.

She looked up at Francisco. His face was expressionless. "I think it's over now. Are you all right?" he asked.

"I'm fine," she managed, though her tongue felt thick and rough in her mouth.

"I must look——" he murmured abstractedly and brushed by her going down the stairs. The sound was decreasing now; it had sunk to muttering and soft weeping. She watched Francisco enter the dining room. Shaking so that she could scarcely walk, she followed him, unable to remain alone on the stairway with her baby.

He turned as she entered the dining room. His eyes were veiled. A look of wry amusement touched his face. He extended his hand to her holding a broken piece of brick, partly whitewashed and partly earth-colored.

"It seems some of my house fell down," he said. There was a great gaping hole in the wall which had before been solid. Debris and broken adobe littered the dining table, having crushed some china and mired in dishes of food set out for the dinner. The room was a shambles, like a house of blocks knocked about by an idiot hand in destructive play.

Petra pushed rubble off a chair and sat down, for her legs would no longer hold her. Earthquake? What was this thing they called an earthquake? Graciano was quieting. She looked up to see his godmother coming in the room.

"Oh," gasped María Luisa, "is he all right? Jaime put me out the window and I was afraid you had forgotten——" She broke off in confusion.

"No," Petra said dully, not even angry that the other girl would think her capable of forgetting her child, "I didn't forget, but Francisco got him for me."

María Luisa's own eldest, a boy of three or four, clung to her skirts and gazed with awe-struck eyes at the gaping hole which had been a wall.

"Francisco—" Don Cristóbal Quixano bounded in—"are you all right? My God, look at this room! Listen, my friend, please: you won't be offended if we go? I must see how things are at San Cristóbal. I'm afraid my *vaqueros* will run away into the hills."

"Yes, of course, you must go to see to your own house. Was anyone home there?"

"Holy Christ, yes, Pedro's wife! Her time is close." Quixano clapped his hand to his brow.

"Pedro has already gone," María Luisa said primly. "He was mounted almost before the earthquake was over. For one so recently praying I would, with all respect, suggest that you watch your language." It was the first and only time María Luisa had ventured to correct her father-in-law in anything.

He looked at her for a moment and then smiled. "How right you are, my love! Run and find Jaime and we shall go. Are you sure," he said, turning to Francisco, "that I can't be of assistance here?"

"Oh no, most certainly not. I believe this is all the damage. We have no way of knowing how bad it was down south. We can manage perfectly here. Please be on your way. I insist. And if there is anything I can do for you——"

"Francisco—" Doctor Vaiz came in—"come and help me—the priest——"

For a moment Petra felt violently ill. The priest! Patricio! She remembered the falling altar. Holy Mother! She started up from her chair and collapsed immediately. Great God, had the world come to an end?

"The mission—I must get to the mission——" The cracked voice of Patricio came to her from the *sala*.

"Mission, my God, man, don't be a fool—I beg

your pardon, Father. Your leg is broken. You can't go anywhere." Vaiz was brusque and harried. "Get me some linen. No, rip it up into narrow pieces——" He gave directions to some unseen person.

Petra held a sort of court in the dining room. Singly and in groups they came. The thought was always the same. . . .

"I must ask that you excuse me and my family."

"We feel that we must leave."

"A thousand apologies, but——"

"In the circumstances, home——"

Home . . . home . . . home. . . . They all wanted to go home. In this crisis they turned to their own land, their own houses, urgent, frightened, wondering if their houses stood, if their servants had run away, if the relatives at home were all right.

Petra mechanically sat and rocked Graciano back and forth. Her hair, still tangled with pearls, streamed over her shoulder and down her back. Her comb had gone. Its teeth had scratched her head, which began to ache dully. The baby was quiet now. She looked in detachment at her skirt. It was torn badly on one side and incredibly dirty. How could it be dirty, so quickly, when only a short while ago it had been shining and lovely?

As the families left one by one, she numbly noted the wailing of the *carretas*. Again and again she heard the hurried departure of someone at a full gallop. Going ahead to see——

Patricio's voice came to her again: "But I must, I must. Can't we fix a litter?" His cry was insistent. "Gabriel is there alone with all those Indians. Suppose he is hurt—killed."

"You cannot," Vaiz said flatly.

"Well, tie it up, put splints——" persisted the stubborn priest. "Hurry!"

"I am hurrying, man." Vaiz had forgotten

again that he was tending a priest. "Unfortunately the good God blessed me with only two hands. And you can't go anywhere."

Francisco came in again. His jacket was gone and his shirt stained. "Petra, Father Patricio's leg was caught under the altar. It's broken badly. Are you all right now? Could you help a little?"

"Yes, oh yes." She started up. Where was her mind? What could she be thinking of to sit here? "Nearly everyone has gone?"

"Yes, most. I'm afraid we'll be shorthanded. Some of the Indians have run away and some won't come near the house."

"Oh, I'm sorry. I . . . what . . . what is there to do?" She looked about, distracted. What could she do? What was there to do in a situation like this? How many Indians had run away? Who was left? Where could she put Graciano?

"These ought to do." Xavier entered through the hole in the dining-room wall, holding two flat sticks for splints. "Isn't this about as long as a man's leg?" he asked, measuring them against his own. Not waiting for an answer, he started at a clumsy loping run across the room. There was a smudge of blood across his face. Then he was gone and Petra and Francisco faced each other for a moment.

"Is . . . is . . . did anyone else get hurt?" she asked shakily.

"No; that is, not much—skinned and bruised a little. Just Patricio when he was caught under the altar as it fell."

Petra began to run over the names of the family in her mind. "Ysidra?" she asked. "Catalina? Guillermo? Padilla?"

"Francisco!" They both turned. Catalina, as if in answer to her name, stood in the dining-room doorway. There was a desperate jauntiness about her, but her eyes were dark pools of fear. Delicately she kicked a piece of broken adobe out of her path and came a step nearer them. "I'm afraid I'm going to have my baby now," she said.

Doña Dolores Acuña ran panting into the room. "I'm staying with you," she said breathlessly to Catalina. "I sent the men home to Las Palomas. Go on upstairs. Do you want to have it here—?" She stopped when she saw Francisco and turned beet red.

"My . . . my daughter . . ." she said lamely, "is . . . is feeling the shock . . . and we believe . . ."

"Yes, of course." Francisco bowed. "Shall I send up Doctor Vaiz when he finishes with Father——"

Vaiz rushed in. "I must go to the mission, Francisco. I'm leaving the priest here."

"To the mission!" Catalina gasped. "You can't! I'm going to have my baby."

"My dear young lady—" the doctor swung around to her, ignoring the others in his urgency—"I'm sorry. The priest will remain here because he has to."

"The priest!" Catalina shouted. "I don't want a priest. I want a doctor! *I'm going to have a baby!*" She dashed up to him clumsily and caught at his lapels.

"Believe me, my dear," the doctor said quickly, "I'm sorry. I had intended to stay, but God knows what has happened at the mission. Please don't be afraid." He beat some of the dust vigorously out of his jacket and struggled into it. "Women have always coped with having babies. It's the poor wretches with broken bones who become confused." He was going out the door. "I'll try to get back——" The sentence was lost as he went into the hall and out the front door.

Petra felt an insane desire to laugh. He could have gone through the hole in the wall, she thought. It would have saved time. She buried her face convulsively over her baby for an instant.

"Francisco—" Ysidra stood in the doorway, calm, unruffled, scarcely even dusty—"my dear, what do you think of carrying Father Patricio upstairs so that when Catalina's time comes——"

"Catalina's time!" Xavier rushed through the door, pushing his mother aside. "My God, not now!" He stumbled up to his wife.

"Yes, now," she cried. "And I'm not to have a doctor. Just the midwife." Her voice rose in outrage.

"Catalina!" She whirled, stunned to hear Francisco's voice. She had expected reprimands from her mother, from Ysidra, but not from Francisco. "Why don't you go upstairs to bed? You will be more comfortable there," he said gently when he had her attention.

The girl seemed to wilt. Her great dark eyes filled with tears. She swallowed with an effort and flung up her head. "You are perfectly right," she said pertly. "Are you sure there is nothing I can do down here first? I won't have much pain for a while."

"No, my dear, we will manage, thank you." Francisco stepped over the rubble and took up her grimy little hand and kissed it. "Now be a good girl and don't make too much noise," he said grinning a little.

Enrique came in wiping his forehead. "I put Father Patricio in a chair as you said to do." He was jacketless, dirty and sweating in the oppressive dust-laden air. "I can't find that woman—that midwife. She's gone."

"Oh, you have to find the midwife," Xavier gasped, suddenly coming to life. His face was gray.

"But, señor, if she has run away into the hills or into town how can I——"

"Never mind the midwife," Catalina said crisply. "My mother is here, and Petra, and the priest——" She stopped; a stunned expression crossed her face. She seemed to crumple and writhe.

"Santa María!" wailed Doña Dolores. "Didn't I say go upstairs? Here, carry her! Help her! No, wait until this pain is gone."

Ysidra moved forward majestically and took calm, almost disinterested command. "Enrique, you and Xavier carry Doña Catalina to her room. There, there, my dear. Is the pain quite gone now? Francisco, please carry Father Patricio up. María-Fe—" she raised her voice slightly, and the other Acuña girl came in, panting a little and tucking up her hair—"would you go with your mother and sister? Petra, put that child down and get to work. There is much to be done. The Indians have almost completely disappeared and the house is a shambles. When you come down, Padilla, please find someone to help you block up this hole in the wall."

Automatically Petra did as she was told, thinking confusedly that she was married to Francisco. Fiesta or no fiesta, she was his wife because the earthquake had come after the ceremony, when they turned from the altar. It was over. They really were married. And there was much to do: scrape the broken crockery . . . take cool wine to the priest who was in a good deal of pain . . . find Catalina's pearl crucifix . . . sweep the dirt out of the dining room. . . .

A few Indians came back, fearful, chastened, shamefaced. She was careful to watch her language before them, who had so lately seen the wrath of God made manifest. Words, confused commands snapped through the sultry air.

Señor Ruiz staggered in. "Don Francisco! Where is Don Francisco? Fire in the *indiada.*"

Panic rose in Petra. Those reed-thatched roofs would go like straw.

"Don Francisco! Don Francisco!" Guillermo, lean, disheveled, holding a whip and a rosary, bounded in through the dining-room wall. "That fence by the canyon fell down. The white mares are out—and their stallion is crazy."

"Don Francisco!" Señora Llanes hurtled through the kitchen doorway, the hem of her skirts drenched. "Where is Don Francisco? Some casks in the cellar have broken. The place is flooded with wine."

One of the kitchen-women came in, pulling at her torn garment, crying savagely. "Adobe fell in the beans. And one of the ovens cracked in two."

María-Fe ran from upstairs. "Where is a bowl, a silver one? The priest wants to bless water."

Then everyone caught his breath as the air was rent by a piercing shriek from upstairs.

It was almost six before the baby came. Catalina was nearly insensible. The midwife had never been found, and the two women, her mother and Ysidra, acted in her place. The younger girl had been sent from the room and gone downstairs to help Petra.

Father Patricio had had his chair pushed up next to the bed. There he waited for the baby so he might christen it. He had refused any narcotic, wanting it saved for those at the mission who might be injured worse than he. The pain in his broken leg bones was sickening. His drawn face was white and shining with sweat as he held out his hands for the baby, which the disheveled Doña Dolores placed in his hands.

"The water!" he murmured. Ysidra set the silver bowl on a small table between his chair and the bed.

"Her name, my child?" he asked of the girl in the bed.

Catalina, her face chalky and hollow, roused herself from a nap of exhaustion. "*Her* name?" Quivering needle points of shock pricked over her body. "*Her* name?" With a wild desperate effort she struggled to sit up. "It's a boy," she said harshly.

"No, no, my angel," her mother said soothingly, "a little girl. A lovely little girl."

Panting, Catalina sat up, shuddering in weakness. "Of course it's a girl," she shrieked, in a cracked hysterical voice. "Of course it is! I never expected anything but a girl. I never expect anything I want."

Enraged, furious, she fumbled wildly at the little table and caught up the silver bowl. Wrathfully she flung it at the pallid priest. Patricio turned in his chair instinctively to protect the infant. The bowl glanced off his shoulder, drenching him with holy water, and crashed clattering into a corner. Catalina collapsed shuddering and sobbing onto her pillow. How she had prayed for a boy! But what did they care? How many candles had she burnt to Santa María, to Santa Catalina! Well, they would never get any more. She lay huddled in a miserable heap, ill with disappointment.

Hastily the breach of manners was covered. She heard them in grim, wrathful anguish. Let them cover it. Let them make excuses for her. She heard words like "hysteria," "travail," "overwrought," "upset." With bitter amusement she heard the hurry and rustle as they got another bowl; somehow it didn't seem fitting to refill the one that lay in the corner. Stonily she heard the tired priest blessing the water. Distantly she heard the whimpering of her baby.

"Her name, child?" the priest prompted gently.

Catalina tried to think. The child had to have a name. She had planned only boys' names. Something like alarm filled her. Why were they naming the baby now? Why couldn't they wait for a proper ceremony? Because . . . because she had come too soon and they wanted to make sure, in case—?

Fragmentary fear for her newborn infant flitted through Catalina's mind. Nothing would happen to it. Surely, even if it were a girl, it would be all right. She must think of a name. What did you name a little girl? All she could think of was Isabela. She had no particular friend with that name, nor was it a family name.

Dully and thickly she mumbled "Isabela" and knew it was incomplete. She was so tired. She said her mother's name after it, "Dolores," and added one for her youngest sister Carmel.

"Carmel." The priest began to intone the words which would name the baby as Catalina sank into sleep. She tried to add a name for her sister María-Fe, but could not summon the necessary strength to utter the single syllable "Fe." Regretting this, she sank into a deep slumber.

Petra gulped back a hysterical wisp of a laugh. How incredibly tired she was! How tired she had been on the day of her first marriage—but for so different a reason! Shining and lovely in white and gold dust, she had been tired from dancing, pleasure, fun. Now in black, dirty and grimed, she was exhausted from plain hard work. Numbly she stripped off her clothes and jewels. Everything she did was an echo, a dark reflection of something she had done before. She wondered if she were through living new things and would go on living echoes and reflections for the rest of her life. Francisco? She knew he was still out with Enrique and Guillermo, clearing up odds and ends. Xavier had long since come back and sat gazing at his new child. The house was an unearthly shell of quiet. Petra washed at the strange washstand slowly, forgetting what she did at times, and staring into space with the soapy rag in her hands. She wished she dared go back to her own room, but she had been afraid that Francisco would come to her there. She could not stand that.

The only sounds in the world seemed to be those she made, the rustle of her clothing, the slosh of the water, the click of her jewels as she laid them down on the wooden stand. She thought of the earthquake again and was suddenly sick. The memory of it came to her at intervals, and always there was this upsurge of illness at the very idea of it. Earth was the one thing a person could depend on. The ground and the soil were always there solid beneath one's feet—except now, of course. It seemed that the very solid earth was a trembling, faulty thing which might shatter and crumble at any moment of night or day. Everything Irish in her soul resented and tried to disbelieve this with desperation and fear. Too many of her forebears had sustained themselves by grubbing in a solid patch of earth for her to credit the fact that the earth was unstable. Again in her mind resounded the rending and cracking of the altar. If an altar to God could fall, what was there to cling to? What stable thing was left?

Of a sudden she was desperately homesick. Not since she had first come over here had she felt this way. She felt incredibly incompetent, ignorant and young. Deep in her mind was the idea that she was really only a child masquerading as an adult, and soon someone would discover her bluff and send her sprawling with a slap. She avoided looking into the glass, for she didn't like to see her saucer-round eyes and unsteady lips. For the first time since she had come to California to be Angelo's wife, she wished to erase it all, forget it, never to have lived it. If only, right now, this minute, she might look across at the bed and it would suddenly be her narrow white bed at home in London! If she could open the window and allow a cloud of mist and fog to billow in! If she could smell again the drenched little garden! If only she could have stayed a little girl forever!

Clutching her nightgown about her throat she went to the door and opened it.

"How are you, Petra?" Francisco asked stepping inside. His face was lined with fatigue but his skin now gleamed with cleanliness. "I stopped to look in on Father Patricio. He was sleeping like a child, from exhaustion I suppose. Are you all right? I hated to leave you alone today, but there was really nothing else I could do."

"I got along very well," Petra answered with an effort, wondering if he would speak of the dress, preparing herself to argue with him.

"I got a look at the baby too." He smiled a little.

"Oh, did you?" Petra had thought for a moment that he meant Graciano. Then: "Oh, you mean Catalina's baby?"

"Yes, it seemed awfully small. It's too little yet to tell what it's going to look like. How is Catalina?"

"All right, I think. I wasn't there at the time. I was busy downstairs. Her mother and Ysidra took care of her."

He sank into a deep chair and was somberly silent for some time. "A rider came from the mission. They needed a few things," he said noncommittally.

Petra's heart missed a beat. "How was it there?"

"Quite bad. It seems we were the lucky ones. I've sent messengers out to the other ranchos to ascertain the damage and offer help if it's needed. . . . The roof of the church fell in."

Petra gasped, "Oh no! Was it empty?"

"I shouldn't be telling you this," answered Francisco tiredly. "I should spare you these details. I can't imagine what makes me so unfeeling. No, the church wasn't empty. They were celebrating noon Mass."

Petra gasped again and sat down on the edge of the bed. Her eyes were wide and dark. "Was . . . was anybody——"

"Thirty were killed," he said flatly. "The altar toppled and saved Father Gabriel from the falling rubble, so that he sustained only slight bruises. Vaiz has been sweating like a slave over the injured ones. I sent several *carretas* of needed articles. I'll have to arrange some way to get Father Patricio back there tomorrow. I didn't wake him to tell him—wrongly, I suppose, as he must want to know."

"Oh no, let him sleep. He'll feel better in the morning," Petra said. Thirty. Thirty people dead at the mission. Thirty people crushed and mangled, and the priest bruised and hurt. And Father Patricio downstairs moaning in his sleep, with his leg broken. The dining-room wall was gone, and the church was without a roof. Everything was wrong. Everything was broken, lopsided and disheveled.

She looked at Francisco leaning his head wearily against the back of the chair, and something stirred in her mind. Apprehension began to rise and chilled her body. She was facing her husband. There was no barrier now, nothing between them. Nothing she could do or say or wish could forestall this inevitable moment.

He was her husband. He was here. Now! She began to cry, hating herself for it.

What a selfish fool she was! How could she think of herself when thirty people lay dead and many houses might have fallen to the ground like shattered toys. Maybe if she had faced it with a sensible mind—maybe if she hadn't vented her silent hate on the altar—maybe——

Who could have thought that Francisco's hands would be so gentle? Who could have suspected he understood how to soothe fright and terror? Who could have thought that beneath the hard, suave exterior was a streak of pure kindness.

He came to her gently. "Petra, dearest, don't." He lifted her in his arms, her gown trailing palely, and carried her to the deep chair.

"I really didn't cheat about the dress, Francisco," she sobbed. "It was the same dress. I . . . I just dyed it, and——"

"I know, I know," he said softly. "Forget about the dress, *niñita*. Don't cry. It isn't worth your tears." Gently he brushed back the streaming yellow hair and dried the tears, kissing her with such gentleness that she scarcely felt his lips, speaking so softly that she scarcely heard the murmuring of his voice. This was peace, sanity, security. How could she have hated him? Who could have thought she would cling to him, weeping for the dead Indians and for the dining-room wall and for Father Patricio who must moan from pain in his sleep?

Petra woke to the singing, which had a mournful and melancholy sound. For a moment she lay in delicious and complete lethargy. A sound of wood hitting wood smote her ears and memory of the dining-room wall came to her mind, and simultaneously heat seared her face. *What a fool she was!*

But who could tell where kindness and soothing ceased and something else took its place? Who could tell in what manner caresses changed until it was too late? Oh, what a clever beast he was! Coming with sweetness and kindness like honey on his tongue and staying through the rest of the black tempestuous night! Hypnotizing her! Making a fool of her!

And what kind of a woman was she?

Wicked, weak, wanton! Little better than the Indian women who cast sheep's eyes at him. And he knew it. How he must laugh at her! A dozen images flashed into her mind, and she faced them with tight lips and glittering eyes. What was wrong with her? Why couldn't she be a good woman? It hadn't been wrong to experience a turbulent joy at Angelo's touch—she had loved Angelo. *She did not love Francisco.* She turned to bury her burning face in the pillow, shaking with shame. What could he see in her? Reluctant bride with whom he might satisfy his stupendous passion? She thought of the gentle, insistent love of Angelo and writhed in humiliation. But at first he had been so tender. How could she have known?

And *sleep!* How could she have slept—slept peacefully and deeply at his side all night? Her mouth pulled downward in a sneer. Mother of God! After that, how could she *not* have slept! Furiously she sat up, wishing the bed wasn't empty beside her, wishing she could hit him, or scratch him, or *something.* Tempestuously she took his pillow and flung it across the room.

Chapter 18

Delfina cried no longer, but lay sodden and limp on the rumpled covers of Guillermo's bed. She looked around the room with swollen red eyes, forgetting to note for the first time how fine a room it was. She moved experimentally and grimaced at the pain of it. She was tired and bruised and old. She would never be young again. Laboriously she rose to a sitting position, feeling the tenderness in her flesh and the aching in her joints. Her face, puffy and blotched, pulled itself into a blank vacant smile. Guillermo, then, was not such a fine man after all. He was not above beating his wife like any Indian. She winced at the remembrance of his rage, but deep in her mind was the knowledge that she could not blame him, and he had been kind. At first there had been a great kindness in Guillermo.

A shiver passed through her, as it never failed to do, when she recalled her wedding night and the morning that followed. She had thought she might appear young and innocent with her bridegroom, but there were apparently things a woman could not counterfeit. Guillermo was not stupid. She remembered waking to find his somber eyes fixed on her, filled with the knowledge that she had come to him damaged and second hand.

He had rolled over, got up and stood before her, good-looking in his slim brown nakedness. "The maid of honor is outside," he had commented laconically. Delfina's blood ran cold. Of course the maid of honor would be out there. How eager would Damacia be to hear whether or not the bride had tasted of the pleasures of love before marriage!

Deflina sat up, her lips pallid. If Guillermo wanted to he could go out wailing and wringing his hands and tell Damacia, who knocked at the door, that his wife had come to him not a virgin. He could cut off her long braids and she would go about shamed and humilated, with everyone knowing that she was sinful and wicked.

Her round little chin came up. "Well, open the door then," she had said, trying to speak naturally, but unable to keep a quaver from her voice.

Guillermo put on some clothing in silence. She had wondered if it would hurt when he cut her hair off. He would probably do it with a dull knife.

He tightened the red sash about his slender middle and went to the door. "Wait a moment," he called. There was a flutter of muffled mirth from outside. The attendants, having slept a little, were ready to continue the fiesta and wanted the bride and groom.

His hand on the knob, he had turned to look at his wife. Something hard washed out of his dark face and his lips moved in a slight grimace. Shrugging slightly he swung open the door to let in the bevy of girls and their escorts.

He bowed before them. "My lovely wife," he said, "is pure as the lilies of the field and white as the snow on the mountaintops."

Never in all her life had Delfina heard such welcome words. No one had noticed the hardness in Guillermo's eyes as the girls rushed forward to help Delfina dress. When he pushed the other men from the room, no one could tell by looking at him that he was anything but a triumphant and completely satisfied bridegroom.

That had been some time ago, and giving Guillermo his due, he had been more than kind ever since. Never by word or gesture had he intimated that he was anything but glad and proud that she was his wife. She rose unsteadily to her feet. Why couldn't she have married him sooner? Why did he have to find out today that he was fathering another man's child? Something like sullen defeat gleamed an instant in her swollen eyes. Well, she hadn't told him who the man was. He could have beaten her until her bones showed naked and she would never have told him. Laughter that was half weeping rose in a strangled gasp. He was hurt and angry and he was running to Francisco, his father, his lord, for sympathy and counsel. Let him run. She wondered what sympathy and counsel Francisco could give him. Francisco, whose wife was the golden Doña Petra. Francisco who had gone to his marriage bed while she received blows at the hands of an outraged husband. The sun streamed in hotly, drenching the room with its glare, laving her in its heat, pricking at her stinging eyes.

Guillermo, confused, furious, anguished, stood before Don Francisco. He made a desperate effort to act the way Don Angelo would have acted—but then no woman would have made a fool of Don Angelo. The wise and beautiful Angelo had known how to handle his women.

Guillermo swallowed and made an effort to speak. "You didn't want me to marry her in the first place, did you, sir?" he asked, hating the unsteadiness of his voice.

Francisco looked at the boy, steeling himself to

remain aloof, noting with affection the superb body, the fine head. "Marriages hurried into are seldom too successful, Guillermo. I am sorry if you have been disappointed."

"Don Angelo's marriage was quick," Guillermo said raggedly, "but he didn't marry an Indian."

"Guillermo," Francisco said gently and paused. Pride seemed to congeal in the boy and knit him together.

"I know," Guillermo said remotely. "I am lucky. I could have expected nothing better. Except that it isn't . . . it isn't——" He stopped a moment, seeming to lose himself.

"She is going to have a child," he said flatly. "It is not mine." Had such a thing ever happened to a Spaniard? What would a Spaniard do? It was incredible that any woman, no matter how bold, would entertain the idea of trying to fool a Spaniard and make him ridiculous. What would Francisco do? Why, kill her, quickly, cleanly, with a certain disdain; seek out the man swiftly and destroy him with ease and detachment. And what did he, Guillermo Estrada do? First he wept, because he was shattered, weakened and dismayed, because he was inferior, because he didn't know how to be a Spaniard, because he only pretended to be a Spaniard, because he was nothing but a savage and a child.

"I am sorry, Guillermo." Francisco was speaking carefully, with something near regret in his tone. "Believe me, I am sorry."

"I should have waited," Guillermo said miserably. "You should not be so indulgent. You should have commanded me to wait, but you were too kind. Indians can't stand kindness, you should know that. They understand only harshness." He sat down, forgetting for the first time in his life to await permission. He felt with a sort of bitter satisfaction Francisco's hand pass over his bent head and rest on his shoulder.

"Don't call yourself an Indian, Guillermo," Francisco said steadily. "You are not an Indian. You are my son whom I adopted. You have a fine future. You will be *mayordomo* of Dos Ríos. This is bad, I know. It is difficult to——"

"But she knew," he burst out harshly. "She knew! She would have nothing to do with me until she needed a husband quickly. Don't you see? I wouldn't mind so much if she had just fallen in love with me and married me. I could have understood that she might have loved someone else before. But it wasn't that." His strong fingers raked distractedly through his tousled hair. "Don't you see, she *had* to! She had to have—just *anybody*."

The words were like acid in his mouth, eating at his soul, corroding his fine and valuable pride, rendering it as dust. In a long-forgotten gesture of childhood he laid his cheek against Francisco's hand.

All the days of his life, ever since he could remember, Francisco had been his rock, his fortress, his protection against the evils and dangers that threatened an Indian. Francisco, the Spaniard, had taken him from the dusty yard at the mission, washed him, taught him to ride, to speak, to think; adopted him, became his father, raised him above his mother's race. Because Francisco willed it so, he was a man instead of a savage, he slept between white sheets instead of coarse blankets, his body was covered with splendid cloth, he rode the best horses next to Francisco, his hair was combed with a silver comb, his food was fine and good. But aside from these, ignoring these, Francisco had been *there*. No matter how great the problem, humiliation, hurt, Francisco was there, strong, intelligent, powerful. He had only to speak for a thing and it was so. Pain diminished instantly, and instantly confusion was gone. Enemies were confounded and dispersed. Everything was made whole.

"How . . . they will laugh at me!" he whispered, his face darkening and burning against Francisco's hand.

"They will not laugh." Francisco's voice held power and conviction. His hands circled Guillermo's face and lifted it. "No one will laugh," he said.

"But who? Who was he?" Guillermo's voice held desperate urgency. For a long moment he did not sense the utter stillness in Francisco's hand, the complete and stonelike stillness of his whole person. Then with dogged, Indian determination, he raised his face and met the eyes of the other man.

As the earth had rocked on its foundation, as it had shaken and quivered in crumbling decay, it shook again for Guillermo. Francisco's hand fell from his face, and Guillermo rose from the chair, not even knowing that he did. He was wounded, maimed, beyond healing. He was sick with a mortal sickness as everything was swept away, all his pride, all his props, all his strength, all things on which he counted and depended. He was left stripped, vulnerable, defenseless.

"Guillermo."

"Oh, let me go," he whispered, and was gone.

Chapter 19

Las Palomas sustained no damage in the earthquake. The servants who had been left swore that there had been only a slight trembling in the ground. So Doña Dolores Acuña decided to remain at Dos Ríos until her new grandchild was well launched in life. She was delighted with the baby and extremely satisfied with Catalina, for the girl showed signs of becoming a conscientious, if not too sentimental, mother. Xavier went about in a happy self-satisfied glow.

Francisco worked like a fiend, spending little time in the house. His excuse for this was that the rancho needed him. It did. There were repairs to make and work to do. He did the work himself, indulging in stupendous labors, as if he took a barren satisfaction in exhausting himself. He turned a blank and expressionless face to complaints about Guillermo, steeling himself to answer them courteously and do nothing about them.

Reports trickled in: Guillermo was drunk; Guillermo was disorderly; Guillermo was vicious and truculent.

"What is the matter with him!" Petra said angrily. "Are you going to allow him to humiliate us in this manner?"

"I can't understand it," Enrique Padilla said savagely. "The boy is bewitched!"

"Have him whipped, Francisco," Xavier counseled placidly. "Whip him yourself. Whipping never hurt an Indian, and it might do some good."

"Perhaps he is ill," suggested Ysidra quietly.

"Yes," Francisco replied in gratitude, "I think he is sick. We will let him alone."

Delfina moved from the great house to stay with her parents. When Guillermo was at Dos Ríos, he stayed there too. The Alcalde of Los Angeles was distressed and dismayed when Guillermo got into trouble there, and sent a special rider to notify Francisco, whose ward he knew Guillermo to be. Francisco, deaf to the family's outrage, saddled a horse and rode to Los Angeles. He paid the fine, settled the damages and brought Guillermo back to Dos Ríos. Guillermo who had always been so beautifully turned out, so fastidious, rode beside him filthy, disheveled and sullen. He did nothing, would listen to no argument. When he had not been drinking, he remained as if drunk on some private bitter liquor of his own. And to the amazement of all, Francisco forbade anyone to take a hand.

"Let him alone," he said, and that was all they could do.

In the meantime the things which needed mending at Dos Ríos were mended. In a remarkably short time everything was again in order. Father Patricio sent Petra one of the mission's yellow rose vines. This she planted outside the dining-room wall. It was little more than a gnarled stump now, but in time it would climb up the wall, obscure the patch and bear pale yellow roses the size of teacups.

As for Petra, she found living with Francisco not so difficult as she had thought it would be. No fault could be found in his conduct toward her, but it infuriated her that their marriage had slipped so snugly into place. It was as if everyone had forgotten that they had ever been anything but husband and wife. She brooded on this fact so often and long that some days the very sight of Francisco was enough to send her into a secret rage. Then too she was disgusted with her own reactions.

There was nothing wrong, really. Women were supposed to submit to their husbands. It was just that she was ashamed of herself. No matter how incensed she became at him, no matter how she fought against him, she could not deny her own traitorous body. She wished she could be completely disdainful and cold, the way she imagined Catalina must be with Xavier. She wished Francisco were completely repellent to her. She wished she could keep from noticing things about him. She was sure that Catalina never noticed Xavier. If you asked Catalina, she probably wouldn't have the faintest idea about the size of Xavier's jacket, or the actual color of his eyes, or the strength of his arm. In a moment of secret, cautious truthfulness, Petra admitted to herself that Francisco was a splendid-looking man. She thought that, for someone else, he might be a splendid husband. But, as her husband, she wished to be coldly disdainful of him. Unfortunately she was either too honest or too wanton to simulate repugnance after a certain time.

And he knew it. What a wise, heartless creature he was! She would turn and bury her flaming face in the pillow, unable to look at him, unable to meet his clear amused eyes. She would twist and turn her body away from him, struggle limply to evade his strong caressing hands, but in the end she would be too weak, too ravished, to do anything but sleep in his arms if he wished it. That was the hatefulness of his coming to her bed. He was the master completely—kindly as a rule—but completely. It was infuriating and humiliating to have him know that she was little better than a wanton who could resist no man's advances. No matter what airs she assumed during the day, no matter how she played the great lady, or the doting mother, he could, with an amused glance, send her into a gulf of embarrassment.

She was upset one day when she noticed the advanced stage of Delfina's pregnancy. Leaving the ironing room, she walked down the hall with narrowed eyes, doing some labored mental arithmetic. Judging from the way Delfina walked, the way she held herself——

"So you noticed it too." Catalina laughed falling into step beside her.

"How far along do you think she is?" Petra asked with a cautious glance around.

"Well, I've seen a lot of pregnant women in my time," Catalina said soberly, "and I would bet my prettiest necklace that it won't come later than the middle of November."

"Well," Petra said doubtfully, "it could come prematurely."

"Well," Catalina said dryly, "if it comes in November complete with hair and fingernails, we can safely assume she carried it the full term." Then, hurriedly: "Hush, here comes Mama!"

Teodoro Acuña rode from Las Palomas to escort his mother home. He was pleasant, poised and beautifully polite as always. He played with his little godson as much as he did his niece, in honest and unalloyed affection. When the time came to leave, he did so with regret. Petra, Catalina and Francisco rode part way with Teodoro and Doña Dolores on the way to Las Palomas. When they paused at last to part company, Doña Dolores turned to Catalina with a frown.

"Please remember, my angel, about keeping oil on the baby."

"Oil," repeated Catalina obediently.

"Plenty of time, lady mother." Teodoro grinned. "Anything else?"

"Nothing else, I guess—" Doña Dolores laughed—"except . . . I . . . did I tell you about heating a cloth for her stomach in case of colic?"

"*Mamacita,* I think you've told me everything about everything." Catalina laughed. "In fact I know so much about babies now that you need not bother to come when I have the next one."

"Not come! How you talk! I wouldn't fail to come."

"When do you expect the next one, Catalina?" her brother teased.

Catalina shot a suddenly malicious glance at Petra. "I had the last one," she said. "It's Petra's turn now."

Petra's face stiffened. "Delfina is next," she said without thinking. "Probably in November."

There was the hint of a reprimand in Doña Dolores' tone when she spoke. It would not be her custom, she implied without saying so, to come to Dos Ríos for the confinements of servants. "In any case," she said, "Delfina and Guillermo were married. . . . It wouldn't be November . . ." She suddenly stammered in embarrassment. There was an uncomfortable moment. Teodoro, sharing his mother's discomfiture, flushed darkly.

Petra saw something flicker for a moment in Francisco's eyes and convulsively tightened her hand on the bridle. *Not Francisco!* Then instantly a flock of small facts flitted through her mind: Delfina's sudden marriage; her strangely large amounts of spending money; the imminence of her confinement; Guillermo's inexplicable disintegration.

Catalina's delighted laugh rang out.

"Look! Teodoro is blushing. Whoever heard of a *caballero* blushing?"

"I think I should be proud if I were able to summon a blush," Francisco commented kindly. "It indicates a certain fundamental decency."

"Catalina, shame!" Doña Dolores admonished, casting apologetic eyes to Francisco.

Petra swallowed a torrent of hot words, hating Catalina, Francisco, and even the thought of Delfina. "We got off the subject," she said outrageously. "We were speaking of children. I don't think I care to have any more for a time." She wanted to add that she didn't want hers confused with those of the servants, but, with an effort, refrained. "On the other hand," she continued quickly, "if I intend having any more, I'd better have them soon." She gazed at Francisco with exaggerated thoughtfulness, appraising him with narrowed eyes, as one might appraise an old horse to estimate how much longer it would be able to support a saddle and trappings. "How old *are* you, sir?" she asked coolly, noting the confusion of the other members of the party.

Something near a grin touched Francisco's lips.

"I'm thirty-nine, Petra," he said.

"Thirty-nine!" Petra said with deep regret, thoroughly enjoying herself now. "I hardly realized that there was that much difference in our ages. It really behooves me to——"

"We must start," the scandalized Doña Dolores gasped. "Really, Don Francisco, I have enjoyed myself tremendously at Dos Ríos. And, Catalina dear, please remember all the things I have told you." She rushed on, her words tumbling over one another in embarrassed haste. There was a rush of good-bys and the Acuñas started for Las Palomas much faster than they would have ordinarily.

Petra, Catalina and Francisco had gone half a

league in the direction of Dos Ríos before the silence was broken.

"Petra," Catalina exclaimed, her cheeks still pink, "how could you behave so!"

"You started it," snapped Petra and would have continued, but Francisco interrupted.

"Catalina, it's a beautiful day. Wouldn't you like a gallop? Why don't you ride back to the house by yourself. I have something to say to my wife."

Both girls stared at him.

"By myself?" Catalina asked uncertainly, not knowing what might happen now.

"Yes, if you don't mind," he said smiling easily and dismounting. The other two horses had stopped when his did, and Catalina flicked distractedly at her horse's mane.

"Well, of course," she said with labored politeness, still not able to leave them.

"My dear wife," Francisco said to Petra, "I was sure of the Spaniards in your family, but there was also the rumor bruited about that some of your English antecedents had their beginnings in a scullery. Judging from your conduct this morning, I am inclined to believe it."

Petra's lips tightened. Just let him say anything about Papa! Then she experienced a little stab of sheer joy. She had angered him. She had disturbed that perfect poise of his. She shrugged elaborately. "I'm sorry you feel you got a bad bargain in a wife," she said, "but since the marriage occurred at your own insistence——"

"I didn't say I got a bad bargain," he said, a hint of laughter in his tone.

"What do you mean?" Petra asked, suddenly wary.

He reached up, expertly snapped the reins from Petra's fingers. Whistling softly through his teeth, he began to tie the horses to the branches of a willow clump. His hat was on the back of his head. The emerald flashed for a blinding instant in the sunlight.

"What are you doing?" Petra asked carefully, holding the pommel of her saddle for balance.

"Tying up our horses," he replied and resumed his careless whistling. When they were tied, he walked around to her side and put his hand on her waist. "I was worried," he said blandly, "about your concern for my approaching old age. I had thought you had full reason to understand my capabilities, but apparently not. I now think it wise to set at rest your fears concerning my feebleness."

Petra's eyes began to widen in dawning horror. She tried to speak but was unable to force any utterance.

Catalina's mouth dropped open and she sat on her horse, hypnotized, unable to move.

"It also came to my mind that you were acting like a little savage back there. It occurred to me that if I treated you like a savage for a while, perhaps you would mend your manners." His hand tightened. He pulled her roughly from the saddle to the ground. His intention was quite clear.

Catalina uttered a smothered gasp and lashed her startled horse into a full gallop.

"Francisco!" Petra found her voice now, astounded, horrified. "Not here on the ground—like an Indian!"

"Yes," he said pleasantly, "here on the ground like an Indian."

She hated him. She hated him. She hated him. She loathed, abhorred and despised him. She longed with a soul-shaking fury to kill him. But she managed to keep some semblance of poise until she reached her room—the one she had shared with Angelo. There she flung herself on the bed in anguished hysteria, weeping from rage and humiliation. When the frenzy had diminished she got up and began struggling with the fastenings of her gown. When she stood white and shaking and half-naked before the glass she saw the marks of his rough handling. She would have bruises, she thought, weeping afresh at this added indignity. Her face was becoming puffy and blotched from weeping. I'm hideous, she said to herself, and was obscurely glad of the ugliness, looking with dull satisfaction at her reflection. Her attendant, Bianca, had come in and, thoroughly frightened, bustled about preparing a bath that Petra wasn't sure she wanted. The Indian remained perfectly silent and proffered assistance with such cringing obsequiousness that Petra was stirred to wonder if she thought her mad. She tried suddenly to regain some semblance of calm. Angelo would never have permitted such a display before a servant. But then Angelo would never have—— Again she was choked with outrage.

After she had washed, she was completely spent. She allowed Bianca to help her into a nightgown. Her arms were incredibly heavy as she lifted them to slide into the white sleeves. From the bed, when she lay down, she saw Bianca tiptoe ponderously from the room. Warning, like a hot wind, swept through her mind.

"Where are you going?" she asked hoarsely.

"Out, doña, so you may sleep," Bianca said placatingly.

"Come here." Petra was scarcely conscious that she spoke. The Indian came, cringing a little before the glitter in her mistress' eyes.

"Listen to me. Tell anyone who asks that I am sick. I have a fever. And listen!" Her voice cracked uncontrollably. "If you tell anything else I'll cut your tongue out—with my embroidery scissors." She added as an afterthought.

The attendant went clay-colored. It was all she could do to keep from falling to her knees. "Oh, my doña," she wailed in mixed fear and outrage, "I never tell tales. Holy Mother, didn't I keep the secret of the doña's first pregnancy? I call to the Virgin to witness——"

"Be quiet," Petra said, pulling up the coverlet with a feverish hand. "Go out now and let me alone."

Bianca scurried out, her body quivering like jelly, her tread thudding on the planked floor.

Petra fell into a choppy, unrefreshing sleep. The room was too warm. She wished sullenly for bigger windows like the houses at home in London, big wide windows that one might open onto a drenching fog.

London. She dreamed suddenly and disjointedly of a London which was hot and breathless; of London houses with strangely slit Spanish windows. When she awoke again she struggled out of bed to get a drink of tepid water. Lagging, she went back to the bed and dropped down on top of the rumpled sheet. The house was completely silent about her. It must be midafternoon. Everyone was in his room for siesta. She lay back with her hair spread damply on the pillow, thinking how she would begin again as if nothing had happened. A dull mottled red crept up in her face. Could she arrange it so that no one else found out. She might have to speak to Catalina. That was easy. She had only to mention Francisco's name and the girl would be all obedience. She could trust Bianca. Poor old Bianca! What had she said—"Didn't I keep the secret of your first pregnancy?" Indeed she had. Uncommonly trustworthy for an Indian. How astounded Francisco and Aunt Ysidra had been the night when she had told them!

First. What had she meant, *first?* Lumbering terror engulfed her. She struggled to a sitting position, completely stunned. She spoke aloud to herself in the silent room. "Why, I'm going to have a baby," she said blankly.

Chapter 20

Petra leaned for a moment against the doorway. She was in rustling black taffeta. The Montoya diamonds glittered at her throat. Her hair and bodice were hung with bits of silver confetti. For an instant she was without the little court that usually gathered about her. The court tonight was for Doña Rosa Acuña y Sal. Petra turned her eyes somberly about the crowded ballroom of the Sal house. So many things seemed to have changed. She was expecting another baby in May, Guillermo was bewitched, and Teodoro had married little Rosa Sal, daughter of Don Sebastián Sal.

Petra turned away and slipped outside for a breath of air. The continuous music had given her a headache. Once outside in the darkness of the low-roofed loggia, she raised her hand and pulled back the black lace of her mantilla to let whatever breeze there was strike her cheeks. It was hot, and she was sick to her stomach. She wondered how much longer she could go before people started to guess that she was expecting again. How lucky that she had brought that corset from England and kept it! Because California women seldom wore them, she had been glad to discard it, but now she was glad to resume its binding, but shielding, encasement. The tight lacings made breathing difficult. Damn Francisco!

"Are you well, Petra?"

She jumped, startled, and turned to face him, feeling uncannily that the very force of her thoughts had conjured him out of the black night air.

"I'm well," she answered distantly, sorry that they were alone together on the loggia. She did not want to regain any semblance of personal footing between them; he had remained impersonal toward her since the afternoon of Doña Dolores Acuña's departure for Las Palomas. Petra wanted to keep it like that as long as she could.

"You aren't dancing," he commented lighting a cigarette. "It made me wonder, for you seldom miss a chance to dance." He regarded her as searchingly as the darkness would permit.

She could find no answer and, being too tired to think of one, remained silent.

He lounged against the adobe wall and looked thoughtfully at the dim fair outline of her face and throat. "If you are ill, Petra, we could make our excuses and go back home to Dos Ríos."

"After only three days?" she asked trying to put sarcasm into her tone.

"Don Sebastián would understand if you were ill."

"We had better stay. There is no point in hurting his feelings." Fragrant smoke eddied about her head and she put up her hand to brush at it. Immediately he tossed the cigarette down and ground it out, offering an apology which she only half heard.

"I'm worried about you," he said thoughtfully after a while. "If you would rather go home, please tell me. There is little rest to be had in a crowded place like this. If you would feel better at home, there would be no question——"

"I would rather stay," she replied bluntly.

"But you aren't having a good time." His voice was gentle.

"I wouldn't have a good time at Dos Ríos either," she said remotely, wishing he would go away and leave her in peace. "Besides," she added as an acid afterthought, "I like crowds. They protect me from things I wish to be protected from." She wondered if his face darkened, but could not tell. Then she turned from him, disgusted with herself. Why did she continually jab at him, trying to torment and annoy him? That was unworthy. If you hate a man, the thing to do is fly at him and rip him to pieces, not pick and peck like a vulture at a carcass. Besides, she must never make him too angry; there were too many things to consider. She must always remember Angelo's child, whose inheritance hung forever in balance. This thought, as usual, angered her.

The germ of an idea began to form in her mind. She would never get anywhere fighting with him. She was no match for him; she couldn't think of anyone who was. Yet in spite of the strength and violence of his nature, he was a gentle person on occasion. He was in love with her. Was it possible that the only weapon she could use against him was this? There had been this breach between them for some time. If she healed it, she would probably incur his lasting gratitude. He was always inclined to be indulgent with those he loved. If he were grateful, would he not spoil her outrageously? Yet on the other hand—— Well, it was worth a try.

She opened her fan, and moved it slowly in the warm air. "I have been very rude to you," she said faintly. "I am sorry."

He strained to see her face in the darkness. "Petra, my dear, I'm afraid I deserve anything I get from you. I'm the transgressor and we both know it. I have apologized before. I do so again."

"Please don't speak of it."

"As you wish, my dear. Am I to take this as token of forgiveness?"

She nodded, suddenly frightened. This was foolish. She should have kept him at bay. But she did not resist him when he moved closer to take her into his arms. For the first time she submitted to him quietly and limply, remaining quiescently in his embrace. His kiss was gentle, but she knew it wouldn't be for long. His fingers caressed the back of her neck, beneath the lace mantilla, and his thumbs were beneath her chin so that he might kiss her mouth. Telltale warmth spread in her body. Crushing a sudden panic, she withdrew a little. "Francisco," she said, her breath coming quickly.

"Yes, my dear?"

"I . . . was wondering if . . ." She paused. How could she say it to him? How could she phrase it so he wouldn't be offended? Angered? "It's so difficult to speak of it . . . but I thought . . . I wondered if . . . if we need have any more children. I . . . haven't been feeling well, really, and——"

"I'm not sure I understand you, Petra," he said quietly. "We haven't any children yet."

"We have Graciano," she said faintly.

After a long pause he said, "Graciano is Angelo's child."

There was a remoteness in his tone which alarmed her. She let her fan fall and dangle from her wrist as she placed her hands impulsively on his shoulders. "Francisco," she said, raising her face to his, "I'm afraid. You don't know how afraid I am. It seems——" Her words were smothered suddenly, as she knew they would be. This time she returned his kiss, clinging to him, while the sudden pounding of her veins caused resentment in that small proud core of her mind which always remained separate to mock her.

"Have you suddenly come to love me?" he asked after a time.

Something in his tone made her push against his chest. "What do you mean?" she asked breathlessly.

"I mean this sudden quiescence, this pliancy, this yielding." His tone was faintly tinged with laughter.

Anger began to rise in Petra. She might have known she could never fool him, not with all the women he had known. She stiffened against the wall. "I'm simply tired of fighting you," she said endeavoring to keep her voice steady.

"But this about children. What point was there in that? You know very well, or should, that I do want other children. In any case, pandering to me the way you just did is no way to keep from becoming pregnant. Believe me," he finished dryly.

She closed her fan with a sharp click. "You are still treating me like a savage? You still don't think I deserve ordinary courtesy? I shall have to be careful or next you will be beating me." Her voice shook with anger now.

"My dear Petra—" He bowed, all Spaniard, but his apology was cut short by Carmel Acuña who fairly danced out the door.

"Don Francisco, there you are! You said you would dance with me at my first ball and you haven't!" She saw Petra and fluttered her fan in sudden nervousness. "That is, of course, if Doña Petra——"

"I'm not dancing, Carmelita," Petra said courteously, feeling suddenly old and sick. Six months ago Carmel had been playing with dolls. "Please go on, sir," she said to Francisco. "I think I'll go upstairs." She swept by them into the lighted ballroom and hurried through.

Her room was hot and close, but it would afford some small privacy for a while. She was rooming with María-Teresa Sal and two of the women guests. Another bed had been moved in making it extremely crowded. Petra longed for her own spacious chamber at Dos Ríos. The Indians had all they could do—during fiesta inclination to work was at a low ebb anyway—and the room was in utter disorder. She didn't light a candle for she shrank in distaste from the clutter. Ball dresses, bangles, shawls, combs, mantillas and slippers covered all available furniture. Perfume had been spilled and the room was rank with the thick cloying scent.

She slammed the heavy door, muffling the sound of music. She stood, loathing the littered room, hating the primly sweet Rosa Sal whom Teodoro had married, hating Catalina, graceful and lovely, surrounded by admirers. She hated little Carmelita, pretty and light as a butterfly, dancing with Francisco. She hated Francisco who knew, always knew, exactly what she was thinking; Francisco who always went free. Her first clenched against her stomach. This damned corset! She couldn't breathe. But she wasn't going to have this baby!

Sinful! Wicked!

She was perfectly still for a moment, wondering if she would be struck by the wrath of God. But she wasn't. Carefully she felt the thought, explored it, and remained whole and alive standing against the door. She wouldn't have the baby. She tested the thought again. How could she keep from having it? Well, Ana had always, until the last time, miscarried. Perhaps the pale Ana had merely been clever. Did a miscarriage hurt? No matter how it hurt, she wouldn't have any baby except Graciano. That would be reward enough. Why not face it? This must have been what was in her mind all along. She had just never recognized it. But she must have known from the very beginning that she could never have any but Angelo's child.

Back at Dos Ríos, some time after the fiesta at Sal's, they christened Delfina's little girl Magdalena. Francisco was named godfather, while Guillermo stared stolidly out the window all through the ceremony. Petra, tightly laced, looking slim as a reed, insisted on being godmother. She felt sorry for Delfina who hadn't stood the birth well and looked fifteen years older than she was. That was the trouble with Indian blood. The women got old so rapidly. Yet once old, they seemed to live forever. Petra thought of the old man and wondered if he were cold. The November wind swirled about the corners of buildings crying like a lost soul. Then she brought her mind back to the ceremony and looked down into the dark little face of the baby she held. She had hoped—Santa María how she had hoped!—that the baby would be white. No such luck. Francisco always went free. No one would ever connect this dark infant with Don Francisco Estrada y Santander. Petra shivered, wondering if the hand of Santa Magdalena herself touched the infant, for as the name was pronounced the infant opened its eyes and, instead of opaque black beads, they were clear liquid green, the green so admired by Spaniards, which usually went with milk-white skin and raven hair.

The baby's eyes closed again and Petra found herself accepting responsibility next in line after its mother's for its religious education and future care. This is Francisco's daughter, she thought.

The service ended, she placed the baby in Delfina's arms, but she thought about it, wondering what would happen to it. She was its godmother, she would have to see that it had some sort of decent start in life, that it made a satisfactory marriage. If only the little thing weren't so dark! But she must not allow it to be lost, she must not allow it to sink into the anonymity of being an Indian—not when Estrada blood ran in its veins. Delfina would tell the child of course; being so much Indian herself she could not keep from it the fact that it was part Spanish. She thought constantly of the baby Magdalena. While she sewed or talked or played with her own child she thought of Delfina's. She awoke in the night thinking of it, seeing those level green eyes in the dark little face. She must not think of Delfina's problems. She must think of her own.

Lying sleepless in her bed she could almost laugh at the grim joke of it. Mother of God, why were women so careful when they were pregnant? She had ridden horseback, she had jumped off the loggia, she had run up and down stairs. What *hadn't* she done? And still the child lay sleeping within her. She dreaded the day it would move. She could not stand that. She twisted, punching up the pillow, and tried to sleep again.

Down the hall Ysidra's door opened a fraction of an inch, and a sibilant whisper reached the ever quick ears of the huge woman on the bed. There seemed an urgency for silence. Ysidra waited for the intruder to speak. The shapeless shadow had walked barefoot down the hallway and edged itself into the darkened room.

"No light." It was the merest breath in the darkness. The small hand of Ysidra which had been about to light a candle halted and she knew that an Indian had entered her room and had sunk to a hulking silent heap beside her bed.

"What?" she asked after a moment.

There was interminable silence while the Indian made up her mind what to say. Ysidra could be patient when the need arose. She lay still, listening to the breathing of the other, knowing who it was.

At last the Indian spoke. "My Doña Petra is ill."

Ysidra had to strain to catch the almost inaudible sound. "Ill? How?" she prompted after another long wait. The Indian became slightly visible. The moon was rising. It gleamed on the rank sweat which had sprung out on her face. Then the idea which fought for utterance seemed to spring through the darkness. "How long since Doña Petra has had her monthly sickness?"

There was a faint sucking of breath. "Long, doña."

Ysidra felt a thrill of anger and chagrin. And the little fiend had taken to wearing a corset. Images of her goddaughter flitted through her mind: Petra running down the stairs; Petra riding at breakneck speed.

"Thank you. Go away. Go back to sleep."

The Indian did not move.

"You are a good woman, a good Christian," Ysidra said. The Indian was afraid. Petra had her cowed. Ysidra's lips twitched in the darkness as she thought of the labored struggle which must have gone on in the Indian's mind before the final decision was reached. How she must have weighed the word of God against other things! How she must have weighed the possible wrath of Francisco—not a light thing to the Indian view!

"I will buy you a present," Ysidra said. Then: "No one will know how I found out."

This seemed to satisfy the other, for she left as silently as she had come.

In the morning Petra had a sudden chill of fear as she heard Francisco coming down the hall. Pleading illness, she had been sleeping in her old room for some weeks, and Francisco seldom had occasion to stop there. Now he came down the hall purposefully, his heels thudding on the planked floor. Something in his stride made her hurry the last few buttons of her dress and turn to meet him as the door was flung open. He entered, shut it behind him and deliberately turned the key in the lock.

"You've given up the practice of knocking?" she inquired sharply. Further utterance died in her throat when she saw his face. His eyes were chips of ice and he was pallid beneath his tan.

"I understand you are going to have a baby," he said.

"Who gave you to understand that?"

"My aunt, a very discerning woman, had the presence of mind to notice your rather bizarre idea of lacing tightly and your sudden efforts at outdoor sports and manual labor."

"I'm afraid—with all respect, Francisco—that my godmother, your aunt, is a busybody. How I clothe and conduct myself is, or should be, my own affair."

"Not when you're carrying my child. How you could be base enough——"

"Don't quibble about my morals!" Her voice rose.

"This is the first time I've ever wanted to beat you," he said softly.

"Go ahead," she invited.

"Not when you're going to have a baby."

"I'm not having a baby."

"I think you are."

"You're mistaken. You have been misinformed. Mother of God, I should know!"

His eyes searched her figure, missing nothing, allowing for the tightly laced corset. He knew every line of her body. "You're pregnant," he said flatly. "Take off those lacings. Do you want to injure the child?"

"Francisco," she said stonily, "I didn't say I wasn't pregnant. I said I wasn't going to have a baby."

He was silent for a long moment. "If you think that, you are a fool," he said at last.

"Don't call me names!"

"When?" he asked stonily.

"I won't tell you," she said turning away from him. He hit her then, the first time he had ever struck a woman in anger. It sent her spinning. She crashed into a chair and fell to the floor. His face was ashen with fury and alarm. She struggled to rise. He strode to her and pulled her up, snapped her up as he would a cornhusk doll.

"Now listen to me," he said tonelessly. "Let us understand this between us. You are going to have this baby. We will not speak of sin and religion, but we will, if we have to, speak of a wife's duty to her husband. Anyhow, you little fool, what makes you think you won't have it, if it has gone this far?"

"Well, if I do, you'll never know it," she gasped, enraged.

"Listen, Petra, you are going to have this baby—and here in my house as the lady of Dos Ríos, even though your natural instincts might lead you to drop it in a field somewhere. Don't set yourself up as an authority here. You will do as you're told—make no mistake about it! Now, *when?*" His fingers dug into her shoulders painfully, but without their support she would have fallen to the floor.

"In . . . in May," she gasped.

"May!" He fell back a little, lessening his painful grasp.

The noise had attracted attention and a crowd

had gathered in the hall. Xavier's voice was raised. "Francisco my cousin, what is it?"

"Are you sure, Petra?"

She nodded dumbly.

"Then why are you laced so tightly?" he said through his teeth. "Mother of God, Petra, do you want to kill yourself!" Ignoring the voices in the hall, he began to loosen her bodice. She sagged limply. In a minute her dress was undone and down over her shoulders. He jerked at the fastenings of her corset, snapping the string like cobwebs. Picking her up, he carried her to the bed and laid her down. "May I get you something? Water? Brandy?" He kept his voice free from alarm at her pallor.

Breathing deeply and unsteadily she turned to look at him, her lips grim. "Wouldn't it be funny if I miscarried now?"

"Most amusing. May I get you some stimulant?"

"No. Get out."

"Not until we understand each other."

"We never will."

"We must, Petra. I don't intend to let you sacrifice any child of mine to your foul temper."

"It isn't temper!"

"Well, whatever it is. I'm your husband," he said softly, grimly, "and you will do as I say. Understand this: you are going to have this baby. And since you're such a husky peasant, you are going to have one every year, whether you wish to or not!"

She rose from the bed, her face twisting in fury. "You pig! You beast! You fool!"

Hit him. Kill him. Blindly she groped for some weapon with which to hurt him. Eluding his grasp she got free and hurled herself, garments trailing, across the room. A chair fell over. Graciano in his cradle began to scream in terror. She grabbed an empty candlestick and flung it. She caught up a bowl and crashed it into his chest. She lifted her sewing box and sent it flying. She lunged for the lamp, got it and threw it straight at him.

Instinctively he twisted. It struck him a glancing blow on the shoulder and crashed with a burst of flame into the statue of the Virgin with Her ever burning candle. Oil splattered, igniting the sleeve of his jacket. His teeth showed white as he beat at it. Footsteps pounded in the hall and bodies hit the unyielding door.

"Listen!" he cried. "By God, you will listen!" With a swooping gesture he snatched the baby from its cradle and raised it in his hand over his head. It screamed with ear-splitting shrillness.

Petra leaped at him, clawing like a mad woman. "Give me my baby!"

He caught both her wrists in his other hand and forced her backward on the bed, nearly breaking her arms. "No." His voice was half drowned by the baby's screams. "By God, I won't! Not until you come to your senses. Petra, listen to me, or so help me God I'll smash him against the wall."

"Francisco! Yes, yes. Give him to me. Anything!"

He pushed her savagely onto the bed. "Be quiet."

"Yes, yes," she sobbed, struggling up. "I will. I will. Francisco, give him to me." She raised one of her released arms and sank her teeth into the wrist to blot out the sound of her hysteria until she could control it.

Silenced, stunned, they faced each other for a moment. Then roughly he put the convulsed baby back into the cradle and snatched up a quilt to beat at the spreading flames which danced over the floor. In a matter of minutes they were out. He flung the charred quilt down and passed his hand over the sleeve of his jacket which still smoked.

Ignoring the clamor at the door, he returned to Petra, who lay white on the bed. "Now listen to me," he said evenly. "We can make a bargain, Petra."

He waited until he was sure he had her attention. "I am sorry that I have been such a husband as to arouse in you only resistance and viciousness. The fault must lie with me. I am sorry. Listen carefully while I tell you this, Petra. If you will please me by having this child, I promise you—you have my word on it—that I shall never approach you again as long as we live, unless you ask me to. Do you understand that?"

She stared at him a long time, sanity returning to her eyes. "All you want is this baby?" she asked in a harsh whisper.

"Yes, that is all. Give me this one child and I shall leave you and Graciano completely alone. That isn't a hard bargain, Petra. You would be rid of me for good."

She turned this thought slowly over in her mind. One baby, just that, and she would be free of him. "About Graciano's inheritance?" she asked doggedly.

"Graciano's inheritance is intact. There will be an equal division; that is all."

Well, it wouldn't be a bad bargain. It didn't look as if she were going to lose this baby anyway. She would probably have it whether she willed it or not. If she pushed him too far in his passionate obsession for a child he might be driven to harming Graciano, and all of Angelo would be lost. She shuddered, remembering his rough grasp on her baby. Then she was seized with a dull lumbering sense of victory. She had won! She was his wife no longer.

"All right," she said. "I will. It's a bargain,

Francisco." Lethargy pervaded her limbs. She was tired to death and the baby was crying himself hoarse. She made a labored movement to get out of bed.

Francisco pushed her back, gently. "Bianca will tend to the baby. You had better rest in case . . . anything . . ."

She relaxed suddenly, almost insensibly. Nothing seemed worth the effort of moving again. Bianca would take care of the baby. Her eyes, still black with emotion, watched Francisco as he went to the door and unlocked it.

The group outside fell back. "Francisco, what is it? What's the matter?" Voices mingled. Horrified glances swept the devastated room and the limp girl on the bed. Bianca, clay-colored, set up a moaning wail which mingled with the screams of the baby.

"Everything is all right now," Francisco said stonily. "My wife is going to have a baby. She has been ill, hysterical. Bianca, go inside and take care of Graciano. Luisa, Damacia, please attend the Doña Petra. See that she is put to bed. Clean up this clutter. The rest of you needn't stay. Thank you for your concern. Everything is all right."

There was no gainsaying the finality in his tone. No one dared question the charred jacket sleeve. The Indian women to whom he had spoken scuttled by him, crossing themselves furtively. The rest turned reluctantly, wondering, conjecturing, but withdrawing politely before his level gaze.

Petra woke and slept and woke and prayed, placating the Virgin for the crime of wishing death to an unborn child; silently pleading and bargaining with the saint so that nothing, after all, would befall the infant sleeping in her body, so she might live up to her bargain with Francisco and be free of him.

She said, "Hail, Mary, full of Grace. The Lord is with Thee. Blessed art Thou . . ." The softness of her desperate whisper hung in the silent room.

Catalina wept, in rage, in frustration. In the privacy of her room, she reviled Petra to her husband. Like a stream of acid the alien words rolled from her pale lips.

She said, "She is a wanton fiend. A woman unfit to be a woman. Little better than a beast. She should die. I wish she were dead. I wish she would die."

Xavier tried to soothe his wife to no avail, tried to stem the tide of her fury, to explain, to excuse. Anger and pain rose and mottled the skin of his face.

He said, "Stop it! You are the wanton, lusting after a man who isn't you husband. Let them be! It is their problem. Attend to your own."

They faced each other, for once with no pretense between them, and looked at each other for a truthful instant.

Guillermo made desperate and passionate love to his wife Delfina, exerting every wile and way he knew to enslave her and make her wholly, submissively his.

He said, "Delfina, love me. Before God, Delfina, I am your husband, and you must love me!" His voice was like the wail of a child lost in a wilderness.

Delfina clung to him, surrendering to his urgency, soothing him like a bride and a mother, stroking his smooth brown body.

She said, "I love you, Guillermo. You are my husband. I will love you until I die." She wished that she could die.

* * *

Francisco sat in almost total darkness in his office. He turned at a sound by the door.

"Francisco?" The shapeless mass of Ysidra stood like part of the shadows.

"I need nothing," he said distantly.

"I am sorry," she said with a faint movement of her shoulders.

He went to her swiftly. "Thank you, Ysidra. I am grateful that you told me." He paused a moment. "I should tell you this—and we will speak of it no more. My marriage is finished."

The eleventh of April Petra gave a small celebration in honor of Graciano's first birthday. Remembering her own childhood birthday cakes, she had decided that she wanted her little son to have one. She did not know how to bake. The kitchen-women stared at her blankly, having never heard of such a thing. It was Enrique Padilla who had suggested riding over to the harbor. He came back triumphantly with the cook of the Boston vessel *Ella Brewster*. This amiable man agreed to prepare a first-rate birthday cake for Graciano's evening meal. There was a wild babbling of confusion in the kitchen as the grizzled sailor set to work mixing up the batter, and he had an extensive and interested gallery.

"My dear child," remonstrated Ysidra, "must you do so much? After all he is only a year old. He will forget it in a day."

"Please, Aunt Ysidra," Petra said. "I'm perfectly all right. I'm not in the least tired." Angered at her godmother's interference she turned quickly to go upstairs. She stumbled and, clutching the newel post, fell heavily to the floor. Hastily she scrambled to her feet. "I'm all right," she said swiftly, but her face had gone white.

Enrique ran in from the patio. "Mother of God! Doña, are you all right?"

"Perfectly, Enrique." She managed a ghastly smile.

Ysidra and Catalina had risen from their chairs simultaneously. Ysidra gestured with her fan. "Be good enough to help her upstairs, Enrique. No argument, Petra! You'll have to lie down a while."

Enrique lifted her and started upstairs. "Perhaps I should go for Doctor Vaiz, doña. I think I know where he is—if he hasn't gone."

"No, Enrique, really. Just put me on my bed. And ask someone to bring Graciano up. It's time for his nap."

"Doña Petra, if you don't mind my suggesting——"

"No, Enrique, my dear. It's quite all right."

"Very well, doña." Frowning, he turned to leave the room.

Ysidra was not to be fooled. She strode majestically into the room, managing with difficulty to keep her face placid and polite. "Petra, my dear, there would be no point in lying to me about it. If the baby is coming, it would be a difficult thing to hide, would it not?"

"I . . . I . . ." Petra said uncertainly, and suddenly gripped the counterpane convulsively.

"Ha! You see. I thought so." Ysidra tossed down her fan and began to loosen Petra's dress.

Labor began almost immediately, sending the house into an uproar. Enrique rode posthaste for the doctor. The midwife was summoned from the *indiada.* Graciano wept inconsolably for his mother and was calmed only by the sailor who continued with the cake and fed him spoonfuls of raw batter.

When Petra saw Francisco, her control snapped. "I didn't mean to do it. I swear to you by the Virgin. I swear——" She sobbed hysterically.

"I know, I know," he soothed her. "Never mind, beloved. It's all right. Everything will be all right." He left the room, sickened by her agony.

The doctor did not arrive until after its birth. It was a boy. He examined it carefully after looking in on Petra and complimenting the midwife on her skill.

"Well," he said to Francisco, "I am certainly surprised. What a husky one!" He squatted on his haunches and looked at the infant in the cradle. "I thought we'd have a struggle to keep him alive, but from the looks of him I don't think you could kill him by force."

Francisco smiled. He could feel nothing but relief that the baby was alive and well. "Perhaps she misjudged the time," he said. "He doesn't look like a premature baby—and I should know."

"This is really economy in a way." The doctor grinned.

"How so?"

"He came on Graciano's birthday. You'll be put to the expense of only one party yearly for both of them. I think it shows good housewifely planning on Doña Petra's part. Now, if she can arrange for the rest to come on April eleventh all will be well."

Francisco smiled politely. There was no point in telling the good doctor that there would not be any others. He said instead, "Suppose we go down and celebrate Graciano's birthday. Petra was determined to have cake for him. An uncivilized food, but I don't think it will kill us."

The next day Francisco came quietly into Petra's room. "You wanted to see me?" he asked politely.

"Yes," Petra answered. She was sitting up with the new baby in her arms and was feeling remarkably well. "We haven't had much time to talk about the baby. I wondered . . . I completely forgot about asking anybody to be godparents." She was a little embarrassed at this remissness on her part. But she had felt so bad and Graciano was such a difficult little boy to manage that she had thought little about the coming baby except that she would be glad when it arrived and the whole business was over.

"I have asked that Doña Dolores Acuña and Don Cristóbal Quixano be the godparents."

"Oh," she said, relieved, "that's nice. They are lovely people. Have you thought about a name?"

"If you agree, I would like to call him for my father: Esteban. Then since he will be the only one, I should like him to bear my name also, Francisco. Then for his godfather: Cristóbal. Then of course: Angelo."

Her head jerked up at this. "Angelo!"

"Yes, but he will be called Esteban."

"You can't name him Angelo," she said flatly.

Color rose into Francisco's face. "I cannot?"

"Certainly not. Graciano is named for his father. Can you have forgotten that?" she asked tartly.

"Well, Petra, merely because one child bears a name is no sign another in the same family cannot. You recall all the Marías in the Acuña family, all the Josés in Sal's family."

"That is beside the point, Francisco," she said firmly but courteously. "I particularly don't want the baby named Angelo."

"I'm sorry you feel that way," he said evenly, "because that is the way it is going to be."

Petra's brows slanted dangerously and she opened her mouth to speak.

"Just a minute, Petra," he forestalled her. "There is one thing which I believe needs clarifying in your mind. It is this: You appear to consider Angelo as some precious possession which belonged solely to you. You ignore the fact that he had some life and connections before he married you. That is a mistake. First he was mine. It is a custom here that when one son dies we give his name to another. If you had never come here, Angelo would still have been my first son, who has died. And I am giving his name to my second son. I am sorry if this displeases you." His voice was calm, almost pleasant.

She remained silent, looking at him with eyes suddenly remote. She was remembering Angelo with painful intensity. Frowning, she brought her mind back to Francisco's voice.

"I said, do you understand?"

"Yes," she said absently. "It's perfectly all right with me, if that's the way you want it. He will be called Esteban?"

"Yes," he said, "Esteban."

She looked down at the strong sleeping infant in the crook of her arm. This was Esteban, another person. Esteban, who seemed, even now, to be remarkably and distinctly Francisco's son.

Chapter 21

The old man leaned against the wall. It was warm and easy against his back. His withered mouth moved in a toothless, faltering smile. One forgot and one remembered. Time went this way and that, backward and forward, sliding at will. He was obscurely glad and thought for a long time trying to remember why he was glad, why the warmth was more comforting than it had been the day before, trying to recall what made the shining suns inside his eyelids more lovely. There was about him in the patio the musical rise and fall of the strangers' mellow tongue, full of ripples and round sounds broken up with laughter. This was good, this dreaming.

After a time he remembered to raise his hands in aimless groping motions to lift the lids of his sunken eyes and look at it all again. It was hazy and indistinct and there was a good deal of moving to and fro, in and out of the sprawling house inside which he had never been. Figures bustled about. Oxcarts stood partially loaded. Someone was either coming to the house of the white man or going away. Before he had time to ponder long on whether they were coming or going, his gaze fell on the tousled curly head of a child, the sun lighting the fineness to gold in places.

Ah-h. It was coming to him now, the reason for

the pleasantness of his dreaming. This was the pleasantness: time had decided to go backward and the little boy had returned. He allowed his eyes to close again and listened for the sounds the little boy made in his play, and now and again he smiled. Time would do well to stay and leave the little boy alone.

"You will probably forget something important," Petra said laughing. "No matter where a person goes and how careful he is, something is always left behind."

Catalina flung a box of combs onto the stacked *carreta*. It was all she could do to be pleasant to Petra. "I've been careful to pack everything." Her house had been ready to move into for five months, and she had found first one thing and then another to allow delay. She had changed, replanned and rearranged her house until it had been fully three years in construction. When finished, it was still only a twelve-room dwelling. She had feigned illness for some time after the birth of her second baby, a boy, whom she had named for her youngest brother, Joaquin. Now little Joaquin was three and her third child, Mario, was nearly a year. He presented such a healthy appearance that she could no longer use his babyhood as an excuse to remain at Dos Ríos.

Xavier had done well in these four years on his rancho. He had made profit on cattle, and had even, much to Francisco's disgust, paid back a portion of the money advanced him.

"But it was a gift, my cousin," Francisco insisted in embarrassment.

"It would be a better gift if you would let me pay a little," Xavier said strangely. "I have never before used money of my own to pay for anything." Francisco was forced to take the payment, which he vowed would be the last.

This suited Xavier, for he was by no means wealthy, and the furnishings of the house had cost a great deal. Catalina had been difficult to please. He was in debt to several of the trading ships but did not worry because he knew that the next time they put into port he could pay them off in hides. Now at last, after years of delay, they were ready to enter the new house and live in it, Xavier was completely happy. He was even a little glad that his mother chose to remain at Dos Ríos, for she and Catalina were not a good combination.

"I'm surprised that you don't object," Catalina said privately to Petra, when Ysidra had announced her intention of staying at Dos Ríos. "After all this is your home and Aunt Ysidra's place is really with us."

Petra had stopped folding the shawl she was about to place in one of Catalina's boxes.

"Well," she said frowning, "I would really prefer that she stay here. She is my godmother, you know. Besides, Francisco would be lost without her."

Catalina shrugged. "Suit yourself. I like this arrangement better myself. God knows we'll have little enough room in that shack!"

"Oh, Catalina, it isn't a shack——" began Petra.

"It's the smallest house I've ever had to live in. And I have three children. I don't know how we'll manage when we have guests."

"Well, you can build on after a while," Petra said placatingly. She was tired to death of Catalina and hastened to forestall anything that might develop into a serious objection to moving. She wanted Catalina out of her house, and she felt she had been more than hospitable. She could not help adding, a little acidly, "If you hadn't wanted so many changes and made the men tear down the walls twice, you'd have had a bigger house."

Catalina refused to answer this, pretending not to hear. It was all right for Petra to talk. She had Dos Ríos!

Doña Dolores Acuña had come down from Las Palomas to the new house with a string of *carretas* containing household goods trailing along behind her. This was followed by half a mile or so of Indians, idlers and stray dogs, who had an interest in the proceedings. She would probably remain with her daughter two or three weeks until everything was in complete order and there had been a fiesta. The estate was finally called La Punta, because of the pointed shape of the outline on the map.

Catalina mounted her horse at last, still managing to look dashing and extremely pretty in spite of having spent a hectic morning getting the last of her things together. The children and their nurses climbed into a *carreta* and the procession formed. Petra and Francisco were riding part way with them. They set out at a walk in order to remain with the *carretas*. There was a wild din of yelping dogs and shouted good-bys as they wound out of the patio and onto the trail which had been worn between La Punta and Dos Ríos in the past years.

About five miles from Dos Ríos the two groups parted after much kissing and calling of good wishes. A hot ball of rage filled Catalina's throat. Sweet Mother of God, what had she done to deserve this? Why did Petra who gave nothing have everything? Think of Francisco remodeling part of the house for Petra and her spoiled child! Petra had for her own use now both her own room and that large chamber which had been Ana's. Think of little Esteban always playing second fiddle to Graciano! And the things Francisco bought her! Just because she had accidentally had a child for him she thought she could ask for anything in the world—and apparently she could. Everything in the world was wrong. There wasn't any justice. There wasn't any fairness. She wouldn't see Francisco again for days, for weeks. There was only Xavier, three demanding children, and the cramped hateful little house at La Punta.

When the Dos Ríos party rode again into their patio they saw a horse with strange trappings tethered to the post. Their pleased surprise was slightly dampened when a servant told Francisco that it was Father Gabriel from the mission, instead of the well-loved Father Patricio. However, they allowed nothing but unalloyed delight to show on their faces when they greeted him.

"Father Gabriel," Francisco said going into the *sala*, "this is indeed most pleasant. I can't think of a time when you have honored my house with a visit before. I am deeply gratified, sir."

Father Gabriel refused, almost brusquely for a Spaniard, the refreshment Petra had started to call for. "I am fasting," he said coldly and turned immediately to Francisco, requesting a private interview. The Estradas covered their surprise smoothly, and Francisco led the way to his office.

The priest seemed to have shrunk. He was thinner, drier, less alive than he had been before. He had ridden to Dos Ríos on a fast day and refused food. He was a holy man, firm in his holiness. Francisco found himself respecting him—never liking him, but respecting him nonetheless. The fact that he had ridden to Dos Ríos instead of walking, as was the custom of the Franciscan Order gave Francisco an inkling that his errand was important.

"Now," the priest said as soon as the door was shut, "I would speak to you of something that is of utmost seriousness to all of Mexico and California."

"Please be seated, Father. You must be terribly tired."

"I do not recognize fatigue," the priest replied sitting down, but not comfortably. He sat on the edge of the hardest-looking chair in the room, and began abruptly. "Francisco, my son, I understand that you seldom indulge in political machinations with other Californians. Is that correct?"

"That is correct," Francisco replied becoming wary.

"May I ask why, Francisco?"

"Certainly, Father. I see no reason to run about looking for trouble. If I have all I need, and everything is running smoothly, I am not disposed to tamper with the existing administration of government. Revolutions bore me. Politics amuse me."

"Concisely put. Patricio told me I might count on your integrity. I had hoped he was right. It brings us then to this point: What have you heard or thought about the movement regarding the missions?"

A guard snapped shut in Francisco's brain. So that was it. He said carefully, "I have heard a good deal, Father. There has been talk of it for years."

"What is your stand?" The question was rapped out in the same tone he might have used in addressing an Indian neophyte, but Francisco allowed no annoyance to show.

"Father Gabriel," he said smiling politely, "that is an extremely forthright question. At the risk of being discourteous I would suggest that you have little right to ask it."

"I am a priest, Francisco. Since when may a man not confide in his priest?"

Francisco was tempted to answer bluntly, but

refrained, saying, "You are a priest, true, but at the moment you are acting in the capacity of a politician. I intend nothing derogatory by that statement. I utter it in all respect. You are a priest, and in confessional I would speak out to you."

Father Gabriel stood up, the scanty color ebbing from his face, his eyes dark and intense. "You are mistaken, Francisco," he said thinly. "There is nothing of the politician in me. I think I have been a priest from the day of my birth. Now I am working, in that capacity, for the good of my Church and my charges. I have every right to use whatever weapon is at hand to further my cause. What these land-grabbing settlers are trying to do is ruin the mission system, render useless all the labor of countless men like me." He stopped with an effort, trying to retain his poise, wiping with a suddenly unsteady hand the film of moisture that appeared on his face.

"Father, I'm afraid you are ill," Francisco said gently. "Please allow me to get you something—a glass of wine, even a cup of coffee."

"I am fasting. I thought I told you." The priest sat down in his chair and Francisco could see the muscles in his thighs jerk from weariness. "You have not answered me," he said after a moment.

"About the missions?" Francisco was on guard. "As you say, there has been talk—but there is always talk, Father. I ask this in all respect: aren't you perhaps attaching too much importance to the legal secularization of the missions?"

"Too much importance!"

"Father, many believe that the mission has served its purpose here. You know that it is one type of colonization. It is never thought of except as a temporary measure, a measure to civilize a place until colonists arrive and establish themselves. They have arrived, sir. California is established."

The priest rose to his feet, his face working. "And those who were here first?" he asked. "Those, my charges, what of them?"

"There are provisions for them," Francisco answered deliberately. "They will be given land as we have been——"

"Provision on paper," Gabriel interrupted scathingly. "And what use is that. I know Indians, Francisco."

"Do you think I don't, Father? I've been in this country for more than twenty years. I've had hundreds of Indians working for me."

"Working *for* you," cried the priest. "That is the key. Of course you have. They have always labored *for* you. They've been the labor that carved this land from a wilderness, and you Spaniards sit back and reap——"

"I have labored, Father. I know what work is."

"Granted, Francisco. You do know what work is—for yourself. The difference is that while you Spaniards have worked for yourselves, the Indians have not been able to work for themselves."

"Well, now they will," Francisco said with some sharpness. "They will be given land and the same chance we all have had to become self-supporting——". Something in the priest's face caused him to stop. "Father, you are ill."

"I am not ill," the priest said faintly, swaying a little. "Perhaps I was foolish to choose a fast day on which to take a long ride but I had a disturbing letter and I had to see you. You are an extremely influential man——" His voice dwindled, seemed to have no strength behind it.

Francisco felt acutely sorry for him. "Will you rest—sleep for a while, Father?" he asked.

"No, I cannot. I have not slept for two nights. Estrada, you cannot be as blind as this. You cannot think that any land given the Indians will remain very long in their possession. You know it will not. My mission consists of eighty-five thousand acres of tillable land and pasture. It is in bearing orchards, fields and pasture. Our herds of cattle, small and large, are the third largest among missions and private ranchos. Who will get it all, Francisco?" The priest's face gleamed in the light from the window. "Who, Francisco?"

"The Indians, Father. They will work as a community. They will be self-sustaining. They will be individual people instead of neophytes of the Church."

"But Indians are children, Francisco. Why do you carry a whip? You carry one because you sometimes have to lay it on the back of an Indian, because they are childish and stubborn and sometimes very stupid. You have to *make* them work, Francisco. If there is no one with authority to make them work, they do not. If they are freed and given the land, they will run riot. They will not think to make any effort until they are hungry and they discover there is no food left."

"Father, please. You excite yourself."

"I know. I excite myself, madden myself, over my children. These are my children whom I see on the brink of being cheated out of everything we have labored to give them."

"Father, no one wants to cheat them."

"You liar!" The priest leaned heavily on the table, his frame shaking. "You are a liar, Francisco Estrada. You know what will happen. You and every other land-seizing ranchero. You know that the Indians can't hold the land. They will run away, become renegades, because that is easier than working. They will die like flies. They will be enslaved. And then all the land will lie fallow and useless. The mission will be nothing but an empty building for field mice. And then who will get the land, Francisco?"

"Father, please! You are ill."

"Who will get it, Francisco?" The priest tried to shout, but his voice failed him and was little more than a cracked whisper. "You will get it. You will step in and take up the land, the planted orchards, the fields, the stock. Efficient, capable, intelligent—Indians will be no match for you and your kind. What can't be got legally will eventually be got illegally."

"That will do. There is no point in this harangue. You are a priest and a sick one, or I wouldn't stand here and allow you to fling recriminations at my head—recriminations for something which has not occurred yet and which——"

"But it will, Francisco," the priest said with an effort. "It will!" He sat down on the chair again, apparently unable to stand. "You aren't a fool. You know what will happen."

"But you have done your work, Father," Francisco said gently. "The mission has served its purpose. The country is growing. The land must pass from Church control, and along with it those Christianized Indians——"

"Control? Perhaps control is the word. But control is still needed."

"There have been abuses, Father."

"There are flaws in everything. If there were perfection, there would be no need to strive for perfection. Francisco, I can tell you the Indians are not ready to pass from Church jurisdiction."

"Domination you mean."

"Domination perhaps. But while they are being dominated, their bellies are full and there is a minimum of lawlessness and crime."

There was silence in the sunlit office.

"Since you have refused to state your stand,"

Gabriel said finally, "I may assume that you are in accord with the wolf-pack."

"No, Father, I am in accord with no wolf pack. I am in accord only with Francisco Estrada. The function of the mission here is finished. The land is colonized and established. If the land passes from the Church to the Indians and then passes from the Indians, there is no reason why it should not pass to me."

The priest regarded him through a long silence. He spoke slowly and carefully, as if he couldn't quite hear his own voice. "You are a grasping, evil man." He stood up, although it would seem impossible for him to, he appeared for a moment so fragile. He raised his bony hand and brought it down with a hard blow against Francisco's face. It cracked out like a shot.

Francisco's face remained expressionless. "I am sorry, Father," he said. "The law is the law and I shall do nothing to stem its course."

The priest left like a gaunt and hurried shade, scarcely speaking to Petra who met him at the door, ignoring the courteous words of Enrique Padilla. Pulling his thin body onto his horse caused sweat to spring again from his face. His sandaled foot kicked the animal's side and made it start at full gallop. He sat his horse badly, awkwardly. Those watching him winced at the jars his body received. They would seem to shake the bones loose from one another.

"Enrique," Francisco said straining his eyes after the priest, "would you ride after him, at a distance, to the mission in case——"

"He is sick?" Padilla crossed himself

"Yes, he is sick," Francisco said. "He is tired and harassed, so don't offend him by letting him know you are following, and when he has reached the mission safely, come back."

Frowning, Padilla mounted his horse and rode after the priest.

Petra caught Francisco's arm in astonishment. "What on earth is the matter? He hardly spoke to me. He brushed right by."

"He is angry, Petra. He is an ill man."

"But even that doesn't excuse—— Francisco!" She stared wide-eyed at the white marks on his face.

Francisco shrugged a little. "It is nothing. Father Gabriel struck me."

Petra's mouth fell open. "Struck you! Oh, Francisco, you didn't hit him back!"

"Don't be ridiculous, Petra; he is an old man." Francisco passed his hand absently over his face.

"What made him do that?"

"He was angry about the rancheros—me mostly. Hello, Ysidra, my dear. You have missed the excitement. Father Gabriel made me a visit."

"I heard."

"But—but why?" Petra insisted.

In the office he told them, speaking mostly to Ysidra, who sat placidly fanning herself in the big chair. He told exactly what had happened and what the priest had said.

"Well, he's right, Francisco," Petra said hotly when he had finished. "You know he is. Can you imagine Ramón or—or anybody here setting up as a ranchero and doing it successfully. And those Indians at the mission aren't any different."

"Petra," he said patiently, "the mission is a frontier establishment. This is no longer a frontier. Control should shift from the Church to the State. The Church is fundamentally for the good of men's souls, not their bodies."

"Well, yes," Petra said confusedly, "but the way he explained it to you, it——"

"My dear girl," Ysidra murmured, "things always sound right. When the rancheros discuss it, their side sounds good. When the priests discuss it, their side sounds good. No one can really tell what will happen until it has happened."

"Well, perhaps that is right, but it seems—— Father Patricio is so good, and——"

"Personalities," Ysidra said. "Of course Patricio is a good man. No doubt Gabriel is too. He is also a zealot. Take the long view. It is their life's work and they hate to give it up. That is understandable, but on the other hand it is not the lifework of the Church as a whole. It will have other projects—many of them. They have prosecuted this project successfully. Now the rancheros and officials believe it has been completed and should be terminated. The Church does not. It is a matter of opinion."

Petra's brows drew down and her eyes held a calculating gleam. She glanced out the window and watched Graciano and Esteban playing in the patio.

"About the land," she said: "will you get it, Francisco?"

"It will belong to the Indians," he said noncommittally.

"But suppose they don't hold it. Suppose they do as Father Gabriel said they would, and go away. What would happen to all the land then? Would it just be wasted?"

"Don't trouble your lovely head about it," Francisco said smiling a little. "Let me do the worrying for the family."

"Francisco," she said uncertainly, "this is the Church."

"My dear, don't worry about the Church. It will undoubtedly be in full existence long after we are dust," he said dryly.

Chapter 22

It was three days after Father Gabriel's visit that a sailor named Adam Langley deserted his ship the *Dauntless*. He hid in the craggy salt-sprayed rocks of Monterey until the *Dauntless* left the harbor. Then, sick from hunger and exhaustion, he staggered out onto the trail. He tried to smooth his thatch of straw-colored hair and brush some of the dirt from his middy and started down the road, weaving from side to side in an almost drunken exaggeration of a sailor's rolling gait.

He might have fallen down by the side of the road and died there. Or renegade Indians might have found him and amused themselves by pulling him to pieces. Or some wandering soldier from the garrison might have placed him under arrest; he might have been interned at the fort and lived to an advanced age very pleasantly waiting for the Mexicans to press some charge against him. Or he might have wandered into the mission and been welcomed with the ringing of bells and allowed to remain as long as he liked.

As it happened, he met Enrique Padilla.

Padilla nearly ran him down, for he was riding into the sun and his vision was obscured. Automatically Enrique pulled his horse up sharply and tensed his leg against the rifle that hung by his saddle. "Good morning," he said politely, ready to shoot the man if he had to. "What happened to your horse?" Then he noticed that the man was a sailor and concluded that he had been thrown. Sailors sometimes borrowed horses and rode about the country during their liberty. This one had undoubtedly lost his horse. Nobody voluntarily walked any place in California.

The man whirled and tried to focus his faltering gaze on the tall Mexican who sat his horse so superbly. Then he appeared to crumple into folds and angles on the dusty road. Padilla knew the pallor of unconsciousness when he saw it and was down from his horse in an instant. He picked up the sailor, flung him over the saddle like a sack of meal and set out for Dos Ríos.

There was an excited hum as he rode into the patio with his find. He had the able assistance of many curious and eager hands in lifting the sailor from the horse.

"What in heaven's name have you got?" Petra asked from the loggia.

"A man," Enrique called gaily. "I found him. An Englishman, I think."

Petra lifted her skirts and ran out to see. It had been a long time since she had seen an Englishman. "Oh," she said disappointedly, "he's a sailor."

"Yes, doña, a sick one." Enrique turned to the cruious Indians. "Here you, stop pulling at the poor man."

"Perhaps we'd better get him inside, Enrique. He must have been starving, he's so thin." Petra led the way inside.

He was placed in one of the small well-furnished rooms which were reserved for more casual guests, people who were strangers to Dos Ríos, but to whom hospitality was extended as a matter of course. He slept almost constantly for three days. The Estrada family bothered him only to see that he received proper food and service. They saw that his clothing was cleaned and returned to him, that his room was kept clean, and that the bowl of money on the dresser, in case he were out of funds, was covered with a clean napkin.

When he felt recovered enough to see people, Petra paid a call to him and tactfully elicited that he had deserted from the crew of his Boston ship. She learned that he had been studying for the law when he was overtaken by illness for which a sea voyage was prescribed. Being of humble resources he had no means of taking one aside from shipping as a sailor, which he did. His plans for a career, he said, did not include becoming a pirate. The ship's master was a brutal and merciless man and trouble had been brewing all the way from Boston. There was talk of seizing the ship. That was mutiny and he wanted no part of it. His only alternative was to desert, and quickly.

He was a pleasant young man, small and wiry with a quick intelligence. The fact that it took him three months to learn to speak Spanish without an accent made him yearn for his studies and vow he had been away from his books too long. During these months he became less a formal visitor at Dos Ríos and more a friend.

"Adam," Francisco said lazily one day as they lounged talking on the patio, "have you thought of teaching as a career?"

"I have tutored a bit," conceded Adam. "I chose law mainly because I have an uncle who will take me into his firm, although even that will afford me little but a clerkship for many years."

"I have had the idea," said Francisco thoughtfully, "of offering you a place at Dos Ríos. My boys will need educating."

"Those little ones?" Adam asked in surprise.

"Graciano is four—" Francisco shrugged—

"Esteban is three. It won't be long until they will be able to do lessons. It's just an idea. There is no hurry. Take your time and think it over. There is no school here worthy of the name. The one in Los Angeles is conducted by a retired corporal who can barely read and write. Anyhow, I hear he beats the students. Petra and I wouldn't tolerate that."

The sharp eyes of the little sailor observed his host. "It appears to me, sir, that an education is not so important here. Life is so simple that there seems no need for learning, except possibly for the pleasure of studying."

"The need will arise, Adam," Francisco replied. "I could offer you a fairly attractive proposition."

"No doubt." Adam smiled. He had been impressed with the obvious wealth and openhandedness of his host. "But there seems little opportunity of making a living here until the children have reached the age for study."

Francisco's laugh rang out. "Living! Adam, you have a lot to learn of Californians. Surely you wouldn't mind being just a guest for a year or two, would you?"

Adam Langley entered into the arrangement with vigor and enthusiasm. He would remain in California to tutor the Estrada children. For this he would receive a handsome wage and the assurance that by the time they were ready for a university Francisco would assist in establishing him as a ranchero. It would take him years to work up from a clerkship in the law office. Here, in the space of ten or twelve years, he could become a landowner, a man of property. Other Americans and Englishmen had filtered into California and it was a foregone conclusion that they married into the better families. It was an intoxicating thought to a boy of humble beginnings. All one had to do was become a Catholic and a citizen of Mexico. Adam Langley swept aside these details. God was God. A church was a church. This was no time to quibble.

In the meantime, he vowed with determination, Francisco Estrada would have no cause to regret his bargain. Adam arranged a small schoolroom and began immediately to teach the children by amusing them. If Graciano had four blocks and needed four more to make a house, how many was that in all? This little boat took on hides and tallow at San Pedro and sailed for Liverpool. Where was Liverpool? Esteban might have as many paper hats as he could count. Graciano might have as many toys as he could identify in three languages. Petra fell in with this idea quickly for she knew that her own scanty learning would not be enough for her sons.

The advent of Adam Langley at Dos Ríos angered Catalina. When she heard it she was hard put to keep her temper. The Dos Ríos children had everything! What of her own? Were Isabela, Joaquin and Mario to get along with what she and Xavier could teach them? It was another reason why she should have stayed at Dos Ríos.

Partially undressed, she stood at her bedroom window and stared into the blackness toward Dos Ríos, wondering, as always, what was happening there. In the few months she had been in her own home, things had run more smoothly than she had expected. Her mother had remained a month in order to get the routine under way. Xavier was completely happy—the only one who was, Catalina reflected bitterly. The children had adapted themselves very well to the new house. They missed the easygoing little cousin Esteban, but were slightly relieved to be rid of Graciano's childish tyranny.

She gripped the ledge of the window and tried to look into the future. It was inconceivable to her that she would live out her life in this house, away from Francisco. She wondered in dull astonishment how she could face a future of seeing Francisco only occasionally, at balls and on holidays. It was incredible that she could endure it, yet there was no possible way of her ever getting back to Dos Ríos—no way at all. That was finished. The black vista of years spread before her. She would have more children, they would enlarge the house, Xavier—entering ranching with vigor—would enlarge his holdings. She would grow older and older and gradually she would settle into corpulent solid middle age. She would be a black-gowned duenna sitting on the side lines of the dance, never having had anything she wanted. It was inconceivable, unbearable, and yet she must bear it. There was no way out.

A rumble of thunder came to her ears. If only she might be struck by lightning and die suddenly and never again face another day! She crossed herself from force of long habit. She shouldn't be thinking things like this. After all there were the children. My God, she loved her children, didn't she? Sometimes she wondered. They were rather nice unspoiled little children. Isabela was a jewel, pretty and quiet, no trouble at all. The two boys Joaquin and Mario were growing to look more like the Acuña than the Miramontes family and were extremely pretty and engaging. She didn't wish them dead—she just wished they might never have been born, that all this need never have happened. She wished only to go backward into her girlhood—before Petra had come to Dos Ríos; before Ana had died. She wished to erase all that. It would be different if she could begin again. If she could do it all over, she wouldn't be so stupidly impatient and Ana would die and she could have Francisco. The force of the thought hit her, as always, so hard that she shuddered in the cool night air. Francisco! Her thought was intense, so concentrated that she did not hear the men in the patio below until they had stormed into the hallway.

"Catalina!" Xavier cried, starting from a sound sleep on the bed. Simultaneously there was a shriek from below and a crash as a body hit the floor. In a matter of seconds Xavier had his robe on and his pistol in his hand.

"Hide the children!" he cried to her. "Hide yourself!" He started to the front hall. The sight that met his eyes was one to strike terror to the soul of a much more fearless man. Two Indians lay on the floor. Baldomero Solan, his *mayordomo*, who had been wakened, stood clasping his arm which streamed with blood.

"Pirates!" Solan managed to gasp and fell face forward to the floor.

"Don't shoot," said the leader and wrenched the gun from Xavier's hand. He swung viciously and hit Xavier across the face with it. "Where do you keep your money, Señor Estrada?" His eyes glittered from a filthy face. Xavier wondered fleetingly whether this was the renegade crew of the *Dauntless* or some Costa Rican vessel.

"I keep it upstairs," he said.

The *mayordomo* on the floor tried to struggle to his knees. "They have made a mistake. They think this is Dos Ríos."

"Upstairs," Xavier cried, trying too late to drown out Solan's utterance, but the pirate had caught the slip. His crew, with drawn pistols, pressed close behind him. He held up his hand to halt them.

"What did you say, my friend?" he asked in meaningful quiet.

Solan realized his mistake and closed his eyes with a moan.

The pirate kicked him in the side. There was the sound of bone cracking and Solan's face went white.

"Wake up, you greaser. What did you say about Dos Ríos?" He drew back his foot again, but before he could kick the bleeding man, Xavier's face twisted, he launched his portly body through the air and the two crashed to the floor. This was a signal for wild confusion. The pirates leaped in like suddenly unleashed animals.

"Wait, wait," the leader said. "Don't kill him." The men left off reluctantly. Xavier, covered with blood, was dragged to his feet.

"Now, Señor Estrada—or is your name Estrada? We were heading for the Rancho Dos Ríos. Is this it or not?"

"It is not," Xavier said with difficulty. "You have miscalculated." There was a roaring in his ears, as in fury the pirate lashed at his face with his fist.

"Stop that!" Catalina's voice cracked out like a pistol shot. The men whirled to see her in the doorway. Her eyes blazed. "Take your hands off my husband!"

"Catalina, run!" Xavier gasped trying to rise to his feet.

"No, Catalina, don't run." The pirate, grinning, strode to her. "So this is Catalina. Well, well, what a pleasant surprise!" He bowed low in mock ceremony. "We were looking for a rancho called Dos Ríos. Apparently we misjudged our distance. Perhaps you can give us directions."

Catalina smiled starkly. She took her hand from behind her back, pressed the muzzle of a pistol in the man's chest and fired. A look of amazement overspread his unshaved features, and he sagged to the floor. At that instant the front door crashed and five *vaqueros* surged inward with bloodcurdling screams. They were Dos Ríos men whom Francisco had sent to La Punta with Xavier. They leaped over his prone figure and two pirates fell to the floor.

Furiously the other pirates launched an attack on the Indians.

"Fire it! Burn it!" one cried flinging a lamp at the wall. It crashed and a wave of flame lapped across the floor.

Xavier rose to his knees and swayed there like a wounded bear.

"My house!" he gasped. "Don't burn my house!"

Catalina turned from the room and raced upstairs, screaming for the rest of the servants. Some answered her bidding and others disappeared, wanting no part of it. She rushed into the children's room and snatched them from their beds.

"Isabela," she panted, "hold onto Joaquin's hand. Don't let go, no matter what." She took little Mario from his bed, dashed into her own room and snatched Xavier's strong silk sash.

Outside she raced for the *indiada.* Joaquin, his bare feet cut on the stones, fell to the ground.

"Bring him!" ordered Catalina over her shoulder. The little girl was deathly white as she pulled her brother to his feet and tried to follow her mother's fleeting figure. Catalina reached the *indiada* and screamed for help. Several Indians fell out of their cabins. She ordered them up to the house. Some went, young men mostly; others turned and fled. Fire from the burning house was lighting the sky. Catalina reached a grove of trees about half a mile away and stopped, panting, her hand clutching her side, her face ashen in the moonlight.

"Now," she gasped, "climb up that tree. Don't come down until I tell you to."

"Mama," screamed Isabela, "we can't. Those men . . . Father . . ."

"Climb up," Catalina ordered harshly, slapping her with numb hands. "I haven't time to argue. Climb up or the pirates will catch you and cut you to pieces!"

Joaquin gave a cry and crumpled to the ground, groveling in horror.

"Mama, don't leave us!" wailed Iabela.

Catalina knelt down an instant and clutched at her little daughter's waist. "Listen, angel," she gasped. "Please take Joaquin up in the tree. You needn't be afraid. If there was any danger Mama wouldn't leave you."

"Mama, please——"

"Listen to me, Isabela. Stop crying. If you hide in the tree and be still—don't make a sound—nobody will find you. Just stay there till Mama gets back."

"But Father——"

"Father will be all right. Now climb up. Hurry!"

She laid Mario on the ground and helped the sobbing child to the first branch. Then she lifted Joaquin. The fire was brighter in the sky.

"Mama, help me. He'll fall," Isabela whimpered trying to hold Joaquin, who was almost helpless with terror.

"No, he won't," panted Catalina. "He won't—he's a big boy. He's Mama's biggest boy. That's right, Isabela—help him. Here, take this sash and tie him in. Go up as far as you can and stay there."

"Oh, *Mamacita*——"

"And be still. Not a sound. I have to go to Dos Ríos. I have to get there and warn Francisco." Seeing that the two older children were out of sight and shielded by foliage, Catalina caught her youngest child in her arms and mounted the first horse she saw. She kicked it savagely and headed into the night.

She reached Dos Ríos a little before four, about ten minutes ahead of the pirates. She slid from her horse, left the swaying animal and dashed through the doorway screaming. In five seconds the house was in an uproar. Francisco routed Padilla out, and Padilla rounded up the *vaqueros* and their arms. When the thunder of approaching horses was heard, Dos Ríos was ready for them.

"Xavier—where is Xavier?" Ysidra gasped, white-lipped.

"At home. Never mind Xavier. Here, take Mario." Catalina fairly flung the child at her mother-in-law.

Graciano and Esteban were crying. Petra, clad in a trailing robe, tried to calm them, wondering frantically what to do. The *vaqueros* prowled swiftly and restlessly about the rooms thirsting for action. The narrow windows were assigned as posts. A group of men were about to go outside in an attempt to ambush the pirates before they reached the house.

"Here, Adam," Petra cried, "you take care of the children."

"No, ma'am," said Adam firmly, pale under his sunburned skin. "You take the babies. I can use a gun. I'm going to be mighty embarrassed if these are the *Dauntless* crew." He took a place near the door.

"Mama, let's go upstairs," howled Graciano. "Take me upstairs." He raised his arms, and Petra struggled to lift him. Esteban looked at her imploringly. "Mama, can I come too? Take me too."

Petra felt Francisco's eyes momentarily on her. Heat seeped into her white cheeks. For an instant she felt ashamed. She bent down, grasped the little boy about the middle and hurried upstairs with both of them.

"Barricade your door, Petra," Francisco called after her.

At that instant there was a fusillade as those outside greeted the pirates.

"They made a mistake, Francisco," Catalina sobbed. Her muscles jerked convulsively from the long ride and she was streaked with sweat. "They thought La Punta was Dos Ríos. They——"

"Yes, my dear. Go upstairs. Ysidra, see that she gets upstairs. Both of you, please now. This is no time——" He pressed against the window, trying to see through the darkness.

"Francisco—" she hurled herself at him—"let me stay with you."

Ysidra's fingers closed on her arm violently. "You come up," she said, her eyes black-red for a moment. "Come up, I say!" She fairly dragged the hysterical Catalina up the stairs.

Petra knelt in her room, clasping the little boys close to her. Graciano wept with abandon, but Esteban, although a shudder went through his small body at every burst of shot, remained dry-eyed, gripping her about the neck urgently.

"They won't hurt Father?" he said once, as a shout arose from below, with the crash of a falling body.

"No," she promised wildly. "No, of course not. Here, boys, crawl under the bed and stay there—right in the middle."

Esteban, gripped her tighter. "Mama——"

"Esteban, don't you trust your father? Shame on you! Do you think he'd let pirates into our house? Now please do as Mama says."

"Fire!" Petra's blood chilled as the cry reached her ears. Unceremoniously she dumped both little boys. Rushing past the window she saw a dull red glow in the patio. Something near fury welled in her. God damn them! She unlocked her door and rushed to the head of the stairs.

"Francisco, they're burning my rosebush. They're setting fire——"

"Go back, Petra. Go back to your room."

Petra stumbled against the quaking form of Bianca huddled in a corner, and tugged at her flaccid arms. "Get up!" she shouted. "Go stay with the boys. Stay there!"

Bianca recognizing the steel in Petra's voice obeyed instantly. The pirates were outside—Petra was here. She scrambled into the bedroom.

Petra flew down the stairs and flung herself at Francisco, caught his bare arm. "Francisco," she gasped, "they are trying to set fire . . . our house . . ."

"Stop it, Petra. You'll spoil my aim. It won't burn. It's adobe." His gun went off with a deafening explosion that made her reel back. He tossed it to an Indian who handed him one freshly loaded.

"But the doors will—the wood——" she screamed.

One window crashed in, and a pile of ignited greasewood was flung inside.

"The floor!" screamed Petra.

Francisco's teeth bared. He started to curse softly. He took aim and fired. There was a strangled croak, and the man crumpled just outside the window. A volley answered from the pirates. A Dos Ríos Indian fell writhing into view.

"Ramón," grunted the savage at Francisco's feet and thrust some powder into the empty gun.

"Where?" Francisco said. "God damn them! God damn them!"

Petra snatched the draperies from the doorway. Adam left his post for a minute, cursing vividly, to help her smother the fire.

"Please don't let them burn my house," she sobbed furiously. "Look at my new curtains." She turned to Francisco imploringly. "My rose-bush——"

Francisco fired again and the bullet lodged itself in the bare chest of an assailant. Dawn was breaking and it was easier to aim.

"That's for your rosebush," he said between his teeth, tossing the smoking gun to the Indian. "That's for your curtains." Again the gun cracked.

"Mama," Esteban screamed from the stairway, "Graciano's looking out the window. He won't stay under the bed." Petra was up the stairs like a shot, sobbing with fear and rage.

But Graciano had started down. He dashed past her. "The old man!" he screamed. He fairly leaped across the hall and into the *sala*. He flung himself at Francisco, grasped his legs. "My old man's out there. They'll kill my old man!"

Francisco caught the child and tried to push him back. "Get out of the way," he grated. "Do you want to be killed?"

Petra stumbled up and sought to pull the enraged little boy away, but he clung, turning his white face up to Francisco. "Get him!" he implored. "Go get my little old man!"

"All right. Stop that! Be still." Francisco pushed the sobbing child roughly into Petra's arms. His face went livid. Recklessly he opened the door and plunged out. They could burn his house and steal his money but he'd be God-damned if they could kill his old Indian. He cursed the unknown hands that had set the old man out before dawn. He grasped him and dragged him into the hall. Several shots rang out. He dropped the old one and slammed the door.

The noise suddenly stopped. The silence was so appalling that they held their breaths. There was a sudden thunder of hoofs—fewer than had come. They were going! They had given up!

She heard Francisco's shout, thick, choked—"Juanito, Fernando, after them!" In the half-light Petra saw lean brown bodies hurl themselves on horses. The air was rent with ancient war cries as the *vanqueros* pounded after the fleeing pirates. *Reatas* whirred in the air. There was the quick dull gleam of a knife.

Then the silence, thick and black as tar, closed again over Dos Ríos. Quaking a little Petra sat on the bottom step of the stairway, her eyes wide, her hair streaming wildly. Francisco stood inside the door, bent forward a little, a grimace of pain on his face. His shirt clung to his shoulders wetly. "Petra," he said almost apologetically, "I'm hurt."

Her knees went weak. Back in the rolling depths of her brain something said, "Petra, I'm falling," but she couldn't think clearly. She rose and took a step toward him hesitantly. She put out her hand to touch his shoulder and drew it back. Not Francisco! The earth might shake, the house might burn, but Francisco was the one unbeatable, unhurtable thing that stood like a rock through time.

"Francisco," she whispered, "oh, Francisco——"

"Don Francisco." It was Padilla sobbing in rage. His lean fingers began to tear away the shirt. "Adam, help me."

Adam stumbled from the other room, shaking burned fingers, cursing luridly in English.

"It is nothing," Francisco said. "Bind it up. I have to get to La Punta."

"I'll go," Padilla argued. "You stay here."

Francisco winced at the touch of Adam's fingers. "Tighter, Adam, so I won't bleed when I'm riding."

"You can't, Francisco." Petra found her voice. "Please——"

"All this sudden regard?"

Her eyes filled. "But suppose you died," she whispered. "I . . . the children . . ."

"I won't die," he said. "Post a guard in case they come back. Enrique, you'd better come with me. Adam, I'm going to leave you in charge here. And if they should come back——"

"They won't," said an Indian rising leanly from the floor. It was Ramón's father. His face was seamed like leather. His eyes were like pieces of agate.

Diego Llanes strode in, breathing hard, his mouth twisting. "Don Francisco, Pedro is dead, Ramón is dead, Rimaldo is dead, and three pirates are dead. The Indians took the pirates' bodies."

"Let them," Francisco said grimly.

"One had a crucifix. He was a Catholic," Diego persisted. "The Indians——"

"Let them," Francisco said harshly. "Diego, if they haven't frightened off all the horses, get some. I have to get to La Punta."

"Get me one too," Padilla said sliding his knife back into his leggings. "My praying didn't do any good," he grumbled wiping his eyes. "I guess I swore too much in between. Your rosebush didn't burn, doña; just a little. It will be all right."

Petra sat down suddenly on the bottom step, her face completely colorless.

"What about Xavier? Joaquin? Isabela?" she gasped with dawning horror.

"That's what I'm going to find out. Padilla, you'd better get some more horses. No telling what we'll find at La Punta." He turned to Petra. "Stop trying to act like a lady of quality," he said forcing a smile. "If you faint, I'll just let you lie here until I get back. Get down to business now and set some order in the house. Try to calm the children. Get a couple of bedrooms ready. Send someone to look for Dr. Vaiz. Send messengers to the surrounding ranchos to let them know in case——"

"Your horse, Don Francisco."

"All right. Now be a good girl, Petra, and do as I say——" He stopped, color ebbing from his face. A look of astonishment flashed for an instant in his eyes. "Get me some brandy," he said thickly.

"You can't go—see, you can't! Enrique will go, won't you, Enrique?" Petra wailed.

"Be quiet, Petra," Francisco said, his voice strange. He turned blindly and went out the door as the sun broke over the horizon.

They set out for La Punta. Padilla alternately raged and moaned because Francisco had insisted on going. Francisco's mouth became grimmer and his lips more colorless.

Toward midday they topped a small rise beneath a grove of trees. "La Punta . . ." Padilla said, his voice suddenly cracking. His horse stopped, and the hand which held the reins of the following horses dropped.

La Punta was a smoldering shell. The adobe walls were partially standing, smoke-blackened. The wooden roof of which Xavier had been so proud was a skeleton of charred flame-eaten timbers. The window frames, doors and floors were gone. Pieces of furniture were stumpy ghosts of charcoal.

For an instant Francisco was violently ill. Xavier's house was gone. And Xavier? . . . His eyes narrowed and flicked about. He began to shake, the strong muscles in his belly and thighs quivering and jerking. Xavier . . . Ysidra's son . . .

"Uncle Francisco——" Like the wail of a lost soul Isabela's terrified voice swept through both men.

"Mother of God, Isabelita——" gasped Padilla.

Francisco's breath whistled through his teeth. "*Niñita!* Quick, Padilla—that tree——"

But the *mayordomo* had already seen the child trying vainly to get down, dangling like a little rag doll, her slim body swinging. He was beneath her in a minute.

"Oh, *niñita*, come to Enrique, little girl." Padilla took the child tenderly in his arms.

Hysterically she twined her arms around his neck and began to cry. "Joaquin can't get down, he's too little. . . . Mama said to stay in the tree."

"Here, baby, come to me. Enrique, get the boy," Francisco said taking Isabela. His eyes roved desperately this way and that in search of Xavier.

Then in the distance he saw him. He was huddled against the irregular pile of stones which marked the boundary of his land. The cross on top was standing drunkenly askew. Wordlessly, Francisco got down from his horse and set the little girl on her feet.

"Stay here with Enrique, Isabela," he said and started to walk to the huddled figure, black rage welling in him. When he reached the crumpled figure of Xavier he thought he could hardly stand. This was a crime against his blood. He fell stiffly to his knees and lifted Xavier's head. The hair was matted with blood and he was nearly naked. What clothing he had was burned and charred in places. He had been beaten about the face and head. Francisco thought he was dead, and chilled when Xavier's eyes opened, stared blankly at him and closed again.

Francisco's body tensed at the thunder of hoofs. A wave of relief washed over him as he recognized his own men. Diego Llanes leaped from his horse. "Doña Petra said come and help you." He crossed himself as his glance fell on Xavier.

"He isn't dead," Francisco said. "See if you can find water and bandages of some sort. Doña Ysidra can't see him like this. We've got to wash him and get him to Dos Ríos. Find a *carreta* or make a litter—he won't be able to ride. Here, you!" He rose to his feet. Two *vaqueros* slid from their horses at his command. "Lay him out flat. And you—" he indicated two others—"I want you to get these children back to Doña Petra."

Each child, slightly calmed now, was placed in the arms of an Indian, who mounted immediately and was off.

Water was brought in a flame-twisted bucket. Francisco began woodenly to wash the blood from his cousin's pulpy face.

In the black of night the slow procession bearing the litter reached Dos Ríos and went into the patio, covered with the red glow of torchlight. Francisco's big body sagged in the saddle as his horse jogged beside the walking Indians. Enrique was wan with fatigue and hunger. They dismounted stiffly.

Petra ran out the door and up to Francisco. "I did everything you said," she cried hurriedly. "O my God! Xavier——" She clapped her hands over her horrified face as the serape which had covered him slid aside.

"He is alive," Francisco said stonily.

"No one has found Vaiz," she faltered forcing her eyes away from Xavier's battered face. "Somebody said there was an epidemic in Monterey and he is delayed. The bedrooms are ready. Catalina and her children are sleeping. Riders have gone out to all the ranchos. Hot food is waiting. . . ."

Her voice dwindled as the Indians carried Xavier inside. Padilla leaned his head against the pommel of his saddle in sheer exhaustion.

"Enrique," Francisco said fondly, "go eat something."

Enrique raised his wan face. "I don't want to eat," he said dully.

"Francisco, are you all right?" Petra faltered.

"I'm fine," he began and stopped, intensity glinting in his eyes. "Who's coming?" They strained their gaze in the moonlight and discerned several mounted men riding hard for Dos Ríos.

"Mother of God!" Padilla fairly sobbed whipping out his knife.

"Wait," Francisco said. "It's Garcia from the Presidio and some townsmen."

At that moment the men swept into the yard and dismounted.

"Great God, Don Francisco, what's happened? Word came of the pirates——" Garcia stopped, staring at the filthy men and the blood-soaked bandage on Francisco's chest.

"They're gone," Francisco said briefly. "Come inside and have dinner. My wife says there's some hot food waiting."

One man from the back of the group surged forward and grasped Francisco's hand, causing him to wince. "Don Francisco," he wailed, "if only I had come in last night! I started to. If I had ridden over I could have helped you. Oh, come, you surely remember me—I am Captain Lopez. My ship *Santa Margarita* put into the harbor yesterday afternoon."

"Oh, yes, Lopez," Francisco said vaguely. "Please come in, sir, all of you."

The man walked beside Francisco as they entered the dim hallway, still speaking distractedly. "I wanted to come," Lopez was saying. "I changed my mind twice. There was so much to be done. On the other hand I wanted to tell you how successful I was with your order. Believe me, sir, no one has ever worked so hard in assembling any cargo as I did yours. And I am glad—this will make you happy, sir—to state that I got every item. Do you hear that, sir, every single item?"

"Wait—wait a minute," Francisco said shaking

his head a little. "Just a minute, my friend. So much has happened. It was such a long time ago. *Santa Margarita,* you say. What did I order from you? Assist my failing memory."

"What, sir!" gasped the captain. "Can you have forgotten? Blessed Mother Mary! Those books! Those dozens of books for your son. I know it's been a long time. I had some trouble—almost lost my ship and was in port seven months getting repairs. But I got them," he finsihed triumphantly. "I got every book you ordered for Don Angelo."

Angelo . . . Angelo . . . Angelo. The name echoed through the dim hallway up the stairs and down. Petra recoiled against the wall, her eyes going dark and her lips quivering.

Francisco leaned over for a moment. "You have done very well," he said steadily. "Due to your long absence and all this confusion with the pirates, you have not yet learned that my son Angelo is dead."

"Santa María, my God, I wouldn't have——"

"Please, Captain Lopez, it is all right. You did not know. Deliver the books whenever it is convenient for you. There are children here who may benefit by them. Now——" He turned to the other men, who shifted uneasily, sorry the captain had not been informed, but it had been so long ago. . . . "Now you gentlemen please go in and eat. I'm sorry, please excuse me. My wife Doña Petra . . . will see that you have everything you need."

There was a rising babble of solicitous speech.

Adam came forward. "Let me help you. I've got some bandages. Don Xavier is sleeping. . . ."

"Thank you," Francisco said as their voices dwindled off.

Petra sagged against the wall. She must go into the dining room and take her place at the head of the table. Turning her face against the plaster in sudden anguish she tried to shut Angelo out. But he was there, his name still echoing in her ears. Angelo . . . Angelo . . .

Chapter 23

The news of the attack by pirates swept the coast and guards everywhere were increased. Pirates were a periodical scourge and much dreaded. Wild rumors flew about regarding the ship. Such a vessel had not been seen, and the general belief was that the depleted crew had sailed to Costa Rica in hope of replenishing their number. For a time people went abroad in groups and well-armed. Many visitors came to view the remains of the dead pirates, which provided an interesting, if rather revolting aspect after the Indians had finished with the corpses. The Dos Ríos *vaqueros* were something of heroes and became insufferable to the visiting cowherds from adjoining ranchos. Many yarns of seeing the pirate ship were brought to Francisco. These he expertly sifted for some grain of truth. Long accustomed to his men, he knew on whose word he could depend, and who could conveniently turn a wheeling pelican into a ship.

In spite of the influx of visitors which necessitated having rooms ready at all times, there was little confusion. Francisco had a passing thought of gratitude for Petra who took charge quietly and competently. Adam, although his agreement had been to tutor the Estrade boys, accepted the two older Miramontes children without a word and kept them all occupied until noon of each day.

Though she was upset, Petra allowed no sign of it to show. She kept busy from dawn to dark until the stream of guests began to diminish, and Xavier seemed on the mend. She was glad when he improved, for she knew he would want to do something about the gutted house at La Punta; if the land remained houseless someone could register a complaint and the grant could be revoked. It worried her that he had accepted with such stoicism the news that the house was gone. She had expected hysteria, but he showed no emotion at all, barely listening when Francisco told him quietly how much damage there was and estimated the length of time to repair it.

Once she surprised Ysidra alone and was startled at the change in her godmother. She had aged and, miracle of miracles, had lost weight. Her skin sagged in new wrinkles and there were black circles under her eyes. In sudden panic Petra rushed from the room. Mother of God, had Ysidra been weeping? The stones in the yard perhaps, but not Ysidra!

Catalina worried her as much as all else. The girl seemed to have fallen into an obscure and inexplicable illness which made her listless and exhausted. She lay for long hours on a couch beside Xavier's bed, rousing herself only when he asked for something between his cracked and swollen lips.

Catalina made herself look at him and decided she must pray for forgiveness for deserting him when he needed her. But she could not pray now. She would have to wait until she wasn't so tired. All she could remember to think about was how hysterical she had been over Francisco's superficial bullet wound, when she had completely forgotten the father of her children and left him in a burning house. A humilating heat crawled into her face when she remembered the spectacle she must have made of herself, riding like a witch though the black night, clutching her almost senseless baby. Francisco must not be taken by surprise. Francisco's house must not be set afire.

She lay, limp and white, on the couch, holding a forgotten rosary in nerveless fingers. She remembered to inquire from time to time about the children, for mothers were supposed to be doting. She remembered to hang anxiously on Doctor Vaiz words about Xavier, because wives were supposed to care for their husbands. She tried to weep a little for her house, for housewives were supposed to prize their dwellings. And when these little chores had been accomplished, she would return once more to the couch and stare out the window at the leaf patterns against the sky. Then she would turn her eyes to the wall and see the leaf patterns there, moving her gaze reluctantly to hold their moving image. Finally they would fade. Sometimes she closed her eyes so as to be thought asleep, but she slept very little. There was too much to think about, and so little energy with which to think.

The first evening that the house was free of guests, Ysidra suggested that Xavier was recovered enough to come down to dinner with the family. Catalina wished in dull resentment that he could be content to lie in bed, but he struggled up and dressed with the aid of his servant. Now she would have to rise from the couch and go down with him. What should she wear? Everything she owned had been burned in the charred shell at La Punta, so the choice was necessarily simple. The sewing women had hurriedly made her two gowns from material at hand, and Petra had lent her some underthings. Carmelita had brought her slippers and stockings from Las Palomas, her other clothing being to small. Catalina chose the prettier of the two dresses they had made, a white flowered one, and held it up before her at the morror.

Mother of God, how ugly she was! Sagging, she leaned against the dresser. Her hair was hanging in straggling wisps, for she hadn't combed it all day. What was happening to her? Was she losing her beauty? She let the dress fall to the floor and frantically caught up a hairbrush. Oh, she couldn't lose her beauty—that was all she had left. Distractedly, hampered by the brush she held, she began to undo the matted braids. Tears of weakness and disgust filled her eyes and spilled over, making crooked paths down her face.

"What is the matter, Catalina?" Xavier asked.

"I don't know," she sobbed weakly. "I'm ugly and dirty and tired."

He looked at her as if from a great distance. "Perhaps you should call a servant. Shall I send for a servant, my angel? Damacia arranges Petra's hair. Damacia does hair well. Shall I call Damacia?"

The dullness of his voice wore against her frayed nerves. "No!" she cried. "Don't call anyone! I'll see to it myself!"

But she made little headway. As she combed one strand free, another snarl developed. She decided to wash and laid the brush down. Then she started to look for the shoes Carmelita had brought from Las Palomas. She halted in her convulsive scramblings and stood with one of the slippers in her hand. It would soon be time for dinner. Xavier was ready and dressed, standing pale and flabby by the window. There was a hum and murmur of activity in the house. Dinner would be served at the scheduled time and she would not be ready. Might she go down like this? She stared dully at the slipper in her hand, at the washbowl with the soap softening in it, at the brush with tangled dark strands of hair. She would never be ready. She was old and ugly.

"I can't go down," she said in dawning wonder.

Xavier turned politely from the window. "Yes, you can go down," he said. "I will call Petra. Petra will help you."

Petra? Would Petra help her get ready? She had helped Petra once, a long time ago. When Angelo had died, she had washed Petra's face and combed her pale hair. She had felt sorry for Petra. Then they had gone to Angelo's funeral. But that was different. She could never allow Petra to help her. María-Catalina Miramontes y Acuña did not require any help.

"No," she said, "it isn't necessary," and was faintly surprised to find that Xavier had already gone. In the distance she heard a shout of delight. Those below were greeting Xavier, welcoming him back downstairs again. He was no longer an invalid. Dimly she heard their voices, unable to distinguish separate words. There was the shrill piping of the children. Somewhere in the medley of sound was Francisco's voice.

The door opened and Petra came briskly in. "Xavier says you aren't feeling well," she said.

Catalina stared at her. Here before her, in rich lovely black, with a fortune of diamonds blazing at her throat, was the lady of Dos Ríos, wife of Don Francisco Estrada y Santander. Catalina pondered on the fact that she could refuse help. She could think of something ugly and cutting to say that would send Petra off in a fury. She would do that. She pondered what to say, and was dimly amazed when the old pattern began to assert itself in courteous restraint.

"I'm only tired," she heard herself saying. "You might help with my hair. It's tangled because I didn't comb out the braids this morning."

"Would you like a bath first?"

"I haven't time. I didn't start getting ready soon enough."

"Well, we'll hold dinner," Petra laughed running to the door. "Rosa," she said to the servant in the hallway, "run down to the kitchen and tell them to wait until I tell them to serve dinner. And, Rosa, find Damacia and both of you come back up with some hot water. And get that powder out of my room, and send Bianca in! Now hurry!"

She turned back into the room. Catalina regarded her with wonder. Petra could keep them all waiting dinner. All she had to say was "wait" and dinner would wait no matter how hungry the family became. She was the lady of this house and the dinner was served at the time she specified. Catalina watched the bustle and confusion that followed her command. She allowed Damacia to tie up her hair. She watched the grunting Bianca and Rosa fill the wooden tub with tepid water. There was a pleasure in seeing her gardenia petal skin emerge from the grime and dirt. There was a luxuriant feeling to Petra's soft powder.

"Would you like one of my dresses? We could tie it in at the waist," Petra offered, laying out the white petticoats.

"Have you something bright?" Catalina asked, suddenly breathless. She was standing, half clothed, before the glass. Her hair, free of tangles tumbled in a black cascade down her back

"Oh, dozens," laughed Petra. "I haven't worn them for years."

She hurried out and came back with several hung over her arm.

"Look," she said, "we could tie this lavender one in at the waist. Or we could call Señora Llanes to run a temporary hem in this yellow——"

"Red!" Catalina startled them all with the eager harshness of her voice. She fairly snatched the last one, red flounced satin and black lace, glittering with jet beads. "Petra, you never wore red!"

"You'll never know how disappointed I was. I put a lot of thought into that dress," she said ruefully, "and when at last I put it on, all the color seemed to go out of me. I just can't wear it."

Catalina examined it, pulling it this way and that.

"Please accept it as a gift," Petra offered. "I'll call Señora Llanes. It's bound to be too long." In rising excitement she caught up her skirts and ran to the door.

"Señora Llanes," she called, "please come up—with some red thread." She turned back to Catalina. "How would you like to wear my rubies? Francisco gave them to me last Christmas, and I haven't had an opportunity to wear them since." At Catalina's look of pure delight, she whisked out the door, leaving it open for Señora Llanes who was coming hastily up the stairs.

"Petra," Catalina cried, "have you got a black comb?"

Petra had and brought it. "Use some of this Chinese perfume," she said admiringly as they surveyed the results of their combined efforts. The servants squatted back on their heels, grins of satisfaction on their dark faces. Ah, Doña Catalina was a beauty! They watched her turn this way and that in the deep red gown. The rubies twinkled like drops of port at her throat. The jet glittered on the black lace. Her cheeks were flushed and her eyes sparkled.

"Not too much perfume," she cautioned. "Are there any red roses?"

Damacia jumped to her feet and rushed from the room. In a moment she was back with a bouquet, the stems still dripping where she had snatched them from their vase. There was a scramble to find the scissors, and after a few silent concentrated moments three half-blown buds nestled in the dark coils of her hair at the base of the combs.

"I'm ready," she said breathlessly.

Petra's laugh rang out. "The men will be glad. They're probably starving. I'll go on down and tell the serving-women. You wait a minute, Catalina, then make a grand entrance." She hurried away, pushing up a loose strand of yellow hair.

When Catalina came down the stairs there was a concerted gasp of appreciation from those assembled in the hallway.

"Mama! Mama!" The child clambered about her.

"Catalina!" Francisco cried.

"Santa María!" shouted Padilla.

"Joaquin, don't——" Petra made a vain grab for the little boy as he clasped his mother's skirt in adoration.

"What a vision!" Adam Langley declared enthusiastically.

"Come. Dinner will get cold," Petra interposed.

Catalina smiled widely, brilliantly, and tossed her head to make the rubies sparkle. She wished there were guests, a hundred people to see her and admire her! She was swept into the dining room in a rush of lavish compliments. She was intoxicated. She was here at Dos Ríos! She was beautiful! Her hand was in Francisco's!

She must laugh and talk, and she found she could scarcely bother to eat. There was so much to say, so much to laugh at. It was like coming alive again after being long dead. Everything was amusing, delightful, exciting. They were all caught up in the sudden inexplicable merriment.

Ysidra wiped her eyes at some ridiculous sally of Adam's. "This is like old times."

"Like old times," Xavier echoed smiling a little blankly. "I will hate to leave it."

"Leave it?" asked Petra. "Do you plan a trip, my cousin?"

Xavier looked nonplused for an instant. "No trip," he said. He turned to Francisco with a shade of pompousness and bowed. "I shall never be able to repay you for all you have done for me, Francisco, but we must really come to some decision about moving."

"Moving?" The grin died on Francisco's face. "Oh, come, Xavier," he said, "where on earth could you go? If you want a cruise up the coast, or even a trip to Spain, I could——"

"La Punta!" Xavier said spreading his hands. "I couldn't think of taking a trip now that everything is finally in order in my house. Surely my wife can find nothing else she wants. I've made it exactly the way she wants it. I love Dos Ríos no less than she," he went on in a thickening silence, "but it is foolish to let the lovely house stand idle. Catalina, my dear, we must really come to a decision on moving to La Punta. It will take about a month to settle. Then we shall have a fiesta——"

Catalina rose to her feet, her face the color of frost. A spoon clicked against a dish. Francisco stood, paling a little, holding out his hand as if to ward off a blow.

"Xavier," Catalina screamed, "it's gone!" She ran to him, clutching the lapels of his jacket. "It's gone!" Suddenly she seemed to shrink and crumple.

Francisco sprang forward and caught her as she sagged against him.

"My dear," Xavier was muttering with vague politeness, "you must really watch the tone of your voice. And we really must go. Francisco, my cousin, don't you think——" His voice dwindled. "Mother?" he asked questioningly.

Francisco helped Catalina to a chair. Ysidra remained like a stone, staring at her confused son. She creased and recreased her napkin between her small dark fingers. Xavier sank into his seat and put his head in his hands. "I'm so tired," he muttered.

The children began to whimper, sensing the strangeness.

"Be quiet, children, finish your dinner," Francisco ordered levelly. "Xavier, I'm afraid you came down too soon. You aren't yourself. A good night's rest will set you right. Here, let me help you upstairs again."

"Yes, help me," Xavier said rising from his chair.

Francisco led his cousin out of the room.

With a great effort Petra roused herself from her bemused silence and forced words from her reluctant lips. "Catalina, my dear, don't be upset. There's been too much excitement. Drink a little wine. Ysidra, will you hand me that glass?" Color flowed into her face, and her hands shook as she passed it to Catalina who touched her pale lips to its rim. "Come now," she said, "Xavier will get a good night's rest and feel fine in the morning. Careful, Graciano, don't spill your water. Watch what you're doing. Ricardo, run get your guitar and we'll have a little music while we finish. Isabela, angel, let Aunt Petra help you cut that."

Somehow she got them all back in their places. The Indian, Ricardo, watched guardedly at the door as he plucked the strings of the guitar. He began to sing softly. Petra had the feeling that everything must be in order when Francisco returned. Catalina, white and strained, could eat nothing. The music drifted about them. Ysidra toyed with her napkin and said nothing. Secretly Enrique made the sign of the cross. Color rose and ebbed in his face.

Petra talked and talked. She felt stupid, inane, but somehow, with the help of Adam's ever ready conversation, she managed to forestall any embarrassing pause. The pattern must be put together again. The same pattern she had so often rebelled against had suddenly become valuable and necessary. There must be nothing abnormal or scandalous at Dos Ríos. She turned her attention to the children and hurried them through their dinners. The nurses hung about the hallway to take them to bed immediately after prayers.

"Prayers are sometimes tedious," commented Francisco closing the door of his office. "Smoke, my love?"

Ysidra nodded with a faint movement and Francisco took a chair opposite hers.

"Well, Panchito," she said after a moment, allowing smoke to creep from her nostrils, "shall we bandy inanities about or shall we come to the point?"

"We will speak of nothing distasteful to you," he said with sudden defiance.

"I wish to," she answered simply.

He settled himself in the chair. "Well then, did Doctor Vaiz hint that this would occur? Did he imply that this would be a natural symptom which would manifest itself in Xavier?"

"No."

Something like a sigh escaped Francisco and he was silent for a long time. "What do you think?" he asked finally.

"I think . . . my son has gone mad," she said with scarcely a break in the even flow of her words. Her eyes were closed and her face was a round blind moon.

"What then?" he asked softly.

A ponderous shrug lifted her shoulders. "I do not know, Francisco."

He leaned forward. "Let us understand one thing," he said with urgency. "I know you well. I have an idea what is in your mind. You think I will object to having a madman in my house. I do not. In no circumstances are you to consider taking or sending him away. Depend on me, Ysidra. Depend on me."

"Very well," she said faintly. She opened her eyes and they were shadowed with a fear she had lived with a long time.

Chapter 24

Petra watched Catalina with a never failing annoyance. Santa María, did the woman never stop preening herself? She seemed, these last two years, to have fallen in love with her reflection. She was forever standing before a looking glass and staring blankly at her image or patting her already neat hair into place.

Laying her sewing in her lap, Petra surveyed her cousin's wife. Catalina had been pretty, then she had been beautiful, now she was exquisite. Her hair shone from tedious hours of brushing, her skin was soft and milky as gardenia petals. Her teeth were like perfectly matched pearls. She dressed with the greatest of care. No trading ship ever put into port without fattening its coffers with sales of silk, satin, lace, damask, linen and fine lawn to Doña Catalina Miramontes y Acuña. Petra marveled at her tireless efforts on her appearance. She seemed to think of nothing else. She was always arrayed in the most exquisite clothes. Nothing was ever out of place. No curl escaped the shining coils of her hair. There was never a burn or stain on the slim beautifully formed hands. She was a jewel of perfection about whom hung the scent of lilacs and sounded the rustle of silk.

Catalina had not resumed any of her old responsibilities since her return to Dos Ríos. She even neglected to buy material for the children's clothes and Petra had to do it. She ignored the workings of the house completely. Deftly she put everything even slightly unpleasant out of her mind. The tinkle of her laughter floated from time to time on the air, as musical and empty as the idle strumming of a guitar. There was little Petra could say, but many times she seethed with inward fury.

"Catalina, my dear," she remonstrated trying to keep her voice pleasant, "will you please look to your children? Am I supposed to discipline them too?"

"Do as you wish, Petra. This is your home. If my children have offended, feel free to mete out the same punishments that you would to Esteban or Graciano." She twisted about to look in the mirror, carefully resetting the comb in her hair. "Do you think this gold has tarnished?" she asked with a faint frown.

Petra gave up. She was sure that Catalina completely forgot her children's existence for days at a time. Soon it was Petra they came to for everything.

"Aunt Petra, Esteban says I'm too little to play."

"Aunt Petra, Mario has fallen and hurt his knee."

"Aunt Petra, Joquin says his throat is sore."

Aunt Petra, always Aunt Petra—never Mama. Mama was something pretty to kiss good night, something lovely to worship from afar. If they were sick, or hurt, or angry, it was Petra to whom they automatically came.

She looked at Catalina now, and her lips pressed together a bit sternly. It was about time for Francisco to come in for the evening meal. Somehow Catalina always managed to have her appearance freshened and be near the entrance. Petra began to notice with dawning wonder that Catalina was always where Francisco would see her. Lovely, immaculate, beautiful little Catalina was always the last thing Francisco saw when he left in the morning and the first thing he saw when he returned at night. Her tinkling, ever good-humored laugh was always near when Francisco was about. Petra wondered grimly how long he could hold out. She had no illusions about Francisco's susceptibility.

He wouldn't dare!

With hands suddenly unsteady she laid aside her sewing and went to stand beside Catalina at the glass, comparing herself with the other woman. Her hair was a pale shining coil. Her face was just as pretty. There was a black comb in her hair, black taffeta rustled when she walked, and at her throat blazed the diamonds. She was a beautiful woman—a satisfying thought. She might be twenty-three, but she didn't look it.

Add that she had borne him a son. She was his wife. Catalina couldn't compete with that. Not that she would dare to think she could. Mother of God, what was the world coming to! If Catalina didn't take care, someone else might begin to see through her stratagems.

At dinner Xavier again spoke of La Punta. A wave of acute embarrassment passed through those at the table. Catalina's cheeks paled and flushed. Petra's jaw line became more pronounced and she hastily turned the conversation into other channels. Mixed with her confusion and discomfort was an acute pity for Xavier. La Punta was real to him. In his bemused mind he could see it as it had stood, the snug little patio surrounded on the three sides by the solid adobe rooms. She paused a moment, a spoon poised in midair. A sudden flush swept her fair cheeks.

As soon as possible after prayers she endeavored to speak to Francisco.

"Yes, what is it, my dear?" he asked glancing up from some papers.

Petra breathed a sigh of relief that Ysidra was not there.

"I want to talk to you about Xavier," she began bluntly. His brows raised slightly and a guarded look came into his eyes.

Petra knew she had begun badly. She could never be Spanish in her approach to any vital question. She was too point-blank. Stubbornly she went on. "Yes, Francisco, he—I don't think there is anything really wrong with him that a little intelligent effort won't cure."

"He has been living in a dream for about two years," he reminded her. "Before we go any farther let us understand each other. I will not send him away, if that is what you are getting to."

She sighed and sat down. There was no point in trying to force him into anything. "Don't make a definite statement about it, Francisco, until you hear my whole idea."

He smiled. "All right, Petra, tell me your idea."

She tried to choose her words carefully, reluctant to offend him. He was so touchy when members of his family were discussed. "You admit that he isn't right," she said. "We all know that, and nobody could be more sorry about it than I. He has a perpetual waiting look that tears my heart out. It seems to me, Francisco, that it's not accepting the facts which has made him . . . different. Suppose—" she clasped her hands together in earnestness, excitement causing her color to rise—"just suppose that, since his mind doesn't fit the facts, we made the facts fit his mind."

He leaned forward. "What do you mean?"

"Well, Francisco, since he is always waiting,

marking time, until he can get back to La Punta—as it was—couldn't you have it rebuilt as nearly like it was as possible? Couldn't—wouldn't—that make it all right? Think: just suppose, say in a year or so, it were done, and one day when he mentioned it, you agreed with him and sent them back again. When he rode up to it, everything would be the same. Do you see? It would be just as if he were going there for the first time?"

She stood up and faced him. "What if he has forgotten about the pirate raid?" she rushed on. "That is all right. Is it so strange? We all forget things. Haven't you forgotten things? What difference would it make then? He thinks he has La Punta now, and we think him mad. But if he had La Punta—don't you see?—he wouldn't be mad, would he, Francisco?"

He rose from his chair, smiling a little. "You make it sound very simple, little one."

"Well," she faltered, "I . . . sometimes remedies are simple. It seems we should certainly try anything——"

"You know, my dear," he said gently, "there is more to ranching than having a house to live in. Do you honestly think him able to cope again with all the duties involved?"

"I don't know," she said uncertainly. "He did so well at first. Remember how pleased you and Don Juan Acuña were?"

"Yes." Francisco stared thoughtfully out the window into the velvet darkness.

"You could help him," Petra offered hesitantly. "What happened to his stock when La Punta burned?" she asked as an afterthought.

"It is intact," he replied absently. "Enrique and I have been looking after his herds. They've increased as a matter of fact. I suppose the only thing lacking is the house. Their orchards have begun to bear. It's good land—too good," he added soberly almost to himself. "If he doesn't take up residence again soon, someone might register a counterclaim."

"That would take his pasture," Petra said sharply.

"It would take everything but the stock," Francisco murmured. He began to walk restlessly about the office. "I would have to discuss it with Ysidra and Don Juan. Enrique and I might go on seeing to the business end for a time until he became sufficiently himself again."

"About the furniture," Petra said thoughtfully: "if we can't get everything they need from the traders, I can spare some things from Dos Ríos. Then, of course Doña Dolores would help—not to mention anyone else to whom we mentioned the need. You know, I think I might even manage to get that large carved chair that stands in Doña Felisa Sal's front hallway. Xavier has always admired it."

Francisco's laugh interrupted her. "You're shameless." Petra had the grace to blush. "Neither of us," he said, "has thought how Catalina might feel about this. After all she is to be considered."

Petra's chin came up. "I don't see why. Xavier is her husband. It would be for his benefit. It would be a poor wife who didn't grasp the chance to do something for——" She stopped, faltering before his suddenly level gaze. "Well," she ended lamely, "their situation is unlike any other situation.

"Yes," he said politely. "Suppose you find her. She should be a party to any discussion about Xavier."

"I . . . I see no reason," Petra began faintly.

"Please be good enough to ask her to come in."

"Very well," she said stiffly, and to show him how little she cared she sent Catalina to him, but she herself did not return. However, the instant she heard the door close after Catalina she regretted it. What would they say? It was her idea! She would never get the straight of the discussion from Catalina, and she would not ask Francisco. Angry with herself for her impulsive disdain, she went hesitantly into the hall where she could discern the faint murmur of voices from the office. That would be Francisco. He would be explaining the idea to Catalina. Petra lifted her skirt and placed one foot on the stairs. Oh, why hadn't she swallowed her pride and gone in? Could she go in now, as if she had been delayed for some reason? Frowning, she hesitated, curiosity burning inside her.

The murmur of Francisco's voice stopped and there was the softness of Catalina's, unintelligible. Oh, this was shameless! She must either go frankly in or else go on upstairs. Gently bred people didn't hang about hallways eavesdropping. She took another step up the stairs. On the other hand, she wasn't eavesdropping because she wasn't actually hearing anything. She stepped down again. Francisco was speaking now. Why didn't he speak up? Oh, how awful! She bit her lip in sudden embarrassment. What on earth would she say if Aunt Ysidra happened to see her.

She was clasping the banister indecisively when Catalina's voice came to her, plainly, loudly, angrily: ". . . won't! I won't! I will not!"

Oh, she couldn't be refusing! Petra's wide gaze fixed itself on the door. Francisco's voice came again, low, controlled, indistinct. Then, after a time, Catalina's voice, strident and frantic: "I can divorce him. I don't have to stand it."

Divorce! Horror washed all color from Petra's face. She heard Francisco say quite plainly, "Are you out of your mind, girl? You'd have to enter a convent."

Then Catalina, passionately: "I don't care. I don't care. I might as well be in one now."

Francisco said, "I'm just trying to . . ." and the rest was lost, for his voice had regained its normal pitch.

Then after a long moment Catalina's piteous wail: "But what about me? Does nobody think of *me?*"

Francisco spoke for a long time, his voice kind and calm. Petra strained unashamedly to hear him. But she could discern only fragments of sentences.

". . . children . . . will marry, but the boys . . . expect to inherit from Las Palomas . . . Teodoro's children to consider . . ."

And at intervals, Catalina's voice, frantic and distracted:

". . . like orphans . . . think of nothing else . . . can be so merciless . . . wife . . ." Then after an interval the phrase: ". . . have been such a good wife!"

Then silence.

She's crying, thought Petra, sympathy for Catalina sweeping through her. What a horrible life! Poor Catalina! Poor Xavier! Poor children! Her hands flew to her throat in a sudden agony of pity. She turned and took a step down, unable to hear the sound of any voice now. Maybe she should go in. Perhaps they had reached a point where any interruption would be welcome. She paused uncertainly before the door, her hand touching the knob. The quality of the silence from the office was strangely tangible, appalling. No voice, no sound of weeping. Why didn't they speak, make some sound, anything? Just the scrape of a chair on the floor? She stared at the blank wood of the door, her heart beating with odd heaviness. *What were they doing?* Convulsively, she twisted the knob and flung open the door.

"Francisco!" She colored violently in outrage at the savage abandon of their embrace. Even when the sound of her voice shattered the stillness of the room, they seemed unable to part, but held each other, swaying, for an instant longer. Petra watched, furious, repelled as Catalina allowed Francisco to put her from him, limply quiescent. His hands at her waist seemed leaden and reluctant. Petra, by the door, could feel the physical wrench of their parting. The very air seemed to surge and vibrate with it. Francisco's face was hard, devoid of any expression, but in the depths of Catalina's great eyes there gleamed for a moment a look of victory.

"Come in. Close the door." Francisco's voice was compressed.

Petra managed to shut the door, then backed up against it, her shaking hands out of sight behind her.

"We must arrange something about the children, Isabela, Joaquin and Mario," Francisco said in a flat, toneless voice.

He was going to ignore it, while Petra stood stiffly by the door in rage; while Catalina leaned forward, breathing quickly, her parted lips quivering as if crushed and bruised.

"About . . . the children?" Catalina asked with difficulty.

"What about them?" Petra was startled at the harshness of her own voice. "What of their own estate—La Punta?" They could not ignore her. She would not permit it.

"Catalina is not going back to La Punta," Francisco said with deliberation. "She cannot. It is too much to ask."

"But the estate?" Petra gasped. "Xavier's boys?"

"I was coming to that," Francisco replied.

Catalina took a step toward him. "Would you like to adopt my children?" Her voice was dim, smothered. "You have only one. You will not have any more. I'll give you——"

Fury, raw and frightening, engulfed Petra. "How generous of you! And if he were your children's father, it wouldn't take you long to become his wife—in a way. Would it? Would it?"

"Petra!" Francisco's voice cracked through the air like a whip. His hand shot out and gripped her arm, shook her. The painful roughness made her lose her breath for a moment and be incapable of speech.

"Catalina," he said, speaking carefully, "I wasn't offering to adopt them. Joaquin and Mario have a father. He may be sick and confused, but he remains their father." His voice became gentler at the rush of defeat in her eyes. "What I was going to say was that, if La Punta is lost, I will see to their inheritance."

"Very well," she said after a disbelieving moment. She spoke absently, staring at him as if she had never seen him before. Then she added hastily, like a child suddenly remembering its manners, "Thank you. Thank you very much. That is very kind of you. Father will be relieved." Her voice dwindled.

"I won't allow it." Petra was shaking visibly.

"You will not?" Francisco's voice was even.

"I . . . I don't care about the inheritance—that's only money. But I won't have Catalina in this house. She cannot remain here. Not after this. You're hurting me." She gasped, wrenching away from him.

"You have nothing to say about this, Petra."

"I have! I have! She has flung herself at you for years like—like a savage. I won't tolerate it.

I'll go to Don Juan. I'll go to Father Patricio. She can't stay here."

"Be quiet! Let her alone!" he said roughly. "There are things you don't understand." Petra fell back before his tone. Even when she had infuriated him, he had never spoken to her like that before.

There was an appalling silence as they stared at each other. Finally Francisco spoke. "What kind of a house have we here, where the people squabble like Indians? Let us all understand this: Dos Ríos will remain the home of Xavier and Catalina as long as they are pleased to stay. As to this—what happened tonight—I shall take pains to see that it does not occur again. Not," he added stonily, "because of any duty I feel to *my* marriage, but because my cousin's wife is inviolate. No more will be said of this interview, or what had passed in this room. We will behave as civilized human beings. No word of recrimination will ever be said of this. Petra, you understand me? Now, this is the end of it. The discussion is finished."

The toneless finality of his voice forbade any answer at all. Petra felt vaguely stunned. Wide-eyed, she watched Catalina grope for her fan, as if by picking up the Spanish fan, she could re-establish the decorous pattern so passionately swept aside for a moment.

"It is late. I must go upstairs." Catalina's voice was calm. No one could tell by looking at the pale beautiful face that she had offered herself savagely and lustfully to another woman's husband. No one could tell that she had offered the very children of her body as a gift, a token, only to have them refused. There was the faint rustle of silk as she left. There hung in the air the faint scent of lilacs. Her step on the stairs was delicate but firm.

Petra looked at the empty doorway in wonder.

She was lost again, beyond her depth. How could she cope with these Spaniards who spoke out in set designs, who seldom made an error and when they did instinctively covered it so carefully that it seemed not to have occurred. Francisco's word was law. He was the master here. If he said a thing was finished, it was finished. Forever after they would behave according to the customs and habits of a lifetime, and with their exquisite, impeccable, Spanish good manners they would bury this until it was out of sight and wholly lost. No one would speak of it ever again. She would obey him. Confusedly she turned her gaze to her husband, feeling a dim sense of surprise. It was true. She knew instinctively that she would obey him.

Catalina had obeyed him. She had picked up her fan, bade them good night and left them as he had wanted her to, as if nothing had happened. Surely, she, his wife, could do no less. Surely she was no less a lady than Catalina. She looked at him an instant longer with wide, unsure eyes. His face was withdrawn, closed. There was no way to tell what thought existed behind its passive quiet.

"If you will excuse me," she murmured formally. "It is quite late."

He bowed. "Of course," he said distantly.

She left the office and mounted the stairs, keeping her back straight with a conscious effort. Her arm, where his rough fingers had gripped it, ached painfully. Even in her room she did not drop the pose. She removed her necklace with careful motions and began to undress, looking at herself formally in the glass, meeting her own eyes with a veiled and blank expression. She admitted to herself for the first time that, actually, Francisco was her husband, and she would have to obey him in any command he chose to issue.

In bed she lay tense and quiet in the darkness, conscious always of the painfully bruised arm, waiting for the sound of him coming upstairs to his room. When she heard him, she lay, holding her breath, until he had passed her door. Then she began, in confusion, to cry.

Petra was amazed at herself during the days that followed. Sedulously she followed Catalina's lead, although at times she ached to slap the other's composed lovely face. She dared not speak of what had occurred to anyone, and, especially during the nights, she was tormented by the thought that Catalina was merely biding her time. Of course Francisco had said he would take pains to see that nothing like that occurred again, but how much pains would he take? Mother of God, she thought savagely, he had only to hold out his hand! He was only human. She wondered in angry distraction why everything had to be so badly mixed up. And yet it was marvelous how things appeared the same on the surface. She and Catalina assiduously "my-deared" and "my-loved" each other. There was never a break in their careful poise. No one would ever know.

This thought, instead of easing her, made her worry more. If he ever did change his mind, and hold out his hand to Catalina, how would she, Petra, know about it? She began to watch them but could detect nothing. It seemed that Francisco was keeping his promise. Out of respect for Xavier, and for no other reason, she thought bitterly.

She wondered if Aunt Ysidra knew. Probably. Francisco made her his confidant in all things. She felt sure of it one day in the *sala* when the three women sat gossiping, apparently unruffled and at peace with the world.

"Did you—forgive this frank speaking, but we are alone—did you hear about Señor Gomez complaining to the magistrate because his wife refused to admit him to her room?"

Petra replied carefully, "I heard something about it, Aunt Ysidra." Catalina seemed intent on her needlework.

"I understand," Ysidra continued, "that the magistrate, a married man himself, ordered that she admit her husband, and decreed that if she refused she be carried off in irons. To me," Ysidra went on placidly, "this seemed a little drastic, considering that Señora Gomez was only thirteen at the time. But it merely points up the fact that laws are compounded oddly regarding the duties of——"

"Yes, of course," Petra cut in, her color a little high. "Is there a law perhaps regarding the privacy of a person's mind and personal affairs?"

To her surprise Ysidra was not offended but flung back her head and gave vent to her wheezing laugh. "Forgive an old woman, my dear girl," she said. "When one reaches my age there are few occupations left save that of busybody."

There. She had slipped again. Catalina would never have spoken so tartly to an elder. Led away in irons, indeed! She knew, with a strange mixture of emotion, that such a thing would never enter Francisco's head, although he was her husband and ostensibly the master. Well, she must think of something else.

A childish uproar arose in the patio, and making a hurried excuse, Petra left them to quell the disorder. Magdalena probably. This idea was confirmed. Joaquin was nursing a broken toy in vocal rage while Magdalena stood sullenly gloating over the damage. The others watched with interest.

"What have you done now?" Petra cried. There was never any coping with this wild little rebel who was her goddaughter. Any other Indian child would have scuttled off in terror rather than face the anger of a white person, but Magdalena stood her ground, looking at her with level insolent eyes.

"She is bad, doña." It was Delfina, who had come up quietly to the group. "Come back to the *indiada,*" she said to the child. "Say to the doña how sorry you are." When the child remained stubbornly silent, she repeated, "Well, come back to the *indiada.* I am very sorry, doña. I try to keep her out back, but sometimes Guillermo does not feel like watching her."

"Yes," Petra answered stiffly thinking she detected a tinge of sullenness in Delfina's tone. She made up her mind she would take no insolence. There was none forthcoming, however, for Delfina turned her attention to her daughter, and when the child still refused to obey, she picked her up and carried her, kicking, screaming and clawing, around the corner of the house.

"Never mind, Joaquin," Petra said soothingly to the little boy whose anger was subsiding. "Perhaps Don Adam can fix your toy. He is very clever at such things. Why don't you ask him? The rest of you run along and play. Play nicely now! No more quarreling!"

That evening, Francisco spoke to her of the child Magdalena. His eyes were hard. "I noticed Concha striking her the other day," he said. "I meant to say something about it. I don't care to have her cuffed about by Indian servants."

A tremor of shock went through Petra. He cared about the child. But of course he would! "Magdalena is a very bad little girl," she said keeping her voice calm. "If she misbehaves—which she does constantly—she must expect to be slapped. Her mother doesn't seem to resent it." That was true. Delfina herself stood in awe of the child and had never been known to punish her. Still there was little she could do if another's outraged hand struck out at her from time to time.

"Why is she so bad, Petra?" Francisco asked frowning. "After all I . . . we are her godparents. We should look after her."

Petra was silent for a moment. Did he think her a fool? "Were you a bad little boy when you were a child?" she asked quietly.

His head came up and he regarded her searchingly for an instant. "I was a very bad little boy. I behaved only when my father was about. Only then." His eyes grew somber. "And later, of course, not even then."

Thank God he didn't insult her intelligence by lying about it! She looked at her hands intently. What he said was true. She had accepted a certain responsibility as godmother. And Delfina had shown herself incapable of coping with the little changeling. Francisco himself dare not make too much a point of interesting himself in her welfare. It seemed, then, to be up to her. Her pulse beat faster.

"What do you want me to do?" she asked and felt slightly ashamed because he looked surprised for a moment at the kindness in her tone.

"I would be grateful if you would take a hand," he said formally. "She seems an intelligent child. It is a shame for her brain and energy to be so misdirected."

She was intelligent, all right, Petra thought grimly. She had to be smart to be so bad. A stupid child couldn't think up half so much deviltry. She hadn't the faintest idea how to go about making a little lady out of Magdalena. She wouldn't be dealing with a stolid little Indian girl. She would be coping with another Estrada. This thought made her start and she recalled wryly how little success she had had in the past in outwitting the Estradas.

"I will be glad to try," she heard herself saying with more authority than she felt. "Of course I imagine Delfina will resent it. I think I would if anyone interfered with me and my children."

Francisco smiled briefly. "No doubt," he said. "What you forget is that Delfina is an Indian and you are the mistress here. Besides, this is an entirely different situation."

She went to bed, her mind buzzing with ideas. She was feeling more confident because Francisco had looked relieved. He seemed to have no doubt that she could handle it. There had been an air almost of friendliness between them.

Her confidence diminished during the days that followed. Getting close to Magdalena was like trying to get close to a small Joshua tree. There was no penetrating beyond the prickly surface she presented to a hostile world. Petra punished the child, only to have the offense repeated. She made her a pretty dress, only to have it ripped and dirtied with wanton heedlessness. She spoke to Delfina and could get no satisfaction at all.

"Her discipline should come from her mother," she said patiently.

"Yes, doña."

"If she is not made to be good in her own home, how can we expect that she will be good outside?"

"Yes, doña."

Petra gave up in despair. Delfina would never lay a hand on the child. She would as soon strike out at Francisco. The fact that the child was his made it seem above punishment or reprimand by an Indian, even if the Indian was its mother.

In the end, the friendship between Petra and the little girl came about in a strange way. There was a fiesta at Las Palomas to celebrate the marriage of Carmelita Acuña to Don Refugio Peréa. There had been a great exodus from Dos Ríos because the sparkling little Carmelita was a favorite with everyone. At the last moment Graciano was stricken with a swift childish illness which sent

Petra into a frenzy of fear, and she had to refuse to accompany the party to Las Palomas. She watched them ride away, and any small regret she felt was smothered in relief because Graciano was sleeping soundly in his bed and his flush of fever was subsiding. She might, she told them, ride over with him in a day or two if he continued to improve.

Dos Ríos seemed an empty shell when the glittering company had departed. She walked about the sun-filled patio idly, wondering how she would occupy her time when she wasn't tending Graciano. There was a drowsy thick quality in the vast silence. She paused before the old man sitting in his accustomed place. He seemed lost in some ancient dream. She turned from him and walked around the side of the house, thinking of Magdalena and wondering where the child was. A few paces from the *indiada* she caught up her skirts and broke into a run.

"Guillermo!" she cried shattering the quiet. "What is the matter?" He sat hunched over before the door, grimed and powdery with dust. A few feet away grazed his horse in its beautiful trappings. He looked up hazily, and Petra suddenly went sick because one of his arms seemed strangely twisted and askew.

"I wasn't thrown," he said thickly. "I wasn't thrown, doña."

Instantly she knew what had happened and ached with pity for him. She went down on her knees in the dust beside him.

"Oh, Guillermo," she said, "your arm—it's broken!"

"But I wasn't thrown," he repeated stubbornly.

"Of course," she said, her voice wavering. "The horse doesn't exist that could throw Guillermo Estrada. I know that. You've just fallen and broken your arm. Did you stumble?"

"Yes, I stumbled."

"Well, I——" She was nonplused at the problem confronting her. Almost everyone was gone. Who was there to send for help? She had no idea how to set the broken arm herself. Well, maybe she could if she had to. She gritted her teeth at the thought. It would be better if Francisco could come back.

"Magdalena," she cried, spying the little girl, "come here."

Pretending not to hear, Magdalena started away in a hurry. In a gust of anger Petra got up and sprinted after her.

"Magdalena," she shouted, "stop this instant!"

At the undeniable authority in Petra's tone Magdalena stopped but refused to turn around. Petra caught up with her and took her roughly by the arm. "Shame on you! Why didn't you come when I called? Don't you know your . . . your father is sick? He's broken his arm." She was panting a little, and when her breath came more evenly, she added, "You ride well, don't you?"

Magdalena permitted herself a small smile. It was well known that she rode superbly, with or without a saddle.

"Everyone has left for Las Palomas, and I want you to ride and catch up with them. I want you to tell Don Francisco that Guillermo is sick. Tell him to come back. Do you understand me?" She tightened her grip on the little girl's arm.

"Yes, doña." The tone was respectful enough but Petra was not at all reassured. There was the frozen look on the child's face that she was becoming used to. Gazing blankly into the middle distance, she would promise anything in order to escape for the moment, and then run away preferring to disobey and take a whipping when she returned.

"You can ride your father's horse," Petra offered. "It's already saddled. And besides," she added illogically, "if you don't go I shall whip you. I really will this time." She couldn't tell whether this threat alarmed or amused the child, for her expression remained the same. Finally the clear eyes focused themselves on the Montoya diamonds.

"If I rode very fast to get Don Francisco would the doña let me wear her necklace? It is a charm necklace. It would protect me."

Petra gasped and her fingers touched the brilliant diamonds. She thought for a moment she would laugh. The Montoya necklace about the dirty little neck of an Indian child! The smile never reached her lips. She had the certain knowledge that Guillermo could die of agony much worse than a broken arm, but if Magdalena didn't get the necklace she would not move one inch after Francisco. Pure Estrada! Petra sighed deeply and unfastened the clasp.

"If you ride very fast," she bargained, "and if you only wear it there and back and return it to me the *instant* you come back—and God help you if you lose it!" She couldn't help adding.

The moment the necklace was about her neck Magdalena's slim brown legs carried her fleetly to Guillermo's horse. Her white teeth bared in a swift grin. The sun struck the necklace in a blinding flash as the horse went off at full gallop. The little girl crouched low in the saddle. The moment Magdalena was gone Petra was seized with misgiving. It would be a long way for a little girl to ride. The Dos Ríos party had a good start. What resistance could Magdalena put up if she met someone who felt that a diamond necklace was not a proper ornament for a small Indian girl? What a risk it was—and yet what other course could Petra take? Distractedly, wondering if Graciano were still asleep, she went back to Guillermo.

"Stand up," she said. "Let me brush the dust off you. Don Francisco is coming back. It will be well to look a little neater." He stood up obediently, but suddenly, gray-faced, he sank down again.

It seemed a long time before she heard the thunder of Francisco's horse. He was down in an instant.

"It's only the arm," Guillermo said rallying a little before Francisco.

"Yes, let me see. Don't get up." Francisco, unmindful of the splendid clothing, knelt down beside him. "Petra, can you get me a couple of small sticks for splints, and your medicine chest? I'll need some bandage."

She ran to the house and got the required items, adding of her own volition a bottle of brandy. She paused for a fleeting instant to listen for Graciano but the house was still. By the time she reached the *indiada* again, the arm was straightened. Francisco's face was grim, and down Guillermo's face ran dark rivulets of sweat.

"Jesús, Don Francisco!" she heard Guillermo whisper through his teeth.

"Listen," Francisco said shortly, "in eighteen seventeen I was mauled by a grizzly. It broke my arm. I set the arm myself, Guillermo, because I was alone at the time. I had to use saplings for splints. I didn't die of the agony. If you don't like the way I'm doing this and prefer to do it yourself, let me know."

Petra was astonished, but an angry comment died on her lips when she saw the effect of his words on Guillermo. The eyes of the two men met for an instant.

"Please continue," Guillermo said woodenly.

"Very well," Francisco replied. "Here, bite on this stick. Let me hear no word until I have finished."

Petra didn't think of the necklace until Guillermo had retired to the depths of the dark little house and Francisco had ridden off again to rejoin the party enroute to Las Palomas. Suddenly panic-stricken, Petra looked about for Magdalena. That little vixen! Uncertainly she walked toward the big house. In the patio standing before the old man was Magdalena. She had been talking to him; the children often did, not knowing whether or not he heard them.

She held out her hand when she saw Petra. "Doña's necklace," she said simply.

Petra took it, a little confused. She had been prepared for battle. "You . . . you rode very fast, didn't you?" she asked lamely.

"Like the wind," Magdalena said complacently, squatting down on the packed earth of the patio. "Father will get well now?" she inquired politely.

For some reason Petra could not detect, they were now friends. Magdalena's attitude was no longer distant and colored with faint hostility. Petra shook her head a little wearily. The old man was making vague, aimless motions with his gnarled hands. She wondered in consternation if anyone had remembered to feed him. The kitchen was deserted at the moment. Just then Graciano's wail carried to her ears. Distractedly she caught up her skirts and ran to the house. He'd wakened all alone.

"Magdalena," she said, pausing at the door, "no one has fed the old man. Could you——"

"I will do it," the child replied turning an unhurried gaze on her. Petra threw her a grateful glance and ran inside.

Magdalena held the food just out of the old man's reach and moved it from side to side tantalizingly. He stuck out his head with his mouth open repeatedly, only to have the aromatic bit of food escape him. He began to whimper in thin anger. Magdalena put it quickly into his mouth. She squatted before him thoughtfully. It had been an interesting day. She had done an important thing, riding out like a *vaquero* . . . not to mention wearing the doña's sparkling charm necklace. The doña must think her a very honest girl. Well, she was. She sighed in satisfaction and shifted her position, extending a bit of vegetable to the old one, watching him as his head moved from side to side in turtlelike efforts to get it. Poor old one!

She would tell her mother all that had happened to her today. "Certainly, I rode after them by myself," she would say. "The doña thought nothing of asking me. She knew I could do it. I rode right up to Don Francisco," she would say. No need to speak of the sudden terror she had felt at his frown. No need to say she had wanted to turn and run because he looked so big and splendid in his brilliant clothing. "Of course I wore the doña's necklace. I can wear it any time I choose. I have only to ask." It had been a nice day. It was fun running about the great dim kitchen making a little fire to warm the old man's food. "Of course I made the fire myself. I found the food too. Somebody had to feed the old man. Doña Petra left it all to me."

She fished a piece of beef from the bowl and fingered it. That was too tough for the old one. She put it into her own mouth and began to chew it with her strong white teeth. Into the withered mouth of the old man she placed a soft chunk of turnip. By the time that was down the beef in her own mouth was chewed to a fine pulp. Carefully she set the bowl down and took it out. Between her brown palms, she fashioned it into a loose ball and placed it in the old man's mouth.

"See how good I am to you, old father?" she asked gently. She was feeling a faint remorse.

What a wicked cruel girl she had been to tease a man so full of years.

"Francisco, something will have to be done," Petra said to him a few weeks later.

"About what?" he asked mildly. Prayers were finished and she had come to him in his office.

"About Magdalena."

He looked surprised. "Why, Petra, I assumed she was getting along splendidly. You were so pleased to have made friends with her."

"Being friends doesn't solve it. I . . . I thought it would," she faltered in embarrassment. "But it doesn't. She is very good at times. That is, she obeys me when I ask her to do something. But——" It had become suddenly a very complex thing: the problem of Magdalena. How could she convey to him the quality of Magdalena's alienness? He sat back, prepared to listen courteously, so she settled down to sort out ideas.

"I think it is the contrast," she said finally. "I give her pretty clothes, and, well, their house has dirt floors and so she ruins the clothes. It would be impractical to have wooden floors put in, although I considered it." She joined his sudden laugh, then sobered, adding frankly, "We can't make too much of a point of Magdalena because we have other godchildren. On the other hand I'm not making much headway. She tries—she does really." Petra's tone became defensive at his quizzical glance. "It's only that I try to make a little lady out of her while she's with me, and then she goes back to the *indiada* with all the *Indian* children." She paused in wonder for a moment. When had she stopped thinking of Magdalena as an Indian?

Francisco was looking thoughtfully out the window. "Yes," he said, "we might have known it would be too difficult for her to reconcile herself to two environments. It sets her apart from her brothers and sisters. She belongs nowhere. Naturally she would resent it."

"I don't suppose it would be practical to think of adopting her outright?" Petra asked faintly. "You adopted Guillermo."

"No, Petra." After a pause he said, "I think the solution is to send her to a good convent."

"Oh, I don't think so," Petra objected hurriedly. "I mean, I remember I was in a convent for a time. I didn't like it at all. I'm sure that Magdalena——" She stopped, realizing with surprise how attached she had become to the child.

"Well, you said yourself that she doesn't fit in here because of the contrast in her surroundings. Part of the time she is supposed to behave like a lady, and part of the time she is forced to hold her own with the children of the *indiada*. A convent, completely away from both these environments, is the logical answer. She would be gently reared then by the nuns, and later perhaps she might make a good marriage somewhere else."

"Well, I——" Petra began uncertainly. She could see the logic of it, but she thought with reluctance of parting with the wild green-eyed little hoyden. "Where would you send her?"

"To Spain or Mexico. The farther the better. The less she remembers of the *indiada*, the more chance the industrious sisters will have of making something of her."

"Mexico, Francisco. Then at least we could see her from time to time. After all I am her godmother. It would be a pity not to. And I'm going to make the trip with her too," she added quickly, as she saw denial in his eyes. "I intend to make the trip to Mexico and stay a few days to see her safely settled." She put such finality in her tone that he was forced to agree.

Delfina made no protest. She received the news

with a gleam of appreciation in her great eyes, as if she had always thought something special should be done for Magdalena. Petra and Francisco made the trip by boat to Mexico and established the thoroughly rebellious child in a convent there.

Looking odd in the new clothing in which Petra had dressed her, she clung with terrified abandon to her godmother. "I will go back with you," she said desperately. "I will always be good. I will never get dirty. I won't tease the old man. I won't fight with the other children."

"But you'll love it here," Petra promised, frankly crying. "And I'll send you presents. I'll write you letters and you must learn to read them. You must be very good and do everything the sisters ask you to."

They parted in the clean bleak office of the mother superior, and Petra, filled with dismay, saw them lead the child from her. She turned away, swallowing her tears. Francisco was standing at the window. She was seized with a sudden gust of anger at his coldness. Did nothing touch the man? But then Magdalena hadn't cried either. During all her angry pleading the clear eyes had remained dry and hard. They couldn't help it. There was that stiff pride in all of them that would never unbend, never relent. She took her cue from him and bade the mother superior a dignified good-by.

On the trip home Petra spoke of the little girl with longing.

"If you had enough children of your own," Francisco said flatly, "you wouldn't miss her so much."

She stared at him in consternation, so seldom was his mask of distant courtesy dropped. Swift color stained her face, and she turned it away from him into the wind. Her hands were holding tightly to the rail. She could feel his somber eyes on her, but it would do no good to look at him, for she could read nothing in his face. She waited, holding her breath, for him to say something else.

"It's getting cold," he said at length. "We had better go below."

In bewildered rage she left the rail and hurried below without his assistance. The rage subsided and she was left with a feeling of desolation which she could not explain.

Chapter 25

Alone in his office, Francisco stared into the diminishing fire. The events which necessitated hiring two foremen instead of one in place of Enrique pressed on his mind. He could feel Dos Ríos spreading out around him in the deepening night like a great sleeping shadow. Dos Ríos, for the Estrada and Miramontes boys. He could see Esteban plainly in his mind. He knew exactly how the child would look spread out in sleep, lax and limp, his hair clinging damply to his flushed skin; warm, strong and sturdy. Esteban Estrada, seven years old, riding like the wind on his fleet horse, over Dos Ríos. Later Don Esteban Estrada, the richest man in California. Francisco smiled wryly. Looking ahead again, dreaming the boy's life away. Seeing him as a man. How foolish that was, when he was so precious as a little boy! Warmth pervaded him and his pulse beat strongly as he thought of the boys, Esteban, Graciano, Joaquin and Mario. Four of them, but always Esteban first.

He thought gloomily of Padilla, staunch and devout. He remembered the breaking, the slight rending, of their perfect understanding. Enrique had regarded him as something between a god and a father. Now Padilla considered him merely a man—which was right of course. But there had been disappointment in falling from a pedestal. A bitterness crept up and filled his throat. He grinned as the old set of excuses and fabrications began to assert themselves and run their familiar course through his mind. Give him ten minutes—fifteen—and he would be able to find no flaw in anything he had done.

As he mused, his heart aching a little for Gabriel with his emaciated shank showing through the charred rent in his robe, he could remember the enticing fields, groves and pastures which lay at waste after they had ceased to belong to the mission and before they had become part of Rancho Dos Ríos. He could recall riding out to look at the rolling miles, knowing that they continued to swell and rise beyond the last rim of vision. They were empty, ownerless land, with a scattered Indian family here and there who had remained half-heartedly to till their own farm after receiving it from the mission. These dots of land could be bought—the rest could be taken.

The mission itself stood a little crookedly as if having grown feeble and doting. Tiles were gone from its once trim roof. Blocks of adobe were gone from the walls. The shrubs and trees had died for want of care. Missionaries had become parish priests. Far-flung, unreachable boundaries had shrunk to dooryard size. Churches had become relics, empty most of the time.

Yet it was hard-won land. Sometimes Francisco thought it had been harder to acquire than the beginnings of Dos Ríos. There had been little satisfaction in the getting of it. To get it, there had to be talk, trickery, underhand intrigue. There had to be slippings and slidings about. There had to be words spoken with two meanings, words carefully chosen. There had to be hairfine lines drawn between legal and illegal. But in the end Dos Ríos was twice as big. Esteban—and the others—

would be wealthy rancheros. The heritage sufficient for two boys had swelled to be enough for four, abundantly, lavishly. Old men became broken and died. Years of time were wasted. Plantations diminished to patios. The church roof caved in like a badly used horse, the ribs of its rafters plainly exposed. He had been sorry for the gaunt old man, Father Gabriel. But even as he pitied him, something cold snapped shut in his brain. This was land. This was wealth. There could be no softness, no quibbling where this was concerned.

There had been criticism and holding back in the eyes of some of his friends, demurs on the part of Acuña and Sal, God-fearing, Church-fearing men. Lines settled themselves about Francisco's face. But men were men, and in the end each had taken his share. All, strangely enough, except Enrique Padilla.

"I will go north, señor," Enrique had said holding in his nervous mount with careful attention. Noonday heat had beaten on their faces. Francisco had found himself almost pleading.

"Stay, Enrique, and take part of this land. We could be next-door neighbors."

The younger man's face was immobile. Nothing showed in his opaque eyes.

"Enrique, you act like a child," Francisco had said harshly. "Don't be a fool. If you don't take it, someone else will—what difference who? The die is cast."

Enrique had bowed, his face glistening with sweat. "I am perhaps foolish." For the first time he spoke with coldness toward Francisco. "But I would always feel guilty. I've known this to be mission land too many years. I've separated your cattle from the mission's for too long. What was the mission's will always remain so in my mind."

Francisco had been silent for a time exploring

with reluctant insistence the feeling of dissent between Enrique and him. "Think it over, Enrique," he said gently. "This thing is done. You took no part in it, but there is no reason you shouldn't benefit. Anyone's gain is always someone's loss. Look at it that way. There is plenty of land here—and already broken and tillable. You can have a great hacienda." His voice stopped as if of its own accord. His arm remained upraised, pointing. There should have been a sea of brilliant grain. There was a lowering cloud, as if a storm had sunk earthward.

Padilla had paled under his tan. "What is that?" he said, but he knew without asking. Fire! In an instant both men spurred their horses. The mission's wheat fields were burning. They rode like the wind, yet scarcely seemed to draw any nearer. They rode in forlorn hope, for they knew they could do nothing but watch it burn, and yet they had to get there—— They had to see it.

Any wind was hot wind. To breathe was to scorch the nostrils. Sweat streamed and brought no relief. The pounding of the horses' hoofs was echoed in the pounding, almost bursting, pulses of the men.

In the mission yard there was pandemonium. Nothing was right. This yard had never slept in the sun! Indians had never drowsed here! This was a portion of hell. Everything was insanity and the priest was a madman.

Father Gabriel was mounting a horse as Padilla and Francisco slid from theirs, the blood fairly bursting from their eardrums.

"Father, Father——" Padilla had screamed rushing after the priest. Gabriel did not hear him. He was gone, off on his wild horse at an incredible pace. He was yelling something disjointed, unintelligible, as he headed for the vineyards. In his skeleton hand a torch burned whitely in the sun.

He was firing the fields. He was firing the orchards. He was firing the vineyards.

The mission was lost to his children, and the Spaniards should have nothing but burned earth for their share. His thin flesh was bruised and grimed. He rode like a comical drunken scarecrow, all sharp lines and angles, with graceless, wildly waving arms. You could laugh at him or weep for him.

His children, the Indians—the few who were left—were engulfed in the hysteria of the old priest. It was a game. It was a nightmare. The priest, like a little stick doll in the distance, rode into the sandy vineyards and, leaving his horse, plunged from vine to vine in a zigzag course. The Indians felt the contagion. They shouted long-forgotten war cries, war cries they had heard only during dances. They were dark demons who took the part of children in the game.

Flame, almost invisible in the glare of noon, had swept the grain fields, burning up the food, twisting the frenzied trees, ruining the fruit, searing the vineyards, rendering the grapes unfit to be trodden into wine.

Those quiet ones who did not join, but did not stop the others, wept and wailed in anguish to see a priest gone mad. Yet there was a fascination here. This was hell; so they were all in burning hell. In the grip of hysteria someone began to ring the bells. There was nothing mellow in the iron throats. There was stridence, hoarseness, discord. They smote the ears of all who heard, mingled with the roar of frantic fire, the war cries and the weeping in a senseless threnody.

When it was over, when Padilla and Francisco had carried the exhausted priest from the vineyard back into the mission yard, the air was crackling with heat. Bits of ash floated and swirled about them like hell snow. The old man didn't struggle against them. Francisco's hand ached where he had beaten out the flame of the coarse habit. Gabriel's emaciated leg showed through, dirty, grimed, and a little burned. He was as light as a bundle of sticks in Francisco's arms. Enrique, unable to speak or cry, had brushed aimlessly at some burned wisps of his hair.

Both men had stopped at the door of the long building. Father Patricio stood there, immovable as an oak, big and hard, his eyes like granite. "Give him to me," he had said tonelessly.

"Patricio—Father—you were here," Francisco had said, his voice hoarse in his parched throat. "You let him——"

"I let him," the other said dully. "It is his work. He may destroy what is his."

The two men looked at each other for a long time. Somehow the elder priest was put into the arms of the younger one.

"Don't say anything, Francisco." Patricio spoke without expression. "There is too much to be said on both sides. Nothing stands alone. Events are a chain. If you do one thing, you must do another. No one is completely faultless—or completely to blame. Go away."

He laid the old priest down on the rawhide bed where he had slept so many comfortless years. They all knew he was dead. Francisco and Enrique turned away, unable to see for the glare, unable to hear much for the din, but they knew that Patricio had begun to weep, and they were bitterly grateful for the noise so that the sound of a strong man weeping would not echo forever in their memory.

"I will go north," Padilla had said, as if the frenzied gap had never intervened. On their horses heading for Dos Ríos, Padilla had said again and again, "I will go north."

"Far north then," Francisco had answered harshly. "Mexico is generous if you settle right below the Russians. They want a chain of Spaniards there. You won't be a poor man."

"I have some money. I have been careful," Padilla had said with half his mind, hearing the crackle of flames eating the wheat.

"You may have anything of mine that you want, Enrique. I owe you that. You will start with an excellent herd. We will drive them up north when you have filed your claim, and every rancho we pass will swell its number."

Now the land was got, and soon Padilla would drive his cattle northward. A small house had been erected and he talked of marrying soon. In a few months he would be gone.

In his place would be Diego Llanes and someone else. Dos Ríos had stretched into twice its size in slumbering hills and valleys which burst into life with crops, produce and food for roving herds of cattle.

A chill crept into the air and Francisco kicked a knot of wood onto the small flame in the grate. A long way from the burning fields of the mission. The mission was a dwindling church and Patricio was its dwindling pastor. The man had aged. Gabriel's scant bones had been buried beneath the altar and he slept, Francisco hoped, in some peace. It was all over now.

It had taken a long time, a toiling and exasperating time. The mission system died hard, in bits and portions. This group and then that. There was much confusion and quibbling. There was much of everything unpleasant. This thing slipped away and that thing was retrieved. Men became vague; their words were veiled and they spoke with a double tongue. The land was somehow portioned out. Some of it was bought, some taken, and some drifted into possession.

In the confused shuffling, missions became churches, settlers became rancheros, and rancheros became cattle barons who didn't know how much they owned. There was nothing left of the burned fields on the new portion of Dos Ríos. They had been reseeded and replanted, and no one could tell where the old Dos Ríos ended and the new began.

Different priests reacted in different ways. Some were angry, outraged men, some were disappointed men, some were bitter men, some were mild men who let fortune take its course and saw the Indians leave them with a minimum of anguish. When it was time to eat and there was no food left, some of the indians returned. When disease overtook them and they died like flies, the priests did what they could and said little or much as was their nature. The mission with the charred fields was forgotten. No one remembered when Dos Ríos hadn't been as it was now.

Francisco knew the line. Because he had known Dos Ríos as well as the palm of his hand, he could see the line. Sometimes he rode to it and stared gravely at the invisible boundary. Sometimes he remembered the old priest rushing from grapevine to grapevine. Sometimes he thought of Patricio and the careful politeness with which they now spoke to each other. Or he thought of Enrique Padilla's withdrawal.

He frowned, coming back to the problem at hand. Who could take the place of Enrique? His holdings were so vast now that two men would have all they could do to oversee them. Leaning back and closing his eyes, he called up all the faces on his rancho, first one then another, examining and rejecting in his mind, thinking with regret of Guillermo who was lost.

Delfina, growing old quickly, remained in the ironing room of the house. Her children played about the doorway of the two-room adobe shack in the *indiada*. Guillermo looked after them half-heartedly as they ran wild with the numerous other children of the rancho. He was never entirely sober, but only occasionally very drunk. He seldom wept, and seldom raged any more. Sometimes when he became bitter and sullen he got very drunk and went into Los Angeles, rode up and down the main road, shouted and fired his pistols. Many times he was thrown in jail.

With money from Francisco Delfina stolidly paid the fines and brought him back to Dos Ríos. She took care of him; she even loved him at times. Most of the time he was little trouble. He sat in the sun before the door of the small house, enjoying the gleam of it on the wall, the leaves and the dark bodies of his children—at least he assumed they were his. He would sit and strum his guitar and sing in a husky voice the beautiful songs that Angelo had taught him so many years ago, for his own amusement and that of any children who cared to cluster about and listen.

It was waste.

Abruptly Francisco rose from his chair and left the house. He walked on feet as silent as an Indian's out of the patio, past the kitchen garden and the melon patch into the *indiada*. Stopping before the rude door of Guillermo's house he rapped with the butt of his whip. The door opened, and when Delfina saw it was Francisco she flung it wide. He could see the quick pulse beating in her throat. They had met each other only impersonally since her marriage to Guillermo.

"Your husband is at home?" he asked stepping inside.

Guillermo rose from the table where he had been seated, and looked with a blank face at Francisco.

"I wish to speak to you, Guillermo."

"Speak then." The tone held neither respect nor disrespect.

"Enrique is leaving Dos Ríos, as I suppose you know. In view of that and the increased holdings I will need two *mayordomos*. Diego Llanes will be one. Would you like to be the other? The requirements are difficult—you know that. Delfina would no longer be employed in the house. You would have your own establishment at the other end of the rancho." His voice was hard. "I ask that in making a decision you consider your children. Good night."

He left the dark little house abruptly. He had cleared the *indiada* and reached the wall of his patio when he heard the pound of footsteps behind him and turned to wait for Guillermo. There was little moonlight and they could not discern each other's features.

Guillermo's voice was harsh. "I could not. I'm no longer a man. I'm a drunken relic."

"There is no man so drunk that he can't become sober."

"You violated my wife."

"She was not your wife at the time."

"You allowed me to marry her and father your child."

"I made a mistake. I offer no excuses. I thought I could make it up to you. Apparently I couldn't. I'm sorry."

There was a long silence. Then Guillermo spoke again, thoughtfully. "What makes you think I have the brains to be a *mayordomo?*"

"I know you," Francisco replied simply. "I

knew you when I took you out of the yard at the mission and washed the dirt off your body. You were reared in my home. I named you."

Guillermo's teeth gleamed suddenly in the darkness. It was half grimace, half smile. He was being offered his manhood again. There had been mistakes. They were past. He would have his own home. His wife would preside at his table in a silken gown, his children grow up to be respected members of the community. He would be the *mayordomo* of Dos Ríos, a job which carried position and prestige. Or he could remain where he was, sitting forever in the sun against the adobe wall, bemused, surrounded by dirt and children. He could grow old there as the Old One had, and Francisco would never send him away and he would always be cared for.

"I will be *mayordomo*," he said.

Chapter 26

Guillermo stopped his horse on the rim of the hill and looked down over the great saucerlike valley. Behind him on each side the hills fell away sharply. The grades were abrupt and steep. He had set out before dawn because he wanted to speak to Francisco on business. He knew, with a solid feeling of accomplishment, that he was an excellent *mayordomo*, and Francisco would listen thoughtfully to any suggestions he put forward. As he started the horse downward, marshaling his facts in his mind, all thought suddenly washed from his brain and he froze into instinctive stillness.

Stampede.

Unmistakably there came to his ears the thunder of a wild undirected herd. Then the cries of *vaqueros*. No. These cries were sharp and shrill. Children! Dos Ríos children. Those wild, willful little boys.

Guided by the sound he turned his horse up the incline to his left, and there across the mesa came a fair-sized herd of steers, ready for market, branded, ear-notched, probably already sold. They thundered directly at him. His horse reared in sudden terror and of its own volition raced for safety. There was no chance of turning the course of the stampede, for the steers were too near the edge of the steep hillside. Grimacing he watched the brown tide of cattle close in and heave over the side of the ravine. Screams of pure animal terror, screams of death, arose from the herd.

The cries of the young *vaqueros* diminished as they dashed up to the edge and peered over in a frenzy of excitement at the mangled mass of lost cattle.

Guillermo spurred his horse to the group which was scarcely a quarter mile away. The four little boys were wild-eyed with joy. "What happened? What are you doing?" Guillermo shouted.

Graciano pushed his hat back so that it dangled down. "We were playing driving off horses," he cried.

"Playing!" Fury rose in Guillermo. Against his will he began to total up the approximate value of the herd just destroyed.

"Yes, you know, the way *vaqueros* drive off wild horses when pasture gets low," Mario supplied proudly. "We drove them off all by ourselves."

Guillermo gripped the pommel of his saddle with dangerous calm. "Those were not horses, as you very well know. Those were valuable steers. I don't know what your father will say to this. I would advise a strong dose of rawhide. Now ride for home—all of you!"

"We are not in the habit of taking orders from a *mayordomo*," Graciano said with dignity. He had a reputation for bad manners. The others looked at him with admiration for his boldness.

"May I ask the young señor what Don Adam is thinking of to let him roam this way?" Guillermo asked. He longed to thrash them all.

"We stole his horse," Joaquin said gleefully. "Don Adam is a long way from home. We're all going to be *vaqueros*——"

"Ride home, all of you!" Guillermo interrupted sharply.

"We may or we may not, as we choose," Graciano said coldly, while the others looked at him uncertainly.

"Maybe we shouldn't have left Don Adam out on the mesa without a horse," ventured Esteban with a little regret.

"Let him walk," advised Graciano. "He is always telling us how people walk everywhere in Boston."

"He will probably be angry," Mario said tentatively.

"Well, Don Francisco will be," snapped Guillermo. "Stay here if you like, but I warn you, *don't drive off any more cattle.*" Furiously he turned. He abhorred all waste, especially when it proved costly to Francisco Estrada. In ill-concealed rage he started again for the house.

By noon the children were coming home at a moderate pace, with many stops and diversions. A time free of all supervision was indeed delicious.

"Wait," Graciano said. The others obediently stopped. "Someone else is coming." He squinted into the distance.

"Maybe Don Adam found a horse," Mario said in rising excitement.

"No. It's Father," Esteban said flatly.

Graciano looked closely at his brother. "I wonder what he'll do," he said softly.

A rueful expression flitted across Esteban's face. "You should be whipped too," he said without malice. They all turned more or less to face Francisco who pulled his horse to a stop before them. The two Miramontes boys swallowed hard and fidgeted with their reins nervously. Esteban visibly braced himself.

Graciano summoned an angelic smile and swept Francisco a bow. "Sir," he began, "have you seen Don Adam? We were enjoying ourselves and——"

"I know," cut in Francisco. "Never mind your

careful words. The damage is done. I came across Don Adam, lent him a horse and he has gone home—in a very bad mood. Also," he continued carefully, "I just happened to ride up on the mesa and was attracted by the sound of cattle bawling. You know something of this?"

The boys looked at one another. Graciano bit his lips, wondering what Francisco would do. He measured the man and for a fleeting moment considered making up a lie.

"You did?" he inquired politely instead.

"I did. I took the liberty of shooting some of them to put them out of their misery. Standing on the edge, I could count nearly three hundred horns. Divide that by two and I come to the conclusion that, at the very least, one hundred and fifty steers went over the edge. Multiply that by the price each brings for the hide, tallow and lard and it represents a staggering sum of money to throw away."

Graciano brightened a little. "But we are rich, aren't we?" he said hopefully.

"And how do you think we got rich?" snapped Francisco. "We got rich because I know how to make money—and hold onto it."

Francisco turned to Esteban. "Why would you do a thing like that? You are intelligent enough to know better."

"I . . . I guess I didn't think about it as money, Father. We were playing——"

"Always think of cattle as money," Francisco said. He took his *reata* and, holding it coiled, looped off about two yards and doubled it. "Get down," he ordered, dismounting. His horse moved a step or two away and began to graze.

"Are . . . you going to whip us?" Mario asked fearfully.

"Yes."

"Wouldn't it be beter to go home first?" Joaquin got reluctantly down from his horse. He spoke in a small voice. "I really think we should be whipped at home."

"Quiet!" Francisco ordered. He knew if he didn't whip them now while he was angry, he wouldn't want to when he got home.

Graciano had sat his horse nervously. He made to join the three boys who now stood on the ground.

"Not you," Francisco said.

Graciano didn't know whether to be grateful or sorry. He stayed on his horse and watched with horrified eyes as Esteban resignedly removed his coat. He laid it neatly on the ground and knelt beside it. A look of acute regret flashed across Francisco's face, and his hand loosened on the rawhide. Then his face hardened. They had to learn. Angelo had never learned anything. He raised his arm and brought the rawhide down across Esteban's sturdy back, cursing to himself the thinness of the shirt.

Graciano watched anxiously as first Esteban, then Joaquin, and then the already sobbing Mario received several hard blows from the end of the *reata*.

It twitched in Francisco's lean fingers when he finished and ordered them curtly to stop crying and mount.

"What . . . what about me, sir?" Graciano faltered.

"You know I don't whip you, Graciano," Francisco answered shortly. "We've had that out before."

"But what are you going to do?" the boy asked, raising his eyes from the *reata* to Francisco's face.

Francisco paused, his hand on the pommel of his horse. The three other children had mounted. Mario's howls had subsided into sniffling.

"You have to do something, Uncle Francisco," burst out Joaquin in an outraged tone. "He did as much as we did. He should be whipped—to death." He finished savagely, furious at the burning skin of his own back.

Francisco's eyes glinted an instant. "Aunt Petra doesn't allow him to be whipped," he said, "much less whipped to death. Rest assured, he will be punished."

"But how?" Esteabn said rebelliously. He loved his brother, but it wasn't fair for him always to go free.

Graciano looked at Esteban, his eyes filled with swift hurt. They all seemed to be uniting against him. He wished for a panicky instant for his mother and gripped the reins hard.

"How, Father?" persisted Esteban doggedly. "It isn't fair."

"Well, let me see," Francisco said. "I can insist that he be kept from going with us to the bear hunt tomorrow."

"No," Graciano said. "I—why don't you let Mother decide?" Even as he said it he colored violently. They all knew how easy Petra was to get around.

"You are a very clever little boy," Francisco said, "but we can't leave it at that. I don't need to explain why. You will stay at Dos Ríos. It's only fair, Graciano. These boys were punished."

"But I want to go," he cried. "I just *have* to go."

"No, I'm afraid you don't, Graciano," Francisco said coiling the *reata* and hanging it on his saddle.

"Your mother will probably stay home with you," Joaquin taunted sarcastically.

"Keep quiet," Graciano shouted. "Listen, sir, why—" he gulped at the enormity of what he was about to suggest—"why don't you whip me too?"

he asked, his voice becoming a little faint. "Then we could all go to the hunt."

Francisco regarded the defiant tilt of the boy's head. Angelo—Angelo in every line of him. He wondered if he could lay a hand on him. If he did, the repercussions would echo to the ends of the earth.

"You don't understand, Graciano," he explained kindly. "Your mother and I have an understanding about that. You realize that you must be punished. The other boys were, and you had a big hand in the mischief."

"I know that," Graciano cried wildly, "but it isn't fair to leave me home when I want to go. They're going. It isn't fair! I've got as much right to be whipped as they have."

"Well, Graciano, that is hardly the point," Francisco began, carefully keeping his face bland.

"My mother has nothing to do with this," the little boy said passionately. "I—I *demand* to be whipped as they were. That's very rude, isn't it? I haven't any manners. I'm the baddest little boy in California. Or *Boston!*"

Francisco glanced at the rawhide hanging coiled on his saddle. "You've never been whipped," he temporized. "You don't know what you're asking for."

Graciano slid quickly from his horse. Tears stood in his eyes. He tore off his jacket and flung it on the ground. He felt on trial, as if the others were standing in judgment over him. His throat filled in his inexplicable longing to be just exactly as they were—not set apart in any way. On the heels of that feeling there welled an abject fear of the rawhide in Francisco's strong hand. With half his mind he wanted to throw himself on the ground and wail for his mother. Never had he wanted her so badly as at that instant.

The thought passed quickly and he stood his

ground before Francisco. "Well, sir?" he demanded.

Reluctantly Francisco took up the rawhide again, measured off the proper length and doubled it. Graciano was a small-boned child, scarcely larger than Esteban though he was older. There was the fragility about him that all the Montoya men had.

As the leather came down across Graciano's shirted back, he tried not to cry out. This was the first time he had every been struck. Acute pain and shock registered on his face.

He felt a bitter triumph on the ride home that he hadn't made a sound. He was positive that he hadn't been spared. His whipping had been as hard as the others', perhaps harder. In a wild mingling of pain and pride he wanted to fling himself at Francisco's feet and cling to him, assure him that he would be good forever, explain to him how much he loved him and that he hadn't really meant to be bad.

"You had better go make your peace with Don Adam," Francisco advised as they reached the house and dismounted. "Now pay attention to what you're doing, Mario. That isn't the way to tether a horse properly." Patiently he took the lines from Marío's grimy little hands and the child watched him intently as the leather seemed to wind itself together magically.

Reluctantly Graciano started into the house, frowning because he had a swift notion that his mother's tears and rage would be harder to bear than the whipping. He pushed open the door to his room, toying with the idea of saying nothing at all. On consideration he had to discard this decision. It would come out anyway. The others always bragged about their whippings once the actual pain was over. When the sting subsided, it was a little exciting. He paused, a half-smile lighting his face. He had had a whipping! Just like anybody else! He stuck out his chin a little, and took a swaggering step or two across the room. And Santa María, how it had hurt! How bravely he had stood it! He gazed into the mirror admiringly. There were clean smudges beneath his wide eyes where the tears had dripped over and been rubbed away. But he hadn't cried *out loud,* like a child. Like little Mario. Poor little Mario—such a baby.

"Graciano!" Petra came in and stopped in her tracks as she saw her son's tear-stained face. "Mother of God, what happened to you!"

He turned to face her, beaming. "I got a whipping!" he said, his voice ringing with pride.

Francisco never knew the stormy scene which passed between Petra and her little son, for Graciano had his way and the whipping was never mentioned. Petra shed secret tears in the privacy of her room over the welts on the child's back. She longed to rush downstairs and speak her mind but swallowed the impulse.

She lay a long time that night staring into the darkness. It was wrong, all mixed up. Graciano's parting words rang in her mind. "Don't say anything about anything!" he had shouted angrily, "I was bad. Everybody else got whipped. They would have laughed at me." Then his tone had lowered. In quick change of mood he thrust his hand lovingly into hers. *"Mamacita,"* he said softly, "do you think he would care if I called him 'Father' as Esteban does? I would like to have him for my father."

It was on the bear hunt that Esteban and Graciano discovered the strangeness of their relationship. After the three-day hunt, the party, its numbers increased by several friends, arrived at Dos Ríos.

Petra, laughing with sheer relief at the safe return, rushed out to meet them. "Graciano! Boys! You're all right?" she called, as they dismounted and trooped noisily into the house.

"We got a bear. You should see him."

"We left him in the south corral. Mother, you never saw such——"

Don Cristóbal Quixano broke in. "Doña Petra, we hope you will excuse our untimely arrival, but we saw Francisco's party and had to join——"

"Untimely!" she said, holding Graciano's hand. "Your visits are never untimely. Please come in. The house is yours."

"And guess what, Mother," shrilled Graciano. "We found out something. I am Esteban's nephew!" He gazed at her, his eyes brilliant at the delightfulness of this discovery.

"And I am his uncle," put in Esteban proudly, "and we are also brothers," he added methodically.

Petra fell back a little, things going slightly out of focus. "What on earth are you talking about?" she said, not knowing whether to laugh or cry.

Francisco, who was accompanying the other men to the back of the house, stopped and turned. "They have just figured everything out, Petra," he said carefully. "It happened night before last. We were sleeping out and they got to talking. It came out that their relationship was a little more complex than Mario's and Joaquin's."

"They are only brothers," Graciano said breathlessly.

"They nearly drove us mad with their continual referring to each other." Pedro Quixano laughed. "It was 'Uncle-brother, what do you think of this?' and 'Brother-nephew, shall we do that?' Such chatterboxes!"

"Why didn't you tell me that Esteban is my uncle?" Graciano insisted pulling at her hand.

Suddenly blinded, Petra turned to go upstairs. "Stop laughing. It isn't funny," she said. "Come with me. You are filthy. Both of you!" She fled.

The children followed her, a little wonderingly. She felt an incoherent resentment against Francisco. He had made a joke of Angelo! He had let them laugh at the mixed-up family relations. He had made light of them. She wasn't ready to explain it all to Graciano yet, she thought passionately. Time later to let him understand how the tangled family had come into being. Francisco shouldn't have taken it on himself. Angrily she splashed water into the wooden tub.

"Come in here and take your clothes off," she ordered sharply.

With strange obedience Graciano did as he was told. Peeling off his grimed garments he got into the tub and began to soap himself. "Are you angry, Mother?" he asked after a time. "Esteban said you were."

Francisco opened the door and stepped inside. Graciano flashed him a grin. "I look paler, don't I?" he asked holding up one clean arm.

"Much paler," Francisco agreed, and turning to Petra he said, "I thought I'd better come in and do some explaining."

"That won't be necessary," she said coldly, giving Graciano all her attention.

"Yes, it will, my dear," he answered quietly. "Go in the other room and dry off, Graciano. I want to talk to your mother."

Petra hastily swallowed a hot countermand. Better let him go, for if it came to a question of whom to obey, she had no doubt that her son would obey Francisco.

"There is really nothing to discuss," she said distantly, drying her hands. "You have chosen to tell them prematurely—when they are too small to understand. You have chosen to make a joke of something important." Hating herself for her weakness, she found that she could not go on.

"I didn't make a joke of it, Petra," he said very gently. "I would hardly make a joke of anything which is as valuable to you as Angelo's memory. And it wasn't premature. If they weren't ready to know the story, it would never have occurred to them to ask. I admit I didn't give it a somber tone, but that is because I don't think children should be burdened with their elders' woes. They are young a short enough time."

"But, Francisco," she burst out, near tears, "they laughed. They were making fun. This—this uncle-brother business——"

"They weren't making fun, Petra. That was the only way I could handle it. The other two—Joaquin and Mario—were there. All of a sudden before I ever noticed it, the thing had developed into something terribly important. You know how children are about any departure from the set pattern. They had teased Graciano until he came close to crying. I couldn't let it spoil his trip. I had to make it seem special. I had to put it in a different vein. The kindest thing I could do was make Graciano and Esteban seem enviable. I wish you could understand."

"When did it come up?" she asked sullenly.

"After we had lain down for the night. There was something about sleeping out that kept the children talking until late—no doors shut in between, no barriers."

Petra could see them, wrapped in their ponchos on the ground or on willow branches, with the wide waste of land around them, the black velvet sky overhead and the clean air sweeping down from the mountains, their young spirits drawn together in intimacy. And from this first serious problem, this first confidence and explanation, she had been left out. Francisco had been in it.

There was a rap on the door.

At Francisco's invitation the door opened and the two boys stood there. Graciano gave Esteban a little shove, came in after him and closed the door with a decisive snap. Esteban was now painfully clean and neat.

"Mother dear," Graciano said in a tone she could seldom resist. He came and took her hand and held it. "Mother dear, are you angry with us?"

"I . . . don't know," she said uncertainly, her eyes filling.

"Well, just be angry with me," Graciano said resolutely disregarding Francisco's faint look of surprise. "It was all my idea. I thought of the whole thing. I don't want you to blame Esteban—for anything."

Petra glanced uncertainly at Esteban standing miserably just inside the door. The child's face suddenly flamed.

"You can see that it's nobody's fault but mine," Graciano persisted.

"Well," Petra said completely out of her depth, "I—I'm not blaming Esteban particularly. I—I just thought you were making fun——"

"Oh no," Esteban burst out, "we weren't making fun. We only——"

Francisco made a slight sound. "Graciano," he said gently, "aren't you a little mistaken?"

"No, sir." Graciano whirled about to face Francisco, his eyes eloquent. "I have it all straight."

"If you have, then I'm mistaken," Francisco answered, "because I seem to remember that although Mario started the discussion, it was Esteban who worked out the relationship."

"Oh, Father!" Esteban cried.

Graciano gritted his teeth and flung his hands into the air. "Santa María! Don't you see," he cried, "you've spoiled it? I know Esteban thought of it. I know that. But if I tell her I did it she won't be angry with Esteban—and she won't be angry with me either."

Color swept into Francisco's face, and his jaw went hard. His eyes flicked over Petra with something like contempt in their clear depths. "That was very clever of you, Graciano," he said steadily. "Did you figure that out or did Esteban?"

"I figured it out."

"I thought you did, motivated, no doubt, by a sincere desire to protect your brother, and a thorough knowledge of your mother's rather strange idea of fairness and discipline."

"I—I suppose so," Graciano said doubtfully.

"Isn't this rather illuminating to you, Petra?" Francisco asked.

Petra had colored violently at the perfidy of her little son. She turned her face and refused to meet her husband's eyes. "I don't think we need discuss it," she said stiffly.

"I do. Doesn't it seem odd to you that one of your children would lie to you to protect the other one? Does that strike you as the action of a normally raised pair of children? One is reluctant to face your anger, the other secure in the knowledge that no matter what he does he won't be punished. Something is wrong there."

"Well, need we discuss it before them? That isn't right either," she said.

"No, perhaps not. Graciano, didn't it occur to you that lying to your mother—even to make sure she wouldn't be angry with Esteban—is wrong?"

"You mean it isn't honest?" Graciano asked, faintly embarrassed.

"Decidedly not honest," Francisco said flatly. "You should always be honest."

Graciano gazed into Francisco's face, with something like awe in his eyes. "Are you always honest, sir?" he asked incredulously.

Petra gave a short unpleasant laugh.

"Well, let us put it this way," Francisco said carefully: "I was always honest with my mother. And you can be no less honest with yours. Now why don't you run on downstairs? Your mother and I will follow shortly."

Petra gave Graciano a quick little pat on the head to show she wasn't angry at his lying. She smiled at Esteban still standing uncomfortably just inside the door. His face lighted up with a sheepish grin, and they went noisily out. Petra and Francisco were quiet as they listened to the boys clatter down the stairs. Something stirred in Petra's memory. Something in the expression of Esteban's face was terribly old and familiar to her.

She was trying to place it when Francisco spoke. "I'm not implying criticism, Petra. The only fault I can find in you as a mother is your marked partiality."

"I love Esteban," she said defensively. "You can't say I don't, Francisco. What kind of a woman would I be not to care for a child I bore?"

"I don't doubt that you love him. You couldn't help yourself. He is a very lovable child. But you love Graciano so much more—and you show it. You are positively mauldin over him. It comes to a pretty pass when an eight-year-old child can outwit a grown woman. That is what happened. Don't turn away. Listen to me. He figured this out all by himself. He knows you so well that he knew you wouldn't be angry with him, and for the same thing you would be angry with his brother. That, you must admit Petra, isn't a healthy attitude for either of the children to take."

"But don't you understand——"

"I understand a lot more than you think I do, my girl. The incident proves that Granciano loves his brother unselfishly. But it's bad for any boy to let another take the blame—even slight—for something he did. If boys do that in small things, it's very likely they would do it in more important things."

"Well, after all, Francisco, why bother with it now? There are guests waiting. What's one little lie?"

"How do you know it's one?"

"What—what do you mean?"

"How can you be sure this is the first time? For all you know, Graciano may have been confessing to numberless infractions which are Esteban's. They have probably worked it out between them. It is a lot easier for Graciano to take all the blame. They know you won't punish him—even scold him. Now I've noticed a lot of meals that Esteban has skipped for misbehaving, though, come to think of it, he has kept out of trouble remarkably well of late," Francisco finished dryly.

"Well . . . it isn't . . . it isn't that I don't love him," Petra began. "It's just that I love Graciano so much I—oh, you don't understand! You can't ever understand anything but what *you* think. I have to hold onto him, Francisco," she cried. "I . . . he's growing away from me."

"Oh no, Petra," Francisco said softly, "he isn't growing away from you. He's just growing up, that's all. You can't keep him a baby all his life." He caught her arms and pulled her around to face him. "My dear, for your own good don't try too hard to hold another person. It doesn't work out. Believe me, I know."

He let her go. "Well, as you said, the guests are waiting. Cristóbal was starving two hours ago. I suppose he'll want his dinner."

"You go down. I'll be down in a moment," she said, her voice sounding muffled and constricted in her throat. As he closed the door, she stared blankly at its polished surface. She remembered now. She could place the memory of that expression which had flitted for an instant across Esteban's face.

It was a reflection of her own father, *her* father in Esteban! She sat down, confused impressions milling in her mind. How many hundred times had she observed that sheepish half-smile on her father's face? She had always thought of Esteban as exclusively and specifically Francisco's son. But he wasn't. He was as much a part of her and her people as he was of Francisco. She explored the idea slowly. Somehow it detached Esteban from Francisco in her mind. The little boy began to emerge as a distinct and separate person, to be thought of alone, apart from Francisco. Her father and Francisco had never met. Papa had died before they even knew such a person as Francisco Estrada existed. And yet in Francisco's son had been a quick reflection, a fleeting image, of her father.

She stood up a little distractedly. Those guests hungering for their dinner. She must go down. Walking down the stairs with a careful, polite smile on her lips, she sensed an integral design, each part bound up inescapably with the others. Never again would she think of herself and Graciano as a separate segment, as Angelo's wife and child. They were all like a tangled skein of thread. It was impossible to tell where one thread left off and another began.

Francisco had been right, of course. Wasn't he always? She went into the dining room, taking pains to be especially pleasant to his guests. She showed extra graciousness to Don Cristóbal, who was Esteban's godfather, knowing it would please Francisco. This caused her a secret wry amusement. Was she becoming like Catalina? Hanging on his every word? Catering to his every wish? Seeking out ways to please him?

* * *

"Now," began Don Adam the next morning during lessons, "if forty steers were driven wantonly over a cliff, and each steer's hide was worth two dollars, how much money would the ranchero lose?"

Sheepish grins showed on the boys' faces. Isabela, looking properly stern, raised her hand as she swiftly figured out the answer.

"Don Adam, don't you think someone could go down in the ravine and get the hides?" asked Graciano.

"We are learning arithmetic, my boy. Don't try to get my mind off the subject." He grinned to take the sting out of the words. "Now," he said, "if a poor man's horse was stolen by young thieves, and he was left to walk—quiet please!—and he was left to walk sixteen miles, how long would it take this poor tired man to reach Dos Ríos if he could walk four miles an hour?"

After a time he said, "That is all of that. We will now begin the other." He took a small leather book from his desk. This was met with whoops of delight. Immediately all attention was focused on the new lesson. Graciano was the teacher in this, and they worked with absorption.

"You are a very good pupil, Don Adam," Graciano pronounced when it was over and he snapped shut the limp leather book. "You may go now," he added with an imperious wave of his slender hand.

Joaquin, Mario and Esteban laughed delightedly. Adam as a pupil instead of a teacher was a very enjoyable person. Woe to him if he missed a response or made a mistake! The children riduculed him mercilessly.

"In what is he a good pupil?" Catalina asked from the doorway, a smile dimpling the corners of her mouth.

They all rose and bowed to her.

"We are teaching Don Adam this catechism so that he can accept the faith and be saved," Esteban said sanctimoniously.

Catalina's laugh trilled out. "So he can be saved and get a land grant?" she asked coming into the schoolroom.

"Something like that, doña," Adam answered grinning, "though it is a comforting thought to know that my soul will be saved, too."

"Don't you think it's good of us to save Don Adam's soul?" Mario asked taking his mother's small fragrant hand.

"I think it's very noble of you—all of you," she said solemnly. "Now why don't you run outside and play? I wish to speak with Don Adam."

Obediently they trooped out, letting Isabela, after some scuffle, go first. Adam and Catalina listened to the diminishing noise as they reached the patio.

"I wanted to ask you about Isabela," she said coming to face him by his desk. "I am very grateful for all you have done for her, but I feel she must have learned enough and should no longer be a burden."

"Burden, doña? As for learning enough, no one ever learns enough," Adam said earnestly.

"But girls don't need to be educated, Adam," Catalina said. "She can read and write, can't she? Isn't that enough?"

Adam laughed. "Well, doña, some hold that learning is no good for a woman, but as for me I would like to keep Isabela in the class. She keeps up the average."

Catalina was frankly puzzled.

"I mean," explained Adam, "That she is the smartest one I have, and the boys keep up because they are ashamed not to. Isabela is a most intelligent child."

When she had gone, Adam took up the catechism again, his bright blue eyes flicking down the pages, queries and responses echoing in his brain. He forgot about Catalina, for her spasmodic little spurts of interest in her children were soon finished. The image of Isabela, however, lingered. Small, compact as her mother, she was pretty and fair as a water color. The mind behind the soft hazel eyes was as keen as his own.

With strange idleness he laid the book aside and looked out the window. Isabela was nearly nine. By the time she was, say, fourteen or fifteen the Estrada boys and her two brothers would have sufficient education either to enter some university or stop studying altogether if they preferred. Then, or before then if advisable, Adam Langley would have completed his journey into the Catholic Church and the citizenship roll of Mexico. He would be a landowner, a ranchero, ready to settle down with a home and children. By that time Isabela Miramontes—— The thought broke off. The childish face swam before his vacant gaze. His ambitious lips shut and he rose to his feet. All in good time. Everything would work out perfectly. Everything was fine.

By the time Graciano was ten he had formed the habit of addressing Francisco as "Father," and Francisco had assumed the responsibility of most of the discipline for him as well as his own son and Xavier's two.

Joaquin and Mario Miramontes resembled the Acuñas and were extremely good-looking and well-behaved. Ysidra said that Isabela resembled the Santanders. She was the acknowledged leader in the classroom, but Graciano was a close second. He showed erratic glints of brilliance, but only when the spirit moved him. Esteban developed into a dependable scholar, but he was frankly more interested in the workings of the rancho than in lessons. He could calculate almost exactly the number of bushels of grain yielded for every bushel sown. He could talk like an adult with the captains and supercargoes who were entertained at Dos Ríos in connection with business. He could estimate almost to a steer the yearly increase in cattle, and the revenue from it.

All the boys were superb horsemen before they reached their fourteenth year. They attended all the rodeos, making themselves useful in running errands and handling small details. Every year from the end of June to the first of October they spent afternoons on the matanza field. They all acquired exquisite proficiency in the use of *reatas* and guns. Francisco was adamant in his standards of excellency. Not one was allowed on the field until he could compete successfully with trained *vaqueros.*

With Graciano, Francisco was especially demanding. He spent countless tedious hours training the boy whose slim hands were so like the beautiful faulty hands of Angelo.

Chapter 27

Esteban looked at the ball costume which Graciano had spread out on the bed. He pursed his lips, and his eyes shone with amusement. "You can't wear it, Graciano," he said. "You know boys aren't allowed to go to balls until they are past twenty. You're only sixteen."

Graciano's brows shot up. "I'm told my father had attended several night dances before he was eighteen. That must mean he started going about sixteen." Graciano smoothed the splendid garments with his slim brown hand. "Isn't this wine-colored jacket beautiful? Look at all the gold."

Esteban burst into laughter. "Pardon me, my brother, but you make me laugh. The way you change fathers!"

"What's so funny about it?" snapped Graciano.

"The way you take advantage! Half the time you refer to my father as yours; the other half you use your own. Graciano, I could weep for shame."

"Go ahead and weep then," muttered Graciano smiling against his will. "It comes in handy, you'll have to admit that."

"Yes, indeed. You manage to get your own way in almost everything. I think it might be nice to have half a dozen assorted parents and play one against another." He picked up the pale wool hat, in the band of which was set a pearl. "This is nice. Where did you get it?"

"It was Mother's. One of a pair of earrings. She lost the other. Don't you think it goes well with the light hat?"

"Beautifully, but I don't think you'll be wearing it to any ball. Why don't you just go to bed along with the rest of us little boys?"

Graciano looked at the big frame of his brother. It was all right for him to say jokingly "us little boys," but when you were little it was a different matter. Instinctively he straightened and glanced into the mirror. Well, he wasn't exactly little. He was about half a head shorter than Esteban when they stood together. It was just that he was smaller-boned, built more slenderly. He gazed gloomily at his reflection. He wished he could stand before Francisco and meet his eyes on a level the way Esteban did.

He straightened again, throwing back his shoulders.

"Have you tried hanging by your neck to stretch?" Esteban asked, laughter running through his voice.

Graciano whirled about, looking for something to hurl at his brother. Esteban leaped off the bed and dived out the door.

Graciano looked at the disordered bed and went to smooth it. He couldn't help smiling a little. It was impossible to stay irritated with Esteban. He regarded the ball suit. Why did women grow up sooner than men did? They started out even as little children. He and Isabela were nearly the same age, but she was considered a grown woman. There was no question about her going to a ball and dancing until early morning. In fact this particular ball was being given in her honor because they wanted to announce her engagement to Adam Langley.

When he went into his mother's room he found her before the glass experimenting with a new comb. It was black wood, set with brilliants. He swept her a bow. "Doña Mother, why bother with new combs when you are as beautiful as you are?"

She laughed at him. "Come in and sit down. Move the dresses off that chair where I can see you. Guess what I did?"

"What?" he asked eagerly.

"You are going to the dance."

"Mother—really? Was Father angry?"

"No, he didn't seem to mind. He laughed and said you'd probably go to sleep in the middle of it."

He laughed easily. "Don't worry, I won't sleep. If you miss me, believe me I won't be sleeping," he said wisely, and Petra grinned at him.

"What a *caballero!* Was Esteban upset when you told him?"

"No, he just laughed." Graciano got up from the chair and took a practice dance step, his eyes gleaming. Petra's breath caught in her throat as she watched him. He stopped at a burst of exaggerated applause from the doorway. Joaquin and Esteban stood there.

Graciano bowed elaborately. "While you boys are sleeping peacefully tonight the applause you are disturbed by will be for my dancing," he informed them.

Even now there was a rising sound of confusion from the floor below. Everyone was making ready.

Joaquin shrugged, shaking his head. "No place to escape to," he said glumly. "Every place I go there are people, people, people either trying on clothes or dancing. Mother has been fixing Isabela up since almost noon. There isn't a vacant chair anywhere. Esteban, did you know that they put two pallets in your room for Mario and me?"

"No, did they?" Esteban asked. "Maybe we could all crowd into my bed; it's pretty big."

"Graciano is sleeping with you," Joaquin said dismally. "The Quixano women are taking his room."

"No," glowered Graciano. "Mother, are they?"

"Well, dear, they have to sleep some place. You boys can all use the same room."

"At least you get to sleep in a bed," pointed out Joaquin acidly.

"There are two mattresses on your bed, Esteban. Why don't you put one on the floor for Mario and Joaquin?"

"Oh, it doesn't matter, Aunt Petra. You know I can sleep on the side of a hill." Joaquin grinned.

"No," Graciano said in a burst of generosity. "Let's go take off one of the mattresses and fix up a bed." He started out the door; the others followed. "We'll put it over by the window. We can move the bureau a bit. Anyway, let's keep it away from the door so I won't fall over it when I come up—late."

The jacket shone like dark wine in the light that filtered out onto the patio. There was the din of music and quick feet. Graciano scowled. They had all known, he thought savagely, that he was too young to be a *caballero*. There were always too many men at a ball, and never enough women! What girl would dance with a boy of sixteen when she could have a grown man of twenty or twenty-five? He kicked a pebble with the toe of his beautiful shoe. He looked hopelessly about the shadowed patio for some diversion. He would *not* go up to bed and admit he wasn't having a good time. He left the patio, feeling badly let down, and wandered out toward the grove of willow and live oak. Under the trees were a couple of oxcart wheels that were used as benches. He could just sit down in the cool night air.

When he reached the dark grove he was vastly annoyed to hear the sound of a scuffle. No peace anywhere! He turned, but was caught by the sound of desperation in a girl's voice. He couldn't understand her, for she spoke in one of the Indian dialects. Indians—well, he could cope with them!

"Who's there? Show yourself!" he commanded sharply and silence fell thickly about him. Becoming accustomed to the darkness, he made out two forms, a man and a woman. The man got up and came to him in a humble shuffling gait. In the patch of moonlight Graciano saw that he was a brave of about twenty, very dark. He didn't recognize him as one of their own Indians.

"Are you of Dos Ríos?" he asked glancing beyond the man to the girl who was endeavoring to hold her torn cotton blouse together. She got up from the ground and sat down on one of the big wheels.

"Yes, don," the man answered.

"New? I've never seen you before." Graciano tried to place the man.

"I came last week, don," the Indian answered. "My whole tribe came to Dos Ríos."

"Well, why don't you go and dance with the others?" he asked idly. He had heard talk of getting another group of Indians for field work and extra cowherds. He supposed Llanes or Guillermo had negotiated with the chief for the removal of his tribe to Dos Ríos.

He turned to the girl. "Why aren't you dancing? The Indians are dancing out back."

"Yes, don," she answered.

"Where does your tribe come from?" he asked sitting down on the wheel beside her.

"From Santa Cruz." She cast a glance at the brave. Graciano noted with sudden interest the smooth glow of her brown skin. Her teeth gleamed. "Make him go away," she said.

Graciano turned to the brave. "Go away," he ordered absently. "Can't you see she doesn't want to be annoyed?"

Without a word the brave left, disappearing among the trees.

"You should know better than to come out here with a man if you don't want to be annoyed," he said with little sympathy. "What is his name?"

"He is Arturo Castro. My name is Margarita. I will marry him someday," she said placidly. "But he wants me to lie with him first."

Graciano grinned suddenly. "I can't say that I blame him."

Her head went back and she laughed delightedly.

"Did you say your name was Margarita?" he asked. "One of my mother's names is Margarita . . . Margarita Petra."

"Oh, that is beautiful!" she said softly. "Is your mother the fair-haired doña?"

"Yes . . ." His voice died out. All at once there was not much to say. He swallowed. "He tore your blouse, didn't he?"

Her dark hand pulled up the cotton cloth carelessly. "I will mend it," she said. "I can sew. My family wishes for me to become a seamstress. They had meant to ask if the house needed someone in the sewing room."

"They possibly do," Graciano said, a slight constriction in his throat. "Very possibly. Señora Llanes is getting rather old. I don't imagine she is much help. Would you like to have me ask?"

"Oh, yes, don," she breathed. "Could you ask? I am living in the house of my parents in the rancheria to the south of the rivers. My father's name is Juan Armijo. His father was a Spaniard."

"I'll ask my mother," Graciano said, automatically doubting her claim to Spanish blood. Her thin blouse slipped down again but she appeared not to notice. "When will you marry this what's-his-name—Castro?"

She shrugged. "Whenever my family says." She leaned back and smiled at him. Her hands were behind her head and her arms gleamed round and golden in the moonlight. "He has been living with our family for two years—since our betrothal. When he can make some money—enough for a house—we will marry."

"Margarita," he said. It occurred to him that Margarita was an exquisite name. He found himself leaning over her. Why hadn't he ever realized what a lovely name it was before?

The music was still loud and spirited. The thud of dancing feet had not abated and it was nearly dawn. He couldn't go in the front door. He was too shaken, too wondering. With an unsteady motion he ran his hands over his face. He felt the yearning for Margarita again, but she was gone. She had faded into the trees and disappeared. Standing by the door with music beating in his ears he felt a sudden sense of irreparable loss. In quick panic he searched his mind for her last name. Then it came to him, a softly spoken word in his brain—Armijo. And she lived with her family in the Indian rancheria south of the rivers. There was only one. She would be easy to find. A delicious warmth pervaded his limbs. But perhaps later she would live in the house—she wanted to be a seamstress. What small hands she had! Heat crawled into his face as he remembered her smooth contours. He had to get away. He must be by himself and think of this new wonder.

Like a bright wraith he slid around the corner of the house and came to stand by Francisco's office window. He tossed his hat in and hoisted himself over the ledge. The hat landed, a pale disk on the dark floor, and rested there. Leaving it where it was he sat down in Ysidra's chair. He had given Margarita his hatband with the pearl in it. Her whisper echoed in his mind, "Give me this, don, to remember," scarcely audible, precious because of its faintness. He had ripped the silver cord from the hat and closed her fingers over it. He would have given her anything. This must be love then! He sat up straight. It was! He was in love. In wonderful content he curled up in the chair. He was in love—and first—before Esteban. His lids drooped and he slept soundly.

Francisco came into the room sometime later and had closed the door behind him before he saw Graciano. He grinned a little. Isabela was betrothed, and pretty soon the people would begin to go to bed—for which he was devoutly grateful. He walked to the chair and stood looking down at the sleeping boy. Gently he cupped the smooth face in his hands and lifted it.

"Graciano," he said softly, "wake up."

Graciano's wide-set eyes opened and he looked blankly at Francisco for an instant. Then remembrance flooded over him, bringing an enticing languor.

"What kind of a *cabellero* are you?" Francisco asked smiling. "It isn't customary for a *caballero* to go to sleep in the middle of a dance. Go to bed, *niño*, where you should have been hours ago."

A quick inexplicable grin, tinged with wickedness, curved Graciano's lips. A gleam of delight showed in his eyes. He rose in cat-like grace and stretched. "I got very tired," he said softly. "You were right, sir. I am much too young for dancing and night parties."

Francisco picked his hat from the floor. "Be quiet when you go to bed. The others will be sleeping. Didn't you have a hatband on here?" he asked.

Graciano took the hat, wondering for an instant what to say. Simple admission seemed best. "Yes," he said noncommittally. "It had a pearl in it."

"Did you lose it?"

"Yes, I must have lost it."

"Well, go to bed. You can find it tomorrow. Good night."

Impulsively Graciano put his arms about Francisco's shoulders and gripped him a moment. "Good night," he said and when he pulled away, his eyes were dancing. Francisco frowned as the door closed. What had the little devil been up to?

Lightly, swiftly, Graciano ran up the stairs. He must tell Esteban and Joaquin and Mario. He paused a fleeting moment before his brother's door. Was Mario old enough? Yes, he was. He must tell them tonight. He would never go to sleep with the knowledge burning in his head like this. He turned the knob and crept in, his teeth gleaming white in the darkness.

He leaped over the sleeping bodies of his cousins. "Wake up," he cried softly. "Esteban, the rest of you, wake up. Oh, come on, Esteban, open your eyes." Esteban groaned and muttered, sleepily fighting Graciano's hands.

"Oh, please wake up——"

"In heaven's name," growled Joaquin, "what's all the racket? I thought I'd never get to sleep because of the music and now you——"

"What is it? What is it? Somebody in the wrong room?" Mario rolled over and slid from the mattress to the floor with a thump.

"Have you been drinking, Graciano?" Esteban said sternly, sitting up in bed. "You've got drunk," he accused rubbing his eyes.

"Yes, my brother, but not on what you think," gloated Graciano. "Sit up now and listen to me."

The three boys sat up. Mario crawled back onto

the mattress and huddled under the covers. Dawn was coming in the window and the room shone with a faint gray light.

"Well," demanded Esteban.

Graciano assumed an angelic expression. "I am in love," he announced softly.

"Santa María!" Esteban whispered savagely. "He wakes us before dawn to tell us he is in love. Go to bed before I beat you insensible!"

"Wait, wait—you don't understand. I—I am having a love affair."

His brother strained his eyes to see Graciano's face in the dim light. "No!" he breathed. "You're joking. Not really!" He clambered to the foot of the bed. "Really, Graciano? Everything?"

"Everything," Graciano returned calmly, surveying the now intent group.

Mario, wide awake now, crossed himself. "How wicked!" he whispered. "What was it like?"

He held them enthralled with his explanation. There was no point in dwelling on his sudden fright and confusion; no need to say he had stolen into Francisco's office and gone to sleep.

"Is it really wildness?" asked Joaquin. "Were you hysterical?"

"I was like a madman," Graciano said grandly. "Afterward I gave her my pearl hatband. Father asked me about it."

"What did you tell him?"

"He assumed that I had lost it and I had to let him think so." He rose and stretched luxuriously. "If you want to ask any questions, do so now. I've got to get some sleep. I'm exhausted," he added meaningly.

Esteban crawled back under the cover and leaned on the pillows with his hands behind his head. "I wonder if I—?" he began tentatively.

"Be careful," warned Graciano in a fatherly tone. "Don't forget you are a year younger."

"But a good deal bigger," Esteban said practically. "Don't worry about me, my boy. I've given some thought to this."

"But you haven't done anything about it?" Graciano said in sudden alarm.

"Well, no," Esteban admitted.

Graciano turned to the others, half naked. "You haven't either, have you?"

The Miramontes boys shook their heads. He sighed with relief and began to strip off his breeches.

Chapter 28

"What about those Indians from Santa Cruz?" Francisco asked Diego Llanes as they watched the workers in the round corral. He kept his eyes on the Indians, giving Llanes a moment to get over his embarrassment and frame an answer.

"I made a mistake, Don Francisco," he answered evenly. "I thought I knew Indians. It seems I don't. Guillermo didn't think they were any good."

"Well, everyone is entitled to a mistake or two during his lifetime," Francisco said easily.

Llanes' horse seemed to share his nervousness and danced from side to side. "I might have known," he said bitterly, "that if they couldn't get along where they were, they wouldn't get along here. Good Indians usually stay where they are and don't move about from place to place."

"Do you think you can get them into shape, or shall we send them off?"

"I—" Llanes hesitated—"I'd like to try a while longer. They are a lazy worthless lot, but there are some decent ones among them. I've taken two *vaqueros* from the group. I believe Doña Petra has spoken of one of the girls to be put in the sewing room."

"She says so, though I wonder that she doesn't take a girl who has been at Dos Ríos longer."

They watched the workers with narrowed eyes. They were doing fairly well, but Francisco knew that as soon as he and Llanes left, work would slack off and time would be wasted.

"Well," Francisco mused, "it is a little early to tell yet. Perhaps when they get used to Dos Ríos, they will prove more tractable. When they come to consider it as home they may be more willing to work." He turned his horse and started away. Llanes rode at his side.

"Are there any particularly bad ones, Diego?"

"About a dozen who are troublemakers. A man named Castro is about the worst. Three of those Armijo men will bear watching. Then there is a particularly vicious renegade, Raul Peña."

"Well, don't look so sad about it, my friend. It is nothing that cannot be remedied. I have to spend a day or two in Los Angeles. Think about it while I'm gone. We need to reach no decision now. We will decide when I return. While I'm in Los Angeles, I'll keep my eyes open and see if I can find some who might take their places."

"Very well, don." Llanes' hat was removed. The two bowed to each other and separated.

Francisco headed back to the house walking his horse, enjoying the warmth of the sun on his face. He was alert for any sign of the boys. He could always tell Esteban at any distance. But they did not come in sight. He assumed that they were busy with their lessons. Adam was not so hard on them lately. He had too much business of his own to attend to. Sometimes he could study with them only one or two days a week.

A look of sober content crept over Francisco's features. What a wild lot they were! Yet he could never be too critical of them, for his own youth was well remembered. It embarrassed him acutely to pull a stern visage and lecture when he knew very well that they broke no more rules than he himself had done—and they knew it too. Most of the time he merely pretended not to see, a subterfuge which stood them all in good stead at times.

He could be fairly certain that Esteban would be intelligent and dependable in most things. Joaquin and Mario could be counted on to follow Esteban's lead. Graciano was the only one to give real concern. Headstrong, not overhonest, but possessing a charm which made it difficult to stay annoyed with him—Angelo's charm, Francisco mused turning into the yard and dismounting.

While he tied the horse, his eyes swept the yard and fell on a girl. Swiftly he began to tick off faces in his memory, trying to place her.

She stood at the edge of the patio, hesitating, looking longingly at the house, and her hands clasped nervously.

"Did you want something, *niña?*" he asked.

The Indian looked as if she might turn and run away, so he waited patiently. She was—or appeared to be—about fifteen. She was barefoot and dressed in a shapeless cotton dress which she had pulled in at the waist to show off her rounded body. She took a hesitant step toward him and, swallowing hard, started to speak. "I have come to speak to the Doña Petra Estrada," she said.

"Well, knock at the door. She is usually in the front part of the house at this time of day." Then remembering, he added, "Are you the girl who wants to sew?"

She nodded wordlessly, her eyes wide.

A smile touched Francisco's lips as his eyes became intent on her necklace. It was a cord of silver, on the end of which hung a solitary pearl of luminous beauty.

He held out his hand. "Where did you get that pearl?"

She very obviously changed color at the coldness in his voice. Her hands clutched at the pearl.

This was the Don Francisco Estrada whose heart when angry was of stone.

"I found it," she said humbly.

"Put it in my hand," he said continuing to hold out his palm.

Wordlessly, with a look of one being crucified, she took it from her neck and dropped it into his hand. He examined it carefully. The cord was dirty, but the pearl hung like a drop of milk, white and shining.

"Where did you find it?"

She appeared completely speechless. Her breast rose and fell with the subdued quickness of her breathing. Then, losing her nerve utterly, she turned and ran like a rabbit.

"Wait!" Francisco called. "Didn't you want to see the doña?"

But she was already gone. He smiled at the flash of her brown shapely legs. He shrugged and went into the house.

Margarita didn't stop until she was well away from the house. The don! She had seen the Don Francisco Estrada and spoken to him! She leaned against a tree to get her breath. Her side ached from the run. She stared at the ground beneath her feet. This was Don Francisco's ground. She looked at it intently, marveling that the very earth she stood on belonged to him. Then she remembered the pearl, and pain and rage rose in her. Her hands came up to clasp her throat where it had hung for so many weeks. It was gone—lost—the lovely milk-white pearl the young don had given her. She caught her breath in remembering him. Her body tingled. She straightened against the tree, recalling that he didn't like it when she slumped. Standing straight, she thrust out her rounded little bosom, feeling that he was looking at her and loving her.

She must have her pearl back. He would get it for her. There was no limit to what the dashing young don could do. He would get her a better one. She could picture his fury when she told him that his father had taken the present he had given her. "He said, 'Put it in my hand,' " she would tell the young don. "So what could I do?" Oh, how his eyes would kindle and glitter! How his lips would draw back with anger!

Then the ever-present worry about Arturo crept in from the edge of her mind. She stared long and morosely at the tree trunk. The joy ebbing out of her, she began to slump a little. Arturo. She could never think of Arturo without seeing his black fingernails and smelling the rank odor of him. And he bobbed up disgustingly. Her family she could pacify by giving presents she had got from Don Graciano, but there was no satisfying Arturo. She began to ponder him, walking slowly away, forgetting to work up her courage to go to the big house again, forgetting a little about the pearl, thinking darkly and fearfully of Arturo.

In the *sala* Catalina observed her daughter with a shade of annoyance in her wide eyes. The child had grown up. All at once she felt old. In quick panic she darted to a mirror and stared for a long intent moment. She was still lovely. Her lips parted in a sigh. Why? she wondered. What did it matter? She turned from the mirror wondering what she could say to Isabela. She was annoyed about so many things. Isabela was so careless about her appearance. Catalina surveyed the neat figure of her daughter. No life. No color. She took little interest in adornment. Her hair—Catalina pounced on that. So prim and neat and colorless.

She had opened her mouth to say something to

the girl when it suddenly dawned on her that in three months Isabela would be married. Then—in swift revulsion—then Isabela might have a baby. She, Catalina, would be a grandmother! This was staggering. She completely forgot what she had been going to say. Panic filled her. What could delay it—just a little while? Anything? But no, it was irrevocable. It would come. They had had the betrothal party over three months ago and they had planned for a spring wedding. Knowing Adam Langley of old, Catalina realized that his Yankee determination would make the wedding occur at the proper time.

She heard a little wheeze of laughter from Ysidra who sat in the corner of the room. How that woman could read one's thoughts. Catalina turned abruptly and left the room.

Isabela glanced up at her grandmother. "Mama is upset about something," she announced composedly, placing her finger in a book to hold the place. "Is it my marriage, do you think?"

"A little, I suppose," Ysidra answered. She had grown much older in the past years. Her eyes were sunk in deep patches of darkness and her face was a network of tiny wrinkles. She got up with difficulty from her chair. "I'm either too fat or too old to get about well," she said; "one or the other. Go back to your book, child. Don't worry about your mother. In all the years I've known her she has never failed to be annoyed at something."

Ponderously the old woman walked into the hall. Isabela bent over her book again, her mind straying to Adam.

Her lips tucked in a moment with a prim little smile. Her eyes twinkled. Busy, busy Adam. A warmth rose in her. How she loved the sandy-haired industrious little man! Kind and decent for all his shrewdness. Sunburned from riding over the rolling acres of his newly acquired rancho, getting the best house for the least outlay of money, seeming to know at a glance every animal he possessed and how much lard could be rendered from its carcass. Clever, prudent Adam, with his hair already receding a little on his domed brow. She sat back contentedly. In three months she would be Doña Isabela Langley y Miramontes. It was a comfortable thought. She would have a husband, children and her own home, and very likely—oh yes, most likely—Adam would someday be the richest man in California.

"There should be a path worn down this hall," Ysidra said going into Francisco's office. "Are you busy? I shall go if you are."

"Only letters," he said rising and pushing the papers away from him. "Come in and sit down." He seated himself again and stretched.

"Go on with what you were doing, Francisco," she said placidly, trying to erase the worry from her forehead, her ears ever tense for the click of a glass against a bottle. Xavier could not be watched every minute.

"Thank you," he answered taking up his pen. "If you hear the boys come in, tell me."

Clasping her hands over her stomach, Ysidra leaned back and closed her eyes. How he doted on those boys! Even as she thought "boys" the image of Esteban rose before her mind's eye. There was something winning about Esteban. He seemed such a well-poised young man, so completely at peace with the world, so steady and dependable. Now, from Adam's tutoring and Francisco's instruction, he promised to be an intellectual replica of his father. Already he was his physical counterpart, not so dark perhaps, but with the same penetrating gaze and subtle humor. It was impossible to think of Esteban without the thought linking itself with Graciano. How odd it was that two such different personalities could be so devoted!

A reluctant smile touched her lips for an instant. That Graciano! A dozen things about him flitted through her mind. How exasperating, how devilish, how difficult and yet how lovable! It was impossible to be irritated with him when he set his mind on pleasing you. Yet at times he nearly drove you to distraction. Angelo all over again. A shadow crossed her mind. Francisco had never been able to cope with Angelo. The shadow disintegrated. Esteban was here to help with Graciano. He respected Esteban's advice when he listened to no one else's.

Shortly before noon the four boys came in. Ysidra grimaced at the clatter they made. "Those spurs," she murmured, but Francisco grinned as he called to them. They ranged themselves politely before the table after bowing to Ysidra.

"I wanted particularly to see Graciano," Francisco said picking up the cord and pearl. "I found your hatband for you. I don't know if it can be cleaned, but the pearl is still good of course."

Graciano's mouth fell open for an instant.

"Why, thank you, sir. . . . Where did you find it?"

"An Indian girl had it, so I brought it back for you. What have you all been doing this morning?"

"You—you didn't do anything to her——" Graciano said uncertainly.

"Do anything? No." Francisco glanced at him assuming a look of surprise. "No. I just saw her wearing it and told her to give it to me and she handed it over." His eyes narrowed. "Did she steal it from you?" he asked blandly.

"No, oh no," Graciano said quickly. "I guess she found it. You remember when I lost it." Color crept into his cheeks.

"As a matter of fact, Graciano," Francisco said slowly, "I remember when you *told* me you lost it.

Perhaps you didn't lose it. Perhaps she stole it. On consideration I realize she must have. Perhaps I'd better have her sent for. We can't have any undue thievery——"

"No. Wait, Father," Graciano stammered. "Come to think of it, I—I guess I gave it to her."

"*Gave* it to her, Graciano?" Francisco leaned back in his chair and looked at the boy, his eyes glinting. "That was very generous of you, Graciano," he said softly. "Are you sure you gave it to her, or did you, perhaps, trade it for something?"

Graciano reddened. Esteban choked. Joaquin sat down on a chair and stared fascinated at his cousin wondering what he would say.

Graciano's head came up. "I traded it," he said shortly.

Francisco regarded him for a long time. "That is very interesting. Tell me—pay attention, all of you—tell me, Graciano, have you initiated your cousins and your brother into the mysteries of love?"

Esteban and Graciano answered together. The first said "no" and the second said "yes." Joaquin prudently kept silent.

"Yes and no," Francisco said thoughtfully. "Apparently one of you is lying. Well, Esteben?"

"It isn't all Graciano's fault," he said placatingly. "He just happened to be the first. I don't imagine it would have been long anyway before I——"

"I doubt if it had entered your head," Graciano said, slightly stung.

Francisco bent his head over the table for a moment. When he raised it, his face was sober.

"I'm terribly sorry, Father, I realize it is sinful——"

"I said nothing of sin," Francisco said with a slight grimace. "I understand this was bound to happen sooner or later. I just thought I'd point out to you that you may as well be intelligent about it."

Joaquin grinned. "Now that I see you aren't angry, I'll admit my share."

There was a quick knock at the door. Petra came in. Graciano cast an imploring look at Francisco.

"Have you changed your mind about going to the harbor after dinner?" she asked.

"No, I'll start when the siesta is finished. I'll probably stay in Los Angeles tonight and tomorrow. Is there anything I can get for you?"

"Yes, if you please. I've made a list. I hope it won't be too much trouble."

Francisco smiled and took the list. He offered Petra his arm and they went into the dining room.

Graciano was nearly asleep after lunch when there was a muffled tap on his door. "Come in," he invited with little cordiality in his tone. Esteban came into the room. "Oh, it's you. Come in and shut the door."

"Yes," Esteban said sitting on the edge of the bed and regarding his brother's slender form. To discourage conversation, Graciano closed his eyes, and the lashes rested lightly on his cheeks.

"You look like a little boy," Esteban said thoughtfully.

Graciano's eyes flashed open.

"Ah, I thought that would wake you up! I wanted to ask you something. I know you've been seeing a lot of Margarita Armijo, and——"

"You haven't been seeing anyone?" Graciano asked pointedly.

"We are talking of you, my brother. Did you listen to what Father said awhile ago? He said, 'as long as you are intelligent about it,' and on thinking of it, I seem to recall that Margarita is betrothed."

"Well, all girls are sooner or later."

Esteban answered patiently, "I know you wouldn't want to find any reason which might make you give her up—and I'm not suggesting at the moment that you do."

"Thank you," Graciano said dryly.

"But I just wanted to impress on you that we don't want any trouble."

"Trouble? Oh, come, they're only Indians. What trouble could there be? Besides—" he smiled suddenly—"didn't you know that's why I keep you around—to take care of trouble. Now why don't you go away? I'm sleepy."

Esteban grinned and rose from the bed. He guessed nothing would happen. And if anything did, he could handle it. But unconsciously he tensed as he thought of Arturo Castro. How like Graciano to rush ahead doing exactly as he pleased, never thinking of possible consequences. He shook his head and went softly past Petra's door, warmth surging through him as he remembered Graciano's confident words.

Chapter 29

The wall looked ghostly in the moonlight. It was of low adobe blocks, surmounted by steer skulls, the horns of which stuck up like white waving fingers. Graciano put his hand about one of them. It was set fast in the mud. His hand was a dark shadow against the white of the bone.

"Margarita . . . Margarita," he whispered, filled with an aching sweetness at the loveliness of her. In the light and shadow he thought he had never seen such a vision. He leaned back against the fence and regarded her. In all the world there were only he and Margarita and the moonlight. Margarita was everything passionate and romantic. He leaned suddenly in sheer joy and kissed her throat.

Her soft laugh pulsed against his lips. It was cut off sharply. She clutched at him in quick dread. "Don . . ." she whispered. Then she wailed aloud, "Oh, don!" and fell to her knees in mortal terror.

Graciano instinctively whirled about. Five Indians stood in a semi-circle about them. He had a flash of pure fear, but managed to flick them all with a swift contemptuous glance. "What do you want?" he asked keeping his voice steady.

"I am Arturo Castro——" one began to say.

"I know who you are," Graciano said impatiently. "Now get out of here. I didn't call for anyone. Get up, Margarita. There is no one here to be afraid of. Well—" he turned back to the Indians—"what are you waiting for?"

There was something in their faces which made his blood congeal in his veins. In panic he computed the distance to the house. It was too far. There was no one else about. A graimace tugged at his lips. Of course, there was no one else about—he had come out here to be alone.

The Indians looked uncertainly at Castro. Graciano grasped at this. If he could intimidate one, the others would follow. They were usually so humble that it took several banded together to arouse courage to face a white person. If one could be shaken, the solidarity of the group would disintegrate; they would cease to be a menace and be only Indians again.

He chose the weakest-looking. "Here, you, what are you doing up here? You are supposed to be on the south range. You're not supposed to be near the house. Get back where you belong or you'll get a taste of Llanes' whip."

"We came up, don," Castro cut in with strange boldness for an Indian. "It is not the practice of my people to let a crime go unpunished. This girl was betrothed to me."

Graciano leaned back against the wall, his mouth going dry. He had to frighten them. He wished passionately that Esteban were with him. One look at Esteban's husky frame would send them scurrying.

"On second thought," he said, "I just might have you whipped myself if you continue to bother me. I have been patient enough. Are you drunk that you haven't the sense to escape while you can?"

It took an effort to keep his voice steady. Castro had taken a step forward. As if given courage, the others closed in a little. Garciano's instinct was to lean closer against the wall, but he forced himself not to draw back.

"Do you want to be punished and sent away?" he asked. "Are you begging for punishment. Do you want to keep your place here on Dos Ríos?"

"We no longer work for Dos Ríos," Castro said seizing the edge of Graciano's finely woven poncho. Fury rose in the boy that the Indian would put a hand on him. He dahsed it away, a glitter in his eyes. For a moment he looked very like Petra.

"Take your hand off!" The words were smothered. The man closed in, and the poncho was muffled about Graciano's head. He fought frantically, kicking, striking out, writhing like an eel—to no avail. There were ten hands against two. The poncho was tight and strong. It twisted about his head, choking him, smothering him.

"It is not my fault," Margarita was screaming in terror. "Arturo, it is not my fault."

Graciano had no time to be amazed at her perfidy. Cold terror filled him as he felt rawhide circle his ankles like a hard snake. Someone hit him in the stomach, crushing all breath from him in an instant. He could hear Margarita's choked pleading. He tried to call Esteban's name but could not.

Before dawn Xavier woke the household singing a love song, instead of a hymn. His voice was coarse and scratchy. Esteban rolled over in bed, wondering if Xavier had gone to bed at all the night before. Sometimes he stayed up all night. As the years passed he had become more confused and lost track of time.

Esteban lay back, amused. How furious Aunt Catalina would be because Xavier had substituted a love song for a hymn! Not that she would show it. She was always very pleasant, but sometimes you could tell by looking at her eyes. He grinned in silent enjoyment. His door opened and in the dim light he saw it was Joaquin. He altered his expression lest his cousin might think the smile meant ridicule.

"Esteban, are you awake?"

"Yes, come in."

"Is Graciano here with you?"

"No," said Esteban. "Why?"

"He's not anywhere. He didn't even go to bed." Joaquin came to the bed softly on bare feet.

"Didn't come in at all!" Esteban slid from the bed, reached for his clothes. In the light from the window Joaquin saw his mouth, drawn and hard.

Apprehension began to stir in Joaquin. "Is anything wrong——He might have slept outside, mightn't he? This once?"

"Not Graciano," Esteban said shortly. "You know as well as I that Graciano prefers to sleep in his bed. Go get some clothes on. We'll have to find him." Something in Esteban's tone, guarded, intent, made Joaquin hurry swifty from the room.

In a very few minutes they met in the lower hall. The household was already stirring.

"Mario *would* come," Joaquin said.

"I can help," the youngest boy said doggedly. "I can always run errands if nothing else. If you don't let me go, Aunt Petra will ask me where you went—and I'll have to tell her."

Esteban slipped his hand over the other's shoulder. "All right, Mario," he said and turned to Joaquin. "We may find him out by that wall—that's where they usually go. Maybe, as you say, he just went to sleep out there. I suppose the house will be in an uproar if we don't get back in time for prayers. God, I wish Father were home!"

The three boys walked their horses until they were well away from the yard. Then they slapped the animals and were up as the horses started. It was a matter of a few minutes' ride to the wall. But which part of it? There was a lowing of cattle and the air was becoming lighter. The ground was wet with dew. Esteban dismounted and walked along the wall. Once or twice he grasped a steer horn in quiet desperation. Graciano might have been here—or there. His hand might have touched this one—or that one. They were all so alike.

"Joaquin, do you see anything—anything at all?" he asked.

Joaquin shook his head. There was nothing unusual to meet the eye. The ground was disturbed here and there, but that could be from anything. Esteban's eyes swept up and down the wall which was nearly a quarter mile long. He began to pace it off, wondering every step he took if he had passed something which would give him a clue to this brother's whereabouts. Never had he felt so childishly stupid and incompetent.

"Where did he say that girl lives?"

"South, wasn't it? By the rivers?"

Without a word Esteban mounted his horse and they headed south at a fast gallop, bending low in their saddles. "It will take forever to get there," he shouted over his shoulder. "Everyone will be wondering where we are. Mother will be frantic."

Those at the Indian rancheria were out and stirring when they arrived. Esteban got from his horse and stopped the first man he saw. About them spread the rounded, reed-thatched huts. Here and there a breakfast of beans and meat was being prepared. Indians squatted around the kettles, dipping their *tortillas* in and scooping out the steaming food.

"I am looking for the family of Armijo," Esteban said shortly. "Which house is theirs?"

An expression of tenseness passed over the man's face. "Armijos have gone from here," he said. Esteban could see his brown belly tighten. "They have all gone."

"Which house?"

The Indian pointed, even then moving away. His attitude said he wanted no part of this, if it were trouble.

Esteban mounted again and they rode to the thatched hut. Even before he went in, Esteban knew it was empty. There were signs of hasty departure. Piles of filth lay about. No stick of furniture or blanket was left. A broken crock lay where it had fallen.

"Here, you!" Joaquin stopped a young girl who was hurrying past. Their sudden appearance at the rancheria had caused considerable disturbance.

"Where have the Armijos gone?"

She shook her head dumbly. "Gone," she said.

"We know that. *Where? Where* have they gone?" snapped Joaquin. "When did they leave?"

"Yesterday," she answered looking uneasily over her shoulder at the group gathering in the doorway of the next hut.

Esteban dropped his horse's reins and stepped over to them deliberately, with no sign of hurry. "Who else speaks Spanish?" he asked.

There was silence and then a brave stepped forward. "I speak."

Esteban looked at him carefully. He was moderately clean for an Indian. "I am looking for a girl, Margarita Armijo. I will pay to know where she is."

There was another period of deliberation, during which the Indian appeared not to see him. "They have gone. They no longer work on Dos Ríos. They went yesterday afternoon."

Esteban waited patiently.

"The man, the woman, and the small children—all but the girl. They left before sundown," the Indian concluded.

"The girl did not leave?"

"The girl was not here, don. She was not here all day."

"About Arturo Castro who lived with them—did he go too?"

"He is gone now."

"Yes, I know that. Did he go with the Armijos?"

"He waited."

"Do you know where he is now?"

There was some consideration. Esteban began to feel dampness inside his shirt. All this took time, too much time. Graciano might be anywhere. He had a wild yearning to see his brother's slim figure.

"I do not know. He went with four other men. They say they do not work on Dos Ríos any longer."

Esteban took some money and held it out to the Indian. It was clear that the interview was over, but he asked another question. "A present for you," he said. "I must find Arturo Castro. I must find him this morning if possible. Can you think where he might have gone?"

The Indian shook his head, accepting the money without comment.

Esteban motioned to Joaquin and Mario. Joaquin leaned far over in his saddle and caught the reins of Esteban's horse. With no sign of haste they joined the group. Esteban mounted. They spurred their horses and went off at a gallop. Clods of earth were flung into the air by the horses' hoofs. The Indian put the money in his belt and went into his hut.

"The only thing to do is go home," Esteban shouted after they had ridden about a league. It was in his mind to get several groups of horsemen to search the rancho from end to end. Llanes and Guillermo could raise three hundred in less than an hour. Graciano had to be found. Sickness boiled in the pit of his stomach. Indians——The thought was not completed, for they saw a horseman directly in their path. It was the same Indian they had talked to at the rancheria. He must have taken a short cut. They pulled up and remained silent, waiting for him to speak.

"I have remembered," he began by saying. "And I thought to ride out and tell you. I am a Christian, don, and desire only to work for myself and my family. I do not wish to place them in any danger. I am a man of peace."

"I am too," Esteban said wetting his lips. "But something has happened to my brother, and I have only a desire to find him."

"I have heard that the Armijos have gone from Dos Ríos because they are afraid of the Don Francisco."

"Have they done anything which would make them fear my father?"

"No, don, but Arturo Castro has—or is. It is his intention to punish that girl Margarita."

"His intention to my brother?"

"He did not say, don," the Indian answered. "He swore only about the girl who has made people laugh at him."

"Where did he go?" Even as he asked the question, Esteban was going over the rancho portion by portion in his mind, ferreting out a place where an Indian would go with a captive.

"He did not say."

"Thank you. I know where he would go," Esteban said. "My father will be grateful to you." He turned to Joaquin. "Will you go with me?"

Joaquin's lips moved slightly. "Why do you even ask?"

Esteban said to Mario, "You can run an errand if you will. Get back to the house and have Llanes or Guillermo rout out some men. Send one to Los Angeles for Father—do that first. Castro will head for the stone caves. That is the best place.

Joaquin and I will go up there. Have some men sent up to help us in case we need help. *Ride!*"

High in the hills where they had had many picnics and bear hunts were the caves. In his mind's eye he could see the rounded, strangely hollowed places in the sides of the crooked hills. Anything could be hidden in that adobe honeycomb. At this moment Graciano——Anger pounded in his eardrums and wet the palms of his hands until the leather he held was slick. Burning in his brain were a dozen fragments of terror tales. A renegade Indian—what wouldn't a renegade Indian do? He felt nauseated again at the thought of anything wantonly marring the smooth flesh of Graciano's body. He tried to think what the renegades could have planned which had frightened the Armijos into leaving without their daughter. Castro had them all cowed. Try as he might, Esteban could not recall Castro's features. They mixed and merged with dozens of other Indian faces.

Esteban and Joaquin were climbing now and the sun beat down hotly on their backs. Of their own accord the horses slackened the pace. This was rough rocky terrain, all uphill by gradual degrees, with the earth split and uneven where chunks of solid rock had been pushed up through the surface in ages past. They were surrounded by little tufts of grass and stringy plants. Trees grew crookedly, branching out at odd angles, and clinging, in a semblance of frozen torture, to the uneven ground. Rocks stacked upon rocks in tipsy unbelievable angles, oddly shaped from rain-washed centuries.

It was nearly nine and the sun was high when Mario flung himself from his swaying horse in the patio of Dos Ríos. He hit the earth with a thud and glanced wildly about in the incoherent hope that maybe, just maybe, Francisco would be there.

"Mario—" Petra dashed out the door—"the boys—where are the boys?" Her face was blanched with fear. "Graciano's bed hasn't even been slept in."

For a moment Mario was unable to speak. His tongue was thick and unmanageable. In an instant the patio filled with people. He clung to the saddle pommel and felt the heaving side of the horse against him. What had Esteban said to do? What came first?

"Llanes!" he shouted. "Guillermo!"

"Llanes isn't here. Mario, *where are the boys?*" Petra laid rough hands on him. He clutched at her wrist. The story spilled out. In spite of everything, in spite of knowing that Francisco was in Los Angeles, he had ridden for many miles holding the image of Francisco in his mind, almost making himself believe that when he came into the patio Francisco would be there to take charge.

In a moment there was wild disorder. Guillermo's voice came to him over the din, shouting orders. His face was harder than usual.

"Don Adam?" Mario gasped.

"Gone—gone!" wailed Petra. Her eyes glittering, she made a dash for one of the tethered horses. Her intent was clear. No Indian was going to lay hands on a child of hers, not while she could ride up to the caves herself, not while she had fingernails and teeth to sink into their flesh.

"No! Doña, no!" Guillermo caught her roughly. The patio had cleared a little. His swift commands had set them all running. Those went for horses. These went for arms. A rider, low in his saddle, turned out onto the road to Los Angeles. His horse scarcely seemed to touch the ground.

"Doña, listen to me!" Guillermo held her struggling form still. In a moment the madness left her eyes and she looked at him. He loosened his grip. "These are Indians," he said. "Indians can deal better with Indians. I will go, doña."

"He is right, Petra," Ysidra said from the doorway, her face ashen. "Go, Guillermo." She added a prayerful certainty, "Francisco will come."

In the cave, Graciano closed his eyes again, not even caring if they saw him. He wished he could close his ears and shut out the sounds Margarita made. She was pleading for her life, sometimes in Spanish and sometimes in her own tongue. He couldn't be sure just what she said for he could not always hear her. In abject terror she was placing all the blame for everything on him. Well, it didn't matter. All the love was lost now. There was no love left in the world. He wondered if he would ever feel anything with his hands again. They felt like stumps of wood from being bound so tightly.

The stick came down on his shoulders again. "Open your eyes, señor!"

He opened them, and retched at the sight of Margarita. How long did it take a girl to die! He tried to speak, but could not utter a sound. He had screamed at them, reviled and threatened them until he had no voice left. They enjoyed the raving. It was no use; it only incited them farther. They had beaten and manhandled him until he was sick to death of them. He had watched with recurring nausea the rising pitch of their frenzy. They talked and drank and worked one another up, feeding on mutual passion until they felt godlike in their excitement. Higher and higher it mounted, making them cry in ecstasy when another blow was struck or another indignity perpetrated. He looked at the wall above Margarita's head, staring hard, trying to lose proper focus so he would see nothing. If only he were blind, deaf and blind! Margarita didn't speak any more, but made little croaking sounds. Finally even they stopped. He hoped she was dead. He tried to pray that she was dead.

"Open your eyes, señor!" Again the stick cracked with a muffled thud.

"Wait!" Another Indian squatted down before the girl and rolled her head this way and that. Graciano's eyes were wide with shock. He waited for the Indian to speak.

"Dead, Arturo," the Indian cried in delight.

Arturo screeched. His voice echoed through the cave. He raised his stick above his head and drove it into the girl, pinning her to the floor of the cave. Then muttering, moaning, chanting, he turned with strange movements to Graciano, the muscles in his legs jerking spasmodically.

Graciano stared at him, hate nearly choking him. The stench in the close cave was suffocating. In madness he wanted to sink his fingers into the dark throat and tear the flesh from it. His lips pulled back from his teeth and he tried to shout his defiance into the other's face. He could utter no sound.

Stooping in convulsive motions, Castro took a clod of earth and forced it savagely into Graciano's mouth. Graciano breathed dirt into his lungs. Strangled, bruised, maimed, mutilated, he would die here with stakes driven into his body by these dogs. Esteban . . . Esteban, he thought as the stick crashed against his head.

Esteban would come. He *would* come. In just a minute, in a second, he must come like a thunderbolt into the foul cave and punish the savages for killing Margarita, punish them for beating him and putting dirt into his mouth.

Esteban was there. *He was!* A garbled picture of Esteban with a fury-twisted face flashed before him. There was a sound of bone cracking and an explosion which rocked them all, tore their eardrums, rang back and forth against the walls. Dust rose, scraped up by boots and spurs. Curses, prayers, obscenities. Esteban's fists, punishing bone and flesh. A dream. A welcome nightmare.

It was all over. Graciano clung to his brother in a grip that would not let him go. "Esteban . . . Esteban," he could only gasp in despair and shock. "They have killed Margarita . . . they have killed Margarita . . . they killed her . . . they killed her . . . they——"

"Graciano, *niño,* please don't. It's all right. Everything will be all right. We'll send someone after them—the rest of them. Guillermo will come, or Father. Oh, look at his head, Joaquin! Get some water to wash his mouth." Esteban began to curse fervently those who had bruised his brother and ground dirt into his tongue and throat.

"Why didn't they stay and fight?" Graciano's ragged voice refused to be still. Joaquin got a hatful of water from a stream, and Esteban, with a torn piece of his sleeve, began to wash the dirt from his brother's face. Joaquin chafed his hands which were nearly black from being bound so long.

"Oh, what fine braves they were," Graciano gasped bitterly, "to kill a girl! Oh, Esteban she was so lovely—you remember how lovely she was—and they—they——"

"Graciano, please——"

Bits of sanity began to filter into Graciano's brain and coagulate; little facts to hold onto. Esteban was here. The cave was quiet behind them. Sunlight lay brightly around them. Two Indians were dead. They lay sprawled in the cave with Margarita. Joaquin, shaking terribly, had tried to lay her out neatly. The others had gone—galloped away like the wind. Now he would lie still and breathe in the dampness of the wet cloth. He would look at Esteban to be sure he was really here. Safety, security. Esteban or Francisco, nothing could hurt them, nothing was equal to them. His eyes closed a moment and then he opened them.

"You said to be careful, and I wouldn't listen," he muttered faintly. Côlor, hot and unhealthy, was beginning to flush his face. His eyes shifted brightly here and there, suspicious even of the bird noises in the trees.

"Forget it. Don't think about it. I'm sorry about the girl—" Esteban looked sad when he thought of her—"but she was dead when we arrived."

Joaquin laid Graciano's hand down, still blue and swollen. "We'd better be getting back, Esteban," he said quietly. "Aunt Petra will be in agony."

Graciano started up, dizziness surging in his head. There was little co-ordination in his muscles. Esteban helped him to his feet. He staggered drunkenly, holding awkwardly to his brother. "My . . . hands . . . don't——" he began.

"They've been bound up too long. They will be all right," Esteban said. "Hold his horse, Joaquin. I'll help him up." His grip on Graciano didn't relax until his brother was firmly in the saddle. "Here, can you hold the reins?"

There was a moment when Esteban looked up at Graciano to make sure he could stand the ride back to Dos Ríos, his mind measuring his brother's strength. He smiled encouragingly at him and held his knee for a moment.

They all saw it too late, heard the whir of it too late. There was time for a split second's disbelief. No! It couldn't be. Those Indians had gone. They had run away. None had crept back. But one had stayed to hide among the rocks and watch them, sliding his hand over his *reata*. It lashed through the air, descended and snapped about Esteban's chest like a snake. He clung for an instant to the pommel of Graciano's saddle, terrified amazement crossing his face. The rawhide tightened. The Indian was mounted. He spurred his horse. It leaped forward. Esteban's hands were ripped from the pommel. He crashed to the ground heavily. He was dragged, bumping, bouncing, snagging, tearing. He gave one hideous cry.

Graciano and Joaquin stood transfixed. Horror washed over their faces. Instinctively they spurred their horses. Forgotten were the damaged hands. As Graciano's horse leaped forward he flung himself through the air onto the rawhide. Anything—anything—to stop its course! He hit it, grasped it and clung, his feet dragging the ground.

At the same instant Joaquin's horse came abreast. He hurled himself at the Indian and they fell to the earth. They groveled a moment together. The Indian jumped to one side, up and away. Joaquin was after him. The Indian's hand closed over a stone. He hurled it straight into Joaquin's face. It gave him the instant he needed. He was up on Graciano's horse and gone.

Graciano realized numbly that the *reata* had stopped. The horse stood nervously, stepping from side to side. The rawhide, loosened, dropped him to the ground. He lay there a moment, then struggled to his knees. He caught a fragmentary view of Joaquin, hunched, swaying, nearly insensible, blood dripping between the fingers he clasped across his face. Graciano, half crawling, half running, started toward Esteban. A strangled sound came from his brother. He stirred once in an aimless, broken motion and lay still, huddled crookedly.

Sobbing, Joaquin picked up a rock and threw it in the direction the Indian had gone. Wiping the running blood from his face with jerky movements he went to the other two. Graciano was crouched, clinging to one of Esteban's hands, his face disbelieving, his mind rejecting the sight his eyes beheld.

"Esteban, you'll be all right in a minute," he was whispering as he kissed one of the hands and smoothed back the matted hair. "Father will come to help us."

They waited, huddling in the sun. Guillermo came in a little while—or a long while. There were many hands to make a litter of branches and a tightly woven serape. The hands were gentle as they lifted the body of Francisco's son and placed it on the litter. A murmur rose from them, part commiseration, part prayer, part fervent anger. Each broken bone was a horror in their eyes. The lifelessness of Esteban Estrada's once strong body was a fantastic and unbelievable thing. There was no place in him for wrenched muscles and torn nerves. Gently, carefully, they began to carry him home.

Dos Ríos land seemed endless. They wound across it slowly, walking the horses. The bearers stepped lightly over stones and rocks. Graciano strained his eyes feverishly into the distance. Somewhere ahead, over that hill or the next, or maybe the next, lay the sprawling house. Mother was there; perhaps Francisco now. A great yearning swelled in him. If they could only get Esteban home! If they could only get him home!

At home Petra waited. She knew by heart every line of the terrain and hills she had stared at so long. She had the whole story from Mario now. Never before had she realized how she depended on Esteban. He would find Graciano and bring him back, she was positive of it. It was a prayer in her mind. She went over all the competent sensible things Esteban had done. There was no possible way for him to fail. He knew the rancho as well as Francisco did. All she had to do was wait. Really that was all. They might be late. They might have got into a fight. They might be hurt a little, dirty, hungry. She stood first at the door, then at the edge of the patio, then out on the road.

When she saw them in the distance she told herself it was only birds wheeling low or cattle on the hill. She must be sure this time. She mustn't run out again only to be disappointed. When she was sure, positive, she started to meet them. Something was wrong. They should be coming fast, galloping in wild disorder, flinging shouts back and forth. But they came slowly, winding, some on foot. Someone was hurt! She began to run, stumbling, her dress snagging on the ground. Her brain was a quagmire of doubt and fear. Which one—oh, which one? She couldn't bear to have any one of them hurt. Sobbing, she tried to recognize the faces. Not Graciano! Not Esteban! Not *either* of them! Her eyes swept the group and fell on Graciano sagging in his saddle; on Joaquin's bleeding face. Esteban? No, not Esteban! The strong one, the big one—not Esteban!

She reached the bearers, unable to speak, her face chalky. With her hand on the litter she walked beside them up the hill into the yard, not seeing anyone, not hearing anything.

She said, "Bring him in, please. . . . That's right. . . . Hold the door, please. . . . Be careful. . . . Up the stairs."

In his room she turned down the covers of his bed. "Help me," she said and they did. She said, "Don't hurt him," refusing to believe he was dead.

The news crept about the house almost silently. Ysidra made a muffled sound, holding onto the newel post at the foot of the stairs. Isabela went up two steps and halted there unable to move. Catalina sat on the edge of her chair in the *sala*, white, stiff.

There was disbelief in the house. Minds rejected the news violently and faces became twisted and pale at the insistence of it. Everything stopped in the weighted stillness which gripped all of Dos Ríos. People could only stand and stare and speak to one another in whispers.

Milling groups increased at the doors, dark faces peered in the windows. Silently the people gathered about Dos Ríos. How long would it take Don Francisco to ride from Los Angeles to find his boy dead—and what would happen then?

Graciano stood at the foot of the bed and thought, Francisco will come home. "Mother," he said. She was sitting in a chair by the window and did not hear him. "Mother," he repeated. "He's going to come home and find me—instead of Esteban."

There was little feeling in him but shame. All the black sunlit day there had been nothing but horror and death. He longed to die with a yearning so great he could not speak again. He was ashamed that he was alive. What could he say to Francisco? No thought in him told him what to do. His facile mind was a dead ash in his head. He wanted to creep away and hide, bury himself deeply in the earth and never see the light of day—never see Francisco. But he must stay, because his legs were numb and he could not move, or because he didn't want to leave Esteban, or because for some reason he had to be here to face Francisco when he came.

The family were like lifeless dolls. Isabela stood silently in the middle of the dining room, staring vacantly at the food which had been spread out when word came that the posse and the boys were coming. She had bandaged Joaquin's face and still held the roll of bandage in her hands. Ysidra had gravitated to her old place in Francisco's office, where she sat heavily. Catalina stood before a mirror seeing nothing. Petra remained at the window in Esteban's room like a statue.

Before she even heard the pounding of his horse's hoofs she knew he was coming. The air was still, but as if in a wind of great strength the people began to move this way and that, fading, disappearing into the walls, the trees, the atmosphere. The groups disintegrated, melted into nothing. Knowledge flicked about unspoken but understood. He is coming now. No one must be here, no one must be visible when Don Francisco found his son.

When he entered the patio it was an empty shell, heavy with silence. He slid from his horse and for an instant stood poised beside it, uneasy that the usually teeming yard was vacant. Then, slowly, with the warm air tugging at his legs, he walked to the door of his house.

He stopped at the door, his eyes strangely wide and clear. He listened but there was no sound in the house. Stepping slowly into the hallway he found it unfamiliar, dim. The silence lay thick about him.

"Esteban?" he said softly and waited. Just beyond the door Catalina was shaken as a leaf in the wind.

"Esteban," he said, his voice held in and restrained. Ysidra heard him and her eyelids drooped.

"Esteban!" It was a broken cry, hoarse and cracked. He crashed up the stairway, shattering all stillness. Plunging down the hallway drunkenly, unbalanced, he came through the doorway of Esteban's room. He stopped by the bed, stunned. He didn't see Graciano, ashen, who had waited. He didn't see Petra, stonelike by the window.

He fell to his knees by the bed because his legs would no longer hold him. He ran his hands over Esteban's body, clutching at the arms, fondling the face.

"Oh, my boy . . . my boy . . . my boy."

Chapter 30

The house was sodden with weeping, the air was thick and old. The people gathered again at Dos Ríos. There was despondency in them, and dull anger. They went about performing their self-appointed tasks listlessly. The women saw that the house was kept in some sort of haphazard order, stopping to wipe their eyes, noticing with a sense of shock something which Esteban had used a few days before. Men sat during long silences, smoking and looking absently at one another, wondering what would happen, where it would end, where Francisco was. Through everything was the constant moaning grief of the Indians and servants. Tears flowed unchecked. They gave vent to their grief and mourned for Don Esteban. It was a house of death and near-death, for Graciano lay in his darkened room scarcely moving on his bed. Joaquin wandered listlessly about, his face bandaged. Catalina went lightly here and there, saying little, accomplishing nothing, her eyes vacant and bewildered. Ysidra was sunk in a dark pool of despair. Xavier wept confusedly.

Petra spent some time with Graciano, who lay wordless and intent, with his fever-bright eyes on the door. She wondered vaguely if her own face would ever regain its natural color. Everywhere she turned, every doorway she entered, she saw

Esteban. Something was there to remind her of his vivid vitality. Francisco? Always her mind came back to Francisco, like all the minds in the house. Where is he now? they thought. What is he doing? Where has he gone?

But they all knew. Ever since he had ridden from Los Angeles and walked into the silent house, ever since he had been swept with the black consuming rage and had come back out of the room, down the hall and again out the doorway, they knew where he had gone.

"Hunting," Guillermo said, his face ugly with bitterness.

"Into the hills," Llanes said shortly.

"Or to Mexico?" Xavier asked blankly. "South? Or do you think north?"

North, south, east or west, it all reverted to Guillermo's ugly word—hunting.

Father Patricio walked over from the mission. He might have come on one of the Church's old horses, or he might have borrowed one, but he walked. The fine warm dust was old and familiar to his feet. Some of it had belonged to the mission and now belonged to Francisco, but he didn't think of that. He was merely a parish priest and he walked to the Dos Ríos house because there was death there. He told himself this, but his throat tightened and filled. He did not feel the rheumatic pain in his legs. He thought only of Francisco, who was his brother in the eyes of God, and whose house was bereaved.

"Yes," he said when he reached the low sprawling house, and the guests told him that Francisco had gone away. "Yes." Somehow he had known that Francisco would not be there. He went in quietly. His brother was gone, and there were things in his brother's house which needed doing. Esteban—his vision blurred suddenly—Esteban had died and must be buried. Someone must take a hand. Things must be carried through to their logical conclusion.

"Mother," Graciano said, his eyes clear for the first time in three days.

She came to the bed and soothed him mechanically. He had lost much weight. The firm flesh seemed to have melted from his bones. With this new thinness and fragility he was the image of Angelo.

"Has he come back?"

"No," she said knowing he meant Francisco.

He began to get up with little strength behind his movements. She tried to make him lie down, but he clung to her stubbornly and got her to help him dress. His jacket hung loosely. His sash, wrapped tightly about his waist, accentuated its narrowness.

He is sick, she thought. He should be in bed.

Numbly, almost wordlessly, he went with her, made her assume her proper place as lady of Dos Ríos. He was like a blade of finely spun steel. He was at her side to keep her from falling when Esteban's body was lowered into the grave. He was beside her, supporting her as she looked, startled and shocked, about the Estrada hillside and saw the graves of all Francisco's children.

He was in constant attendance when everyone came back to Dos Ríos to wait. They didn't know exactly what to wait for. But they were Francisco's friends, and they would wait for him to return. If, when he returned, he had need of them, they would remain. If he did not, they would go. The house was filled to overflowing with quiet waiting people.

One day ebbed into the next and still he did not come. One week went by, another and another.

"Mother—" Petra listened to her son's question which had been striving for recognition in her own mind—"why aren't there any others? Why am I the only one?"

She could not answer him. She stood struck dumb, for it seemed that Angelo stood before her with questioning eyes. She turned and went into her own room.

Well, why? Because she must mourn for a ghost. She buried her tearless face in her hands and stood silently in the center of the room. For a ghost she had wasted her brain and body for many years, until the house, in the end, was as empty as when she had come to it. She had done nothing, been of no use at all.

She raised her head and Angelo—no, Graciano—stood in the doorway. There was no escaping the wide-set searching Montoya eyes. She turned her back to him, but she had seen the sudden rise of color in his face.

"Mother," he said gently, "there is still time——" The word hung in the air between them.

"You are only thirty," he said.

"Thirty-two," she answered dully. Her lips flattened and twisted whitely. "He would have no use for such as me."

"Is it that you still love my father?"

She thought of this for a long time, revolving the idea clumsily. Yes, she would never stop loving Angelo. Her love for him had held a sweetness and newness which nothing could replace. She would have loved him until the day she died, but there was nothing in it now of the thunder and need and sweeping fulfillment. It was a dream, diaphanous and lovely, and she had made the sweet dead thing take the place of all else. She had held it so close that she had been unable to see beyond it. She turned to answer Graciano, but he was gone.

News came. It skimmed through the air over the hills, rushed in the courses of the two shallow rivers, was repeated by the grains of dust. Words whispered from person to person. Sentences half spoken and dying out. Eyes meeting and lowering. Francisco Estrada was coming home. He was coming back slowly, walking his horse, a different horse. Step by step he was coming down California from the craggy mountains and redwoods of the north to the flat rounded hillocks of the south. Somehow they knew exactly where he was each hour of the day. Fresh word went out and eddied about in gusts of silent knowledge. News came when he was riding across the tip edge of Rancho Soledad de Santa María, and when he reached Santa Barbara. Word came when he passed through Las Palomas at night, and when he entered and left Los Angeles. And confusion and anxiety came when they knew that now—this minute—he must be crossing the line of Dos Ríos land. He came slowly.

Those who through the leaves of trees or from the blind windows of flat little houses saw him coming sent their words down with the rest. He was different now. There was little of Spanish grandee in his form. He was filthy, unshaved. His clothing was the color of earth and clung in shreds to his gaunt body. Dried blood was on his hands and leggings. Hatless, sunburned, he came on slowly. They could not understand why so slowly. They waited for him to pass. Those he had passed remained quiet behind the leaves of the trees, or in the blind windows of their houses, or sat like statues on their horses. Their eyes had swept his figure sagging in the saddle, picking out this and that to relate to others, noting the dirt, the stains, the different horse. Sometimes soon and sometimes late, their eyes fell on his belt. They seldom believed what they saw the first time. Eyes played tricks, but they knew finally what they saw there—little twisted, wrinkled bits of something, dried and black with bobbing tufts of hair on them. Jerking and jumping as if half alive, the dried things hung. And sooner or later the onlooker realized that these were scalps which dangled at Francisco's belt.

Those who were Indians and saw the scalps counted them and remembered that three men had got away. He had come from the north, and they were astonished that a white man could trace three Indians in a forest and find them all. As he went slowly by, those who were religious crossed themselves, and those who were not gazed after him in solemn wonder. Deep in their brains was the knowledge that the souls of the three renegades hung at his belt. The souls would not be taken in the Estrada family and released, but would hang forever to the bits of twisted skin and twirling hair.

He came home, looking neither left nor right, seeming to feel his way across the land, and rode again into the patio. He sat for some time on his horse, not moving. Again there was only stillness to greet him, for the people hung back in strangeness, in deference, or fear, or grief. At last he got stiffly from his horse, which stumbled and then stayed still where he left it.

He stopped in the doorway, unable to see clearly in the dim hall after the bright sunlight.

"Graciano," he said after a time. Xavier made a confused motion toward the stairs. Francisco walked past his friends and family and mounted the stairway silently, like a man in whom age rests heavily, whose bones are brittle and old. At Petra's door he paused.

She started from her chair, shaken with a deep humility at the sight of him. She took a hesitant step and stopped, for he did not see her.

Graciano turned from the window to face him.

"Graciano," Francisco said vacantly. His legs

seemed to buckle under him. Graciano, the slim one, the weak one, was at his side in an instant, supporting him so that he would not fall to the floor. Caressing the blood-blackened hands, kissing the dirty face, Graciano helped him. Francisco clung to him as he fell to his knees. There was a weighted disbelief in Petra. She turned her head away, knowing painfully that Francisco was going to weep.

The sound of it was terrible, loud and coarse, weeping which strangled a man unused to weeping. It smote the ears of all who heard it and rendered them speechless. For a time they were—Indian and white—conscious of nothing except his grief. His wrath was spent, and this was his sorrow. It rocked the air in the house. The blocks of adobe were dulled with the echo of it. It seeped into the walls and rafters and clung there in whispers of strange sound. They could do nothing but wait, breathless and still, feeling the blackness, the obscenity, the dreadful intimacy of a strong man made helpless and shattered.

The next day they began to go home. There was no service they could perform. The only balm left for him was time. Esteban was gone, lying on the Estrada hillside. It was better that they go. Petra moved about like a ghost, uttering bewildered words, breaking off her sentences and forgetting what she had meant to say. Francisco came down among them and spoke the correct words, but they were not sure that he knew he spoke. Graciano was always at his side, much thinner from his illness, much paler, his great eyes burning. He was different, older, more tired. No one guessed the dark unbelievable thoughts which had been born and lived and died in his brain while he washed the stains from Francisco and secured fresh clothing for him.

When the house was emptied of people, no

member of the family thought to follow his ordinary tasks. Even Adam did not stir himself, but sat stonily, thinking of all the fine knowledge he had put into the good brain of Esteban.

Guillermo went into the kitchen finally to tell the women to prepare food. They must eat. His eyes were swollen, but he stolidly went about building a fire and organizing a meal. The women did not resent him. It was not so strange—a *mayordomo* in the kitchen—no stranger than Don Esteban being dead. It was all a part of the wrongness, the newness. They would never find anything strange again who had heard Francisco weeping.

Petra stood before his doorway, knowing she must go in to him, wondering dully what he would say to her, wondering what she had to say to him. The time when she could come to him was past. It was too late now.

She went in and sat down, looking at him and wondering if she could even pierce the veil of abstraction and kindle a look of real recognition in his face.

Ysidra struggled up from her chair, clumsy, graceless and ugly, knowing it and not caring. She was old, terribly old. Petra turned her eyes back to Francisco. He was old too. The firmness of his jawline sagged. There was a looseness beneath his eyes. His hands lay listlessly on the arms of the chair. He did not rise in quick politeness when his aunt stood and walked ponderously to the door.

"I'm tired," she said and turned the knob with an effort.

"Yes," he said abstractedly, "yes," and after she had gone, he continued to look at the place where she had been, as if he had not seen her go. Petra observed the room grow gray in the failing light. There was grayness between her and Francisco. She rose and went to stand before him. She was tired to the bone. Slowly she sank to the floor beside his chair, her eyes lingering on the lines of his face, her hands yearning to reach out and touch him. She must explain to him that he was not alone. She too had lost a son. She opened her lips to tell him, but the proper words did not come.

"I love you, Francisco," she said humbly. "I love you."

She did not know she was crying until his voice came to her through the grayness.

"Don't cry, Petra," he said gently and lifted her up. She huddled in his arms, miserable and lost.

"Don't cry, beloved," he whispered, his lips kind and loving against her face.